www.MinotaurBooks.com

The premier website for the best in crime fiction.

Log on and learn more about:

The Labyrinth: Sign up for this monthly newsletter and get your crime fiction fix. Commentary, author Q&A, hot new titles, and giveaways.

MomentsInCrime: It's no mystery what our authors are thinking. Each week, a new author blogs about their upcoming projects, special events, and more. Log on today to talk to your favorite authors. www.MomentsInCrime.com

GetCozy: The ultimate cozy connection. Find your favorite cozy mystery, grab a reading group guide, sign up for monthly giveaways, and more. www.GetCozyOnline.com

MINOTAUR BOOKS

Praise for
Michael Koryta

Envy The Night

"Revenge drives this superb stand-alone . . . Koryta's dialogue is as sharp as the knives his characters wield, and his plot twists at the most unexpected moments. This thriller places Koryta solidly in the company of the genre's most powerful voices." —*Publishers Weekly* (starred review)

"Michael Koryta earns a seat at the high table of neo-noir crime writers by putting a fresh spin on the fathers-and-sons narrative." —*The New York Times*

"Gallows humor leavens this heart-pounding thriller . . . Take yourself to an island, pull up an Adirondack chair, and scare yourself silly with this one." —*Boston Globe*

"Superb writing and storytelling from Michael Koryta . . . *Envy the Night* represents his best work to date." —George Pelecanos

"Koryta's skill as a writer—and as a crafter of complicated plots—will fascinate." —*St. Louis Post-Dispatch*

"A great new stand-alone novel. *Envy the Night* is a story full of family history, with a likable protagonist and a strong sense of place . . . Koryta's characters are irresistible." —*Charlotte Observer*

"This diabolical novel, laid out in simple but eloquent prose and pitch-perfect dialogue, heralds a changing of the guard. I have seen the future of 'The Best Mystery Writer in America' and its name is Michael Koryta." —*New York Times* bestselling author Ridley Pearson

"One of the year's finest crime novels."

A Welcome Grave
Nominated for a Quill Award

"Stylish . . . well observed." —*The New York Times*

"Addictively readable. . . . There are no stereotypical characters, no predictable plot lines. . . . Readers who enjoy
authors like Steve Hamilton, Michael Connelly and Dennis
Lehane should add Michael Koryta to their reading lists."
—*Chicago Tribune*

"A nuanced, mature novel that proves both the depth of
Koryta's talent and the vitality of the PI genre."
—*New York Times* bestselling author Laura Lippman

"Sentence for polished sentence, no one in the genre writes
better." —*Kirkus Reviews*

"Edgar-finalist Koryta stakes a claim as one of today's pre-
eminent crafters of contemporary hard-boiled mysteries . . .
Despite Koryta's youth . . . his haunting writing and logi-
cal, sophisticated plotting rival that of established stal-
warts like Loren Estleman." —*Publishers Weekly*
(starred review)

"If you haven't already discovered Michael Koryta...now's
the time. *A Welcome Grave* is his best book."
—*Toronto Globe and Mail*

"The Rust Belt never looked so scary . . . a nightmare chess
game." —*Rocky Mountain News*

"For a while now Michael Koryta has been called one of the rising young talents in crime fiction. I say enough of that. *A Welcome Grave* proves the promise. Koryta is one of the best of the best, plain and simple. With stories like this, his Lincoln Perry is going to be around for a long, long time."
—Michael Connelly

Sorrow's Anthem

"Sometimes a book grabs you and stays in your memory long after the rest of the in-box's contents have been flushed away by new arrivals. Koryta's second mystery about Cleveland private eye Lincoln Perry has this kind of hold on me . . . Dashiell Hammett of *Red Harvest* would appreciate the tangle of high-level political and police corruption of *Sorrow's Anthem*, but anyone who mourns for lost friendships will add a more visceral reaction."
—*Chicago Tribune*

"Perry is an appealing fellow, and Koryta is a straightforward storyteller, but the real pleasure here is touring the back streets of C-Town. . . . Nominated for an Edgar Award for best first novel at the age of 21, Koryta is now 22, but *Sorrow's Anthem* is no sophomore slump."
—*The Washington Post*

Tonight I Said Goodbye
2005 Edgar Award Nominee for
"Best First Novel by an American Author"

"The 21-year-old author excels at building characters and story, making this one of the best mystery debuts this year."
—*Library Journal*

St. Martin's / Minotaur Paperbacks by

MICHAEL KORYTA

Envy the Night

A Welcome Grave

Sorrow's Anthem

Tonight I Said Goodbye

Envy the Night

Michael Koryta

St. Martin's Paperbacks

This is a work of fiction. All of the characters, organizations and events portrayed in this novel are either products of the author's imagination or are used fictitiously.

Reprint of lyrics appears courtesy of Dax Riggs and Fat Possum Records.

ENVY THE NIGHT

Copyright © 2008 by Michael Koryta.
Excerpt from *The Silent Hour* copyright © 2009 by Michael Koryta.

For information address St. Martin's Press, 175 Fifth Avenue, New York, NY 10010.

Library of Congress Catalog Card Number: 2008018094

ISBN: 0-312-35741-9
ISBN: 978-0-312-35741-2

Printed in the United States of America

St. Martin's Press hardcover edition / August 2008
St. Martin's Paperbacks edition / August 2009

St. Martin's Paperbacks are published by St. Martin's Press, 175 Fifth Avenue, New York, NY 10010.

10 9 8 7 6 5 4 3 2 1

For Dennis Lehane, who remembered the elevator

Acknowledgments

Deepest gratitude to Dennis Lehane, Roland Merullo, Christine Caya, Sterling Watson, Meg Kearney, Laura Lippman, and all others involved with the Writers in Paradise program at Eckerd College in St. Petersburg, and the low-residency MFA program at Pine Manor College in Boston, where this book was born.

The Willow Flowage is a real place, albeit one with which I took plenty of fictional liberties, and I'm grateful to my father for introducing me to it, and to Dwight and Fran Simonton for being gracious hosts over the years and providing some wonderful background information. Also to Jim Kiepke for always finding the fish.

Ryan Easton guided me through details related to cars and the body shop business, and my sister, Jennifer, advised on dealing with stroke patients. If I got anything right, the credit is theirs, and if I got it wrong, the blame is mine.

Thanks, as always, to my agent, David Hale Smith, and to the St. Martin's Press/Thomas Dunne team for their wonderful work, particularly Pete Wolverton, Andy Martin, Katie Gilligan, and Liz Byrne.

Further thanks to:

Michael Connelly, Bob Hammel, Laura Lane, Gena Asher, Don Johnson, Robert Pepin, Louise Thurtell, and Lawrence Rose. And to all of the booksellers, reviewers, and magazine publishers who do so much to help, particularly

Jim Huang, Jamie and Robin Agnew, Richard Katz, Jon and Ruth Jordan, John and Toni Cross, Otto Penzler, Barbara Peters, Lynn Kaczmarek, Chris Aldrich, and Janet Rudolph.

I envy the night
for its absence of light.

Dax Riggs, "Ancient Man"

One

Frank Temple III walked out of the county jail at ten in the morning with a headache, a citation for public intox, and a notion that it was time to leave town.

It wasn't the arrest that convinced him. That had been merely a nightcap to an evening of farewells—Frank hanging from the streetlamp outside of Nick's on Kirkwood Avenue, looking down into the face of a bored cop who'd seen too many drunks and saying, "Officer, I'd like to report a missing pair of pants."

It hadn't been the hours in the detox cell, either. Frank was one of six in the cell, and one of just two who managed not to vomit. Sitting with his back against the cold concrete block wall listening to some poor son of a bitch retch in the corner, Frank considered the jail, the people who checked in and didn't check out the next morning, the way he would. He considered the harsh fluorescent lights reflecting off gray and beige paint, the dead quality of the air, the hard looks the men inside developed to hide the hopelessness. It would be the same when the sun rose as when it set, except you wouldn't be sure when that happened, couldn't even use the sun to gauge the lack of change. He considered all of that, and knew that if he could understand only one thing about his father, it was the decision he'd made to avoid this place.

This was the second time Frank had been in a jail. The

first was for a drunk driving charge in a small North Carolina town two years earlier. He had failed the Breathalyzer but requested field sobriety testing anyhow, his booze-addled brain sure that he could pass. After watching Frank stumble and stagger through the first exercise, the cop put an end to it, said, "Doesn't look like your balance is too good, kid." Frank, leaning against the car for support, had waved him closer, as if about to impart a secret of the highest magnitude. The cop leaned down, and when he was close enough, Frank whispered, "Inner ear infection."

He had the cuffs on and was in the back of the car before he was finished explaining the connection between one's sinuses and one's balance. His was not a receptive audience.

So this was the second trip to a jail, and even if his father hadn't found a coward's way to avoid a life sentence, the number would be the same. Frank wouldn't have visited. But he also couldn't hide the thought, listening to those drunks mumble and belch and vomit beside him, that maybe the reason he put himself in situations like this was because he wanted a taste. Just a taste, that was all, something he could walk back into the free world with and think—*that's what it would've been like for him.*

He'd been chased into the night of drinking by one disturbing phone message and one pretentious professor. The message had come first, left by a voice he hadn't heard in many years.

Frank, it's Ezra. Ezra Ballard. Been a long time, hasn't it? You sound older on your message. Anyhow, I'm calling because, well . . . he's coming back, Frank. I just got a call from Florida telling me to open up the cabin. Now, I'm not telling you to do anything, don't even care if you call me back. I'm just keeping my word, right? Just keeping my word, son. He's coming back, and now I've told you.

Frank hadn't returned the call. He intended to let it go. Knew that he should, at least. By the end of the day, though, he was done in Bloomington. A single semester of school— his fifth college in seven years, no degree achieved or even threatened—and Frank was done again. He'd come here to work with a writer named Walter Thorp (*Walt to my friends, and I hate all of them for it*), whose work Frank had admired for years. Bloomington was closer to home than Frank had allowed himself to come in years, but Thorp was a visiting professor, there for only one semester, and he couldn't pass up that chance. It had gone well, too. Thorp was good, better even than Frank had expected, and Frank had worked his ass off for a few months. Read like crazy, wrote like crazy, saw good things happening on the page. The last week of the semester brought an e-mail from Thorp, requesting a meeting, and Frank used that as encouragement to push Ezra Ballard's call out of his mind. Focus on the future, don't drown in the past.

That was his mantra when he went to the cramped office on the third floor of Sycamore Hall, sat there and listened as Thorp, glancing occasionally at that gold watch he always wore on the inside of his wrist, complimented Frank's writing, told him that he'd seen "great strides" during the semester, that Frank clearly had "powerful stories to tell." Frank nodded and thanked his way through it, feeling good, validated in his decision to come here, to ignore that phone call.

"I've never done this for a student before," Thorp said, arching an eyebrow, "but I'd like to introduce you to my agent."

Frank couldn't even feel the elation yet; this was that much of a surprise. Just looked back at Thorp and didn't speak, waited to see what else would be said.

"In fact," Thorp added, tracing the edge of his desk with a fingertip, eyes away from Frank's, "I've already mentioned you to him a few times. He's interested. Very interested. But he was wondering—we both were, really—have you ever given thought to writing nonfiction? Maybe a memoir?"

Frank got it then. He felt his jaw tighten and his eyes go flat and he stared at the old-fashioned window behind Thorp's head and wondered what the great writer would look like flying through it, landing on the terrace three floors below.

"I only ask because your story, and the way it intersects with your father's story, well, it could be quite compelling. To have that in addition to your own narrative gifts, Frank, is quite a package. Nate—he's my agent—he thinks the market would be fantastic. You might even be able to get a deal on just a synop and a few sample chapters. Nate thinks an auction would be possible, and that's the sort of circumstance where the dollar figures can go through the—"

He had the good sense not to follow Frank out the door and down the steps. Ten hours later, Frank was in the jail, all the amusement left in his drunken mind vanishing when the booking officer looked up from the paperwork and said, "No middle name?"

Nope, no middle name. Too bad, because going by your middle name was an easy thing—provided you had one. But he didn't. Just that Roman numeral tacked on the end, Frank Temple III, the next step in the legacy, a follow-up act to two war heroes and one murderer.

They'd put him into the detox cell then, left him there to wait for sobriety, left him with swirling thoughts of his father and Thorp and the message. Oh, yes, the message. He'd deleted it, but there would be no need to play it again anyhow. It was trapped in his brain, cycled through a dozen times as he sat awake waiting for morning.

He's coming back.

He was not allowed to come back. Frank and Ezra had promised one another that, agreed that they'd let him live out his days down there in Miami so long as he never tried to return, but now there was this phone call from Ezra saying that after seven years the son of a bitch had decided to test their will, call that old bluff.

All right, then. If he would return, then so would Frank.

He was northbound by noon, the Jeep loaded with his possessions. Except loaded wasn't the right word, because Frank always traveled light so he could pack fast. The quicker he packed, the easier it was to ignore his father's guns. He didn't want them, never had. Through nineteen states and who knew how many towns in the last seven years, though, they'd traveled with him. Other than the guns, he had a laptop computer, two suitcases full of clothes, and a pile of books and CDs thrown into a cardboard box. Twenty-five years of life, it seemed like he should have more than that, but Frank had stopped accumulating things a long time ago. It was better to be able to move on without being burdened by a lot of objects that reminded you only of where you'd just been.

West through Illinois before heading north, to avoid the gridlock and construction that always blanketed Chicago, then across the state line and into Wisconsin as the sun disappeared, the destination still hours ahead. Tomahawk, a name Frank would've dismissed as cliché if he'd written it for a North Woods lake town. The town was real enough, though, and so were his memories of it.

His father wouldn't be there. Devin Matteson would be. If Ezra's call was legitimate, then Devin was returning for the first time in seven years. And if Frank had an ounce of sense, he'd be driving in the opposite direction. What lay ahead, a confrontation with Devin, was the sort of possibility that Grady Morgan had warned him he *had* to avoid. Grady was one of the FBI agents who'd brought down Frank's father. Grady was also a damn good man. Frank had been close to him for a while, as close as he had been to anyone for a few months during the worst of it, but then the media sniffed that relationship out and Frank left Chicago and Grady behind. They hadn't talked much since.

He drove past Madison in the dark and pushed on. He hadn't eaten all day, just drank Gatorade and swallowed ibuprofen and drove, hoping to do it all in one stretch, with just a few stops for gas and to exercise sore muscles. Before he reached Stevens Point, though, he knew he wasn't going to make it. The hangover had killed his appetite, but he'd needed food if he was going to stay awake, and now the fatigue was beginning to overpower him. There was a rest stop ahead, maybe the last one he'd see for a while, and he pulled off and parked. Lowered the driver's seat as far as it would go, enough to let his legs stretch a bit, and then he slept.

It was a Big Brother kind of thing, no doubt about it, but Grady Morgan had kept an active monitor on Frank Temple III for seven years. It wasn't proper, or even really legal, because Frank had no role whatsoever in anything that could still be considered an active investigation for Grady. But nobody had noticed or cared or commented yet, and as long as they didn't, he'd keep watching. Without a touch of remorse. He owed the kid at least this much.

The feelers Grady had out there in the world, computers that ran daily checks on Frank's fingerprints and Social Security number, had been quiet for a long time. As had the phone lines and the e-mails and the mailbox. No word from Frank in quite a while, and there were times when Grady ached to speak to him, check in, but he didn't. He just went to work every day and eyed the calendar that showed retirement was not far away and hoped that Frank would continue to stay off the radar screen. Grady didn't want to see a blip.

Here was one. The wrong kind of blip, too, an arrest in Indiana, and when it first came through to his computer Grady felt an immediate sick swirl go through his stomach, and he actually looked away from the screen for a moment, not wanting to read the details.

"Shit, Frank," he muttered. "Don't do this to me."

Then he sighed and rubbed a forehead that was always growing, chasing the gray hair right off his skull, and he turned back to the computer screen and read the details of the arrest. When he got through, he let out a breath of relief.

Public intoxication. That was it. The second arrest in seven years, the second time Grady had felt this chill of sorrow, and the second time he could roll his eyes and chalk it up as No Big Deal, Kids Being Kids.

He hoped.

As he pushed back from his desk and walked to the window and looked out at the Chicago skyline, he sent a silent request to Frank Temple III somewhere out there across the miles.

Tell me it was just fun. Tell me, Frank, that you were out with some buddies having beers and chasing girls and laughing like idiots, like happy, happy idiots. Tell me that there was no fight involved, no temper, no violence, not even a closed fist. You've made it a long way.

A long, *long* way.

Frank III had been eighteen years old when Grady met him. A slender, good-looking kid with dark features contrasted by bright blue eyes, and a maturity that Grady hadn't seen in a boy of that age before, so utterly cool that Grady actually asked a psychologist for advice on talking to him. *He's showing nothing,* Grady had said. *Every report we've got says he was closer to his father than anyone, and he is showing nothing.*

He showed something in the third interview. It had been just him and Grady sitting in the Temple living room, and Grady, desperate for some way to get the kid talking, had pointed at a framed photograph of father and son on a basketball court and said, *Did he teach you how to play?*

The kid had sat there and looked at him and seemed almost amused. Then he'd said, *You want to know what he taught me? Stand up.*

So Grady stood up. When the kid said, *Take that pen and try it to touch to my heart. Hell, try to touch it anywhere. Pretend it's a knife,* Grady hadn't wanted to. All of a sudden this was seeming like a real bad idea, but the kid's eyes were intense, and so Grady said what the hell and made one quick thrust, thinking he'd lay the pen against the kid's chest and be done with it.

The speed. Oh, man, the speed. The kid's hands had moved faster than anybody's Grady had ever seen, trapped his wrist and rolled it back and the pen was pointing at Grady's throat in a heartbeat's time.

Half-assed effort, Frank Temple III had said. *Try again. For real this time.*

So he'd tried again. And again, and again, and by the end he was working into a sweat and no longer fooling around, was beginning to feel the flush of shame because this was a *child,* damn it, and Grady had done eight years in the Army and another fifteen in the Bureau and he ran twenty miles a week and lifted weights and he could beat this kid . . .

But he couldn't. When he finally gave up, the kid had smiled at him, this horribly genuine smile, and said, *Want to see me shoot?*

Yes, Grady said.

What he saw at the range later that afternoon—a tight and perfect cluster of bullets—no longer surprised him.

Seven years later, he was thinking about that day while he stared out of the window and told himself that it was nothing but a public intox charge, a silly misdemeanor, and that there was nothing to worry about with Frank. Frank was a good kid, always had been, and he'd be absolutely fine as long as he stayed away from a certain kind of trouble.

That was all he needed to do. Stay away from that kind of trouble.

Two

Frank woke to the grinding of a big diesel motor pulling away, sat up, and saw gray light filling the sky. When he opened the door and tried to get out of the Jeep his cramped muscles protested, and he felt a quick razor of pain along the left side of his stiff neck. He was hungry now, the alcohol long since vanished from his cells and the Gatorade calories burned up. He took the edge off with a Snickers bar and a bottle of orange juice from the vending machines, ate while he studied the big map on the wall. He'd come closer last night than he'd realized; Tomahawk was only one hundred miles ahead.

The closer he got, the more his resolve wavered. Maybe it would be best to pretend he'd never gotten that message from Ezra, didn't even know Devin was on his way back. Maybe he'd just spend a little time in the cabin, stay for a weekend, catch some fish. It would be fine as long as he didn't see Devin Matteson. If he stayed away from Devin, if it was just Frank and Ezra and the woods and the lake, this could end up being a good trip, the sort of trip he'd needed to take for a while now. But if he *did* see Devin . . .

What are you doing here, then, if it's not about Devin? he thought. *You really think this is some sort of vacation?*

Whatever part of his brain was supposed to rise to that argument remained silent. He drove with the windows down as the gray light turned golden and the cold morning air began to warm on his right side. Past Wausau the smell of the place began to change—pine needles and wood smoke and, even though there wasn't a lake in sight, water. There would be a half-dozen lakes within a mile of the highway by now. He knew that both by the change in the air and from the map in the rest stop, this portion of the state freckled with blue.

The smells were triggering a memory parade, but Frank wasn't sure if he wanted to sit back and watch. It was that sort of place for him now. The deeper he got into the tall pines, the faster the memories flooded toward him, and he was struck by just how much he'd loved this place. It was one thing to recall it from somewhere hundreds of miles away, and another to really be here, seeing the forests and the sky and smelling the air. Maybe he'd stay for a while. The summer stretched ahead of him, and the money wouldn't run out. Blood money, sure, and spending it while hating the methods that had earned it made Frank a hypocrite at best and something far darker at worst, but it was there.

The first few times he and his father had made the trip, the highway had been two-lane this far north. Then the tourism dollars began to knock on the right doors down in Madison, and soon the four-lane was extending. Frank's mind was on the cabin, and he blew right past the Tomahawk exits before remembering that he had nothing in the way of food or supplies. He'd have to come back down after he'd unpacked, grab some lunch and buy groceries and then head back to the lake.

He exited at an intersection with County Y, a narrow road slashing through the pines, and had gone about a mile down it when someone in a silver Lexus SUV appeared behind him. From the way it came on in the rearview mirror Frank knew it was really eating up the road, had to be doing seventy at least. As the car approached, it shifted into the oncoming lane, the driver planning to pass Frank without breaking stride. Had to be a tourist, driving like that. The locals had more class.

It was that thought that made him look at the license plate.

He probably wouldn't have done it otherwise, but now he wanted to prove his theory correct, so his eyes went to the plate.

Florida.

The car was gone in a silver flash then, swerving in ahead of him and pulling away. The muscles at the base of his neck had gone cold and tight and his breath seemed trapped.

Florida.

It didn't mean anything. A strange little touch of déjà vu, sure, but it didn't mean anything. Yes, the Willow Flowage was an isolated place and a damn long drive from Florida, but there were several million cars with Florida license plates. There wasn't even a *chance* that Devin Matteson was driving that car.

"Not a chance," Frank said aloud, but then that message from Ezra filled his head again—*I got a call from Florida . . . he's coming back*—and he pressed hard on the gas pedal and closed the gap on the silver Lexus. A closer look was all he needed. Just that minor reassurance, enough that he could go on to the cabin laughing at himself for this reaction.

He kept accelerating, closed until he was only a car length behind. Now he was leaning forward, his chest almost against the steering wheel, peering into the tinted rear window of the Lexus as if he'd actually be able to tell who the driver was.

There was only one person in the car, and it was a male. He could tell that much, but nothing else. He pulled a little closer, almost on top of the Lexus now, staring hard at the silhouette of the driver's head.

"It's him." He said it softly, exhaled the words, no justification for them at all but somehow he was *positive*—

Brake lights. A flash of red, one quick blink that he saw too late because he was too close, and then he hammered the brake pedal and slammed the wheel left and hit the back corner of the Lexus at fifty miles an hour.

"*Shit!*"

The back of the Jeep swung right with the impact, then

came back to the left and sent the front end sliding, a fishtail that was threatening to turn into a full three-sixty. Even as the skid started Frank could hear his father's voice—*turn into it, turn into it, your instinct will tell you to turn away, but you've got to turn into it.* He heard it, recalled those old lessons in the half second that it took him to lose control of the car, and still he turned away from it. It had happened too fast and the instinct was too strong. He turned away from the skid, the tires shrieked on the pavement, and then any hope of getting the car back was gone.

Frank was saved by bald tires. He'd lectured himself on the tires a dozen times, thinking they'd kill him someday if he didn't get them replaced, but instead they saved him. The pavement was dry, the Jeep was a top-heavy vehicle, and if the tires had been able to grab the road well he probably would have rolled. Instead, because there was hardly a trace of traction left on the worn rubber, he slid. He saw whirling trees and sky and then the Jeep spun off the shoulder and into the pines. He heard a crunch and shatter just as the airbags blew out and obscured his vision, and then he came to a stop.

The airbag deflated and fell away, leaving his face tingling, and for a few seconds he sat where he was, hands still locked on the steering wheel, foot still pressed hard against the brake, blood hammering through his veins. It was amazing how fast the body could respond—you'd spend an hour just trying to wake up on a normal morning, but throw a crisis out there and the body was ready for a marathon in a split second. He reached over and beat the airbags aside with his hands and saw spiderwebbed glass on the passenger window, the door panel bent in against the seat. Bad, but nothing terrible. He could probably drive away.

What about the Lexus? Devin Matteson's Lexus. He was sure of it again, absolutely certain, and without any pause for thought he turned and reached behind his seat, found the metal case, flicked the latch and opened it and then he was sitting behind the wheel with a gun in his hand.

Reality caught up to him then. *Sanity* caught up to him.

"What are you doing?" he said, staring at the gun. "What the hell are you doing?"

He slid the gun back into the case and closed it and opened the door—after a glance in the sideview mirror to make sure he wasn't going to step out in front of a truck, survive the accident only to get squashed when he was on foot—and then got out of the car. He walked around to the front and saw that he wouldn't be driving anywhere. The right front tire was blown out and the wheel bent inward, crunched down beneath the mangled front quarter panel. If he'd handled it right, turned into the skid instead of away, he might've been able to keep the Jeep straight enough to avoid the trees. Then he'd be left with a dent and a drivable car, instead of this mess.

He'd lost track of the Lexus at the moment of impact, and now he was surprised to see how far behind him the car was, a good hundred feet at least. The driver had made the shoulder as well, but the car was facing the wrong direction and angled against the trees that lined the road.

Looking up at the car made his previous suspicion come on again, and again he thought of the gun, had to shake his head and move away from the Jeep before the urge to go for it got any stronger.

"It's not him," he said. "It's not him."

At that moment the driver's door on the Lexus opened and Frank's breath caught and held for a second until the driver stepped out onto the road.

It was not Devin Matteson. Not by a long shot. Even from this far away he could tell exactly how ludicrous the idea had been, could tell that he'd just caused a dangerous accident over an utterly absurd moment of paranoia.

He walked toward the Lexus as the driver began to survey the damage to his vehicle. Frank's first thought, watching him—*the dude's on speed.*

The guy, tall and thin with a shock of gray hair that stuck out in every direction, was dancing around the Lexus. Literally dancing. He'd skip for a few steps, twirl, lift both hands to his face and then prance back around the other side. He was talking to himself, too, a chattering whisper that Frank couldn't make out, and he seemed completely oblivious to the fact that there'd been another car involved in the collision.

"Hey." Frank got no response and walked closer. "Hey! You okay?"

The guy stopped moving then and stared at Frank in total confusion. Then he looked up at the Jeep and nodded once, figuring it out. Up close, Frank saw that he wasn't too old, maybe forty, the gray hair premature. He had a long nose that hooked at the end and small, nervous eyes set above purple rings that suggested it had been a while since he'd had a full night's sleep. His hands were still moving, too, fingers rippling the air as if he were playing a piano.

"Yes," he said. "I'm okay. Yes, everything's fine. You don't need to worry about me. I'll just call Triple-A. You can go on now."

Frank raised his eyebrows. "Just call Triple-A? I hit *you*, man. You're going to want to hang around and get this worked out for insurance."

The guy was shaking his head. "No, no, I hit my brakes, just slammed on my brakes, not your fault at all."

Not his fault at all? What the hell was he talking about? Frank had been tailgating so bad he'd slammed into him as soon as the guy slowed. It was clearly Frank's fault. The guy must be nervous, that's all. Shaken up. Collision like that, at nearly highway speeds, who wouldn't be?

"What I'm saying is, we need to call the police," Frank said. "Get an accident report made, so we can make this square with the insurance company, right?"

The gray-haired guy winced and rubbed his forehead as if a pain had developed there. He probably had a bad driving record. Maybe a few accidents, and driving a car like that Lexus, his insurance rate already had to be high. He was worried about the money. Didn't understand that Frank was liable for all the damage.

"Tell you what," the guy said. "It'd be a big help to me— a *big* help—if we didn't get an accident report made."

So he'd been right—bad driving record. Unless it was something more serious. Hell, maybe the guy *was* on drugs. Frank frowned, studying him closer, looking for the signs. He just seemed amped-up, that was all. Buzzing. His eyes were clear, and he was cogent enough in conversation. A Starbucks addict, maybe.

"I'll pay for your damage," the gray-haired man continued. "I know what you're thinking—as soon as I can, I'll take off and stiff you on the bill. But I promise that won't happen. We can take care of it right now. Find a repair shop, and I'll take care of the bill beforehand."

"I hit *you*," Frank said again.

"Don't worry about that. It was my fault, my responsibility, and I don't want an accident report made, okay?"

Frank shook his head and walked a few steps away, looking at the Lexus. It was even more beat to shit than his Jeep. The front end was crumpled, there was a gash, maybe three feet long, across the passenger side of the car from the contact with the trees, and steam was leaking out of the hood.

"Please," the man said, and there was a desperate quality to his voice that made Frank look back with surprise. Whatever trouble this guy had with his driver's license—if he even had one—was serious. Frank stood there on the shoulder as two cars buzzed past them, nobody stopping, and looked at this weird guy with the nervous hands and panicked eyes. Why not give him a break? It was Frank's fault, so it was only fair to let this guy handle it in whatever way he wanted.

"All right," he said, and the look on the gray-haired man's face, the way it broke with relief, was enough to convince him he'd made the right call.

"Thank you. Oh, man, *thank* you. I'll call a tow truck. The car's got a navigation system, you can find anything with it, we can pick any repair shop you want, I'll show you the choices . . ."

Three

Jerry was staring at Nora's ass again, in that way he had where his eyes seemed to bug right out of his head, nothing subtle about it, but she wondered if she was allowed to care today—she'd done the same thing that morning as she got dressed, looking her butt over in the mirror like some sort of sorority girl instead of a woman with wrench calluses on her palms. You did something like that, could you get upset when a guy allowed himself a stare? Maybe she'd earned the leer. Karma.

The glance in the mirror was important, though, a morning reminder that Nora was still very much a woman. This before putting on the jeans and the heavy work shirt, tucking her hair into a baseball cap so it wouldn't hang free and invite a painful accident. She'd learned that lesson one afternoon when she'd used the creeper to check up on Jerry's work and rolled right over her own hair. Stafford Collision and Custom was open by seven thirty, and from then until six or six thirty when she shut the doors and turned the locks, Nora would interact with few females. It was a man's business, always had been, but she liked the touch she brought to it and thought the customers did, too. Granted, they were her father's customers and probably kept returning more out of loyalty—and pity—for Bud Stafford than for his daughter, but the shop still did good work. On those rare afternoons when a particularly difficult job was done and the car driven out of the shop, Nora might even let herself believe they did a better job now. She wouldn't admit it to anyone else, of course, but she did have an eye for detail that her father couldn't touch. Too bad an eye for detail wasn't enough to keep the bills paid.

The phone rang out in the office, and Nora straightened up and looked back at Jerry, who promptly flushed and averted his eyes. Even when you *didn't* catch Jerry, he thought you had. Jerry would've made a piss-poor criminal.

"I'd like you to take another pass over that front quarter panel," Nora said.

"Huh?"

"Nice orange-peel finish in the paint, Jerry. I know you can see that, and *you* know how I feel about it. Doesn't matter if it disappears in the shadows, you can see it in the sun, and that's when people care about their cars looking the best. They go home and the first sunny Saturday morning they wash the car and wax it and see that orange peel. And then you know what happens? They don't come back."

She walked away from him, got into the office just in time to grab the phone before it rang over to voice mail. She was always forgetting to take the cordless handset out into the shop with her, and she knew they'd lost business because of it. When a body shop doesn't answer, people just call the next one in the phone book; they don't wait and try again. She'd been one ring away from losing this call.

"Stafford Collision and Custom, this is Nora Stafford."

She sat on the edge of the desk and took notes on one of the old pads that still had Bud Stafford's name across the top. The caller wanted a tow truck for two cars that had wrecked up on County Y. Her last tow driver, who'd also been a prep man and part-time painter, had picked up a drunk driving charge three months back and to keep him would have required bearing an insurance rate spike that she simply couldn't handle. In reality it was a welcome break—the shop's financial situation was going to dictate firing somebody anyhow, and the drunk driving charge gave her an excuse. She'd let him go and couldn't afford to hire a replacement. But two cars—including a Lexus—that was business she couldn't turn down, either. Jerry could drive the tow truck, but he wasn't covered by the insurance policy, and she needed him to finish repainting that Mazda this morning. She'd have to handle this one herself.

She got the details of the wreck's position and promised to be out within twenty minutes, then went back into the shop and told Jerry where she was going. He just grunted in response, not looking at her.

"What's the problem, Jerry?"

"Problem?" He dropped the rag that was in his hands. "Problem should be pretty obvious. You got me wasting all my time *re*painting work I shouldn't have had to *paint* in the first place."

She waved a hand at him, tired already, the argument by now just like the dying water heater in her house—too familiar, too annoying, too expensive to fix.

Jerry was a body man, a fine body man, none better in town. Didn't have the eyes for a top-quality paint job, but that wasn't the problem so much as the way he felt disrespected when asked to paint. If she could afford to bring someone else on board, she would, but that explanation hadn't appeased him.

"Jerry, this is not a big deal. If you'd done it right the first time, I wouldn't have asked you to repaint it. Instead, you half-assed the job and then tried to make up for it with the buffer, like usual."

"Damn it, Nora, last time I painted cars it was with—"

"Single-stage lacquer, spray it on, buff it pretty, don't have to mess with no damn clear coat . . ."

Nora mocked his voice perfectly, capturing the drawl so dead-on that Jerry pulled back in anger and grabbed his rag again, tightened his fist around it. He was a small man, only a few inches taller than she was, but strong in the wiry way that comes from years of physical labor. What was left of his hair was thin and brown and damp with sweat.

"All right," he said. "So I've told you before, if you remember all that. Think you're clever saying it back to me,

I 'spose. But if you was clever you'd understand, instead of using it to make fun of me. Your daddy understood. I'm not a combination man. I do body work. Been doing it since back when you was playing with dolls and putting on training bras and learning to paint your nails."

Same old shit. He'd start bitching about his workload, then begin with his what-a-pretty-little-girl-you-are routine, slighting her gender either directly or with what he thought passed as slick humor.

"Tell you something, Jerry? When I was learning to paint my nails, I was also learning how to paint a *car*. Now it's time that you do."

She turned and walked away from him, heard the *bitch* muttered under his breath and kept on going, out of the shop and into the tow truck. Sat behind the wheel and let the engine warm and lifted her hands to her face and thought, *I would've cried about this. A year ago, maybe even six months ago, I would've cried.*

Not any more, though. No way. But was that entirely a good thing?

She wasn't going to think about it. Pointless exercise. What she needed to think about was the cars waiting for her up on County Y. That was more than a pleasant surprise—it was salvation. She'd spent the morning trying to determine which bills she could be late on. It was down to that now, down to creating a rotating schedule of missed payments because otherwise she simply could not keep the doors open. Now here was a phone call offering enough work to keep those wolves distracted, if not completely at bay. And to think, she'd been one ring away from missing it altogether.

It felt longer than twenty minutes. The gray-haired guy kept up a constant stream of chatter, the words sounding more nervous each time there was a pause, as if he were scared of silence. When a car passed by, though, he'd stammer the way you do when you lose your train of thought, stare intently at the vehicle until it was out of sight. A couple of times, people slowed and put their windows down, ready to offer help, and the gray-haired guy just waved them off and shouted that everything was fine, go on, have a nice day.

It *was* a hell of a nice day, though. If the Lexus driver would shut up for a few minutes, Frank wouldn't have minded it at all, standing out here. It had been a long time since he'd lived in the city, so it wasn't as if he'd arrived in the woods fresh from garbage-riddled streets that stunk of exhaust fumes. Even so, this place felt different. For one thing, there wasn't a building in sight. Turn right, turn left, see trees and blue sky, nothing else. A pair of hawks rode the air currents high above, staying on the south side of the road. Must be a clearing back there, something offering prime hunting ground for the birds. Frank could've watched them for a long time, if this jazzed-up dude would let him. Instead, he was busy fending off meaningless questions and observations.

He was relieved when he saw the tow truck at the eastern end of the road, and a minute later it had pulled up beside them. The driver opened the door, and Frank felt his eyes narrow, saw matching surprise on the gray-haired man's face. The driver was a woman, and a good-looking one, that much evident even with her face shadowed by a baseball cap. She hopped down onto the road—the truck was too high for her to just step out; she couldn't go an inch more than five-three and might go an inch less—and walked around to face them.

"Sorry about the wait, guys. I got moving as fast as I could."

"No problem," Frank said, and he was going to shake her hand when the gray-haired man interrupted.

"If it's no trouble, can we do this car first?" He pointed at the Lexus.

The woman wore jeans and boots and a denim work shirt, sleeves rolled to expose thin forearms. There were grease stains on her clothes, and both the pants and shirt were loose, giving her a shapeless look. She didn't wear any makeup, but her eyebrows—not a feature Frank would ordinarily notice—had been carefully attended to, well shaped. Cool green eyes, now fastened on the Lexus driver.

"There a reason that one needs to go first?"

He gaped at her for a second, then looked at Frank and forced a smile.

"Well, I was just hoping . . . I've got a meeting to get to, and I was sort of—"

"In a hurry," the woman finished.

He nodded.

"Right," she said. "Well, I can give you the first tow unless this gentleman has an objection."

Frank shook his head.

"Great," the woman said. "Here's how we're going to do this—I'll get the Lexus rigged up, tow it back to the shop, and you guys can ride with me, unless you've got someone coming to get you."

This time Frank and the gray-haired man shook their heads in unison.

"Okay. Well, probably be easier to figure out your situations from town, unless you'd rather stand out here on the edge of the road."

"Sure," the gray-haired guy said. "Town's fine." But he was looking down the road with a frown.

The woman walked over to the Lexus and knelt beside it, studying the front end. Frank turned away when she bent over to see under the bumper, not wanting to stare. When was the last time a guy had wanted to check out a tow truck driver, anyhow? She straightened up and walked back to the truck, climbed in and put it in reverse and had the thing centered in front of the Lexus in half the time it would've taken Frank.

"I have to winch you out of that ditch before I can get it ready to tow," she told the gray-haired guy. "Looks like the Jeep is sitting clear enough already."

She hooked the winch beneath the front bumper of the Lexus, went back to the truck, and turned it on. The chain went taut and the gears hummed and the Lexus slid away from the trees and up the ditch, shedding a tangle of branches and broken glass in its wake. When she had the car on the flat surface of the road, she shut the winch off, went back and fussed with the chains for a few seconds, and turned to the car's owner.

"This thing's all-wheel drive. We should use the dolly on the rear wheels to keep from hurting your axles or transmission. The thing about that is, we also charge an extra thirty dollars to use it."

The gray-haired man stared at her, mouth open about an inch. Didn't see many women winching your fifty-thousand-dollar car out of a ditch.

"Uh, yeah, sure."

She raised her eyebrows. "You're okay with that?"

"You think that the dolly will save time?"

"It'll save your transmission."

"Whatever. Faster the better. I want to get moving."

She went back to the Lexus, and Frank thought her stride was slower, almost as if she were screwing with the guy because he was in such a hurry. It made a wry smile build on Frank's face, and he turned before the Lexus driver caught it.

Once she had the wheel-lift under the front end of the Lexus—looked like a set of mechanical arms wrapped around the wheels—she strapped the tires to it for added security and disappeared behind the car. Frank and the gray-haired man stood together in silence, waiting. Eventually she walked back around to the front, gave the wheel-lift one last look, and then made a small nod of satisfaction and turned back to them.

"Go on and get in. Short straw gets to sit in the middle."

Frank got to the passenger door first, pulled it open, and slid across to the middle seat as the gray-haired man climbed up beside him and the woman got behind the wheel.

"What's your name?" Frank asked her.

"Nora Stafford." She took one hand off the wheel and extended it. When they shook, he felt fine bones on the back of her hands, the skin smooth and cool, but hard on the inside, beneath her fingers.

"I'm Frank."

"Good to meet you, Frank." She put the truck in gear and checked the mirror. "Who's your buddy?"

"You know, I didn't make his acquaintance yet, just his car's," Frank said.

"My name's Dave O'Connor. Sorry. Should've introduced myself earlier. I'll be paying for this, which brings up a, uh, a question. I was wondering . . . see, I'm from out of town, and I need this done fast, but, well, I don't have my credit cards on me."

"Credit cards?" Nora turned to him with surprise. "Sir, I think you're going to want to make an insurance claim on that."

"No, we're not going to do that."

"Um . . . I don't mean to tell you your business, but this job is going to be several thousand dollars," Nora said.

Frank shifted in his seat. He'd hit the guy, and his insurance should be paying for the damages, but the gray-haired man had been adamant.

"So what I was wondering was, I mean my question, well, could I give you cash? Because I've got some cash on me, see. And if I gave you that, you know, to get started, and then I could come back with a credit card or call you and give you the number . . ."

Nora's face hardened just a touch, barely noticeable, a little frost in her eyes even though she didn't take them off the road. There was something about the edge she showed in that moment, like the way she'd slowed down just because the gray-haired guy was in a hurry, that Frank found damn appealing.

"Two cars, both with substantial damage," she said, her voice friendly. "Parts and paint alone are going to run up a decent bill, Dave. That's without labor figured in."

"I could give you two thousand dollars today. Surely that's enough to get started? You aren't going to burn through two grand in the first day."

Nora kept her eyes ahead, and so did Frank, but in the few seconds of silence that followed he felt a shared curiosity with her—*no credit cards on you, but two grand in cash?*

"Well . . ." Nora nodded her head as if in discussion with

herself. "Two thousand dollars is a sizable down payment. The bill for this work will run well over that, but it's certainly enough to get us started."

They were on the highway now, southbound toward Tomahawk, the tow truck's engine throaty, straining to get its load up to speed. Nora's thigh was warm against Frank's. He looked at her hands on the steering wheel, saw no wedding ring. So it wasn't her husband's body shop. This was just what she did, drive a tow truck in a town like Tomahawk? A young girl, intelligent, with perfect teeth and eyebrows?

"You guys have someone to come get you?" Nora asked.

"Nope," Frank said, and Dave O'Connor shook his head.

"I've got to get something figured out," O'Connor said. "Like I told you, I'm in a bit of a hurry. Got a meeting that won't wait all day for me."

"A meeting at the Willow?" Frank asked.

"No. I, uh, I've got to get to . . . Rhinelander. Little bit of a drive left to make, so, you know, got to figure something out."

Rhinelander. He'd been westbound on County Y, headed for Rhinelander? That was an interesting route, considering County Y took you out to the Willow, across the dam, and then looped back down to the old highway and into Tomahawk. O'Connor had been driving the exact opposite direction from Rhinelander, and not toward any highway where he could correct his course.

"Any chance you'd have a car you could rent me?" O'Connor asked Nora.

She shot a sideways glance at him. "I don't rent cars. I fix them."

"You don't have anything around the shop? It'd be one day. *One* day, and I'll give a couple hundred cash for it. I've got to make this meeting."

Nora let a few cars pass before she answered.

"Only drivable vehicle I could give you—unless you want to drive the tow truck—is a beat-up old Mitsubishi that probably can't do more than fifty without blowing up."

"That's fine. I'll take it."

"And if it *does* blow up on you, I'm certainly not going to take responsibility. I'm doing this as a favor."

"It's not a favor. I'll pay you—"

"You won't pay me anything. Sounds like you need something to get you to Rhinelander, and the Mitsu will do it. Slowly."

"I appreciate that," O'Connor said. "It'll be a huge help. Save me the time of renting a car, and I don't have time to waste."

Something else it would save, Frank thought, staring out at the lumber truck ahead of them, was the *process* of renting a car. You couldn't do that with cash—and Mr. Dave O'Connor seemed damn concerned with sticking to cash.

Four

Took Nora ten minutes to get Dave O'Connor in and out of the body shop. He had the cash out before she was even in the door, put it in her hand and waved away her offer of a receipt, said he knew she was trustworthy and he was in a hurry, now, could you show me that Mistubishi you were talking about?

So she took him out back and showed him the car, a rusted blue box of a thing they used for errands, running back and forth to the auto parts store. Had four-wheel drive, but that was about it. Windshield wipers were shot—how many times had she asked Jerry to replace them?—and two of the windows hadn't moved in the better part of a decade. Dave O'Connor looked at it as if it were the next year's model of his fancy Lexus. Took the keys and tried to press more cash in her hand.

While declining the money for the third time, she realized she was hustling him out of the shop almost as much as he was hustling her, and she knew why. There was something *off* about this guy, and, yeah, it started with the cash-only thing and the I'm-in-a-big-hurry thing but went beyond those, too. A meeting in Rhinelander? What the hell was he doing on County Y, then? License plate from Florida, no less. And the mannerisms, the tension . . . she pushed it out of her head. He'd given her more than enough money to hold the job, and it didn't seem likely he was going to dash off and leave his expensive car. If he did, hell, she'd make a fine profit off that. How long did you have to wait to claim a mechanic's lien?

So she let him take her car and drive off, didn't fill out any of the standard paperwork, just accepted his money and his promise to return Monday. Even a few months ago she would never have believed she could agree to something as crazy as this, but a few months ago the shop's debt was merely threatening, not suffocating her in the way that it was now. She stood in the parking lot and watched him go, two grand in cash in her pocket. It was enough to justify the breach of protocol. She was in a dream world when she walked back into the shop, and pulled up with surprise when she saw the young guy standing there, Frank. How old was he, anyhow? Appearance said he'd be a few years her junior, maybe twenty-six, twenty-seven. Acted older, though. Carried himself all steady and sharp-eyed, the way a man who's seen a lot will do. The way her father had.

"Hey," she said, and for some reason she tugged off the baseball cap, shook her light brown hair out.

"Hey. You get things settled with that guy?" He stepped closer to her, an easy smile on his face but the eyes not matching it, too thoughtful. A nice-enough-looking guy, runner's body, good skin. Needed to grow the dark hair out, though, lose that military cut that made him look even younger than he was.

"A pocketful of money to prove it," she said and gave him one raised eyebrow that made him nod.

"Feel safe about getting that Mitsubishi back?"

She laughed. "If I never see it again, that'll only save me money."

"Different sort of guy, wasn't he?"

"Seemed a little on edge."

"Uh-huh. Got a gun out of the glove compartment when he was moving his things into your car, too."

That stopped her. Not just because of the gun, but the way he said it. Relaxed. Casual. And how had he even seen that? When O'Connor was busy switching his gear from the

Lexus to the Mitsubishi, she'd been standing right beside him, with Frank all the way back at the shop, leaning against the wall.

"Handgun," he said. "No big deal, I'm sure. Lots of people carry them."

She didn't say anything, just stood beside the door and stared at him.

"Look, I didn't want to worry you," he said. "It's meaningless."

"I know that. I was just surprised you saw him with it, that's all. You were standing all the way over—"

"Good eyes. I've got good eyes."

"I guess so." Pretty eyes, too. Nora always liked blue eyes on a guy with a dark complexion. Something about the contrast. She pulled open the office door, stepped inside with Frank behind her.

"I'll go back and tow your car in just a minute," she said. "You know what you're going to do for a ride?"

"I'll figure something out."

"Where were you headed?" If he said Rhinelander, she was going to be awfully uncomfortable.

"The Willow. Staying at a cabin up there. I've got some errands to run in town, though, groceries and the like, so I'll deal with them first."

"You aren't going to rent a car?"

"No need. Once I get up there I don't plan on leaving for a while."

She pushed her hair back over her ears, the baseball cap still in her left hand. Over Frank's shoulder she could see Jerry standing at the row of lockers along the far wall, getting ready to take a cigarette break. The doors to the paint booth were still open and the lights were off, which meant the Mazda wasn't drying, which in turn meant Jerry hadn't repainted that quarter panel yet. Good thing he was taking a cigarette break.

"Tell you what—if you can kill the afternoon in town, I'll drive you up to your cabin tonight," Nora said, refocusing on Frank again. "Come by around six?"

"You don't need to—"

"It's not a problem."

"All right." He nodded. "I'd appreciate that."

"Sure. Six o'clock, right?"

"Six o'clock."

Thing was, Jerry didn't dislike women. Was rather fond of them, in fact. In their place. And their place was not in a friggin' *body shop*. Shit. Standing in the paint booth and listening to the tow truck growl as Nora set off on her second trip, he wondered just what he'd done to earn this fate. Working for a woman, him, best body man in the damn town. Could he find work somewhere else? Sure. But even if Nora was a righteous bitch four days outta five, she was also Bud Stafford's daughter. And if Bud ever got better, came back to run the place again, Jerry wouldn't want to make eye contact with him knowing he'd left the girl on her own.

She'd told him to redo the clear coat on the Mazda. Redo it, like he'd painted the thing the wrong color or something. Hell with that. Somebody needed to look at the Lexus, and Jerry didn't think Nora was the one for the job. Car all beat up like that, there was some work just to figure out what all was wrong. If she wanted the Mazda fooled with again, she could wait till Monday, or do it her damn self.

Jerry found the keys to the Lexus and pulled it into the shop. *Shee-it,* what a car. More bells and whistles than anything he'd seen. More than anything he'd want, too.

Once he had the car inside, he got to work inspecting the damage. Hood would need to be replaced, plus the front quarter panel, and the front passenger door. Now, if it were Jerry's car he'd probably handle that door and the quarter panel with a liberal amount of Bondo, a spray gun, and a buffer. But he didn't imagine the Lexus owner would agree.

Problem with these fancy new machines was all the shit you couldn't see. Sensors and computer chips and whatnot. Some of them would be up under the bumper, so he'd have to figure out what the hell they all did when he took that off. Probably want to replace the bumper assembly, too. Make a few extra bucks, get the job done right. Nora herself would appreciate that outlook, if she ever climbed down off her damn broomstick to listen to him.

He dropped onto his back and slid beneath the front of the car, wrench in hand. Way the front was punched in, there could be some damage to the internal workings. He got the splash shield off and—wait a second, what in the hell was this?

A thin black box, about the size of a remote control but without the buttons, was mounted on the bumper reinforcement. One of those sensors he'd been worrying about? Those were usually wired in, though, and this thing just sat there by itself. Jerry tapped at it gently with the wrench, and the thing slid around a bit. Reached out and got his fingers around it and pulled. Popped right off. It was held on with a damn magnet. Two thin wires trailed out of it, and he followed them with his fingers, found another box, this one larger, and popped it free, too.

Pushing back out from under the car, Jerry sat up and studied his find. The smaller device was plain black plastic with a magnet on the back and a small red LED light in the center. The other thing, the bigger one, looked like some sort of battery pack. First thing he thought of was one of those GPS units. Buddy of his, Steve Gomes, had one he took hunting. Tracked your position. The Lexus had a navigation system, so it would need a GPS unit, but wasn't that inside the computer?

That's when he got it. The magnets were there so you could attach the thing to the underside of the car, on the frame. Attach it without the owner knowing. But whoever put this one on, they went even a bit further. Popped out the bolts and got it inside the splash shield on the bumper reinforcement, where it would be protected from water and road debris and couldn't possibly fall off.

"Who are you, friend?" he said, bouncing the black box in his hand and staring at the Lexus. Nora said the guy gave her cash, didn't show a driver's license or credit card, anything with his name on it. Stupid of her to let him go like that, no proof of identity, but two grand in cash had a way of convincing even the strictest person to let a few details slide. Couple kinds of people in this world liked to move without identification, and a smaller number of those were going to have someone tracking them. Drug dealer, maybe? Bank robber? Could there be cops on the way, following him with this gadget?

Jerry walked into the office with the device in his hand, opened the mini fridge, and pulled out a can of Dr Pepper. Jerry drank three or four Dr Peppers a day. Kept him fresh. He dropped into the chair behind the desk and cracked the top on the can, took a long swallow, and considered his find. No matter the explanation for the black box's presence, Nora was going to be damn interested in it, and, possibly, so would the cops. Should they call the cops, though? Did they have any reason to? Maybe not. Maybe it was best just to pretend they'd never seen the thing. He could put it back inside the splash shield, send it on its way without ever knowing what it was doing there. That would be Nora's call to make, not his.

He should have heard the husky growl of the tow truck engine, but the black box had taken his mind deep into other places, and he missed it. When Nora entered the office, he was still in her chair, with his boots propped up on her desk and the soda can in hand. Her face twisted at the sight.

"Tell me," she said, "that the Mazda is done, Jerry."

"Listen, Nora—"

"No." She leaned over and slapped at his boot, trying to knock it off the desk. His foot didn't budge. "I will not *listen,* because I've heard them all already. Every excuse and problem and complaint that you utter. None of them are new, not anymore."

"Wait a sec—"

"If my father had *any* idea the sort of work ethic you exhibit down here, he'd be disgusted. Absolutely disgusted. The last thing I said before I left was that I wanted you to finish that Mazda, and instead you spend your time sitting at *my* desk drinking a soda?"

"I just sat down two seconds ago. Reason was, when I

started taking that Lexus apart . . ." The little black box was in the hand not occupied by the Dr Pepper. He started to lift it above the desk, thinking to drop it in front of her, shut her up, but she started in again.

"Lexus? I didn't ask you to do a thing to that Lexus, Jerry! I specifically said the Mazda needed to come first. What can't you follow about that?"

Jerry kept his hand below the desk, closed his fingers around the black box, felt his jaw clamp tight.

"Would you *please* go get some work done?" Nora said. "Please do what I already asked?"

He slipped his hand into the pocket of his coveralls, dropped the plastic device inside, and swung his boots off the desk and to the floor.

"Yes, sir, boss. Don't let me bother you anymore."

On his way back through the shop he stopped at his locker, placed the tracking device inside, then slammed the door shut and locked it.

Five

Ezra Ballard, a few hundred yards out on the lake, spotted the blue car shortly after noon and knew that the two on the island were no longer alone. The car, some sort of beat-up Jeep, was parked in the woods across from the island cabin—a cabin that had, for almost two days, been home to a gray-haired man and a blond woman. Technically, that was Ezra's business. He didn't own the cabin or the island, but for many years he'd been entrusted with their care. Same with the cabin down on the point, less than two miles away. Two cabins that, at least in Ezra's mind, still belonged to men who'd been buried long ago.

Twice a year the Temple boy mailed Ezra a short note with five hundred dollars inside. The note always read *Thanks for keeping an eye on the place*; the money was always in five one-hundred-dollar bills, the envelope always void of a return address, but a phone number would be included on the note. Ezra would spend the cash on whatever expenses he might encounter keeping the cabin in good shape and save the rest. Seven years young Frank had kept that up, and though Ezra wondered when he'd return to the place, he never wondered *if*. The boy—hell, he wasn't a boy anymore, was he?—would be back, but not until he was ready. Maybe Ezra would still be around, maybe not. Something like that, it took time to make your peace with it.

Circumstances with the Temple cabin had been consistent,

and Frank's boy seemed to understand the situation, had made no effort to contact a Realtor or a lawyer. The Matteson cabin, here on the island, was a different matter. After Dan died, Ezra hadn't heard a word from the family. Sent a few letters, made a few phone calls, and finally received a curt order to ready the place for sale—this from the son, Devin. When Ezra explained that the island couldn't be sold—it was part of a legacy trust that would either remain with the family or revert to the state, and good luck convincing a judge to break that—Devin swore at him and hung up. Never called again. This was before Frank Temple had taken his own life and Devin's role in that situation became clear, before a few conversations with Frank's son that Ezra probably never should have allowed to take place, before a final call that Ezra had made to Devin.

In the years that followed that last call, Ezra had never heard from Devin or anyone else about the island. He hadn't expected to, though. His message had been succinct enough: If Devin came back, Ezra would kill him. For seven years it seemed that Devin had believed the promise, and he damn well should have. Ezra was not a man given to idle threats, and he certainly was not a man with light regard for killing. Not anymore.

Though the cabin had sat empty for years, Ezra kept the place in shape, paying property taxes and all expenses out of his own pocket. Nobody other than Ezra had been inside until this week. Just two days ago a bizarre phone message had been left, someone claiming to be Devin telling Ezra the cabin needed to be "opened up for guests."

The call had sucked the breath from Ezra's lungs, the brazenness of it, the *audacity* almost more than he could get his head around. He'd never expected to see Devin again, believed that the island cabin would sit empty until after Ezra was gone from the world, and even in the corner of his mind that recognized there was at least a *chance* that Devin might show up, he never imagined a call like that. So casual, so flip. A taunt, like after all these years he'd decided Ezra was a harmless old man.

Ezra had called Frank's son—probably a poor choice but, again, there was a promise to be kept—and then visitors had arrived at the island, but Devin was not among them. Not yet.

Now there was this second vehicle. With opening weekend of the fishing season a mere week away, Ezra had decided to run some of the bays and islands, getting depth readings and trying to find new spots to catch walleye. It was on his first run across the lake that he'd noticed the car, and now he'd spent most of the afternoon anchored off the opposite shore, using a pair of binoculars to watch the island. His first idea was that there had been a new arrival. That changed around midafternoon, when the gray-haired man moved the car.

He and the woman had arrived in a Lexus SUV that had disappeared this morning. Now the gray-haired man took his boat back across the inlet, got into the blue car, and drove it out of the mud and back up the hill. At the top of the hill, he went off the road and into the grass, right into the pines. Drove it as far into the trees as he could, till the boughs swept over the roof and pushed against the side of the car to the point that he had trouble opening the door to get back out. Only reason you parked a car like that was to hide it. He'd gone too far, though; the car was hidden from the logging road, but he'd driven it right up to the edge of the tree line, so the sun caught it and reflected the glare of glass and metal across the lake. Hard to see unless you were on the water. Hard to see unless you were Ezra.

Ezra had been on the Willow for most of forty years now, taking fish out of the lake's waters and deer and bear out of its surrounding woods. Best guide in Oneida County, that was what people said. The people were right, too. At least when it came to hunting. Out in the woods with a rifle in hand, there wasn't anybody better than Ezra. Thing was, he preferred fishing. He was good at it, sure, but not the natural he seemed to be when it came to stalking prey with a gun.

This was about to become a busy time of year, too. The season opened for walleye, pike, bass, and the other game fish on the first Saturday of May, which was in one week. From that point on, Ezra had a full calendar. It was no time to worry about a cabin that hadn't been used in years. But there sat that damn car, shining against the blanket of trees, inviting everybody and their brother to slow a boat and stare at it and wonder if someone was using the Matteson island. Questions would be headed his way, and maybe he should have some answers ready when they did. Problem was, this gray-haired guy clearly wanted that car hidden, and of the men Ezra had known who hid cars, exactly zero of them were guys he wanted to deal with.

It being Friday, and a full workload arriving out of the blue like that, Nora was in a good mood as the afternoon wore down. Good enough mood that after she'd towed the Jeep in, she picked up lunch for Jerry, one of those Angus burgers he favored. An obvious peace offering, and one that seemed to make Jerry feel awkward, shuffling around and trying to stay mad at her for that oh-so-demanding request to do his job correctly. They didn't talk much for the rest of the day, but there were no blowups, either.

She spent the afternoon with the computer, going over finances. It was her own laptop, and she'd devoted countless hours to slowly transferring all of the paper files Bud Stafford had used. Tedious work, yes, but now they were more organized, more efficient—and lacking enough jobs to make it pay off.

Jerry had given her his damage assessment on the Lexus. "Uh, you got your quarter-panel issues, you know, and you gotta get down in there, too, plus there's the light and your, uh, you know the bumper issues, plus there's the airbag and your, uh . . ."

From that she managed to cull an actual estimate, printed it out, nice and official. She was reviewing it when someone pulled into the front parking lot, got out of the car without shutting the engine off, and opened the office door. Four o'clock on Friday afternoon was an unusual time for business.

The visitor came through the door and stopped, ignoring

Nora to look around the room with open curiosity, as if he were on a museum tour. Big guy, too, a fancy knit T-shirt stretched over his chest and shoulders, loose jacket over that.

"Can I help you?" she said.

He had a bizarre silver belt buckle, a sort of rippled pattern, like latticework. Not ridiculously large like some of those western things, but ornate, flashy. Nora had always found that a man who believed a belt buckle should be a fashion statement was not her kind of man.

"I hope I'm in the right place," the guy said. "Friend of mine called and asked me to grab some things out of his car. I think he left it here . . ."

"What's his name?"

The guy just smiled at her. Patient, as if she'd asked a worthless question but he was willing to ignore it.

"The car's a Lexus SUV."

"I didn't ask for the car's description. I asked for the guy's name."

"Vaughn," the guy said. There was a hitch in his voice, though, like a game show contestant who second-guessed his answer at the last minute.

The longer he stood in the office, the more space he seemed to fill. She had trouble meeting his eyes as she shook her head.

"I'm sorry. Nobody named Vaughn has a car in here."

"I'm rather certain he does. Perhaps there's been some confusion over the name."

"If there has been, then the car's owner will need to come in and explain that to me. I'm certainly not allowed to release personal effects from a vehicle, sir."

"How about we give him a call, together? You can ask . . ."

Dave O'Connor had left no phone number—or any other form of contact information—but even if he had, Nora wouldn't have called. O'Connor had been weird enough, but this guy was almost threatening.

"No," she said. "If the car's owner—whose name is not Vaughn—calls me and explains this, then we'll see how we can proceed. Until then, I'm afraid not."

The guy's eyes darkened and he seemed ready to object when the office door opened and Jerry ambled in, a socket wrench in one hand. He gave Nora and the guy a casual glance and then knelt in front of the little refrigerator she kept in the office, pulled out a can of Dr Pepper, and cracked it open before walking back into the shop. The visitor watched him go.

"It sounds to me like you might have the wrong body shop," Nora said.

For a long moment he didn't answer, just stared at the door Jerry had walked through as if it were something that called for real study. Then he nodded.

"Of course. That must be it. Apologies."

He gave her a mock bow, lifting his hand to his forehead, then opened the front door and walked back into the parking lot. She stood up and went to the window in time to see him climb in the passenger side of a black sedan. That was why he'd left the engine running—he wasn't alone, wasn't driving. She got a clear look at the car as it pulled out to the street, a black Dodge Charger, one of the newer models. She'd made the mistake of complimenting the look, only to have Jerry ridicule her. *Nora, it's a* four-door. *That ain't a Charger, it's a joke.*

She couldn't read the license plate, but the colors told her it was from out of state. Wait, those colors were familiar. A smear of orange in the middle of a white plate with some green mixed in. She'd just seen that on the Lexus. Florida.

It wasn't five yet, but she turned the lock on the front door as she stood there gazing out the window. The odd feeling that had convinced her to get Dave O'Connor out of her shop and back on the road without any of the normal procedures had just returned, only this guy with the belt buckle made it swell to the edge of fear. He'd called him Vaughn. She had no proof that the Lexus driver's name was actually Dave O'Connor. All that cash, the hurry he was in, the gun Frank had seen, none of it suggested anything good. Add a fake name to the mix, though, and she was beginning to feel stupid. She'd gone for the money despite all the obvious objections, let the guy dictate the situation. It wasn't easy to imagine her father handling this in the same way.

Nora walked out of the office and back into the shop, watched Jerry working on the Lexus. The car was empty. Dave O'Connor had cleared all his things out when he left, including that handgun in the glove compartment. So he hadn't called someone to come pick anything up.

"Jerry," she said, "can you give me a minute?"

She wanted to talk to him, explain the situation and ask if he'd found anything in the car, more cash or guns or, well, *anything*. But when he turned around he had that irritated sneer on his face, ready to argue or mock her or do anything but listen.

"Well?" he said. "You got another problem needs me to fix it?"

"No, Jerry. It's just . . . I was thinking . . ."

"Hope you didn't hurt yourself." That passed for humor to him, real wit.

"I was thinking you can go home early," she said. "That's all. It's Friday, and we got some nice work in today, and you've done a good job this afternoon. So go on and get out of here. Enjoy the weekend."

She walked away as the first flush of gratitude mixed with shame crept onto his cheeks.

Six

Getting out a little early on a Friday was no reason to disrupt your normal postwork routine, so Jerry drove directly to Kleindorfer's Tap Room, had himself a bar stool and a Budweiser before the clock hit five. Carl, the bartender, took one look at him coming through the door and asked if the Stafford girl had finally fired him. Jerry didn't bother to dignify that with a verbal response, electing instead to go with a simple but clear gesture.

It was early enough that the room was almost empty, a couple of out-of-towners drinking Leinenkugel in a booth, nobody at the bar except Jerry, nothing on the TV except poker. Give it a few minutes, they'd switch over to that show where the black guy and the white guy argued about sports, neither of them knowing a damn thing to start with. Jerry and Carl tended to have better ideas than those two.

Jerry sipped his beer and watched the muted poker game and simmered over Carl's comment. It had been a joke between friends, no offense meant, but it riled him anyhow. Not so much at Carl for saying at it, more at his own life for the circumstances that produced the line. Jokes about working for Nora were constant. Could hardly get through a day without hearing one. She'd been there almost a year now. Showed up from Madison dressed to the nines, walked into the body shop wearing jewelry and perfume and with her long fingernails polished and told Jerry she was the new boss. Wouldn't just own the shop, she intended to *run* the shop.

The afternoon Bud Stafford had his stroke, it had been Jerry who found him slumped under a Honda, his shirt smeared with primer from the fall onto the hood. Jerry knew it was bad; his hands shook while he dialed for the ambulance. At the time, though, he'd seen two possible outcomes—Bud would die, or he wouldn't. The end result, this half-death, was a twist Jerry hadn't considered. Nora'd called a few days after the stroke to ask him to keep the shop going while Bud was in the hospital. A week after that, she was in town and in charge. Jerry had tolerated it, because he figured Bud would come back. That's what she kept telling him, insisting to him. Bud was going to be fixed up, and then he'd be back and she'd be gone, back down to Madison, finish up graduate school in *art history,* of all things.

He still couldn't get his mind around that. Bud had been cutting that girl checks for years, putting her through school. Reasonable thing to do, providing the kid would accomplish something, walk out of there with a piece of paper telling the world she was useful, an engineer or an architect or a doctor, but Bud could never say what the hell she was going to do. Most practical man Jerry'd ever seen walk the earth would just shake his head and smile and say, "She's a damn smart girl. I'll let her learn, and when she's done with that, she'll do something big. Guarantee it, my man. She'll do something big."

Well, she wasn't doing shit that Jerry could see except bitching a blue streak about things she didn't understand and losing them business. End of every month, Nora would tell him that they'd kept the bill collectors at bay again, like it was something to be proud of. Didn't realize those bills were paid only through a sort of pie-in-the-sky expectation that Bud would be back eventually. It kept a meager supply of work coming in. And, Jerry had to admit, kept him in the shop. So who was he to criticize the customers who did the same thing?

Ten, maybe fifteen minutes had passed while Jerry

brooded—enough for a completed Budweiser and the order of a fresh one—when the door opened and closed behind him. Regulars finally showing up, he thought, until the new arrival sat down beside him. Long, lean guy with a shaved head and a tattoo on the back of his left hand, a weird symbol that meant nothing to Jerry. Had a camouflage jacket on over jeans and a T-shirt. Seventy degrees today, and both this guy and the one who'd come into the shop office to talk with Nora were wearing jackets.

Jerry turned back to the TV, and the new guy didn't say anything for a few minutes, not till Carl brought his drink— vodka tonic—and returned to the other end of the bar.

"You work down at that body shop, don't you?" the guy in the jacket said. "Stafford's?"

Jerry turned and offered his favorite expression for making new acquaintances—sullen, with the lip curled just enough to imply a little disrespect.

"I don't think I know you, pal."

"My apologies," the guy said, making a little bow of his head. "Name's AJ."

Jerry didn't answer, just drank his beer and looked at the TV.

"So you work at the body shop, correct?"

"Uh-huh. And I don't give free advice on cars, and I don't look at them after work on a Friday. So you got one that needs fixing, bring it in Monday morning and we'll—"

"The car I'm interested in is already there," the guy named AJ said, and Jerry paused with the bottle back on his lips but no beer flowing yet. He lowered it.

"The Lexus?"

AJ smiled. "Either you guys don't have much business, or you're a smart son of a bitch, Mr. . . . ?"

"Dolson. Jerry Dolson." He took another drink and turned all the way around to face AJ. "You want to tell me what the deal is with that car? Who the hell you are, and who's the fella you're looking for?"

AJ reached into the front pocket of his jacket and came out with cigarettes, shook one out, and offered the pack to

Jerry, who accepted. They lit up and smoked for a minute, neither saying a word. A group of five came into the bar and settled onto stools beside Jerry, talking loud and laughing, yelling drink orders at Carl.

"You work for that girl?" AJ said. "She really run the place?"

Jerry scowled. He had enough headaches over working for Nora without some stranger walking into a bar and pointing it out.

"She doesn't run shit," he said. "I worked for her daddy for, hell, a number of years. He had himself a stroke, and for some reason the girl decided not to sell the place. Got this idea of keeping it going till Bud comes back. But you want to know who *runs* that place, you're looking at him."

AJ sucked at his cigarette and nodded, like this was just what he'd expected. "She doesn't seem like the car-fixing type."

"She ain't."

"Problem is, she also doesn't seem like the question-answering type. Friend of mine stopped by today, had a few inquiries to make about that Lexus you mention. The girl, she wasn't too cooperative. Put on a bit of an attitude."

"That's Nora, all right," Jerry said. He finished his beer, and before he could wave for another, AJ did.

"I got this one."

Jerry didn't thank him, just accepted the drink and consumed a few swallows of it, feeling a nice light buzz beginning. Beer in his right hand, cigarette in his left, a fine start to the weekend.

"Now, you want to come in here and tell me that Nora gave you a headache, that's fine," Jerry said. "But you just said that she, how'd you put it? That she wasn't the question-answering type."

"That's right."

"Well, seems to me I just asked you a question of my own. Don't recall it getting answered."

He felt a smug smile growing as he lifted the cigarette back to his lips. This guy think he was a total idiot? Come in here and bitch and moan about Nora, get Jerry loosened up to the point that he'd just forget about his own questions?

"Fair enough," AJ said. He was using his thumb to clear a streak of condensation off his vodka glass. Not much of the vodka was gone.

"What I'm saying is, you want me to talk to you, you're damn well gonna need to talk to me first," Jerry said. "I don't know you, I don't know the son of a bitch drove that Lexus into the tree today, and I don't have an interest in either one of you. Yet."

AJ made one more swipe at the glass with his thumb, then lifted it and took a long drink before speaking, his eyes on the bar.

"Man who drove that Lexus, he's of interest to me, Mr. Dolson. Not to you. Understand?"

"What did he do, steal something? Drugs, or money?"

AJ shook his head.

"What, then? What are you talking about?"

Silence.

"Your problem," Jerry said, "is that you put that cute little box on the underside of the car instead of sticking it to the fella himself. You found the car all right, but your boy isn't with it. Tough shit, huh?"

He laughed, and AJ lifted his eyes from the bar and locked them on Jerry's, and then the laugh went away. This guy talked easy, voice soft and calm, but there was a steel edge inside him. It showed in the way he kept rubbing that glass with his thumb. Some people would do that out of boredom or nervousness. With this guy, it was different. Like with each stroke of his thumb he was tamping down embers in a place nobody else could see.

"You're an observant man, Mr. Dolson," AJ said, his voice tighter.

"Wouldn't have seen it 'cept I had to take the car apart," Jerry said, and suddenly he was wondering if he should have played this card, let the guy know he'd found the tracking device.

"What did the girl say when you told her?"

"Haven't told her."

"So you found it and . . ."

"Threw it in my locker and figured I'd think on it for a day or two."

Something loosened in AJ's face.

"You told me you don't know me, or the guy who drove the Lexus," he said. "Told me you aren't interested in us. And I say that's just right. You shouldn't be interested in us. We're about to move right out of your life. But you can make some money before that happens. I expect you understand that's an opportunity not to let pass by. Easy money, from someone who has nothing to do with you?"

"You want the car?" Jerry said. "I ain't gonna let you steal that car, man."

"I don't give a shit about the car. I want to know where its owner went. His name is Vaughn. I need to find him. Like you said, none of this has anything to do with you. No reason for you to protect him. Am I right?"

Jerry nodded.

"So you've got a decision to make, and as it stands now you've got no reason to support either option. How about I give you one? A thousand dollars cash. I'll put it in your hand the minute you tell me where he went."

There were more people in the bar now, and it felt too hot and too crowded. Jerry sipped his beer and squinted. Had that flushed, dizzy sensation like he'd get about seven or eight beers from now. Wished everyone would lower their damn voices, stop shouting and carrying on. He stared at the floor, trying to steady himself, saw that AJ wore a pair of shiny black boots, one of them tapping off the bottom rung of the bar stool. Tapping, tapping, tapping. Jerry got lost watching them.

"Not interested?" AJ said. "Okay. Then we'll go on and get out of your life. Just like we would have anyhow. Only you'll have nothing to show for it."

"He didn't tell Nora where he was going," Jerry said.

"He's not going to abandon that car. He might not show up for it, not for a while at least, but he'll check in. He doesn't want you guys to call the police, run his license plate, anything like that. You'll hear from him again. When you do, I want to know about it. In exchange for the thousand."

Jerry drank the rest of his Budweiser fast, some of the beer foaming out of his lips and dribbling down his chin, then slid the bottle away.

"How do I get in touch with you? *If* I decide to."

AJ wrote a phone number on a bar napkin and passed it to him. Jerry glanced around, curious if anyone was watching him take this guy's number on a napkin like he wanted a date.

"All right. I'll see what I can do."

"Excellent decision," AJ said. "How do you feel about five hundred bucks up front?"

"Feel fine about that."

"Give me the device you took off that car, and I'll give you the five hundred. Gesture of good faith, on both our parts."

"Can't do that."

"Why not?"

"Shop's closed, and, uh, I don't have keys anymore."

His face burned when he said it. There were plenty of problems between him and Nora, but losing his keys, that was the most serious one. She'd come down one weekend and found him using the paint booth to put a fresh coat on Steve's boat. Sort of thing he'd do from time to time, favor for a friend. Bud had known, and hadn't cared. But Nora, she accused him of undercutting the business, of stealing paint—which was a bold-faced lie, Steve bought the paint— and disrespecting her. Demanded his keys. He'd never been as close to quitting as he was that day.

"You can't get in all weekend?" AJ said.

"Not without Nora, and it sounded like you didn't—"

"No." AJ shook his head. "I don't want her involved."

"Well, Monday, then."

AJ nodded after a long pause, resigned, and got to his feet.

"All right. You get in touch Monday, and I'll get your wallet stuffed fat, Mr. Dolson. And now I'll leave you to the rest of your evening."

"Not till you buy me another beer, you won't," Jerry said. He felt good about saying that, pleased with the tone, insistent, demanding. Like he was in control.

AJ settled his tab, left a fresh beer in front of Jerry, and walked out of the bar, his boots loud on the floor. Jerry gave it a few seconds, then got to his feet and went to the window, leaned on the jukebox with a cigarette in hand and studied the cars in the parking lot, looking for AJ. Didn't see him. How the hell had he gotten out of there so fast? Then his eyes rose from the cars and found him across the street.

It made Jerry frown. The guy wasn't from town, he was certain of that, so he didn't arrive in Tomahawk on foot. He had a car, but it wasn't here now, which meant somebody had dropped him off at Kleindorfer's Tap Room and gone elsewhere. Now this guy, AJ, he was walking in the direction of the body shop. Rankled Jerry a little. What did he need at the body shop after Jerry'd agreed to help him? He considered driving down there. It held him at the window for a moment, but eventually he shook his head and went back to the bar. The shop was closed, Nora was gone, and if this yahoo had any ideas about breaking in he'd just set off the alarm and draw the cops out. It was Friday evening, and Jerry's vested interest in Stafford's Body Shop was on hold till Monday.

Seven

Nora hung the CLOSED sign on the front door as soon as Jerry left, and turned off the lights in the office with every intention of leaving early herself. The weekend stretched ahead, a chance to relax, get some much-needed Nora time. She'd spend an hour or two with her father and then be free of all responsibilities until Monday at eight. There was a pang of guilt at lumping the visit with her father into the responsibilities category, but she didn't think anyone would blame her. They were difficult visits.

She was locking the back door of the shop when she remembered Frank. *Damn it.* She'd told him six. So used to staying late that it had seemed the most appropriate time to suggest. Now, with the shop closed and a sudden yearning for a shower and a change of clothes in her mind, that extra hour was torment. She stayed at the door for a moment before turning the lock back with a sigh and stepping into the shop. There was nothing to do but wait.

It was dark inside, lit by just one emergency lamp above the door. Nora made her way through the room without bothering to turn on the lights, so familiar with the building that it was easy. She knew the placement of every tool by now, and knew their purposes. Navigated around the chain fall in the corner, frame rack beside it, paint booth behind that, toolboxes lining the walls. When she got to the office door, she took her keys out of her pocket but didn't use them.

There was a stool beside the door, and rather than enter the office she just sank onto the stool, pulled her feet up onto the seat and hugged her knees to her chest, sat there smelling the paint and the dust and staring at the shadow-covered room. Instead of building a garage divided into separate bays, her grandfather had simply jammed everything into one large warehouse, a space that cooked you in the summer and chilled you in the winter. Her father had upgraded the equipment over the years but never considered a new building. Though earlier in the day she'd told Jerry she'd been learning about the work that went on in here since she was a girl, she really remembered being inside only a handful of times, usually accompanied by her mother, who stalked around the place with an expression of haughty distaste.

They'd gotten divorced when Nora was six. It had been a marriage of whim and romance: Her mother was from old money in Minneapolis, and her father was third-generation Lincoln County, Wisconsin, son of a body shop owner who also drove a plow in the winter. He'd been bartending at a supper club up near the Willow when twenty-two-year-old Kate Adams arrived for a vacation with her parents and some cousins. The family bored her; Ronald "Bud" Stafford did not. He was tall and good-looking and appealing in a way that only an outdoorsman can be, but also quick with a joke and a compliment. It was supposed to be a summer fling. Only problem was, Kate didn't realize that until Stafford had replaced Adams at the end of her name and a baby was on the way.

If there'd been good times when she was a child, Nora couldn't remember them. Couldn't remember the bad times, either, just a vague sense of tension. After the divorce Kate moved back to Minneapolis with Nora in tow. Nora's relationship with her father had been slow building at best. He would come to Minneapolis about once a year, usually around Christmas, take her down to the Mall of America and patiently wander through girls' clothing stores with her, laughing at the way she insisted on trying everything on. Her mother had only permitted a few visits to Tomahawk when Nora was young, and always came along, as if she were afraid Nora would never come back if left alone for a few days. It wasn't until high school that Nora finally began to make a weeklong trip by herself in the summer. She and her father started writing letters more frequently then, a couple of times a month, exchanging photographs—her in a prom dress, him with a thirty-six-inch northern pike—and news. From the time she was a little girl he'd promised to put her through college. Her mother had remarried by the time Nora was ten, remarried to plenty of money, but on that issue Bud was firm—*he* would pay for college.

He and her mother just couldn't live together, that was all. Everything Kate had found so charming about Tomahawk that first summer disappeared under a blanket of snow in November, and even when the thaw came and the tourists returned the luster was gone. And for Bud Stafford, moving to Minneapolis wasn't an option. He'd been born into a pocket of the earth he considered superior to all the rest, and he'd never leave . . .

Someone was at the door. Nora put her feet back on the ground and started to stand up as the door opened. Not the front door of the office but the back door. *Frank*, she thought as the knob turned and the door swung inward. Had to be him. Then the visitor stepped inside, and as his silhouette filled the space she saw it was too tall, too broad. Without even seeing his face she knew him. It was the man who'd come by to ask about the Lexus.

She didn't say anything, didn't take a step forward. If the lights had been on, she would have, but since they were off, and the stranger clearly hadn't noticed her standing back here in the dark, she kept silent and watched him.

He stood just inside the door and didn't move. Letting his eyes adjust to the dark, maybe. Turned the knob back and forth, then looked from it back up across the room, probably thinking the door would've been locked if the shop were empty. It was dark, though, and the sign outside said CLOSED. After another hesitation, he swung the door shut very slowly, so it hardly made a sound as it latched. Then he walked farther into the shop, toward the Lexus that sat in the middle of the room, surrounded by its own trim pieces.

She should have said something as soon as he opened the door. Called out in a loud, authoritative voice, stopped him. But she hadn't, and now he was inside and moving in a way that unnerved her. Cautious, on the balls of his feet, with attention to quiet. It was just past five on a weekday, in town, with plenty of people passing by outside, and this guy had walked into a business, that's all. Somehow it didn't feel like that, though. More like she was standing in a closet watching someone crawl through a window and into her home in the middle of the night.

Stop it, she thought. *It's your business, you're in charge, and this asshole has no right to creep in here.*

It wasn't much, one brief bout of internal scolding, but it was enough to get her moving. She stepped to the side and reached out and up, flicked the light switch, and said "You want to tell me what you're doing?" in as hard a voice as she could muster.

He moved at the first sound of her voice. Whirled and came toward her, fast and aggressive, and she had the sudden thought that surprising him like that had been a bad idea. The overhead lights were long, old-fashioned fluorescent tubes, and they didn't snap on like an incandescent lamp would. There was a hint of a glow, followed by a short humming sound, and then the room filled with light. By that time the guy had closed the gap between them to about five feet, and Nora stepped back, stumbling over the stool. When she pulled up short, he did, too, but her sense of command over the situation was already gone. He'd frightened her— she knew it, and he knew it.

"I said—"

"I heard what you said." His eyes took in the room around them, seeing the emptiness, the dark office behind her. It was obvious that she was alone. She wished she'd stayed on the stool, kept the lights off, just waited and watched.

"You have no right to be in here," she said. "Can't you read the sign out front? We're—"

"Closed," he said and took another step toward her, that damn belt buckle glinting under the fluorescent lights. "Yeah, I saw the sign. You usually sit here in the dark after you close up?"

"Maybe I should start to more often, if people keep breaking into my shop. Now get out. You want to talk to me, I'll be back in on Monday."

"I didn't break in anything." He was one pace away now. "Door was unlocked."

"I want you out. I don't know who you think you are, walking in here like this, but I want you out right now. I told you before, if this car's owner wants to call me, he can. Otherwise, stay the hell away from here, unless you'd like me to call the police."

"No, I don't think I'd like that, at all," he said. "And neither would you."

The phone was in the office. All those times she'd had to rush back in to catch a call because she'd forgotten the cordless unit paled in comparison to this. Her cell phone was in the truck, where she always left it because she couldn't be bothered with personal calls during the day.

"Get out," she said again. He was in her space, almost chest to chest, and she'd backed up against the office door, which was still locked. To open it she'd have to turn her back to him, and that didn't seem like a good idea.

"You're going to listen to me, hon, and listen good," he said, and a sour chill went through her stomach, the words and tone sounding like something a drunk would say as he advanced on his wife with a belt in hand. "You got no problem here, okay? Just tell me where the guy who drove this car went, and I'm gone."

"I'll ask you one more time to leave. Then I'm calling the police."

He didn't say anything. She gave it a few beats of silence and then went for the office door. The keys were already in her hand—had been since she sat down on the stool—and she reached for the lock, standing so close to the door her nose almost brushed it when she turned. Had the key raised but not inserted into the lock when his hand closed around her wrist.

Her first reaction was to reach back with her free hand and claw at his face. A year ago, it would've made an impression, too—long, French-tipped fingernails—but you didn't work on cars with nails like that. Now her fingers slid harmlessly over his cheek. So she twisted and kicked at his knee, using her heel instead of the front of her foot. Caught him on the side of his knee, so his leg buckled, and for a moment he was off balance and she thought she'd get free. He didn't lose his hold on her wrist, though, used it instead to jerk her forward and spin her around and then she felt a wrenching pain in her shoulder and her face hit the door and she knew it was going to get very bad, very fast.

Eight

The sign on the door said CLOSED, and there were no lights on in the office. Frank was early, too. So had she forgotten, or was she planning to come back? It was only five twenty. He stood on the sidewalk in front of the body shop with two full grocery bags in his hands and wondered what the hell he should do.

She didn't seem like the type to forget. Too put together and in control for that. Things had gotten a little hectic there, with the gray-haired guy rushing everybody, and it was possible. She'd said six, though, and that was a while off, so maybe he should just wait.

He set the bags down by the front door and looked around, wondering what Nora Stafford drove. The only car parked on this side of the street was a black Dodge Charger a block away. No cars in the handful of parking spaces in front of the shop. Maybe she'd gone out on another tow. He'd check to see if the truck was still parked behind the shop. If not, he'd wait. If so . . . maybe wait a little less.

Leaving the groceries where they were, he walked around the building and into the back parking lot. There was a wire security fence around the lot to protect the towed vehicles, but the gate was open, suggesting she hadn't left for the day. He went through the gate and into the parking lot and saw the tow truck parked there, his battered Jeep behind it. Okay, she wasn't out on a tow. But the gate wasn't locked, either. So where the hell had she gone?

At first, he thought he'd imagined the cry. Short and muffled, not a scream but a mild sound of outrage, or maybe pain. He tilted his head and listened and heard nothing but silence. Took a few steps toward the back door. Still no sounds, but now he could see light on the other side of the door. Then something fell inside, a clang of metal on concrete.

He saw them as soon as he opened the door. A tall man with his back to Frank, shoving Nora Stafford against a tool-box on the far wall. He had her arm twisted behind her back and his other hand covered her mouth while he used his weight to keep her pinned against that toolbox and spoke in a low voice. Frank probably could have made out the words if he'd tried, but he was already moving, crossing the concrete floor fast and quiet, sidestepping enough to keep himself positioned behind the tall man's back, out of his line of sight.

It was maybe fifty feet from the back door to where they stood, and Frank made about forty of it before the guy heard him or sensed the motion. He twisted his head, saw Frank coming at him, and shoved Nora Stafford away. A small pile of bolts and a socket wrench hit the floor with her, bouncing off the concrete in a jingle of metal as the tall man reached under his jacket and brought a gun up.

For his thirteenth birthday, Frank Temple's father gave him a musty hardbound book with a blue cover. *Kill or Get Killed*, the title. A close-quarters combat text. His grandfather's book, then his father's, now Frank's. *Read it,* his father told him. *All of it.* Frank had. Two weeks later, his father challenged him to try to take a gun out of his hand. The first of many lessons.

The gun facing him now was a 9mm automatic, and the man who held it was used to the sight of a gun having some stopping power on its own, because he kept lifting it, passing over Frank's body and aiming for his face. He wasn't planning to shoot. Frank knew that as he closed the rest of the distance between them. Put a gun in the face of most people, they'll stop moving. That was the expectation. The reality was going to be a little different.

Frank's first strike, delivered a quarter of a second before the next, was with the edge of his left hand on the wrist that held the gun. He moved his head down and to the right as he did it, and then the gun was pointing harmlessly away from him. The second strike was really two at the same time—he hit the tall man's chin with the heel of his right hand while he brought his right knee up and into the groin. It was a simple move, using the momentum he already had from his forward rush, but it was effective. He actually missed with his knee, hit on the inside of the man's thigh instead of the groin, but since the guy's head had already snapped back the blow was enough to keep him going. He hit the same toolbox that he'd pinned Nora Stafford against, and now Frank caught the man's wrist with his left hand and slammed it into the metal edge of the toolbox. The gun came free and bounced away. Frank ignored it, got his hand behind the other man's neck while he released his wrist and then slammed him forward, using his leg to upend him and spill him onto the floor.

The guy took the fall well, rolled back onto his feet and lunged upward just in time to be greeted with the socket wrench Frank had recovered from the floor. He laced it downward with an easy stroke, about fifty percent of his strength going into the blow, but it was plenty. Caught the guy right across the back of his skull and dropped him back onto the floor.

It should have been done, but Frank was caught by the tide now, unsatisfied with just how damn easy this had been, wanted to grab that gun off the floor and put it to the bastard's knee and blow a cloud of blood and bone onto the concrete. He went for the gun, saw it wasn't on the floor, and looked up to see Nora Stafford standing with the weapon in her hand. Her eyes moved from Frank to the man at his feet, and then she held the gun out.

"Here."

It was a Glock, no safety to remove, just squeeze that

trigger and watch the thing kill. Frank knew the gun well. By the time it touched his palm, though, the flush of rage was gone, a cool calm sliding back into its place. He slipped the Glock into his waistband, cast one glance at the unconscious man on the floor, and then turned back to Nora Stafford.

"It would seem," he said, "that you should probably call the police."

Frank was worried about her until she came back out of the office. Was she going to fall apart, get hysterical, give him another problem to deal with before the cops showed? Then she stepped back into the room and stared at the tall son of a bitch stretched out on the concrete and he knew she was fine. The look was laden with anger and disgust, not fear.

"You're early," she told Frank.

He nodded. "Didn't want my milk to spoil."

A smile tugged at the corner of her mouth. "Wouldn't want that, no. Thanks for the help. He just walked right in here . . ."

"You don't know him?"

"No. He came in this afternoon and asked about the Lexus."

Frank tilted his head. "Car that I hit?"

"You got it."

He blew out a long sigh as a siren began to close on the body shop and looked to the side, where the partially disassembled Lexus stood.

"That guy was all wrong. Shit, I'm sorry. I should have said something earlier. Had a bad sense about him, but I was trying to ignore it. Figured it had nothing to do with me."

That was total bullshit—Frank's original sense about the guy was a personal thing indeed, but he didn't see what would be gained from explaining that to Nora.

"I had the same sense, and told myself the same thing," she said, "but I didn't count on this."

She was holding her right wrist with her left hand, rubbing it gently, and Frank saw for the first time the dark red streaks left on her skin, left by a firm and no doubt painful grasp.

"You okay?" he said.

"Fine." She dropped her arm as if embarrassed to have her pain noted.

"What did he want?" Frank gestured at the unconscious man with his toe.

"To know where your buddy in the Lexus went."

"No kidding?" Frank looked at the guy on the floor. He'd arrived pretty damn fast after the car was left at Stafford's Collision and Custom. And if he didn't know where Dave O'Connor had gone, then how had he found the Lexus?

Frank slid the Glock out of his waistband and looked at it. Good gun, not uncommon, but the sort of thing preferred by people who knew what they were doing. The guy he'd taken it from hadn't been that bad, either. Just hadn't expected Frank to be any good, that was the difference. The way he'd shoved Nora past him and cleared the gun in one swift, easy motion . . . he'd been around.

"He told me the guy's name was Vaughn," Nora said.

"What?"

"Dave O'Connor, right? That's what he told us his name was. This guy, he said the person driving the Lexus was named Vaughn."

"You see a driver's license, any sort of ID?"

She shook her head, and he saw a spark of irritation in her eyes. Maybe at him for asking, maybe at herself for not getting it.

"Anything in the car?" Frank asked, but the sirens were in the parking lot outside, and Nora walked away from him, toward the door. The guy on the floor was starting to come back, rolling his right foot a little, eyes still closed, left side of his face pressed to the cold stone.

The cop came in with Nora, and Frank was surprised to see it was just one guy. About forty, ruddy faced, thick fingers. He was speaking into the microphone near his collarbone as he entered, reporting his position and situation, casting a scowl at the sight of the body on the floor. When he was done talking into his radio, he withdrew a plastic bag from his hip pocket and reached out to Frank.

"Gimme the gun." His badge said *MOWERY.*

Frank dropped the gun in the bag, and Mowery sealed the plastic lock and jammed the gun, bag and all, into his belt. He nodded at the man at his feet.

"His gun."

"That's right."

"You took it from him."

"Uh-huh."

"After he pulled it."

"Yeah."

Mowery studied Frank as if he weren't sure he believed it. "What'd you hit him with?"

"Hands, at first. Then a wrench."

"That seemed like a wise idea to you? Swinging on a man with a gun?"

"It worked."

"Hmm." Mowery squatted beside the tall man, whose eyes had fluttered open, leaving him staring blearily across the floor. "Looks like he's 'bout ready to rejoin the world. Best that he do that with his hands cuffed, don't you think?"

"Nobody else coming?" Frank said.

Mowery gave him a sour look. "We got a lot of county and few cars to cover it right now, son. You really think I need to bring all of them off the roads, help me deal with this? Seems to me it isn't that difficult a situation."

Should've been here five minutes ago, Frank thought. *Like to see* you *come across that room when he showed the gun.*

Mowery got the cuffs off his belt and fastened the man's hands behind his back. The prisoner was fully conscious by the time the second cuff snapped shut, twisting his head to try to look back at Mowery. The movement didn't work so well; he made a soft grunt that seemed driven more by nausea than pain and laid his cheek back on the concrete.

"I hit him pretty well," Frank said. "Might have a concussion. Maybe need an ambulance."

"He isn't gonna die in my car before he gets to a hospital." Mowery leaned over and flicked the man's cheek. "You with us, asshole? Want to walk out to the car with me, get that headache checked?"

The guy grunted again, and Mowery wrapped one hand over the handcuffs and the other in the guy's shirt, then hauled him upright with a jerk.

"You can stand," he said, as the man's legs started to buckle. "Stand *up*, damn it!"

Excellent procedure, Frank thought. *Way to be concerned with the potential medical condition. Should be filming this for a police academy.*

"All right," Mowery said when his prisoner held his own footing. "Let me get him in the car, get him down to the hospital. Don't want the son of a bitch dying on us, do we? I finish with him, three of us are gonna talk."

The tall man's movements seemed steady enough heading across the room to the door, shuffling along without comment, casting one long, hard stare at Nora as he passed her. She gazed right back at him and flicked her middle finger up. Mowery, walking behind his prisoner, reached out and grabbed a handful of the guy's short hair and twisted his head away from Nora.

"You don't look at the lady, shithead. You don't even *look*."

They stepped out the door. Frank and Nora walked that far and then stopped, standing just inside as Mowery guided the tall man toward the police cruiser parked about twenty feet away, a Lincoln County Sheriff logo on the front door. Mowery opened the back door of the car, put his hand on the back of his prisoner's head, and started to shove him into the seat. He was facing the inside of the car, and when a man rose from behind the trunk, on the opposite side, Mowery never saw him. Had no idea trouble was at hand until Nora shouted, and Frank went through the door and started toward them as the new man, wearing a camouflage jacket and black boots, hit Mowery in the side of the head with a handgun. Mowery fell into his prisoner, the two of them tumbling into the backseat in a crush of bodies, and then the gun swung down again and Mowery's nose shattered and blood sprayed the inside of the window.

Frank had taken a few steps toward them when the new man whirled and lifted his gun, and just as he'd been so certain before that there *wouldn't* be any shots if he kept moving, this time he knew there would. He lifted his hands and backpedaled, and for a moment he was sure the crazy bastard was going to fire anyhow. Then Mowery, sliding down out of the car to the ground, reached out and got his fingers in his attacker's shirt, and that was enough to draw another whip of the gun. It was two seconds of distraction, but it got Frank back inside.

He grabbed Nora around the waist and pulled her into the body shop and swung the door shut behind them with his free hand. Nora's feet tangled with his, and she started to fall. He let her go, turned away as she hit the floor hard on her ass, reached for the dead-bolt lock and turned it. He banged his hand over the light switch and dropped to the floor, and then it was just the two of them inside the dark room and Mowery outside with his prisoner and a man with a gun.

Nine

They'd been closed for the day. That was the first thought Nora had, lying on the cold concrete floor with paint chips under her palms and dust in her mouth. She'd locked the door and hung the CLOSED sign, ready to drive home and take a shower. Should be curled up on the couch now with a pillow under her head and a warm sunset filling the living room. Instead she was here with a wounded cop and two gunmen outside and an oddly capable stranger crouched beside her.

"He might've killed him," she said, pushing upright. "Do you think he could have—"

"Get the phone," Frank said. "Call 911."

He disappeared then, slithering off into the darkness almost noiselessly, toward the row of toolboxes on the far wall. His motion was enough to propel her own, and she started for the office on her hands and knees, went about ten feet before she felt foolish and stood up. If they were going to start shooting through the walls, they'd have done it.

The thought had hardly left her mind when the gunshots started. Four in succession, muffled by the walls of the building but somehow seeming the loudest sounds she'd ever heard. She was back on the floor before the final shot was fired, pressed down into the dust and grime. In her mind, holes opened in the walls and bullets tore through and sought her in the darkness and found her in an explosion of black pain. But the shots had been directed somewhere else; there was no sound against or inside the building. The cop, then. Mowery.

"They killed him," she said, and Frank's answer was immediate.

"Tires."

"What?"

"They shot the tires on the police car."

She rolled over and chanced a look back at the door, expecting to see him there, surveying the scene. There were only shadows, and she finally found him across the room, a long ratchet in his hand.

"How do you know?"

"You could hear them pop."

Could hear them *pop?* She'd heard nothing but the shots, was *still* hearing the shots, rattling around in her ears as though the bullets remained active, floating out there somewhere, looking for a destination, for *her*.

Frank crossed the room, the ratchet dangling in his right hand, but his walk was unconcerned. He reached for the dead bolt, and she hissed at him in shock.

"What are you doing?"

"They're gone," he said and opened the door. Nora braced for more gunshots, but none came. Frank stood in the doorway for a second, and from the floor she could see past him to the police car, which now rested on its rims, the tires reduced to cloaks of flabby rubber. The back door of the car stood open, and Mowery's body was slumped behind it, only his legs visible to Nora.

"Make that call," Frank said, and then he stepped outside.

She'd left the phone on the stool by the office door when Mowery arrived, and when she reached for it she saw the ugly red marks on her wrist. The pain in her arm and shoulder seemed to pulse faster now. When the 911 operator answered, Nora's explanation came out in a voice she'd never heard—too fast, too high, on the edge of hysteria. She brought it down with an effort, explained what had happened to Mowery, and then disconnected despite the operator's attempt to keep her on the line. She went to Frank, walking to the open back door, one she passed through countless times each day, now looming like the most treacherous of gateways.

Frank was kneeling beside Mowery, and there was blood on his jeans. He'd stretched Mowery out on the gravel, and the cop made neither motion nor sound. Frank turned to her.

"Ambulance on the way?"

"And the police." She took a single step outside, pulling against the strings of a fearful desire to cling to the safety of the building. The parking lot was empty except for Mowery's car.

"They're gone?" she asked.

"Yeah. Probably not far, though. No cars in the parking lot except this one, and the only one I saw on the street was empty, so that's not where the second guy was waiting."

"They came in a Dodge Charger the first time."

He looked up. "New model? Kind of sporty-looking thing?"

"Yes."

"Well, that's what was parked out front, but it was empty when I got here. So I don't know why the first guy went after you alone. Where was his friend? Why'd he wait on the cop before he decided to help him out? Doesn't make sense."

He said all of this while working on Mowery, checking his pulse and loosening his shirt collar.

"Is he okay?" Nora asked.

"He's not going to die, but he's not going to feel or look right for a while, either."

She rocked up on her toes to look past Frank's shoulder at the cop, and when she saw him her eyes seemed to swim out of focus, everything a blur of red. She sucked a breath in through her teeth and forced herself to look again. His nose was almost unrecognizable, turned into a bloody smear across the right side of his face, and shredded lips revealed broken teeth.

Frank pulled his own shirt off and used it to wipe gently at Mowery's face. Then he sat back on his heels with a frown, studying the unconscious cop before leaning forward to move him again. He tilted him off his back and onto his side, tucked the shirt under his head, and worked on the angle of his neck until Mowery's face was pointed slightly down, toward the pavement.

"Shouldn't you leave him on his back?" Nora said.

"I don't know how well he can breathe. There can't be much air going through his nose, and if he's on his back all that blood goes into his throat. I want it to drip away from his throat."

Nora looked away again and took the door frame in her hand, squeezed it tight.

"I almost missed that phone call," she said, and if Frank heard her he didn't respond. He wouldn't know what she was talking about anyhow. Wouldn't know that the Lexus had been one ring from being bound for someone else's body shop, someone else's life.

Report a routine assault, and it takes a while before the cops finish sorting it out. Report an assault *on* a cop, and watch that time frame expand.

Frank told the story six times to three different cops—everybody seemed to want to hear him run through it twice—after Mowery had been taken to the hospital. He was semiconscious when the ambulance got there, but in no state to explain the attack to his police brethren. That put it back on Frank and Nora, who had an intensely interested audience. Seemed to Frank that it must have been a long time since someone bloodied up a cop in Tomahawk.

They started at the body shop, walking two of the cops through it step by step, then went to the police station to explain it to a third, this time on tape. By the time they were done, the sun was gone and the small town was quiet, moving on toward nine in the evening.

One of the officers dropped them both off at the body shop. The groceries were still sitting on the sidewalk out front. Probably not a good idea to try that milk, Frank thought. Man, what a day. Twenty past five, you're worried about keeping your milk cold. Five thirty, you're worried about staying alive.

"If I hadn't promised you a ride," Nora Stafford said, staring at his groceries, "I wouldn't have been here when that asshole showed up. I would've been home already."

"Sorry."

She shook her head. "No, I'm just thinking. If I hadn't promised you the ride, I wouldn't have been here, right? But if I hadn't promised you the ride, *you* wouldn't have been here, either. And if you didn't show up . . ."

Neither of them said anything for a minute after that. Nora shook her head, snapping away from all those possibilities.

"My point is, you *still* need a ride, don't you? And I'd say it's the absolute least I can do."

She managed a smile at that, and Frank felt better. She'd handled the first round well enough, better than most would have. It was the second, that guy rising up out of nowhere and taking Mowery down, that had shaken her.

They walked back into the rear lot—you could see Mowery's bloodstains on the gravel, but Nora kept her eyes high—and out to a little Chevy pickup with the Stafford Collision and Custom logo emblazoned on the side. Frank opened his Jeep and got to work transferring his belongings into the bed of the truck. Nora helped silently. When everything had been moved, Frank paused to get a fresh shirt out of a suitcase, the blood-soaked one having departed with Mowery. Then he was in the passenger seat and Nora was behind the wheel and they were northbound, headed out to the Willow twelve hours after he'd expected to arrive.

"Temple the Third," Nora said as they pulled away from the last stoplight in town.

"What?"

"I heard you give your name to the cops. Frank Temple the Third. Sounds fancy."

He looked out the window. "Not really."

"If you have a son, would you feel obligated to name him Frank Temple the Fourth?"

"No," Frank said. "I certainly would not."

He wished she hadn't overheard him with the cops. He'd gone through the internal bracing that he always did when he gave his name, watching the cop's eyes and waiting for recognition. There wasn't any, though. It had been a few years since his father made headlines.

"You up here by yourself?" she asked.

"Yeah."

"From?"

"All over. Chicago, originally. I've moved around."

"But you've been here before."

He turned back from the window. "You say that like you're sure about it."

She flicked her eyes to the rearview mirror as she accelerated onto the highway.

"You call it the Willow. Not Willow Flowage, not the flowage, but the Willow. First-timers don't say that."

"Interesting. If I want to impersonate a real tourist later, I'll keep that in mind."

"But I don't see any fishing tackle in your stuff, which makes you a real mystery. Everybody that goes to the Willow in May is going to fish. I think you got here about a week early, though. Season hasn't started yet."

"I may do some fishing. The gear's already up at the cabin."

"Really? You own the place? Nice."

"It's my father's."

"Is he joining you? A little father-son bonding?"

"He's dead," Frank said, and she winced.

"I'm sorry."

"That would make you one of the few." Then, to fill the awkward pause, he said, "What'll you do with that car? The Lexus."

"I'm not going to fix it, that's for sure. Minute I hear from him, he'll hear from the cops."

"They ran the VIN and the plate, right? Did they tell you who owned it?"

He was thinking of that powerful and total conviction he'd had when he saw the Florida plate. Devin Matteson's car. He'd been *sure* of it in that moment. Sure of it and reaching for his gun.

"If they already know, they didn't tell me," Nora said. "I bet it's stolen, though. As crazy as all this got, I'm almost positive they won't be able to find out who that guy was from the car."

"Maybe."

She shot him a glance. "You disagree?"

"Not necessarily. I'm just thinking about how fast his buddies showed up. Guy wrecks his car out in the woods, nobody else around except me, and then people immediately are looking for him at your shop. They knew the car was there, but they didn't know where he was, or even what name he was using. How?"

"That's a fancy car. Has the navigation system, the satellite link. Maybe they used that somehow? Called Lexus and reported it stolen or something, got the satellite to position it."

"Could be." Frank was thinking about other methods, though. Things like tracking devices, which, when mixed with men who carried Glocks and had no problem attacking strange women, did not present an appealing scenario.

"All I know is I want that damn car out of my body shop," Nora said.

"Aren't the cops going to impound it?"

"Yes, but I need to get it put back together first. Can't tow a car that's in a dozen pieces, you know? I'll call Jerry in the morning, ask him to come in and put the parts back on so I can get it out of my sight. He'll demand time-and-a-half, I'm sure, but I don't care. I want it gone."

There was vehemence in her voice that Frank hadn't heard before. It was as if she blamed the car.

"Where do you live?" he asked, looking for a more relaxed topic of conversation.

"Almost up to Minocqua. You're not far out of the way for me at all."

"You always lived here?"

"Nope. I've been here for about a year."

It was a disclosure that presented all sorts of questions—where was she from originally, what in the world had brought her to a body shop in Tomahawk—but Frank didn't ask them. She was quiet for a bit, as if waiting for the inquisition. When no questions came, she offered another of her own.

"When was the last time you were up here?"

"Seven years ago."

"That's a long time. How do you know the place is still standing?"

"Guy named Ezra Ballard checks in on it, keeps it in shape."

"Well, no wonder you're so relaxed about it. Nobody in the world's more reliable than Ezra."

"You know him?"

"Everyone does. He's one of a kind. Supposed to be the best guide in the area, too. At least that's what I've been told."

Frank nodded without comment. A hunter without peer, that was Ezra's reputation. The stories Frank knew were probably far from those Nora Stafford had heard, though. A different sort of prey.

They were on Willow Dam Road now, the Chevy's headlights painting the pines with pale light, and at Frank's instruction Nora turned left, toward the dam. This was maybe a quarter mile from where the wreck had taken place. He'd been that close to his destination. Once they were across the dam and past the Willow's End Lodge, he instructed her to take a right turn onto a gravel road leading to the lake.

"You're lucky to have a place right on the water," she said. "That's tough to find at the Willow, with all the development restrictions."

"Yeah." Frank's interest in conversation had vanished when she made the turn, taking all the moisture in his mouth with it. This felt stranger than he'd expected, and he'd expected it to be damn strange.

They rumbled past the three-way fork that divided the gravel road into separate drives, and Frank told Nora to stay left. Then they were past it and facing the cabin.

"Home sweet home?" Nora said.

"Yeah. This is it."

He sat there silently until he felt her curious eyes on him, and then he shook his head and opened the door and stepped out into a cool breeze that came at him like a kiss. In front of him the dark lawn ran out to a hand-laid log wall that stood above the beach. Since it was still spring, the water would be high enough to bang against the logs when the wind blew. By midsummer, it would be down, fed out of the dam regularly to replenish the Wisconsin River and its valley. Stars and a half moon hung above the lake, everything pristine until Frank turned his head a touch to the right and saw the blinking red lights of a cellular tower miles away. He remembered when the cell tower went up. His father hated the tower. Loathed it. One night, sitting with the Coleman lantern crackling beside them, he'd taken out a gun and emptied a clip in the direction of the tower, the bullets dropping harmlessly into the water. They'd had a hell of a laugh over that.

"Beautiful," Nora said softly, and only then was Frank aware of her standing beside him.

"Yeah," he said. "It's all right."

He turned back to the truck, and she went with him, grabbed one of his bags out of the bed, and started for the cabin.

"Just set it down outside the door," he said. "Thanks. I'll get the rest."

"I'll help you get everything inside. It's not a problem."

"*No.* Thank you, but no. Just set it outside the door and I'll take care of it."

She stood with the bag in her hand and cocked her head, puzzled. Then she raised her eyebrows and made a slow nod—*whatever you say, psycho*—and dropped the bag to the ground in front of the door. Frank felt a surge of irritation and embarrassment at his snapped words, but he couldn't help wanting her gone. He didn't want anybody walking into that cabin with him when he stepped inside for the first time in seven years.

"Okay," she said. "Well, then, I guess I'll take off."

"Thanks for the ride." He pulled a few more bags out of the truck. "Really, this was a huge help. I didn't want to spend the night in a hotel."

"Hey, least I could do."

They stood there awkwardly for a few seconds, facing each other in the dark. Then she moved toward the truck, and he lifted two bags to his shoulders.

"I'll give you a call soon, let you know what sort of time frame to expect on your car," she said, pulling the driver's door open. "Should get it done a lot faster now that the cops are taking the other one."

"Thanks. Let me know what you hear from the police, too, okay?"

"Sure."

She got in the truck then and started the engine, and Frank turned away so as not to be blinded by the headlights, reached in his pocket and closed his fingers around an old and well-remembered key chain, and went to the door.

Ten

Looking back, Grady figured at least one reason he'd grown so attached to the Temple boy didn't involve guilt. He understood something about family legacies. About becoming something you didn't want to become simply because it was what you knew. What you'd seen, what you'd been taught, what ran through your veins.

Grady lived alone now, in an apartment that was about the same size of the kitchen in the house he'd shared with Adrian, and though it still felt relatively new and certainly nothing like home, it had been nine years since he moved in. *Nine years.*

His father had been a good-natured drunk who never lifted a hand to his son, not once in all those twelve-beer nights. Instead, he'd come through the door unsteady and mumbling, walk into Grady's room, and apologize. Sometimes they were short speeches; sometimes they went on for an hour or more. Tearful, choked-voice monologues in which the old man would take blame for all the wrongs of the world, acknowledge they were all his fault. He was sorry for being a bad father, sorry for being a bad husband, sorry they didn't have more money, sorry they never took a vacation, sorry Grady was an only child, sorry their landlord wouldn't allow pets because every boy should have a dog.

There were nights when Grady would lie there and wish his dad would just come in swinging, the way drunks were supposed to. *Hit me, damn it,* he'd think, *slap me around, do anything but this crying and apologizing, you pussy.*

He never hit him, though. Just kept right on apologizing until the day he had a heart attack on the corner of Addison and Clark, walking into Wrigley for a baseball game. Grady, who'd been home from college and waiting at their seats inside the park, was sure his father would have apologized for that, too, if only he could.

He'd made up his mind, though, that he would not become his father. No chance in this world. He'd make some mistakes, sure, but he would not let remorse over them haunt his days, not spend his life apologizing for faults that he never attempted to correct. He'd be assertive, he'd be strong, and any character flaws acquaintances might whisper about during parties would be borne forth from those qualities. *Too cocky,* they'd say, *too stubborn, too sure of himself. Never admits when he's wrong.*

He'd been wrong with Frank Temple. Hadn't admitted it. Made his mistake, moved on. Except for those computer checks. Except for those. One of the reasons he kept monitoring the kid was that Grady knew a few things about legacies. But his had only been, well, pathetic. Not dangerous, not in the way Frank Temple's could be. The kid wanted to beat it, wanted to leave that bloody coat of arms behind, but it wasn't going to be an easy task. And Grady surely hadn't helped him. If anything, he'd given him a firm push in the wrong direction. What he'd done in his time with seventeen-year-old Frank Temple III was his greatest professional and personal shame. With the exception of Jim Saul, an agent down in Miami, it was also a private shame. Nobody else knew the way Grady had manipulated that kid. Frank surely did not, and that, more than anything else, was what kept Grady checking the computers, always monitoring the young man he hadn't seen in years and wondering what it meant that he'd show more devotion out of guilt than he ever had out of love.

The case against Frank's father had been a huge story—nothing attracted attention like the story of a federal agent turned contract killer—and when it broke the accolades and praise were rolling in and the media was loving the Bureau, loving Grady. What they didn't understand was that when Frank's father killed himself he had effectively aborted the future of the investigation. He'd known so much, could have provided information that would have taken Manuel De-Caster down, destroyed one of the deadliest and most powerful crime entities in Florida, hell, in the country. It had been shaping up to be one of the most significant organized crime prosecutions in years, and then Frank Temple II lifted his gun to his lips, squeezed the trigger, and killed the case along with himself.

So even as the story was arriving it was dying, and while the media didn't understand that at first, Grady and Jim Saul sure as hell did. All they had left was Frank Temple III. The boy was supposedly closer to his father than anyone else had been, and the stories of his unusual education, the molding process that had been going on, were legion. He'd even made a trip down to Miami with his father, and there had been at least a short visit with Devin Matteson.

It was for Devin that Jim Saul most hungered. Devin was a phantom, involved in every level of DeCaster's operation, investigated by the DEA and FBI and Miami PD for years without a single conviction. Temple was supposed to be the first domino, Matteson the second, but Temple had managed to go down without touching any of the others. They could start the chain over with Matteson, Saul was sure. And there was a chance, maybe even a strong one, that Temple's son knew far more than they dared imagine. It would take a little bit of a sales pitch, that was all. A few talks about betrayed legacies, a few reminders of just how much Devin deserved his share of the punishment, what a shame, no, what a *crime* it would be to see Frank's father alone bear that load.

He'd walked into that kid's house knowing the truth, but with a promise—a professional oath—not to share it. Nothing evil in that, right? Except he'd shared another story and passed it off as the truth, a story that filled a grieving child with white-hot hate and a vendetta.

Grady had spent some time on it. He and the boy had a good many conversations about those things before Frank's mother grew concerned and a newspaper reporter learned of the unusual bond and began to ask for interviews and the whole thing fell apart, leaving Frank with his hate and Grady and Saul with nothing to show for the ploy.

It had been worth the effort, though. That's what they'd told each other early on, that if it had paid off and the kid actually knew something and shared it, well, then it absolutely would have been worth it. You had to prioritize, after all. Without the boy, they had no case, and they needed a case.

Except they already had one. While Grady was down in the basement of that house in Kenilworth, showing Frank pictures of his father with Devin Matteson and talking of loyalty and betrayal, trying to build enough hatred to coax a reaction, a group of rookie agents in Miami were working the streets and chasing bank records, and a few years and two ugly trials later DeCaster was in prison. No help needed from Frank Temple III, no lies to a grieving son, a *child,* required.

It was the sort of thing that was hard to put out of your mind.

Grady kept his eye on the kid, though, and found a measure of relief in each year that passed without incident. Frank was making his own place in the world, and it looked like a peaceful one.

Had looked that way, at least, until the day after his arrest for public intoxication down in Indiana, when Jim Saul called Grady at home on a Friday night and asked if he'd heard about Devin Matteson.

Grady took his feet down off the ottoman and set his beer aside and leaned forward, his grip tight on the phone.

"Heard what about him, Jimmy?"

"He's in the hospital down in Miami, with three gunshot wounds. Looked like he was going to die when they brought him in, but he's been making a furious recovery ever since.

You know the kind of shape that prick was in. Ironman, right? He's conscious again, and it's almost a sure bet he'll make it."

"They have the shooter?"

"Nope. And if Matteson knows, he's not saying. But somebody plugged him three in the back, and you know how he will want to handle that."

"Personally," Grady said, and he felt cold. "What do you hear on suspects?"

"Could be anybody. If they've got good leads, I'm not aware of them."

"Temple's son was arrested in Indiana night before last. Public intoxication. When was Matteson shot?"

"The day before that," Saul said slowly. "And how do you know the Temple kid was arrested for a PI?"

"Word travels," Grady said.

"Right," Saul said. "Well, I thought you'd like to hear about it. And if I hear something new, you'll be the first to know."

They hung up, and Grady dropped the phone onto the cushion beside him and stared at the wall.

Devin Matteson shot in the back, Frank Temple III arrested for drinking in Indiana a day later. Celebration, maybe? A few champagne toasts to the dead?

No. No, that couldn't be it. The kid was doing fine, and Matteson had any number of enemies. The list probably grew by the day.

Frank had wanted him, though. Frank had wanted Matteson *badly,* and by the end, when Grady was trying to make amends, he'd urged the boy to put that away. Told him that he'd *have* to ignore it if he wanted to stay away from his father's sort of end. Frank had accepted it, too, at least verbally, but Grady remembered going back to the range with him a few weeks after the lies had started, remembered the look on Frank's face and the perfect cluster of bullets in the target. He'd known damn well the kid was seeing Devin Matteson down there.

And whose fault was that, Grady? Whose fault?

He picked up the beer again, drank what was left, and stood up to go after another one.

"I should have asked about the wounds," he said aloud, talking to his empty apartment. That would have settled it. Because if there'd been more than an inch or two between those bullet holes, then Frank Temple III hadn't been pulling the trigger.

Ezra Ballard ran an electric fillet knife down the perch's side in a smooth, quick stroke. Turned the fish over and repeated the motion. Moved the filets to the side and then lobbed the fish head over the fence and into the dog kennel. Two of his hounds hit the fish carcass together. There was a soft growl, the sound of snapping teeth, and then the winner retreated with his prize.

Last summer, an architect from Madison had given Ezra a nice lecture after watching him feed the leftover fish to his dogs. Fish in that condition wasn't suitable for dogs. Could do serious harm. Ezra had tried to stay polite, listening to him. Finally Ezra asked him if he had any experience with bear hounds. No, not with bear hounds, the guy said. Plenty of experience with dogs, though. What kind of dogs, Ezra asked. Pugs, the guy said. Took all Ezra had to smile and nod, wait till the guy wrote out the check and went on his way. Pugs.

Ezra had selected all four of his hounds when they were just weeks-old puppies, watched them in their litters and picked up on traits of personality that set them apart. Trained them himself, spent long summer hours in the woods and brush with them, teaching them to work as a team. Though the hunting season wasn't till October, you could run bear in the summers in Wisconsin for dog-training purposes. On days when he didn't have to guide, he generally loaded the hounds into their crates and into the back of the truck and set off to take advantage of the free time in the way he loved best: out in the woods, alone except for the dogs. Of course, it wasn't like being alone at all. The dogs were Ezra's family.

More than pets, more than friends. And when the air turned chill as fall began to lose its early skirmishes with winter, and the dogs bayed long and loud in the dark woods, Ezra with gun in hand as they chased their prey? Then, the dogs were something altogether nearer to his heart: comrades.

Boone, a six-year-old bluetick, was the pack's alpha male even though he wasn't the largest. Bridger (they were all named after famous woodsmen—Boone, Carson, Bridger, Crockett) was bigger in size, taller and fifteen pounds heavier, but he lacked the aggressive edge that dogs respected in a leader. He was a diplomat, Ezra had decided, whereas Boone tended toward the preemptive strike. Ezra felt closest to Boone, but he spoiled Bridger and tried to put out the idea that he was the favorite.

He cleaned a final fish, tossed its remains into the kennel, and then gathered up the filets and his knife, turned off the floodlight above the cleaning station, and went into the house. He cooked the fish and ate it with potatoes and carrots that he'd seasoned and wrapped in foil and cooked outside on the propane grill, ate at the kitchen table, facing the mounted head of a ten-point buck he'd taken five years earlier. Everything from the décor of his room to his clothing to his daily activity told him what he was, reminded him of it, pushed the essence of his life into him from the outside. He was a fishing and hunting guide, a woodsman, a local. His clients knew it, his friends knew it, his neighbors knew it. After nearly forty years, he was starting to know it, too. Mission accomplished.

You became what you wanted to become. That's what Ezra believed. You could become it if you tried hard enough, could take what you really were and change it, force-feed yourself a new life until it became your old life, too, blurred together until a better self emerged.

He'd spent twenty years in Detroit and another four in the jungle trying to decide what he'd be if he could choose. Nothing stopping him, he'd move back in time, open up the west with Frémont and Carson and the others who were there, see this country in all the beauty it had once held.

Reality did stop him on that one, and so he chose the next best thing, a life spent on the water and in the woods and far away from the urban world of greed and hustles and constant violence that he'd known growing up. He'd been twenty-five when he arrived here, a young man with an old warrior's body count behind him, had no idea where to find a walleye, no idea how to track a deer or run a bear. He learned those things, and now he taught those things, and there were moments when it seemed that the perception of others—that idea that he'd always been here—was true.

He finished his meal and washed his dishes and gathered his car keys and went out to the truck. Took Cedar Falls Road to the logging road, went bouncing over the uneven track. Anybody else would spend hours, maybe even a full day, trying to locate that car from the land. Ezra was different, though. A tree that looked identical to the rest stood out as a landmark to him, each bay and inlet and island as familiar as the houses of neighbors in a suburb. He knew the gray-haired man had taken the logging road, and he knew which fork of it he'd followed.

The road went on a good half mile past the point where Ezra brought his truck to a halt, but he didn't want to drive all the way down to the water, have his headlights visible from the island. He took the rest of it on foot, the wet earth sucking at his boots. Here the soil was almost boglike, holding moisture long after the last rain had passed. The lake was surrounded by more than sixteen thousand acres of forest that were protected by the state, home to bear and deer and three wolf packs. Home to Ezra.

There was a boat ramp farther south, but Ezra knew people who used this logging road as a put-in area for canoes, saved some paddling time if they were headed north. You'd put your canoe in the water and take off across the lake, splitting either north or south around an overgrown island with a few NO TRESPASSING signs posted. The only privately owned island in the entire flowage, out of more than a hundred possibilities. It should never have been privately owned, either. Dan Matteson's grandfather had won it in a bizarre legal case.

Matteson's grandfather, a Rhinelander native, had owned forty acres of good timberland several miles east of the Willow and adjacent to hundreds of acres owned by one of the state's major paper mills. When the mill accidentally clearcut his property, he sued. The case had gone to arbitration, and the arbitrator had decided to award Matteson property of comparable value instead of cash. Back then most of the land around the flowage was owned by the paper mills rather than the state, and the arbitrator had issued Matteson a small tract on a point of land on the eastern shore and one of the only islands in the whole lake that was high enough to avoid regular flooding. The total land came to just under five acres, a fraction of what he'd lost, but the arbitrator argued that it was waterfront property and therefore worth more. Matteson had accepted, and now, sixty years later, there remained one privately owned island on the flowage.

Dan had grown up around here, and on long days and longer nights in Vietnam, he'd talked of the place. To Ezra, who'd never been more than forty miles from Detroit until he shipped out, the flowage had sounded like a dream world. Miles of towering dark forests, pristine lakes, islands. The island that Dan owned held appeal that Ezra couldn't even put into words, but the longer they stayed overseas the more attached he grew to the idea of the place. He couldn't go back to Detroit. Not if he hoped to avoid the sort of existence he'd left behind.

Just before he'd enlisted, Ezra had gone out with his older brother, Ken, to settle up a debt. The sum owed was four hundred dollars. Ezra had held the arms of an alcoholic factory worker while his brother swung on the guy with a bottle. When the bottle fractured, Ken had hit him one more time in the face, a driving uppercut, and the jagged glass bit into the unconscious man's chin and continued upward, peeling a strip of pink flesh off the bone from jaw to eye socket. They'd left him in the alley after emptying nine dollars from his pockets. The next day, Ezra went to talk to a recruiter.

As his tour wound to a close, and the prospect of returning home became more real, Ezra made an official request to Dan: Could he head up to this place, this Willow Flowage, for just a few months, until he figured something else out?

You're shit-brained, Dan had said. *It's going to be winter, man. Three feet of snow on the ground, you want a cabin with no electricity?*

Snow doesn't sound so bad right now, Ezra answered.

Dan had agreed to it. He headed south for Miami while Ezra went north, Frank Temple taking his job with the marshals and landing in St. Louis at the time, right in the middle.

Miami ruined Dan. The Willow saved Ezra. Absolutely *saved* Ezra. It was hard living but clean living, where you invested your strength and sweat into clearing snow and starting fires, not breaking legs and wielding guns. And there were certain moments, when the evening sun cast a pale red stain across silent snow or when an early spring wind blew up out of the lake with a surprising touch of warmth, that made you want to drop to your knees and thank whatever God you believed in—or maybe one you hadn't believed in—for putting you in that place at that time.

Ezra had been on the island five months when he learned his brother's body had been found in the trunk of a Caprice off Lafayette in Detroit. He skipped the funeral. That summer, Dan and Frank came up for a visit, and Ezra made his pitch. He and Frank should pool resources and buy the additional parcel Dan owned on the point, build a cabin there and create a camp that they could share and pass down to their families. It was the sort of grand plan you can only have when you're young and friendships seem guaranteed to last forever.

Go on, Dan had laughed. *I'll sell you the land, man. But I'm not spending much time out on that damn island, middle of nowhere and nothing to do.*

Then sell it to me, Ezra suggested, the island already sacred ground to him.

Dan shook his head. Slow, with some of the mocking humor gone from his face.

Nah, he said. *I can't sell that one. Not the island. It's in a trust, a legacy deal, to keep the state from taking it. The island goes way back in my family, you know that. I've got a son, and it'll be his someday. I want it to be his.*

So he'd kept his island but rarely appeared there, and Ezra and Frank built a cabin on the smaller parcel around the point and shared some summers and memories. Now, with a few decades of separation, Ezra could look back on it and see that it had been the bellwether, Dan's life moving in a different direction, to a place hidden from Ezra and Frank. The real shame was that it hadn't stayed that way for Frank.

Ezra had lived in the lake cabin for a time, but as soon as he could afford to he bought more land a few miles up the road and built his own house. Eventually Frank Temple bought the lake property in full, put it in a legacy trust for *his* son. Now it had been years since anyone spent a night in either the lake cabin or the one on the island. So much for the legacies.

As he reached the top of the hill he left the road and moved toward the waterline, reentered the trees near where he imagined the car to be, and found it easily. Driven right up to the last tree, all those boughs mashed against it, bleeding sap onto the roof. He ducked beneath the branches, his jeans soaking in moisture when his knee touched the grass, and then came out at the back of the car. Reached into his shirt pocket and withdrew his lighter, flicked the wheel, and held the flame close to the bumper, so he could read the license plate.

It was local. Wisconsin and Lincoln County. That was a surprise. He memorized the numbers and then took his thumb off the lighter and let the flame go out. He hadn't expected a local vehicle. The only people he believed should have access to the island cabin were some thousand miles away. The Lexus had carried a Florida plate, as expected, but now it was gone, and this old heap with a local plate had taken its place. Why?

He left the car and returned the way he'd come through the silent woods. When he reached his truck he decided to go the Willow Wood Lodge instead of home, have a drink and do some thinking before calling it a night. No tourists, this time of year. There were six cars in the parking lot when he arrived, laughter carrying outside. He walked in and found an empty stool at the far end of the bar, had hardly settled onto it before a glass of Wild Turkey and an ice water were placed in front of him. Carolyn, the bartender, didn't need to wait on an order.

"Glad you came in," she said. "Been meaning to give you a call."

"Yeah?"

"Dwight Simonton came in about an hour ago. You know Dwight."

"Sure. He's a good man."

"He said somebody's down at the Temple place. Said there was a fire going outside, somebody sitting there."

"Right idea, wrong owner. Somebody showed up at the island cabin."

Carolyn shook her head. "Dwight said it was the Temple place."

Ezra frowned. "I don't think so. I was just out there today, had a look at it from the water. Nobody's staying there. Been so long since anyone visited either one of those cabins, Dwight probably was confused. Heard something about the island cabin, got it mixed up."

Now Carolyn leaned back and raised her eyebrows. "Come on. Not a soul who lives on this lake doesn't know the Temple place, after the way that crazy guy went out. Dwight told me the fire was right down on the point. You think Dwight can't tell a fire on the island from one on the shore two miles away?"

She was right; Dwight Simonton wouldn't have made that mistake. He and his wife, Fran, had owned a place up here for more than a decade and were the closest things to neighbors the Temple cabin had. If Dwight said it was the Temple cabin, then it was the Temple cabin.

"You don't think," she said, lowering her voice and leaning closer, "it's his kid?"

Of course it was his kid, responding to the message Ezra himself had left, but rather than confirm it, Ezra simply shrugged.

"That'd be something," Carolyn said.

Yeah. That'd be something, all right. Ezra finished his bourbon without a word, tossed some money on the bar, and got to his feet.

"You going down there?" Carolyn asked, her face alight with curiosity.

"Figure I ought to."

She was ready with another question, but Ezra turned away and went to the door, stepped out into a night that now seemed electric. First there'd been the beautiful woman and her gray-haired companion in the Lexus. Then the Lexus was gone and the man hid a new car in the trees. Now someone, probably Frank's son, was back at the Temple cabin. Ezra didn't like the feel of it, the way this group was gathering on his lake. He was responsible for them, he knew. A generation later, maybe, but he'd brought them here all the same.

Eleven

The letter was right where it belonged, framed on the wall beside the corresponding Silver Star. Frank read it while he drank his first beer, read from the date right down to President Harry S. Truman's signature.

In grateful memory of Major Frank Temple, who died in the service of his country in the military operations of Korea, on August 22, 1950. He stands in the unbroken line of patriots who have dared to die, that freedom might live, and grow, and increase its blessings. Freedom lives, and through it he lives, in a way that humbles the undertakings of most men.

The letter had hung above his father's childhood bed, the only tie Frank Temple II ever had to the soldier who'd died in Korea, leaving a wife six months pregnant with the son who would bear his name. Frank Temple II grew up without knowing a father but knowing plenty about his legacy—his name was a hero's name. During D-Day, on beaches filled with heroic acts, the first Frank Temple and his comrades still stood out. Using grappling hooks and ropes, his Army Ranger battalion scaled the cliffs at Point du Hoc, stone towers looming a hundred feet over the sea and protected by German soldiers with clear lines of fire. Into the teeth of that rain of bullets climbed Temple and his fellow Rangers. Casualties were heavy, but the mission was accomplished.

A tough act to follow, but Frank Temple II had done it for

forty-five years. He had his war, Vietnam, where he served as a member of a specialized group so covert and so celebrated that it was still the subject of speculation decades later. MACV-SOG they'd been called: the Special Operations Group, elite soldiers whose chain of command seemed to end with the CIA instead of the Department of Defense. Temple II had matched his father's Silver Star and Purple Heart, then come home to a career as a U.S. marshal, fathering a son who—of course—bore his name, his father's name.

"You've got a lot to live up to." That was his mantra for Frank, a thought shared with the same casual frequency most people used for "Good morning," a constant reminder that Frank's was a line of brave men and heroic deeds.

The hell of it was, Frank had always believed him. Believed *in* him, which was even worse. All the hero bullshit, the talk of honor and courage, it seemed to come from his father's core. It was sacred. Right up until his father killed himself and a team of FBI agents arrived at the house, three months before Frank's high school graduation, he'd believed in his father.

Now, sitting beside a fire with a lukewarm beer in hand, he wondered how long that would have continued. If his father had never been caught, if those FBI agents had never showed up at the door, would they sit here together, sharing a laugh and a beer, Frank steadfast in his faith in the man across the fire from him? Or would he have grown wiser with age, smelled the lie in his father's words, seen evil in eyes that had always looked on him with love?

He would've been proud today, Frank thought. *The way I brought the socket wrench down, the sound it made on the back of that guy's skull, yeah, that's Daddy's boy right there.*

He laughed at that, the sort of laugh you can allow yourself when you're drinking and alone. Laughed for longer than he should have, then lifted his beer to the cabin, a toast to his return. This was their place, a spot of memories shared only with his father, no interlopers here.

He wanted to spill some tears, weep for his father. It had

been four years since he'd last been able to do that. Driving through the Kentucky foothills in the middle of the night, listening to a radio station from some town he'd never heard of when the Pink Floyd song "Wish You Were Here" came on, began chewing at the edges of his brain, then danced right through the center of it when one softly sung line— "Did they get you to trade your heroes for ghosts?"—wafted out of the speakers.

There'd be no tears tonight, though, and maybe those he'd lost on a lonely highway in Kentucky would be the last. If this place, with all its good memories, didn't affect him in that way, then no place ever would.

He wouldn't cry for his father here at the Willow, but he might kill for him. If Devin was really coming back . . . damn, but that would feel good. Frank could do it, too. Bet your ass he could do it. Years of lessons didn't disappear that quickly, not when they were taught by somebody as good as his father.

There'd been a day, sometime in the summer when he was fourteen, that his dad first broached the subject of justified killing. Really laid it out there. They'd been downstairs in the mat room, working out, Frank attacking and his father defending, blocking most of his attempts easily, but every now and then Frank would sneak a blow in. When he did, his father would smile. Glow, almost.

They'd finished and were sitting together with their backs against the cold concrete wall, breathing hard, and his father had said, *There's a lot of bullshit to what I do, son. And to what I did. With the marshals now and the Army before.*

Frank thought he meant bullshit as in boring work, red tape and bureaucracy. That wasn't it, though. As the sweat dried on Frank's neck and back and his heart rate wound down to a slow, steady thump, his father had explained what he meant.

We chase down guys who are evil bastards, Frank. I mean evil, *you understand? Guys who steal and kill and rape and commit any other manner of crime, anything you can think of. Some of them go to prison. A lot of them don't.*

They get off on some technicality, get some lawyer pulling tricks, whatever. But they go right back out on the street and hurt somebody else. I'm not saying the system doesn't work sometimes . . . I'm saying it doesn't all the time. There are guys the system can't touch who aren't worth the air they're breathing. And there's a way to settle it. A natural way.

A natural way. That's what his father thought of killing. That it was the most natural thing in the world, an inherent solution to human conflict, ageless and unsurpassed.

Frank hadn't said anything for a while, until it became obvious his father wanted some sort of response. Then he'd asked what all of that had to do with the Army.

It's the same thing. There's this system in place, right, governments and generals and all the rest, and they're supposed to keep the peace, and everybody wants them to do it without firing a shot. But you know what? They can't. Because there are evil people in the world, son, and they're going to keep doing evil things. And that keeps people like me in demand. People like me, and your grandfather, and you. Somebody who knows how to use a gun and knows when to use it.

That was the first time Frank had been officially included in the list, and it made his head go a little light, the honor of that shared company hitting him deep in his fourteen-year-old boy's heart.

A few years later, his father's body in the ground and face on the front page of the newspaper, the sad truth of moments like that one began to show itself to Frank. He understood what his father had been doing, understood that he'd been rationalizing with himself as much as he'd been offering a philosophy to Frank. But he believed what he said, too, and Frank saw the horror in that, saw the fallacy and savageness and the justification. Yes, the justification. It was still there. Smaller, maybe, weakened, maybe, but not obliterated. It couldn't be. Because his father, evil man or not, was dead, and Devin Matteson—evil man for sure—was alive and free. Cut a deal, hung Frank's father out to dry, and then walked away from it. No punishment, no penance, no pain. He deserved some of all of that. Damn sure deserved some pain.

There'd been another conversation down in the basement that stood out in Frank's memory, and again the true significance hadn't hit for a few years. They'd been down there working on elbow strikes—vertical, horizontal, front, rear, up, down, Frank's dad always demanding greater speed, greater power—while his mother played Tom Petty music loud upstairs, trying to drown them out, unhappy with the violent lessons her son was taking to so well.

That day had been, Frank would later learn, exactly one week after his father came back from Florida having killed two men to avenge Dan Matteson's death. One week living with the reality of it, maybe a couple of weeks of dealing with the decision itself. He'd paused to sip a beer—it was the first time Frank could remember his dad bringing anything but bottled water downstairs with him—and he'd studied his son with a critical eye.

Frank, he'd said, *suppose somebody takes me out one of these days.*

It had still seemed like a game right then, and Frank had answered, *That can't be done, nobody out there good enough,* in a flip, teasing voice, thinking they were just working up to some of the chest-thumping bravado the old man liked to get into during a hard session. His eyes were different, though, darker and more intense.

It can be done, Frank. Probably will be done, someday.

Frank didn't answer.

Suppose it happens, his father had said, *and suppose you know who's responsible. What would you do?*

Still no answer.

Frank? What would you do?

Kill him, Frank said, hating how weak his voice sounded, like a little kid. *I'd find him and I'd kill him.*

Pleasure in his father's eyes. Respect. He'd nodded, finished his beer, and said, *Damn right you would. Damn right.* Then he'd laid a hand on Frank's shoulder and said, *You're a good boy, Frank. Check that—you're a good man.*

A few years later, Frank had been able to flash back on that conversation and once again see what had been working beneath the surface, see the rationalization, the justification, but there'd been something else there, too: a promise.

I'd find him and I'd kill him.

Frank Temple II had killed himself. No scores to settle. None.

I'd find him and I'd kill him.

Frank had endured a lot of pity over the years, some genuine, some false. Sometimes it would be expressed directly to him; other times it just showed in their eyes. *Poor kid. Imagine having such a monster for a father.* The problem, though, the one that Frank saw and nobody else ever could, was that he'd been a good father. Was a murderer, sure, got paid for it, yes, but while that might be enough to define him for the rest of the world, it didn't work for Frank. Didn't replace seventeen years of love. He was a good father. Frank wished he hadn't been, at times. Wished that he'd come home drugged out and violent, knocked Frank and his mother around, threatened the neighbors, that he'd done all of those things that a murderer should do in his own home—but he hadn't. He'd been quick with a joke and a kind word, supportive, interested. When Frank was eleven years old and struck out with the bases loaded to end his Little League team's season, his father had held him in the car as he'd cried in shame and said, "Don't worry, kid, next year we'll cork your bat," and the tears had turned to laughter.

Even those lessons in the basement—which the TV people had fixated on and manipulated to make his father even more of a monster, this man who would ruin a child with violence—they'd been the products of love. His father had seen a different world than most, a world of constant violence. He was preparing his son to go into it, that was all. Saw no other way to raise him than to make him ready for the worst.

"Welcome back."

The voice came from just over his shoulder. Frank's only thought as he whirled to face the speaker was that the man had approached in total silence. It was that realization almost more than the voice that allowed him to place his visitor.

"Uncle Ezra?"

A child's nickname, but it was the first thing that entered his mind. The man stepped closer, out of the darkness, and offered his hand.

"Good to see you, Frank."

Frank got to his feet and accepted the handshake. He was taller than Ezra by several inches, and though he had been since he was in his teens, it still surprised him. The man was bigger in his memory, and quiet and capable, with a habit of sliding out observations that would be the envy of any late-night comedian, delivered in the same slow, soft voice, the jokes usually coming and going before anyone realized what had been said and got to laughing.

"You given up on motorized travel?" Frank said, waving a hand at the dark woods from which Ezra had emerged. Hell of a way to make an appearance.

"Nice night for a walk."

Anyone else would have started with the questions then: When had he arrived, why didn't he call to say he was coming, how long would he be staying? Ezra offered none of them, though, just settled onto a stump beside Frank and said, "Cabin was in good shape." A statement of fact, but one he wanted Frank to acknowledge.

"Of course," Frank said, and he sat, too.

"You intending to let this fire go out?"

It was close to going out, though Frank hadn't noticed that as he'd sat alone with his beer and his memories.

"Uh, no. I just—"

Ezra knelt beside the fire pit and adjusted the wood, fed a few fresh logs into the pile. The flames licked at the fuel and grew, the glow lighting Ezra until he stepped back, satisfied, and returned to his stump. Frank was staring into the fire, but Ezra sat sideways, so his eyes were never directly on the flames. Frank had asked his father about that once years ago. *He doesn't face the fire because he wants to keep his night vision,* his dad had said. *It's an old habit, buddy. One that lingers.*

"Boat's in the shed," Ezra said, "but I took the motor off and put it in the cabin."

"I saw that."

"Figured the shed might make an easier target if somebody wanted to break in. But I come around enough that most people know better."

"Yeah. I appreciate that."

"Hell," Ezra said, poking at the fire with his boot. It got quiet after that, just the fire popping and hissing and the trees creaking in a steady wind. There'd been loons when Frank was a kid, lots of them, but tonight he had yet to hear one of those haunting calls. He'd been up in the summer on every trip but one. That year, they came in the dead of winter for a weekend of ice fishing. Frank had been prepared for a long, cold tramp over the ice to a small hole you sat beside on an overturned bucket or a stool. Instead, Ezra had driven them out onto the lake in a half-ton pickup truck, driven right across the frozen water without any hesitation. Frank, sitting between the two men, the gearshift banging against his knees, had been sure that the ice would break somewhere out in the middle of the lake, swallow them up, Frank finishing his run as a twelve-year-old blue corpse. The ice had held, though, and Ezra's fishing shanty was small but warm. They'd pulled northern and bluegill out of the ice, and his father and Ezra had told stories while sipping bourbon-laced coffee.

"I got your message," Frank said. A fast tremor was working in his chest, just the thought of Devin out there on the island enough to build the anger.

"That seems to have been a mistake."

It was silent, and then Frank said, "What kind of mistake?"

"He's not here," Ezra said.

"Devin."

"Anybody else you'd be asking about? Yes, Devin. He's not up here, Frank."

"But somebody is?"

"Yes."

"Who?"

Ezra hesitated, then shook his head. "I don't know. It's a man and a woman and they're both strangers to me. Might be Devin's renting the place."

Frank felt that tremor fade away, something—was it disappointment?—taking the anger's place. It was crazy to be disappointed, though. Crazy. Because if he'd *wanted* Devin up here, then what, exactly, had he been hoping for? There was an answer to that one, and he didn't want to dwell on it. Couldn't let it into his mind for even a minute. Grady had told him that many times.

"It's good to see you," Frank said, and though he'd spoken mostly to fill the silence and take his mind away from Devin, the words were true.

"You ain't kidding, son. Been a long time."

"Going to be tough," Frank said. "Being up here."

Ezra didn't look at him. "I would imagine so."

Frank, who just moments earlier had been so grateful that Ezra *wasn't* talking about his father, suddenly wanted to. What the hell did you say, though?

"Good memories, up here," he offered. "Less so in other places. But up here, mostly good."

"He wasn't a bad man, son. Wasn't a perfect one, either, but hc damn surc wasn't the way they made him out to be."

"Tell that to the families of the people he killed," Frank said, and he was surprised by the weariness in his own voice, the aged sound.

He finally heard a loon then. It cut loose from somewhere across the lake, the sound unlike anything else, riding the wind across the water to their campfire. He thought maybe they were both grateful for it. Something to listen to, something to stop a conversation that was going nowhere good.

"Like I said, I'm glad to see you, Ezra. Don't want to make you have conversations like that. I'm sorry."

"No need to be," Ezra said. "And I think you do want to. Be surprised if you didn't, at least."

Frank didn't respond to that. He was stuck in a memory, another night around another fire with his father and Ezra. He'd been fifteen at the time, and his father decided to show off some of the tricks he'd worked so hard to teach his son, show off those unholy fast hands. *Watch this,* he'd said to Ezra, *watch how damn quick he is.* They'd gone through the usual routine, his father with the gun and Frank trying to take it, or maybe the other way around. He didn't remember the details of that night's game anymore, just remembered that when Ezra had said, *Yeah, you're real fast, kid,* his voice was sad and he wouldn't look at either of them.

"I thought it was a bad idea, calling you," Ezra said. "I'd promised to do it, but I still thought it was a bad idea."

"It wasn't."

"Then what are you doing here?"

"What do you mean?"

"Why did you come up, Frank?"

He didn't answer. Ezra looked at him for a long time and then nodded as if the question had been answered.

"We agreed to let it go," he said. "A lot of years ago, we agreed to let it go."

They had agreed to some other things, too. Like the fact that the Willow was sacred ground, and that Devin—who'd betrayed two generations of loyalty and friendship that were anchored in this spot—should never be allowed to return to it. They wouldn't pursue him, would let him sit down there in Florida for as many years as he could last, but they also wouldn't tolerate him returning to this place. Not unchallenged, at least.

"That's really what you want to do?" Frank said. "Let him come up here and sit in the cabin, have a nice little vacation, enjoy himself? He brought my dad into it, Ezra, used a lot of bullshit about loyalty to set the hook, and then he turned around and gave him up to buy himself immunity."

"You think I've forgotten? I'm just wondering about your intentions."

"I'd like to ask him some questions," Frank said.

"That's all?"

"That's all," Frank said, but he was thinking of the guns inside the cabin, beautiful, well-engineered pieces of equipment that had not been built to ask questions.

"Where'd you come from, anyhow?" Ezra asked, and Frank returned to the moment. "Postmarks on those letters bounced around a bit over the years."

"I was in Indiana."

"Working?"

"Taking classes."

"What sort?"

"Writing. Had ideas about a book, but maybe a screenplay would be better."

"I think that's just fine," Ezra said, and he seemed legitimately pleased. "You were a storyteller even as a kid. I remember that."

"I just remember listening to the stories."

"Well, sure, back then we had a good many more to tell than you. But I remember you had a way with it. Tell a story about a bike wreck and make it sound more exciting than anything I had to offer about a battle or a bear hunt."

Frank laughed. Storytelling had been a big part of those trips, and eliciting any positive response from Ezra, a smile or a nod or one of those low, soft laughs, had been a serious reward.

"How long of a drive is it?" Ezra said. "Up from Indiana?"

"Took about ten hours."

"Good trip, I take it?"

"Those hours I mentioned, that's driving time. I left out a few hours of fun that started because I had a car wreck with someone I thought was Devin. He wasn't Devin, but based on the guys who came after him, he's not exactly peaceful, either."

Ezra turned almost fully toward the fire and lifted his eyebrows in a way Frank had seen a thousand times before, usually in response to something his father remembered that contradicted Ezra's memory.

"You want to provide a bit more detail on that?" Ezra said.

Frank provided the detail. Ezra listened quietly, shaking his head from time to time or making a quiet murmur of appreciation, but not speaking.

"Hell of a welcome back to town," he said.

"No kidding."

"I know Nora Stafford. Knew her father better, of course, but she's a good girl. You sure she's all right?"

"Other than the scare. I'd be surprised if the car she loaned out is ever returned to her, though."

The half of Ezra's face lit by the firelight went hard, his jaw shifting and eyes narrowing, and then he turned away and was entirely in the darkness.

"What kind of car you say that was?"

"It was a Mitsubishi SUV. Probably twenty years old. Little box of a thing. Blue paint, lots of rust."

"Plate number six-five-three-E-four-two," Ezra said, and Frank sat forward on the stump and stared at the older man.

"I don't know if that's the number. But you do. Want to explain that?"

Ezra sat quietly for a long time, as if there were a decision to be made and he wouldn't be rushed toward it. At last he got to his feet.

"Let's you and I take a drive."

They walked back up the gravel road and then out to the Willow Wood Lodge without Ezra volunteering a word, no hint where they were headed. Got into Ezra's truck and drove north, went across the dam and took Cedar Falls Road. Then it was left onto an uneven dirt road through the trees, Ezra taking it slow. He stopped the truck in the middle of the road, turned the lights off, and cut the motor.

"Now we walk."

For ten minutes, they walked without speaking, the only sounds those of breathing and sticks breaking underfoot. As they pushed up a slope covered in pine needles, one of the loons called again, and the sound seemed less magical than before. Chilling, now. A note of warning.

They went up the hill and back into the trees, and then a dark shape showed itself. Ezra knelt and flicked a cigarette lighter to life. The glow caught a rusted blue bumper and a Wisconsin license plate. Nora Stafford's car.

"How'd you find this?"

"Saw him pull it in this afternoon while I was on the lake."

"So he dumped it here," Frank said. "Left it in the woods and had somebody come get him."

Ezra shook his head, then extinguished the lighter. When he spoke again, his voice floated out of the blackness.

"Got in a boat and went out to the island."

Frank's eyes had been stunned by the brief light, and he blinked hard and searched for Ezra's face in the darkness.

"Devin's island."

"Yes."

"You told me he wasn't—"

"He's not here, Frank. I don't know who these people are, but Devin is not here."

Good, Frank thought, turning back to look out across the dark water toward an island he couldn't see. *Because if he were, I'd take that lighter from your hand and swim out to that cabin, set the place on fire and watch it burn and make sure he went with it. I'd watch it burn and savor every minute, Ezra. Make my father look like a preacher.*

"But they're connected to him," he said. "That explains the guns."

"I expect so."

"So where's Devin?"

No response.

"I knew it was him," Frank said, speaking to himself as much as to Ezra. "Saw that damn Florida license plate, and between that and the message you'd left, I *knew* it was him, that he'd come back. I wasn't wrong by much. Not by much."

It was quiet for a while, Frank's mind filled with things like ghosts and legacies and the sort of fate he had long wondered if he could avoid. The answer was here, a rusted-out car hidden among the trees.

"I think," he said softly, "that I'd better call Nora Stafford. If this guy's staying in Devin Matteson's cabin, he and everyone around him are a hell of a lot more dangerous than I thought originally."

Twelve

It was long past visiting hours, but they let her in anyhow. Nora was well known by now at the Northwoods Nursing Center. The woman who staffed the front desk gave her a disapproving look but didn't ask questions or attempt to stop her, just offered a single curt nod, and then Nora turned the corner and walked to her father's room.

"Dad?" She spoke as she opened the door and stepped inside, and Bud Stafford twisted his head to see her, a smile crossing his face. It was this moment that broke her heart—that immediate smile. He was always so damn glad to see her. Other patients in the center weren't able to recognize their loved ones. With Bud it was just the opposite; he couldn't follow conversation well, couldn't process simple details, but he absolutely recognized his daughter. Somehow, on a night like this, that made it harder.

"How you doing?" She leaned over and kissed his forehead. He struggled with the covers, made it clear he was trying to sit up, and she helped him get upright before sitting in the chair beside the bed.

Nora had heard the phrase *wasting away* a million times in her life, never stopped to give it any real thought until her father's stroke. That was exactly what was happening, though. He just . . . faded. The strength had gone first, then the size, leaving a frail man where a powerful one had existed.

"Hello." The single-word greeting came a full minute

after she'd come into the room. It took his brain that long to catch up to the events, then search for the proper reaction to them. When you kept the conversation slow and simple, he could develop a bit of a rhythm, and the sense of truly *communicating* with him was better. Get too much going on at once, though, or going too fast, and he became helplessly lost, often resorting to repeating the same word or phrase over and over. It reminded Nora of the ancient computer she'd used in college. You'd ask the thing to run new software and get nothing but that silly hourglass symbol, a promise that it was processing, but you knew it would never yield results.

"Hello," she said. She thought it was important to always go back and match his place in the conversation, make him feel less overwhelmed by it. "What was dinner?"

"Yes." He smiled at her again.

She waited for a few seconds and saw there would be no response tonight. Sometimes he followed the questions, the simple ones at least. More often he did not. The stroke had affected his cognitive and motor skills. On the right day, he could move around just fine, albeit a little slowly. The problem was, you never knew when the right day would be, or the wrong day. His balance could be fine for a while and then completely disappear. He'd be crossing a room under his own power and then suddenly look as if he were on the deck of a pitching ship. This was the reason a return home was impossible, at least right now. He needed twenty-four-hour care, and they couldn't afford that.

"Good day?" she said, emphasizing the question. The more you did that, the more likely he was to understand that he was expected to provide an answer.

"Good day. We had the birds."

That meant they'd taken him outside, to a patio surrounded with bird feeders. That was a highlight of his existence now.

"Do you have cars?" he said. This joined the smile as the two constants of every visit. Sometimes he'd be unusually adept at following a conversation; other days he struggled with the simplest exchanges. The one question he *always* managed was: Do you have cars? He didn't remember that he'd owned a body shop, or at least he was incapable of expressing that he did. When she tried to explain anything about work to him, he tended to get hopelessly confused. But he asked that question about the cars because somewhere in his fog-shrouded brain he knew it was important, critical, that without cars there would be serious problems.

"I have cars," she said. "We have cars."

He nodded, his face grave. Hearing that answer always reassured him. She looked down at him and felt his love even through the veil of confusion. It was a sensation she could remember so well from those visits when she was a girl, one of unusual staying power. There were few things that caught your breath more than looking at another person and feeling the intensity of his love for you. Seeing it in all of its layers, the depth of the adoration, of the pride, of the fear. Always the fear. You looked at the ones you loved and in that moment you were terrified for them, for all of the things that could go wrong in the world, the car accidents and the illnesses and the random violence that could reach out from the darkness without a note of warning and claim the ones you cared about most. It wasn't until the stroke, until the first time she saw the shell that had been left behind where her father belonged, that Nora truly understood just how unbreakable was that link between love and fear. They belonged together.

There was a notepad on the table beside her, filled with scrawled attempts at his name. That meant it had been a therapist day. Three times a week, an occupational therapist named Jennifer came to work with him. She'd made remarkable progress, too—he tied his shoes slowly but competently now, and a few months ago, when he was still in acute care at the hospital, Nora would never have believed that would be possible. The fine motor skills were more difficult. Anything requiring dexterity was a challenge.

"You want to try your name for me, Dad?" She passed him the notepad and the pen, which he took carefully, his

face set in a frown of concentration. The expression remained as he carefully laid pen to paper. The first three letters of his first name—Ronald—came easily enough. Then
he hung up on the *A.* She watched him hesitate, write the
letter, hesitate, write it again. And again. *R . . . o . . . n . . .
a . . . a . . . a . . . a*

She stopped him after the fourth repetition. "You're
stuck, Dad. You already wrote that one. Try the *L.*"

He stopped writing to listen to her, head cocked slightly,
then went back to the paper and wrote the *A* again. *Perse-
veration,* that's what the therapist called it. When the patient
would get stuck on a word or an action. It was a frequent
problem with her father. For months, he'd been unable to
switch from brushing his teeth to combing his hair. Something about the action with the toothbrush dominated his
brain; he'd take the comb in his hand and stare at it in bewil-
derment, mime the motion he'd used with the toothbrush,
never get the comb anywhere near his hair. He was over that
now, at least with the comb. Jennifer had solved that problem by changing the order of his bathroom procedures, putting the toothbrush last.

"Let me help." Nora leaned across the bed and took her
father's rough hand in her own, guided him through his
name. It was a regular part of her visits, but for some reason
on this night it cut through her with a sort of fresh agony
she hadn't felt since the early days with him in the hospital.
He was her father, a strong man who was supposed to care
for *her.* Today, a day on which she'd been attacked, when she
needed his support the most, she was helping him write his
own name.

The realization brought a stinging to her eyes and a thick-
ness to her throat, and for a moment she just sat there, leaning on the bed and holding his hand and fighting tears.

"Done?" he said.

That brought her out of it. She sniffed and got a laugh out
and shook her head.

"No, Dad. Not done. Let's try again."

They went back to the writing, with her guiding his hand and naming each letter as they wrote it.

Driving home in the dark, hours after she'd expected to be there, her thoughts turned to Frank Temple. Excuse me, Frank Temple *the Third*. There were stories behind Mr. Temple, she was sure. He was a little too calm in the situation they'd encountered today, a little too . . . *familiar*. If he were older, she'd suspect he was a cop, or maybe a soldier. Had the right haircut for a soldier. But he couldn't be any older than she was, and if forced to guess she'd actually say he was a few years younger. So where did that odd poise come from?

He'd been attractive at first, charming and funny in a low-key way, but then there was that strange outburst at the cabin. He'd practically shouted at her when she went for the door, made it seem as if he couldn't get rid of her fast enough. What was he so worried about? Afraid she'd throw him onto the bed, force herself on him in some show of gratitude? Please. Nora had tired of the regular routine of turning down dates from her customers—some of them offered sweetly if a little awkwardly, others in lecherous fashion—and maybe, *maybe,* she'd flirted with Frank just a bit earlier in the day. By the time they'd reached that cabin on the Willow, though, all she wanted to do was get his gear out of her truck, visit her father, and get home and into bed.

Home. That was how she thought of it now, although it was still a decidedly foreign and amusingly masculine place. At first she'd hesitated to make any changes, feeling like an intruder in her father's house, wanting him to return from the hospital and find everything as he'd left it.

As the weeks turned to months, though, she'd become more of a realist. When he came home, he'd still need her there for at least a while, so it was fair that she begin to think of it as her home, too. The hideous old curtains went first; then she repainted the kitchen and deposited the bizarre "jackalope" creature—a rabbit head with deer antlers, some friend's idea of high humor—into the basement. A day later, she felt guilty about the damn thing and brought it back up, hung it on the wall where it had been. Gradually the place began to take on a quality that was more comfortable. She was working on a mural in the back bedroom, a tropical scene she hoped he'd appreciate. If he didn't, she'd hand him a roller and a can of that flat white paint that covered the entire house and let him do his worst.

Much as she loved him, he would not have been a good day-to-day father. Nora realized that now, but she'd believed otherwise as a child. In those days, struggling to adjust to a stepfather whose attempts at warmth seemed all too false, she'd been able to build Bud Stafford into a fantasy figure. It wasn't difficult; in their rare times together Bud was attentive and thoughtful and funny, a strong man layered in self-confidence.

Nora began to see her mother as weak, money-hungry, someone who'd sacrificed passion for comfort. Only a fraction of that was true—the trade of passion for comfort. At this point in her life, Nora was certain her mother's only passionate relationship had been with Bud. She was equally certain, though, that they could never have lasted together. Bud had taken Kate's natural adjustment struggles to Tomahawk as a sign of weakness, deriding her instead of aiding her, using her privileged upbringing as a constant tool for teasing, because behind the teasing he could hide his insecurities. A family was certainly part of Bud Stafford's vision for himself, but it was a family built on his own terms, and Kate hadn't agreed to those. Had they loved each other? To this day, despite all the exchanged jabs, Nora believed that they had. Maybe still did. But they couldn't live together.

The problem was that after the divorce Bud had decided he couldn't live with anyone. It was a fine way to be when you were young and strong and always in control. The years caught up with you, though, devoured the youth and the strength and in the end even the control. Bud had no say over his existence now, and that, perhaps more than anything, held Nora in Tomahawk. Did she want to spend her life here, running a body shop and conducting empty visits at a nursing home? No. Nor did she want to fail, either, to lock the doors and shutter the windows and leave her father with a kiss on the cheek and a town full of people who admired him but couldn't care for him.

So what *did* she want? How would it end? It was a question she'd been determined to ignore at first, firmly believing he'd return to the shop healthy and ready to work. Each passing month added weight to the reality, though, and she knew now that he'd never be back. Meanwhile the calls from Minneapolis and Madison had crested and faded, family and friends who'd been anxious to know when she'd return now giving up hope or losing interest. Back home life was plowing ahead, passing her by, and here she was in Tomahawk, lost in a routine of body shop business and nursing home visits.

She couldn't let the business go under, though. Couldn't close those doors and hang the FOR SALE sign and let two generations of sweat and blisters and bruises disappear as if it had never meant a thing.

The one thing she still hadn't gotten used to about her daily routine was the dark ride home. Still couldn't relax driving anywhere out here at night. When the sun went down, the familiar ceased to be familiar, all landmarks hidden by shadows, everything beyond the reach of the headlights an unknown. They illuminated nothing but trees and pavement. She'd flick on the brights and then be dismayed when she saw how little it helped. You could see maybe an extra ten feet ahead, three to the sides, but for what? Nothing out there but more trees and more pavement, and the brights only made the surrounding shadows grow longer and seem darker. Many times when she left 51 she'd make it all the way home without passing another car, and that was a seven-mile stretch. Back in Minneapolis, you couldn't go seven feet without passing another car. The first few weeks up here she'd actually come close to panic attacks during the drive home, everything looking so damn similar that she could have been on the wrong road, headed in the wrong direction, completely unaware.

Empty and alone and dark. That was what she'd thought of the place at first, and though she'd grown fond of many things about it as time passed, the night drive was not one of them. That was a time that hammered the old mantra— empty and alone and dark—back into her brain, left her longing for bright lights and loud music and the voices of strangers.

There was a light on at the house when she pulled in, and usually that was enough of a reassurance, but today the uneasiness followed her out of the truck and stayed with her until she was inside. Nothing shocking about that—it hadn't been the most carefree of days. Well, it was done now, would be nothing but a memory by morning, fast on its way to becoming a story she would actually enjoy telling at parties, soaking up the way people's eyes widened and their jaws hung slack when she described the gunshots echoing outside of her father's shop.

Yes, soon that's all it would be. A memory and a story.

She'd eaten no dinner, but the effort of preparing food seemed too much and her appetite too little, so instead she settled for pouring a glass of red wine and moving into the living room. *Say this much for Dad's furniture,* she thought, *it looks like something you'd want to hide even at a garage sale, but it's comfortable.*

She sank into one of his overstuffed couches and kicked her shoes off, unbuttoned the denim work shirt and slipped out of it, down to the sleeveless white shirt she wore underneath. Feet up on the coffee table and wine in hand, she exhaled slowly and lifted her glass to the jackalope.

"Rough day. How about you?"

It took one glass of wine and thirty minutes of bad TV before she gave up and decided to call it a night. She was exhausted, and tomorrow wouldn't be a typical Saturday— she needed to get up early and track Jerry down, coerce him into getting the Lexus back into one piece. Once that was settled, she could turn it over to the police and, hopefully, have the whole miserable mess done.

Halfway to the bedroom, she remembered that the police might have used the shop number instead of the house if they'd learned anything or had any more questions. It was probably too late for that, but she was curious, and it was worth checking. She dialed the shop number and waited until she got to voice mail, then punched the pound key and entered the password. One message waiting, the robotic voice informed her. The police, surely.

It wasn't the police.

Hello, I'm calling for Nora Stafford. This is Frank Temple. Listen . . . if you want that Mitsubishi back, I know where it is. But we're going to need to talk some things over first. I think I might . . . there's a chance I might know a little bit about that guy. Vaughn. I'm not sure of anything yet, but I've got some things that I should probably explain to you before anybody tries to deal with this guy. I'd like to talk to you, and then, you know, probably to the police. We'll see.

He left his cell phone number, which she already had, and hung up. Nora stood in the dark living room with the phone to her ear for a minute, then punched the button that replayed the message. Listening to it again, she felt a twist of fear begin to counteract the sleepiness created by fatigue and wine.

Frank Temple knew where her car was? And, apparently, something about the man who'd taken it? Where, in the time since she'd dropped him off, had he stumbled across *that* sort of information, alone in his cabin on the lake?

I'd like to talk to you, and then, you know, probably to the police. We'll see.

We'll see?

Thirteen

He woke to the sounds of birds, but it was anything but pleasant. Harsh, angry caws, shrieked in rage. Frank rolled onto his side and lifted his body on his elbow, squinting against the sunlight that filled the room and searching for his watch. He found it and checked the time—ten till eight.

The birds were still going at it with shrill screams. He shoved the covers back and stood up, the floorboards cool on his feet. Wearing nothing but his boxers, Frank walked through the cabin, unlocked the door, and stepped out into a cloudless morning. The sun shone bright but cool, the lake glittering beneath it, pushed by a gentler version of the previous night's wind. The sky was so bright, particularly to eyes that had just left sleep behind, that he didn't see the osprey until it completed its dive.

The bird came tearing down toward its nest, then redirected at the last second and shot skyward again, releasing another shriek. There were osprey nests all over the lake, constructed on posts out over the water. What made this one so angry?

He figured it out when the osprey made its second dive. Just as it neared the nest, another bird spread its wings and bobbed up on the thick piles of sticks, matching the osprey's scream with one of its own. This bird was larger, and unlike the osprey its head was pure white. There was a bald eagle in the osprey's nest. No wonder the other bird was pissed.

He was watching the osprey circle, no doubt plotting another dive, when an engine came into hearing range, a car approaching down the gravel drive from the main road. He turned back toward the sound as a pickup truck rumbled into view. Nora Stafford.

No real surprise. He'd expected her to call, but maybe she had; cell phone reception was sporadic out here, even with that damn tower disrupting the night sky. As he watched, she pulled in beside the cabin, shut off the truck, and stepped outside. Too bad he wasn't wearing any clothes. On the plus side, at least his underwear was clean.

She was walking toward him when the osprey dove again, announcing it with the loudest scream yet, and he turned away from Nora to watch.

The bird folded its wings, turning itself into a compact little missile, and hurled down, pulled off without hitting the nest. This time the eagle, perhaps bored with the dispute, took to the air with a shout of its own. Frank could actually hear the sound the eagle's wings made when they flapped; there was lot of wingspan there. Then both birds were airborne. As the eagle flew away from the nest, out toward open water, the osprey followed, buzzing the bigger bird like a fighter pilot before pulling away for good, the eagle headed toward the opposite shore, the nest empty again.

"I didn't think eagles fought with each other."

Until Nora said that, Frank had almost forgotten she was there. He'd been that entranced by the brief aerial battle. Now he turned back to her.

"One was an osprey. I think it took exception to the eagle using the nest."

"I guess so." Nora looked away from him again. "I'm here because of your message. It was awfully cryptic."

"I'll explain," Frank said, "but do you mind if I put on some pants first?"

"I was going to suggest that."

He went into the bedroom and pulled on jeans and a sweat-shirt while she waited at the kitchen table, then stopped by the bathroom to rinse his face with cold water and brush his teeth. Not yet eight on a Saturday, and Nora was already in motion. Either she was an early riser or his message had scared her.

When he came back out of the bathroom she'd left the kitchen table and was standing in the living room, looking at the framed Silver Star and the letter. She turned to him and pointed at the medal.

"Your grandfather's?"

"Uh-huh."

"So they gave him the medal after he was dead? That's so sad. I can't imagine what your grandmother thought about that. Proud among other things, I suppose."

"I suppose." There were a couple of ways to approach this conversation, and ordinarily Frank would have favored the less-is-more variation. While Nora was due a warning, a sense of what sort of trouble had arrived with that Lexus, she didn't need to know any information about Frank or his father. But there was something in the way she was studying the medal that twisted him away from that instinct, made him want to tell her the whole damn story. *Listen to me, please, listen because I've got to tell you the way it happened, I've got to tell you the way he really was.*

It shook him, this sudden desire to open up. He'd spent a long time working to avoid anything like it, perfecting that flat gaze that was designed to say, *I've got no story for you at all. Nothing to tell. Sorry.*

Now it was different with Nora just because she was staring at the damn medal? Was that it? No, there was something else, something in the way she talked and held his eyes and how she'd handled herself in the heat of it all yesterday that suggested a quality of . . . what? Judgment withheld, that was it. Consideration before conclusion.

"I'm surprised you got the message so early," he said and walked out of the living room and into the kitchen, got the coffeemaker running just so he could have a task to engage in instead of standing there with her, staring up at the starting point of the legacy.

"I checked it last night." She returned to her seat at the table. Today she was dressed less like a mechanic, having traded in the heavy denim shirt for a blue tank top worn over loose white linen pants. These clothes showed much more of her body, a very nice body, and taking that in Frank understood why she probably went for the shapeless look at work.

"I'm going to be honest," she said, dropping the friendliness, her words cool, "I thought about showing up here with the police. In the end, I decided I'd give you what you asked for, the chance to talk through this, but I also didn't like what you said on that message last night. You made it sound as if you knew more than you told me yesterday."

"I might know more than I told you yesterday," Frank said, pouring the water into the coffeemaker, "but I didn't at the time. Everything you—and the police—heard from me was accurate. I'd never seen that guy before, Nora. That's the truth."

"You said you knew where my car was."

"That's right."

"How can you possibly—"

"Ezra Ballard found it."

"Where?"

"Hidden in the woods about two miles up the shoreline." She pulled her head back. "On the Willow?"

"Yes." He finished setting the coffeemaker and turned to face her, leaning against the counter. "That guy, Vaughn, he drove it down there as soon as he left your shop yesterday, tried to hide the car in the trees. Ezra was out on the lake, watching."

"You're sure it's my car?"

"I'm sure. He took me to see it last night."

"So Vaughn dumped it."

Frank shook his head.

"No?"

"No. He's staying here. Ezra saw him go out to an island. There's a cabin on it, has been for years. Apparently this guy is with a woman out there. Just the two of them."

She took that in, nodded. "Okay. Well, that's good news, isn't it? I can get my car back, and we can tell the police where to find this guy."

Frank didn't answer.

"What else do you know?" she said, watching his face carefully. "Frank? What else do you know about him?"

"About him? Nothing. I know something about the cabin he's staying in, that's all. Something about the man who owns it."

"And what's that?"

"That he's a killer."

She looked at him for a long time, while the coffee burbled on the counter and the wind picked up and buffeted the cabin.

"You mean he's a murderer? Some sort of psychotic?"

"A professional."

"A professional." She echoed the phrase as if it were in a foreign language.

"Yes." The coffeepot was full, and Frank turned and lifted it free and poured, held a cup out to her. When she shook her head, he took a drink from it himself.

"You're serious," she said. "I can see that you're serious. That the guy who drove that Lexus is some sort of assassin."

"No." He shook his head. "I don't know if he is. In fact, after seeing him, I'd have to say he is very far from that. What I'm telling you is that the man who owns that cabin is. So if this guy with the Lexus, if he's working with him or friends with him or whatever . . ."

"It's not good for me," she finished.

"*Maybe* it's not. Like I said, Nora, I don't *know* anything here except what I've told you. Whether this guy is someone for you to worry—"

"How do you know that about the owner, though? He just came over once to make some neighborly conversation and told you that he kills people for a living?"

He looked at her and remembered what she'd said about his grandfather's medal—*proud among other things,*

I suppose—and then he blew over the coffee cup and took another drink. "He worked with my father."

Those cool eyes she had were beginning to falter. Beginning to let some fear in. "Your father."

"Frank Temple," he said. "Same name as mine. That doesn't mean anything to you? Never heard of him?"

When she shook her head, he was surprised. Always was, when someone *hadn't* heard of his father. In Frank's mind, everyone had heard of him, talked of him, still did. In Frank's mind, his family's shame was still dinner table conversation across the country.

"All right," he said. "I guess I'm glad about that. He made the news a while back. National news. Pretty big story."

"For?"

"For killing people for money," he said, and then he held her eyes and drank more of the coffee and neither of them spoke.

"I'm sorry," she said eventually.

"You don't need to be. I'm just telling you so that you'll understand how I know these things."

"So your father and the guy on the island, they *both* kill people for money? This is some sort of retreat for assassins?"

He set the coffee down on the counter, kept his eyes on the floor.

"My dad served in Vietnam, part of a pretty elite group, very good soldiers. He made some friends there. Ezra Ballard was one. A man named Dan Matteson was another. They were from three different parts of the country, but after the war, they wanted to stay in touch. Stay close. Dan had property up here, and Ezra moved up and then convinced my dad to build a cabin with him. Thought they could use it as a way to stay together as the years stacked up. Dan kept the island, and my dad and Ezra bought this place."

"Is Ezra . . ."

"No." Frank shook his head. "He's not part of the mess, Nora. Don't worry about that. He's a good man."

"But your father and the other guy?"

"Dan Matteson got into trouble right after the war. Essentially he was a mercenary. Went into corrupt, beaten-down countries and took a lot of money to fight for one side or the other. He got into something in Central America, I'm not sure what, but he made some contacts out there and got involved in the drug trade. When I say drug trade, I don't mean street corner deals, either. I mean dealing in *weight,* smuggling planes and boats, not dime bags. Became a very big deal with some very dangerous people in Miami. When I was a kid, I got to know Ezra pretty well, but Dan was never around. I never actually met him."

"Your father was working with him the whole time?"

"No. My father was a U.S. marshal. From every account I've heard, he was a good one for most of his career. An honest one."

Frank lifted his eyes again, found hers. "When I was a sophomore in high school, Dan Matteson's body washed up on the beach in Miami. They identified him through dental records, because he was missing his hands. His hands, and his eyes."

It had to be so strange for her, so unnerving, to hear him explain this fun little family history. She took it well enough, listening silently and watching his face.

"Matteson had a son named Devin. By then he was working in the same world as his father. I think he's about fifteen years older than me. After the body was found, Devin gave my dad a call. Made this pitch. This request for my father to help him avenge Dan's murder. Find out who did it, settle up."

"And he did it," Nora said softly. Then, when Frank nodded, "That doesn't sound so evil. I mean, the people he killed, they were the ones who'd murdered his friend?"

"Some of them were," Frank said, "but he didn't stop there. By the time they sorted that out, Devin's boss made him another offer. My dad took it. And another after that. Last count I heard, he killed five people on contract. There might have been more. This while keeping his marshal's badge. I'm sure he had access and information that was awfully appreciated by Devin and the rest of them."

He paused, then said, "Eventually, the FBI got Devin into

a jam, and to get out of it, he offered to trade some information. He gave them my father. Told them the information they needed to know to get the case moving, but Dad got wind of it, and he killed himself before there was an arrest."

The refrigerator kicked on beside them; for a while the only sound in the cabin was the whirring motor. Then it switched off again, and Nora spoke as if it were a cue to end the silence.

"I'm sorry, Frank. The way you reacted last night when I asked about your father, it should have told me—"

"That he was a killer?" He laughed. "No, I don't think it should have told you that. You've got nothing to apologize for. The only reason I'm telling you this is that I don't like Vaughn having a connection to Devin Matteson. It appears that he does."

When she spoke again, her voice was guarded and her eyes downcast. "And I'm supposed to believe that this connection between you and Vaughn is an honest coincidence. That you've never met him, don't know anything about him, and somehow still manage to be involved with the cabin where he ended up."

What should he tell her? That he'd come up here because Ezra's message had made him suspect Devin was returning, that he'd caused the accident with Vaughn because he thought it was Devin in the car, that he'd reached for his gun as soon as the Jeep was at a stop? Not a real reassuring sort of explanation.

In the end, all he said was "Well, you can imagine I'm not real pleased by that little twist, myself."

She was quiet, and he could tell from the set of her mouth that she didn't like the answer. Well, fine. He didn't like it, either, but that didn't change a damn thing.

"What does that mean?" she said. "You don't like the connection, and I understand your reason, but how does it change anything for me?"

"The people Devin runs with . . ." Frank swung his body off the counter and walked to the big front window looking out on the lake. She turned her head to follow him. "They're dangerous, obviously. And what they do, Nora, it's not penny ante. Whatever's going on, there's probably a lot of money involved."

She forced a laugh. "Okay, I'll let him keep the car. How about that? Just pretend I don't know where it is, don't know any of this."

"That's a good idea," he said, still with his back to her. "It's not the only problem, though. Vaughn's not the only problem. There are the two guys from last night."

She was sitting half turned in the kitchen chair, twisted to look at him, and he could see understanding begin to grow on her face.

"You mean they might come back."

"Like I said, I don't know anything about them, or Vaughn, but I know some things about Devin. One of those things is that the people surrounding him will be professionals. Professionals don't like to leave loose ends. You were face-to-face with that guy yesterday. So was I. We both saw him attack you and saw his buddy attack that cop, and our testimony could put them in jail for a long time. You and I have just become loose ends. If these guys really are involved with Devin Matteson or anyone close to him, then that's a very serious concern."

Fourteen

Steve Gomes had wanted to take his boat out that morning, but Jerry passed on the offer and headed for the library. Though not much of a reader, he was a regular patron. The Tomahawk library had a handful of computers with Internet access, and Jerry had recently discovered the online auction sites.

Jerry's dad had owned a liquor store, an occupational choice less than pleasing to Jerry's mother, a woman who went to church on Sundays *and* Wednesdays. Rare was the week that passed without a bout of criticism of Rob Dolson's work, that selling of sin. There was one element of the liquor business, and one element only, that pleased her: the presence of mirrors. Alice Dolson *loved* mirrors, and her husband received plenty of them, shipped in from Stroh's and Anheuser-Busch and the rest. Though she loathed the products they advertised, Alice couldn't help but like the mirrors. Her favorites were the Scotch mirrors. *Much more elegant than those silly beer mirrors,* she'd insist. *If you ignore the brand name, they're really quite beautiful.*

So Rob Dolson hung on to the mirrors, and when he died, Alice kept them. She'd passed a few years later, leaving Jerry a fifty-year-old collection of bar mirrors. They decorated his home and filled his garage now. He'd hoped to build the collection, but classic mirrors were hard to find—or so he'd thought until he discovered eBay. If he felt a bit fruity shopping for antiques on the Internet in the library (and he did), it was easy enough to dismiss that with the recollection that the mirrors were, of course, advertising alcohol. Nothing embarrassing about that.

He'd found a nice Genesee mirror with paintings of men engaged in various outdoor pursuits, the slogan reading *The great outdoors in a glass,* when his phone rang. Steve Gomes had talked him into canceling the landline in favor of a cell a year earlier, telling him that the cell had free long distance and none of those bastard telemarketers calling. What Steve had failed to anticipate was that Jerry made few long distance calls, and didn't mind talking to a telemarketer in the evening, providing it was a woman with a nice voice and he'd already consumed a brew or two. He had the cell now, though, and when the damn thing rang he saw that it was Bud Stafford's home number. Nora's home number, now.

Jerry turned the ringer off and matched the glare from the front-desk librarian with one of his own. Who couldn't appreciate the Benny Hill theme song, anyhow? When he'd learned that was one of the ringer options, he'd been as good as sold.

Two minutes later, the phone rang again.

"It's a *Saturday,*" Jerry growled. Nora had no right to bother him on a Saturday.

This time the librarian lobbed a heavy sigh with her glare, and Jerry stood up and took the phone outside onto the sidewalk. Nora deserved a lecture for this one.

"You never heard of a day off?" he said when he answered.

"Just rumors," Nora said.

"That ain't funny. I'm down here at the library and you got my phone ringing and bothering—"

"You're at the library?"

"Ain't the point, Nora. Don't matter where I am. Point is, it's Saturday, and that's a day off."

"How'd you like another day off, Jerry?"

"What do you mean?"

"You come in today, for just a few hours, and I'll let you

take Monday off. You'd be trading eight hours of work for about two or three, and you're already in town. Tell me what the downside of that is."

No downside that he could perceive, other than caving in to her request. He was silent, thinking it over.

"Time-and-a-half, Jerry. That's what I'll pay you if you come in today."

"What the hell do you need me there for? We don't have anything all that urgent."

"We do now. I want that Lexus put back together, and I want it put back together fast."

"Nora, that car is not a one-day fix. Hell, we're gonna need parts that'll take a day or two just to get—"

"You're not fixing it. You're just putting it back into one piece so I can get it out of my shop."

"Guy wants to take it somewhere else?" This was not good. Jerry had a thousand bucks riding on that car.

"The police want to take it elsewhere."

"What?"

"I don't want to get into it on the phone, Jerry, but I need that car back together, and I need it to happen today."

Shit. If the cops were already onto this car, he might have lost his chance at the grand already. Of course, that AJ character had offered him half of that if he could get the little tracking device, and Jerry had turned him down because he didn't have access to the shop over the weekend. Well, he did now.

"All right, Nora. I can come down there. Time-and-a-half and Monday off, I'll come down there."

"The very soul of generosity."

"No problem," he told her, and then he disconnected the phone.

This was working out to be a fine weekend. He had little on his plate for the rest of the day, and now he was going to make time-and-a-half *plus* the five hundred AJ had promised him in return for that tracking device. That Genesee mirror had just become much more affordable.

He went into the library, purchased the mirror, and logged

off the Internet. Giving the librarian a mocking wink and salute, he walked back into the sunlit day and reached into his pocket and extracted the bar napkin he'd put there when he left the house that morning. AJ was probably going to appreciate this phone call just as much as Jerry had ended up appreciating Nora's.

He answered on the second ring, and Jerry told him the situation while he walked away from the library and down the hill toward the river. The Wisconsin rolled right behind the library, wide and languid at this spot, a water skier working up by the bridge.

"Deal still stands—you get the tracking box, I get the five hundred?"

"You want to take me up on that deal." AJ's voice was different today. Kind of uneasy, wary.

"I *will* take you up on it. If you ain't interested anymore, though, shit, it's no skin off my back."

"I thought you couldn't get in the shop on weekends."

"I just *told* you, she's paying me time-and-a-half to come in."

"And she didn't tell you why that was?"

"I assume the boy you're so interested in is coming back for the car." Jerry didn't want to repeat Nora's reference to the cops; it seemed like something that could kill this deal before he made a dime.

"That seems unlikely."

"Well, I don't know. I'm just saying if you want your gadget back, now's the time to get it."

"You're asking me to come back to that body shop?"

"Man, I ain't asking you nothing. I'm telling you I can get my hands on the thing. That's all."

AJ went quiet for so long Jerry thought he'd hung up.

"You there?"

"Yes. All right. You get that tracking device, and return to the bar where we talked yesterday. Go there at seven o'clock."

"And you'll bring the money."

"Yes, Mr. Dolson. I will bring the money."

*   *   *

Being alone in the shop again wasn't a good feeling. Believe it or not, Nora was anxious for Jerry's arrival, something that had never occurred before. Frank Temple had offered to come into town with her, but she'd declined, disliking that maiden-in-distress vibe of relying on some strange male for protection. Besides, she was still reeling from what he'd told her. A *hit man*? At the Willow Flowage?

She wanted to consider it a joke. Might have been able to, were it not for the sorrow she saw in Frank's eyes as he'd told her the story. That haunted look he wore when he talked about his father was chilling. If he could conjure that up just to screw with somebody's mind, he needed to head to Hollywood on the next bus, get to work winning his Oscar.

So then it was real. That stirred a queasy blend of emotions within her, one that would hopefully be quieted once the Lexus was out of her garage and into police hands.

She left the office and went out into the main body of the shop and looked at the Lexus, sitting alone under the glare of the fluorescent lights. Since she'd taken over the shop, she'd found herself unappreciative of most of the new cars that came in. They had no personality, no soul. The old cars, your '55 Chevys and '68 Mustangs and any of a two-decade stretch of Cadillacs, those cars were like friends. She felt not unlike a doctor while tending to them, considered the removal of rust and addition of fresh paint to be healing effects, and she was sorry to see them leave the shop. It wasn't that she loathed the new cars; they just didn't inspire any feeling within her. Until this one.

She hated it now. Feared it. Just standing in its presence and looking at those twisted and crumpled quarter panels on the floor beside it was creepy. She was shaken by the sense that the piece of plastic and metal was somehow aware of her fear, was studying her now like a large strange dog unfenced and unchained.

Her sophomore year of college, she'd taken a trip to Rome with some classmates, an art history study project that her stepfather had financed without so much as a blink. Her mother had made the request, and after he'd written the check, she leaned down and kissed his neck, nipped his earlobe, and rubbed his back as he smiled distractedly and turned back to his desk. Nora, standing in the doorway watching it all, felt a cold ripple spread through her stomach.

That trip got off to a bad start. Due to delays from bad thunderstorms over the Midwest, Nora missed a connecting flight and had to wait for nine hours in LaGuardia, alone. To pass the time, she visited the airport bookstore and grabbed the first Stephen King paperback she saw, *Christine*. For most of the layover, she huddled in a corner seat in the terminal with that book, amazed at King's ability to make even a *car* seem scary. That was a real miracle of storytelling, she'd thought, to give menace to a car.

This Lexus, though, put King's '58 Plymouth Fury to shame. It wasn't something out of a book, it was real, felt firm and cold under her hand, and its presence had already produced the most terrifying moment of her life. She caught herself rubbing her wrist as she looked at the car. There were thin blue lines on her flesh now, reminders of fingers closed over her arm.

A sudden, powerful rattling at the side door made her jerk, and when she stepped backward her foot hit the front bumper, which was resting on the floor, and nearly put her on her ass.

"Nora! Let me in."

Jerry. She put both hands on her temples, took one long breath, and then moved to the door.

"Take my keys away, and then you can't even unlock the door when you know I'm coming?" He entered the shop with customary good cheer, griping and scowling. It must be exhausting to be Jerry, carry all that hostility at all hours of the day.

"After last night, I'm never leaving a door in this shop unlocked again," she said. "Not when I'm alone, at least."

That caught his attention, made him tilt his head and lift one of his wild eyebrows.

"What do you mean?"

She told him what had happened and was surprised by his face as he listened. He looked concerned in a way she wouldn't have imagined he could be, concerned and almost guilty.

"Shoot, Nora. I can't believe that. This fella walking in here and putting hands on you . . . shoot." His chest filled with air and he looked around the shop as if hoping to find the culprit still on the property. "You say they hit Mowery, hurt him bad?"

"He looked *real* bad, Jerry."

"I known that old boy since I was a kid. Sure, he's given me a hassle a time or two, but he also drove me home from Kleindorfer's once when he sure as shit didn't have to. Other guys, situation like that, they just take your ass down to the drunk's cell." His hands had curled into fists at his sides.

"I didn't know him," Nora said, "but I was scared for him. I want to go down to the hospital today, see if he's all right, and thank him."

"Yeah." Jerry's eyes weren't on her, didn't seem to be on anything in the shop.

"What's wrong, Jerry?"

"Nothing. I mean, shoot, just what happened, that's all. I wish I'd been here, Nora. Got in the habit of cutting out ahead of Bud at quitting time, but I shouldn't do that with you. Shouldn't leave a woman alone in a place like this."

"I'm not your responsibility, Jerry. Don't worry about that." She was touched by his concern, though.

"Well, that's the last time, you hear? This is a good town, Nora, a darn good town, but in the summers you get people coming in from all over, people you don't know and can't trust. Long as that's going on, I shouldn't be leaving you alone around here."

He looked up at her with a surprising sincerity in his face and said, "I'm sorry, Nora."

"It wasn't your fault. And I really do appreciate you coming in here to get that stupid car put back together and out the door. I'll be glad to see it go."

"No problem." Then, banging his fist on the hood of the

Lexus, "You think the son of a bitch who drove this thing is going to come back for it?"

"I don't know, but I don't want it here if he does. I've heard some things I don't like, Jerry. Things that scare me."

"What do you mean?"

She didn't want to give him the whole story, hadn't yet decided who she *was* going to give that to, but she was also worried and wanted to talk. It was one of the problems of her existence here; she was an outsider, a strange woman in a strange role, and her only confidant in the entire county was a man who needed help to write his own name. She and Frank still hadn't come to an agreement on whether she should even tell the police about the Mitsubishi. It would be nice to talk things over with someone.

"I've got a lot on my mind with this thing," she said, pointing at the Lexus. "Last night was bad enough, but this morning I talked to the other driver, and he . . . he offered some theories I don't like."

"The kid?" Jerry frowned. "Where'd he go, anyhow?"

"He's staying at the Willow. I drove him out last night." Best not to mention her return trip and invite more questions she wasn't comfortable answering.

"What's he know about it?"

She hesitated. No, it wouldn't do to share any of this with Jerry. For one thing, he ran his mouth, and for another, he elaborated. Even a toned-down version of Frank's account would soon be the sole topic of conversation over the bar at Kleindorfer's, only by the time it got there it would probably involve terrorists and nuclear weapons.

"He saw a gun in the Lexus," she said. "The guy took it with him." This wasn't a lie, and hopefully it would be enough to appease Jerry.

"You tell the police that?"

"Yes."

"They say anything about this car? Have any, uh, ideas of what's going on?"

"Not last night. I don't know if they do today."

He wouldn't look at her. "Get on out of here. I'll have this thing done fast."

"I'll wait on you."

He turned back to her, shaking his head emphatically. "No, you don't need to do that. Tell you what—you go on down to the hospital like you said, check in on Mowery, tell him old Jerry says hello. Then I'll give you a holler on the cell phone when this fancy-ass thing is ready to go."

"I think there should always be two people in this shop, Jerry. Until the car's gone, we should both be here."

He lifted a hand to his forehead, rubbed above his eyes like an exhausted man with many miles ahead. "I leave you here on your own last night for all that shit to happen, and now you want to stay around for me. Want to keep *me* safe."

It wasn't a complaint; he was more musing to himself than talking to her.

"I just think it would be safest for both of us."

"I got something to tell you, Nora." He looked anguished. "And I want you to understand this first—I didn't know nothing about this car or what had happened to you at the time, okay? I mean, shit, if I'd known what happened . . ."

"Jerry, what are you talking about?"

He lowered his hand and walked past her, to his locker. Pulled it open and reached inside and withdrew a small plastic box. Even when he passed it to her and she held it in her own hands she had no idea what it was.

"It's a tracking device, Nora. Sends out a signal, and if you got the receiver you can follow it along." He ran his tongue over his lips. "It was on that car. I pulled it off the bumper reinforcement yesterday."

She ran her fingertips over the smooth plastic. This was the secret. This little thing was the source of the chaos. It had brought those bastards into her life.

"You found this yesterday afternoon?"

"Yes."

"And you didn't tell me."

"I'm sorry, Nora. I just . . . I don't know what to say. I wasn't thinking, that's all."

"Okay." Perhaps she should have been furious, screaming at him right now, blaming him. Instead, all she felt was confusion. Was this discovery good or bad? Would the device help her, or was it an increased risk just to hold it in her hand?

"I'm sorry," Jerry said again.

"It's all right. You're telling me now. That's what counts."

"Hang on," Jerry said. "There's more."

Fifteen

Frank had no intention of watching the Matteson island—no conscious intention anyhow. When he got the boat in the water and the motor fastened onto the transom, his only thought was of taking a ride, seeing the lake again.

He made it all of five minutes with that as the morning's lone goal. Out of the little bay and around the sandbar—the lake was still high enough that he probably could have gone right over the top of the bar, but old habits guided him around it—and then, just after he hit the main body of the lake, he opened up the throttle and pointed toward the Four Islands. Past them and around the point, out into the more desolate stretches of the lake, was the Matteson place. He had to see it. Just a look.

It was twenty minutes with the little outboard running at full throttle before the island came into view. There were so many islands out here that it could get confusing; half of them looked like the shore from a distance, and then you'd be around them and into a bay that looked big enough to be the main portion of the lake and suddenly you were damn lost.

Toward the northernmost reaches of the Willow the lake became more desolate, and tucked into the eastern shore was an area called Slaughterhouse Bay, so named because of the liberal collection of stumps and dead trees that protruded out of the water and could easily and swiftly ruin a boat.

Navigating among the dozens of stumps, even at slow speeds, was treacherous, and though Frank and his father had always assumed it would be a treasure trove of pike and perhaps bass, they'd never taken a good fish out of the bay. It was an eerie spot, particularly at dusk, when the partially submerged trees blended with long shadows and made the place look almost like a Florida swamp.

Skirting the bay and its stumps by several hundred yards, Frank crossed Slaughterhouse Point, approaching the head-waters where the Tomahawk River fed the flowage. Between Slaughterhouse Point on the south side and Muskie Point on the north, lying offshore of hundreds of acres of unbroken forest, he found the Matteson island. After a seven-year absence, maybe it should have been difficult to locate, but he didn't have any trouble. The place was burned deep in his memory.

Although there were dozens of good-sized islands on the flowage, few would have been hospitable to development even if not state owned. The waters in the flowage fluctuated too much; in a low-rain year the lake was responsible for feeding much of the Wisconsin River valley, and the dam would be opened to the point that the lake level would dip as much as much ten feet below the norm. A high-rain year, they'd close the dams up and the lake would rise dramatically, creating an ever-changing landscape that turned islands into mainland one summer and partially submerged them the next spring. The Matteson place was an exception due both to the high bluffs that bordered it and its placement in the middle of the lake. The water would never reach the ground level upon which the cabin was built, and any major recession simply expanded the beach below the bluffs.

He passed the island on the west side, keeping about a hundred feet out, saw the roof of the cabin and two of the *NO TRESPASSING* signs, then circled and was ready to head back when he saw the woman.

She was walking out into the lake, waist deep now, testing the footing and moving slowly. What in the world was she thinking, going for a swim in this lake in April? Even though the air temperature was unseasonably warm, at least ten degrees above normal, the water would be frigid. She didn't seem concerned, though.

Frank didn't react to the sight of her, didn't slow or cut the motor or do anything else that would make a clear show of his interest. Instead, he turned his head and stared straight out over the bow and gave the throttle an extra twist, picking up speed. He took the boat out into the lake, angled away from the island. The day had risen clear and beautiful, the breeze warming as the sun rode higher, everything reminding him of a number of days spent on this water with his father. He'd been ready for the memories today, but now they were sinking away, pushed down by that woman in the water.

She was a beautiful woman. Even from fifty yards out, he'd seen that. Tall and elegant, and from the short look he'd gotten at her body, it probably seemed more suspicious that he had *not* slowed the boat to stare. She would be used to stares.

Dave O'Connor, or Vaughn, or whoever the hell the gray-haired man really was, did not seem a match for that woman. He was such a strange-looking man, so nervous and awkward. On the other hand, he drove a Lexus and had thousands in cash on him, along with a gun. Maybe she was the sort who was attracted to money or danger.

That was another problem with Vaughn, though. He didn't seem like a dangerous guy. Even with the gun, even with the duo that had shown up on his heels, he didn't fit the mold. Those guys at the body shop yesterday had been a different story. Vaughn didn't seem anything like them or like other dangerous men Frank had known. Didn't seem anything like his father.

There he was, though, sitting in Devin Matteson's cabin with a woman who could turn heads from across the lake, two gun-toting badasses in pursuit. Nothing about that scenario felt right to Frank. Not after the time he'd spent with Vaughn yesterday.

He brought the boat around in a circle and ran back across

the lake, a little farther out this time. She was leaving the water, and he could see another figure on shore. The distance was too great for a definite identification, but he assumed it was Vaughn.

Down maybe three hundred yards to an osprey nest, then back around for another pass, watching that island. This time he couldn't see anyone on the beach. They'd gone inside, maybe. Or he'd spooked them. In retrospect, this was a pretty stupid approach; if he wanted to watch them, he should just anchor somewhere and *watch* them, the way Ezra had yesterday. These continued passes were more likely to attract attention. His father would have pitched him overboard if he'd been here to witness it.

Enough with the half-assed surveillance attempt. They were gone, and he'd already made one pass too many. Better to continue on, leave those two to their own affairs and hope his didn't coincide with them again. Nora Stafford had left his cabin with a measure of uncertainty, but he suspected what she planned to do now was simply get that Lexus off her property and leave the Mitsubishi in the woods. As he'd told her, there was a good chance it would still be there long after Vaughn left. If not, he'd pay for the rusted old heap himself. It was a better option than calling the police out to the Matteson place and attempting to repossess the vehicle. The less interaction Nora had with Devin Matteson's associates, the better.

He found himself alone in North Bay, no other boat in sight, and cut the motor. The flowage would never seem busy, but during fishing season there would be plenty of other people out and about. Today, though, it was empty.

The sun was unhindered by cloud, and he pulled his shirt off so he could feel it on his skin, take in this moment and this place. They'd caught a lot of fish out here, shared a lot of laughs.

A harsh ringing spoiled the silent day then, sounding louder on the water than it ever would back on land. He couldn't believe he got cell phone reception out here. That damn tower that had irked his father so much was doing its job. He took the phone out, saw the same number he'd dialed the previous night to leave his message for Nora. She was back at her body shop.

"Hello?"

Static and garbled words, Frank catching no meaning at all. He took the phone away from his ear, looked at the display again. Still connected, but showing just one bar, a weak signal. Okay, maybe the tower really wasn't anything but an eyesore. He tried again.

"Nora? I can't hear you. Nora?"

More garbled words, but this time he caught a few. Something about a tracking device. Fighting a surge of frustration, he asked her to slow down and repeat herself. Instead, the call was disconnected. Perfect.

He sat down in the boat and looked out across the water, then sighed and turned back to the motor, adjusted the choke and pulled the cord, brought it thundering to life. He didn't have a clue what that call had been about, and until he did, anything pleasant about this morning was ruined. He'd go back to the cabin, call Nora, see what the hell was going on.

"Damn it." Nora smacked the phone with her palm, turned it back on, tried again. This time it didn't even ring, just rolled over to a message saying the mobile user was unavailable. She wondered if he'd caught any of what she said. No way to know. Okay, what now? She wasn't ready to go the police with Jerry's story, not until she'd had a chance to run all of this by Frank, hear his opinion. He knew more about these guys than she did. It would be great if she could get him to come into town, talk things through, but Frank's source of transportation was sitting in the back of her tow lot, so he wouldn't be making any more surprise appearances. It was a long drive out to his cabin, but she didn't know what else to do.

"Jerry." She walked out of the office and into the shop. He was standing over his toolbox, next to the Spraybake paint booth. Outside the day had to be warming, because it was growing stuffy in here despite the concrete block walls and corrugated metal ceiling that usually helped keep it cool.

"Yeah?" Jerry had kept his eyes away from hers ever since he'd told her about the man named AJ, and now he stared at the floor.

"I'm going to get Frank and bring him down here."

"He the kid?"

"Yes." Didn't seem like any kid to her, but if that's how Jerry recognized him, fine. "I want him to be down here when we talk to the police. Like I said, he's got some ideas that they need to hear."

Jerry frowned and spun a ratchet in his hand, the whirring clicks loud in the quiet room. "What sort of ideas has he got?"

"He thinks he might know something about who these guys are, and who they work with."

"How?"

She lifted her hands. "I don't know, Jerry. I'm just telling you what I've heard. He also claims to know where the guy who drove that Lexus is staying. And now I've got to leave and pick him up so we can talk to the police."

"All right. I'll get this car put back together as much as I can, so they can tow it."

"I'd rather you don't."

"Huh?"

"I mean, I don't want anyone left alone in the shop." She tried to put proper concern into her voice, but only a portion of it was for Jerry's well-being.

"Don't worry about me."

"Jerry, I'd really prefer—"

"You don't think you can trust me." He straightened and looked at her for the first time, defiant. "That's what's going on, isn't it? Before I told you about the deal that guy cut me at the bar, you were ready to leave me here, go down to see Mowery. Told me that we needed this Lexus back in one piece fast, for the cops. Now why has that changed?"

They looked at each other for a long moment, and then his face softened and his shoulders sagged.

"I'm *sorry*, Nora. You don't even know. I can see where you wouldn't think real well of me right now. You and I, we've had our problems. But I'll tell you this—ain't a man in this world I respect more than your daddy. Not a one. And the reason I'm still here is I know it's what he'd want me to do. Help you out, keep things running till he gets back on his feet. It's not just about the shop, it's about you. I wanted to make sure you were okay, too. Always did. So when you tell me about last night . . . about these bastards walking in here and treating you like that . . . maybe you don't see how personal that is to me. Okay? And all I can say is, I'm sorry."

Though Jerry asked about Bud's condition constantly, Nora had never been entirely honest with him in her reports. One reason was that her father had absolutely no memory of Jerry, and she knew that would hurt him. Now she wished he *could* remember Jerry. Bud would have liked this story.

"I appreciate everything you just said, Jerry. And I know I haven't been a real easy transition for you. Let's not worry about it, okay? You get the Lexus put back together, and I'll bring Frank Temple down, and then the three of us will talk things out and call the police."

He tipped two fingers off his forehead in a little salute and turned back to the car. She crossed the shop, stepped out the side door, and pulled it shut behind her, making sure that it locked.

When she was gone, Jerry got to work. He started with the hood, which he'd removed completely since it was damaged beyond repair. A day earlier, he'd have just tried to jam the bent piece of metal into the backseat with as many other loose parts as possible, tell Nora that it didn't matter what condition the car was in if they were just transferring possession to the police. After her story, though, no chance. He still knew how to bust ass, how to do a job right, and after hearing what had happened, he'd be doing a lot more of it. Wasn't his fault, he understood that, but it didn't do much to ease the guilt. Fact was, while he was drinking beers and cutting a deal to sell equipment that wasn't his, Nora was back here with some bastard shoving her into a wall. If the kid hadn't showed up when he did . . . Jerry didn't like to think it through much beyond that point.

He wrestled the banged-up hood back into place on the car, fastened it as tight as it would go. The damage kept it from closing all the way, but it was attached and would stay on. By the time he was done with that, a good sweat was working its way across his scalp.

"Too damn hot," he said aloud. He didn't want the shop opened up like they kept it during the week, let people think they could stop by with a car, but having some fresh air wouldn't hurt, either. A crack in the overhead door should do the trick. He crossed to the garage door opener and hit the button, let the big door rise about two feet off the floor, and hit the button again, freezing it there. Already he could feel a breeze shove through, sliding over his feet. That would help.

It was a pain in the ass putting a car back together without assistance, but Jerry had gotten better at that in the last few months. Nora was always trying to help, and, to be fair, usually *could* help, but he preferred to do things himself. To fasten the bumper onto the front of the car, he got one side lined up and bolted loosely, then walked into the paint booth and retrieved a rack they used for drying parts, brought it out, and set it up under the bumper in a way that kept the thing level and positioned well enough that he could get the bolts lined up and tightened. He dragged the creeper over, hitched up his pants, and settled down with his knees and face pointed up at the ceiling. Using his heels, he shoved backward, and the creeper slid under the car so he could get at the bumper bolts, leaving only his lower body exposed.

It was dark under the car, and he had to feel with his fingers to get the wrench in place. Once he had it set the procedure was simple enough, working the wrench with a practiced motion. He'd been on his back under a car since well before he could drive one, watching his daddy labor over a fastback Mustang that he'd bought wrecked, with visions of restoring it to Steve McQueen quality. He'd never gotten it done, but he'd hooked his son on cars. Thirty years later, Jerry was still with it.

He got the bolts on the driver's side fastened and was working the creeper over to the passenger side when he heard the overheard door rattle ever so gently. It was just a slight shake, one that could have been from the wind, but when he turned his head to look he saw two feet. Someone was walking the length of the door while Jerry lay there on his back and watched. Someone in polished black boots. Jerry knew those boots. He'd seen them tapping a soft beat off a bar stool not twenty-four hours earlier.

The son of a bitch was back. This time he didn't have a friend in Jerry, either; what he was *going* to have was a wrench upside his head. Jerry had extended his feet, ready to use his heels to pull himself forward and out from under the car, when he saw a hand appear next to the boots, and then a knee. AJ was coming inside. Crawling under the door and coming inside.

He was a coward for doing it, knew this well, but Jerry pushed with his heels instead of pulling, slid all the way under the Lexus. There was something about this that took him from angry to scared in one blink. What was the guy thinking, crawling into the shop like that? They'd agreed to meet at Kleindorfer's hours from now. So why violate the plan, take this sort of risk?

Resting on his back on the creeper, his nose a few inches from the rear transfer case, Jerry kept his head rolled to the left so he could see his visitor's approach. AJ crawled under the door and straightened up, and then all Jerry could see was his feet as he walked into the shop. Then the feet passed out of his field of vision and he was reliant upon only his ears, listening to the slow claps of boot heels on concrete.

He held his breath in his chest like a dear secret as the boots came and went again in his sight line. AJ seemed to have made a full circle of the shop, was now probably standing in front of the Lexus. Peering into the office, maybe, seeing that it was dark, seeing that the place was empty.

Now, if he'd just crawl back under that door and walk away, Jerry could get up and lower the garage door, lock the place up tight, and give the cops a call. Nora hadn't planned a course of action yet, but this was the second time one of these bastards had broken into the shop, and that was crime enough. Even if Jerry took some heat from the cops, they needed to pick these boys up. Somebody had to answer for Mowery.

There was the metallic bang of a gear engaging, and then a loud hum as the garage door lowered and thumped to a stop against the floor, closed tight. The sound made Jerry lift his head too far and too fast, his forehead making solid contact with the transfer case. He blinked hard and dropped his head again. Why had AJ lowered the door? What the hell was he thinking of doing now?

"You going to stay under that car all day, Mr. Dolson?"

The voice drawled out of the air above him; Jerry could still see no boots to tell him where the man was standing. He was caught. Damn it. Now a dose of embarrassment mingled with his fear. Hiding under the car like a little girl under her bed. That wasn't right, and he should've known it from the start, met this bastard on his feet and with the wrench in his hand. Using the self-reproach as fuel, Jerry slammed his heels onto the floor and pulled himself forward, out from under the car and right into the barrel of a gun.

Sixteen

Frank tried calling the body shop as soon as he got back to the cabin, where a steady cell signal came through. Voice mail. A second try found the same result. He didn't have a cell number for her, either, so the trip back to the cabin now seemed to be in vain.

He pulled the boat higher onto the beach and was half-way to the cabin when his phone rang again, an unfamiliar number on the display. He answered, heard Nora's voice say his name, and was surprised by the strength of the relief he felt.

"Yeah, it's me. I just tried calling you back at your shop."

"I just left it," she said. "Are you at your cabin?"

"Yes."

"Good. I'm on my way. I'd like you to come into town, and of course you can't do that because you have nothing to drive."

"Something happen?"

"You suggested we leave my car where it is, not bring the police out there, because it might be better for me. Safer. Right?"

"Right."

"Okay. Now, if I told you that the two from last night were going to be at Kleindorfer's Tap Room at seven tonight, would you still say I should keep my distance? Or does your advice change at that point?"

"Tell me what happened," was all he said.

The story she told wasn't a surprising one, not really, but even before they hung up he knew his response would be different from hers. He was unsettled by Nora's obvious enthusiasm for bringing the police in. If her body man was honest about the situation, and there really was a meeting scheduled at this bar, yes, he could see the appeal of setting a trap. So would the men who'd set the meeting, though. It went back to what he'd already told her repeatedly: These guys were pros.

He didn't blame them for recruiting her employee as an ally. That had the touch of professional work, too; why risk a strong-arm move when the tickle of a little cash in the palm accomplished the same thing?

They'd played it both ways, though, and that was what he didn't understand. Why recruit the body man and attack Nora the same night? Why take a step to avoid a strong-arm move and then still *make* the strong-arm move?

Because they weren't together.

No, they hadn't been together. That was one of the concerns he'd pondered as Nora drove him to the cabin, one of the problems he couldn't resolve to his own satisfaction. Why had the second man waited until after his buddy was in handcuffs to help? He'd waited because he wasn't there yet. It hadn't been a *wait* at all; he'd arrived at that moment and been forced into action. So that meant that the second guy was the smarter of the two, probably. He'd been at the bar trying to buy off Nora's employee while his friend had been, what, stationed back at the shop to see if she moved the Lexus outside at closing? That made sense. Only the guy stationed at the shop hadn't been patient enough. He'd gone into action, and his friend had to pull his ass out of the fire. Now their presence in town was anything but discreet.

Frank walked back to the cabin thinking about that final realization: These two guys, if there were only two, now understood that their situation in Tomahawk had changed. It was a small town, a town where gossip spread fast and strangers stood out, and now everyone would be talking about them, the police looking for them. It added an element of pressure. Would they wait patiently for a meeting with Nora's employee? He knew *his* answer to that, and it wasn't comforting.

He unlocked the cabin door and went inside, washed up, and changed into a clean shirt. Then he put the suitcase aside and pulled a metal case onto the bed, flipped the latches and opened the lid, and withdrew the two holstered and well-oiled handguns beneath.

His father's guns: a 10 mm Smith & Wesson and a .45-caliber Glock. They should have been the day's project. He'd thought about taking the boat out to the right spot, Muskie Point, maybe, or somewhere among the stumps of Slaughterhouse Bay, and feeding the guns to the lake. It would be a most heavy-handed gesture, yes, but it was one he still wanted to make. He wanted to hold his father's violence in his hands, feel the heft of it, and then leave it behind in a place without regrets, a place of clean memories.

They wouldn't be sinking today. He knew that as he recalled Nora's voice on the phone, all that excitement because she thought this meeting represented the end of the problem. Frank knew it was anything but that. Jerry was just another loose end, and, sadly, another loose end connected to Nora.

He had the Smith & Wesson in its shoulder holster and concealed under a thin jacket by the time Nora arrived.

Spend enough time around firearms, and they'll fail to inspire the same sense of terror that might catch a novice, even when the weapon in question is pointed at your heart. Jerry wasn't thrilled to see it, no, but he wasn't about to wet his pants or anything, either. Guns were guns. Only thing to worry about was the man who held it. And that man hadn't shot him yet.

"You don't look happy to see me, Mr. Dolson," AJ said, sliding his thumb up and down the stock of the gun the way he'd handled the vodka glass the day before.

"I'm not. We had an agreement, and this ain't part of it. Why don't you go on down to Kleindorfer's and wait for me, like we planned?"

"You were down here with the girl," AJ said. "Your boss. She have anything to tell you?"

"Nope."

"You're a bad liar, Mr. Dolson."

Jerry worked his tongue over his teeth and steeled his eyes against the other man's empty gaze.

"And you're a Grade A piece of shit, buddy. Coming in here and beating up a woman."

"I didn't lay hands on anyone."

"Then your buddy did. Which makes you both Grade A pieces of shit, all right? Now you get the damn gun out of my face and get on your way."

"We had an agreement."

"I don't make agreements with people who beat up women."

"All the same, one was made. And I'm going to need that tracking device."

"Don't have it."

"Who does?"

He started to say Nora's name, then stopped. It was wrong both ways; first of all, it might send these assholes back after her, and, second, she didn't even have it. Thing was still sitting in his locker, waiting to go to the police.

"Put that gun down," Jerry said.

"That will make you comfortable? Maybe then we can talk this through, work something out?"

Jerry wasn't about to talk anything through, and any chance of working something out had ended the minute he heard what happened to Nora. He didn't like staring into that tiny muzzle, though, so he nodded.

"Maybe we can."

AJ pistol-whipped him in the face. Jerry had time to lean backward maybe six inches and half-lift the wrench in his hand before the gun caught him just under his right eye and knocked him back into the Lexus. His ribs slammed against the grille, the wrench fell from his hands, and then he took another blow from the gun, this one across the back of his head, right near the top of his neck. It brought him down almost to his knees, hanging on to the car to keep from hitting the floor. All wasted effort, though; the third swing was harder than the first two, and it took all the resistance out of him, left him stretched on his back with one leg hooked over the creeper, looking at the corrugated metal ceiling that now bloomed with a dozen colors.

Jerry watched the colors dance and bit down on the tip of his tongue, trying to clear his head. It didn't work. He bit harder and tasted blood but still the room reeled, and when he felt someone moving his hands he could make only the slightest resistance. A cord bit into the flesh of one wrist, then the other. AJ was tying his hands.

"Is the girl coming back?"

Jerry didn't say anything. When he tried to pull his hands forward, he felt unyielding resistance. He was tied to something. Maybe the Lexus. He heard AJ walking away, blinked hard, strained to lift his head. The gun was out of sight now, but AJ was at Jerry's toolbox, had the drawers open, was lifting a ten-pound maul out. No, no, no. Put that thing down. Please put that thing down.

"Is the girl coming back?" AJ repeated, his back to Jerry as he hefted the maul, took a practice swing.

"Yeah." Jerry's head was clearing fast now, and the pain was no longer a presence in his mind.

"How long till she does?"

"Maybe an hour."

"She go to the cops?" AJ was standing over Jerry, the maul held down against his thigh.

How to answer that? Instinct said to tell him no, but why? If the guy thought cops were on the way, maybe he'd cut this short. Was that a good thing, though?

"Mr. Dolson? Jerry, buddy? You want to give me an answer."

Split the difference, maybe. Tell him she was planning to go the cops, but hadn't yet. Was that good?

"She went to pick up that kid. I think they're . . . could be they'll go to the cops. But that ain't my fault. That's your buddy's, man. You hit a woman, then knock a cop around like that, you've got to expect—"

"What kid?"

"One who jacked up your friend last night."

"Why's he involved?"

The pain was coming back now, but so was his sense of guilt. He shouldn't be giving this asshole so much information. Shouldn't be rolling over like this.

"Don't know."

There was a whistle of metal through air as the maul came down, and Jerry had just enough time to tense before it caught him square in the hip. A hellfire shot of pain cut through his leg and into his stomach, filled his chest. He arched his back and hissed through clenched teeth.

"Want to answer that one again?" AJ said.

"He thinks he knows something about you."

"About *me*? How does he know something about me?"

"I'm not sure, man." He had his eyes squeezed shut against the pain but still sensed the maul being lifted again, yelled out, "I *don't* know, okay? She didn't say. Just told me that she needed to talk to him to decide what to tell the cops. The kid thinks he understands something more than the police, and he thinks he knows where your boy went, the one drove this car."

"He knows where to find him?"

"I think so."

"Where?"

"I don't know."

"You're a lying piece of shit. *Where?*" The maul was drawn back again, and as much as Jerry wanted to look strong, he couldn't help but cower.

"*She didn't tell me.*"

"But she knows."

"Yes. Maybe. I mean, the kid says he knows."

"And she went to get the kid. Where was she going to pick him up?"

"I don't know."

"You're lying again. Where did she go?"

AJ's voice had intensified, and this time Jerry knew he had to shut up. *Had* to. If he told this asshole, the guy was going to leave immediately, chase after Nora. Jerry wasn't about to do that to her. No chance.

"Where did she go?" AJ repeated.

"Tell you where *you* can go. Straight to—"

This time the maul was swung with far greater force, straight into Jerry's thigh. He heard the bone snap a tenth of a second before he felt it, and this time he couldn't make a sound, couldn't have screamed if he wanted to. The pain slid into his brain like a fast-moving storm cloud and he faded beneath it. AJ's voice was somewhere outside the cloud, questioning him, maybe the same question or maybe another; he no longer could translate the words of his own language.

"You're going to die."

He got that sentence, held it for a second, figured it out. Yes, the man was telling the truth. Jerry was going to die.

"One more chance, Mr. Dolson."

So maybe he was not going to die? One more chance. That meant a chance to live, right? Had to. Jerry tried to look at his leg, expecting to see bone and blood. There was nothing of the sort. Just his jeans going down to a foot that he could no longer move. Could he? He tried and nothing happened. Or was he even trying? So hard to tell. So hard to know what to do.

There was something between his eyes and that immovable foot now, swinging in the air. What was it? Oh, shit, the maul. He remembered the maul. It was what had caused all of this. Thing shouldn't even be in the body shop. It was for splitting wood, but he'd brought it down because it was heavier than the hammers and easier to use than a sledge, a good all-purpose pounder. He hadn't considered this purpose.

"*Where did she go?*"

Where did she go. That question again. Asking about Nora. Don't tell him. Remember that, Jerry. Don't tell him.

The pain's going to come back soon, going to make you forget some things, but don't forget this.

"You've got to start talking again," AJ said. "Does she have the tracking device? I don't think she does. You said it was in your locker yesterday. I bet you still have it. You wanted that money."

AJ moved away and the pain moved back in. Jerry took in a long breath and choked on it. There was so much spit in his throat. Or was it blood? You wouldn't bleed in your throat from a broken leg, would you? No. No, that didn't seem to make sense. His leg was in two pieces. That didn't make any sense, either.

"Thatta boy," AJ said, and a locker slammed shut. What was he so happy about? Oh, right, the tracking device.

"You got it," Jerry said. Tried to say, at least. The words were tough to form. AJ had the tracking device now, so he would leave, right? He would leave now, go away and let Jerry alone.

"Yes," AJ said. "I got it. But that's not the only thing I need. Where did *he* go, Jerry, old buddy? Where is the guy who goes with the car?"

Jerry didn't know. Nora hadn't told him. Maybe Nora didn't know. He couldn't remember anymore. Wait—AJ had the tracking device, and that meant Jerry had failed. That was the whole point, wasn't it? Not to give him the tracking device. No, the point was Nora. Not to tell him where Nora had gone. Where *had* Nora gone? The Willow, that was it. She'd gone after the kid at the Willow.

"What's that?" AJ was standing above him now. "What are you saying?"

He'd been talking. No good. Don't talk, Jerry. Keep your damn mouth shut, for once in your life.

"Willow?" AJ said. "Is that what you said? Keep going. Keep talking."

Don't keep talking. Don't say a word. You almost made a mistake, a bad mistake. Don't say anything, Jerry. Bite down on your tongue. Is that your tongue? Doesn't matter. Bite it. Bite it and hold it and don't say a word.

"Okay," AJ said. "I think you're running out of usefulness. Good news is, you're not going to feel that leg anymore."

The maul was gone, discarded in favor of a knife with a small blade. Good. Jerry didn't know if he could take another swing from the maul. Snapped that bone, probably the thickest bone in his body, like it was a piece of rust. No, he couldn't take another one like that. But the knife wasn't good, either, was it? Not in AJ's hand. He should ask AJ to stop. Just stop and go away. Jerry was hurt. Couldn't he see that Jerry was hurt?

Seventeen

"It's not going to be quite that easy," Frank Temple said as Nora drove down Business 51 and into Tomahawk. He'd been offering so many comments of this sort that she was beginning to feel uncomfortable with him. Even if everything he'd told her was the truth, it seemed odd to be *so* leery of calling the police. She was telling him, flat-out, that there was going to be a meeting with Jerry and these guys, and he was still trying to discourage her from calling the police. Who did that? Any normal person would be *ordering* her to call them. So was there something more involved here? Was the man in her passenger seat connected to these guys somehow?

"I'm not saying it's going to be *easy*. I'm saying, if they do it right, this is a good chance. These guys think Jerry's working *with* them, Frank."

"I don't know if they really believe that."

"Well, they agreed to the meeting. And at the time that he set it up, he was all about giving them that tracking device, too. So I don't think his demeanor would have done anything to create suspicion."

"Guys like these don't need something to *create* suspicion, Nora. The idea of going for some sort of trap with a handful of small-town cops whose idea of high crimes probably includes poaching seems like a piss-poor plan to me."

"You spent this morning convincing me that I should be terrified of these men."

"That wasn't the idea."

"Well, it was the effect. You do that, and then I tell you that there's a good opportunity to have them arrested, and you're trying to discourage it. Forgive me if I say that doesn't seem right."

"All I've said, Nora, is that I'm not sure you appreciate the background these guys have."

"You don't know what their backgrounds are. You said that was just a lot of guessing."

"Very educated guessing."

"In your own opinion, sure. I don't know if the police, if the people whose *jobs* it is to deal with situations like this, would agree."

She was snapping at him now and didn't want to be, so she stopped talking before any more hostility crept into her words. He was quiet, looking out the window, and she felt a quick pang of foolishness and guilt. Why, though? Why *should* she believe him? He was a twenty-five-year-old kid who wanted to be a writer, for crying out loud. Just because his father had killed some people didn't mean he was James Bond. And who knew if any of that was even true? What she should have done was get on the Internet and see if she could verify his story.

It was ridiculous not to go to the police. Ridiculous, and probably dangerous. She didn't really know Frank Temple or anything about him, and that odd sense of trust she had in him could be simply the product of the way he'd come to her aid. In fact, she was pretty sure she'd read something like that in a psychology class. Her emotions from the previous night were causing her to put too much faith in him, when he could be just as dangerous as the men she was worried about.

"I'll let you talk to Jerry," she said, "but then I'm calling the police. Okay? This is *not* your decision. I was the one they attacked yesterday, that damn car is in my shop, and it's my responsibility."

He just nodded.

"So it's up to me to decide what we do, and we're going to call the police and give them that little box Jerry found and tell them about the meeting. I can't make you tell them any of the things that you told me this morning, and I won't try. That's up to you. But I will tell them everything I know."

Again he didn't say a word. *Fine,* Nora thought. *In an hour or so the police will be dealing with all of your strange moods, not me.*

She drove into town, into the shop parking lot, through the open gate, and parked just behind the building, facing Frank's Jeep. As she opened the door and stepped out, she saw that one of the overhead garage doors hung about two feet off the ground. Probably getting too stuffy in there for Jerry. Might as well open it up all the way.

Frank was out of the truck and walking beside her as she went to the side door, which she found was locked. She rapped on the door, and they waited. There was an awkward tension now; Frank's silent, blank-faced reaction to her rant in the truck left her uncomfortable. It would be nice if he'd responded, or at least if the silence seemed like a response, as if she'd angered him and he was sulking about it. Instead, he was impossible to read, just stood there with every thought and emotion tucked in a locked box and hidden from the world.

Jerry must have the radio on, because he didn't hear her knock. Or he'd reverted to typical Jerry form and chosen to ignore it. She got out her keys and unlocked the door and pulled it open, held it for Frank.

"Thanks." He walked past her and into the shop, and she followed, letting the door swing shut behind her. She'd made it maybe two steps inside when he whirled back to her, put his hand on her shoulder, and guided her backward.

"Outside."

"What?"

He didn't answer, just kept his hand on her shoulder while reaching for the door handle. Her confusion switched to irritation, and she twisted free from his grasp.

"Let go of me. What are you doing?"

He had the door open and was reaching for her again as she stepped around him and saw the blood.

It should have induced immediate terror, maybe, but instead her reaction was simply to follow it with her eyes, some natural curiosity telling her to find the source before she responded. There was a drain in the center of the concrete floor, a big rusted grate with nickel-sized holes, and a thin trail of blood was leaking into it now. Up from that the flow widened, and then she saw Jerry.

He hung in an awkward half-lean from the front of the Lexus, his hands bound to the car's grille with a length of wire, his head flopped sideways onto his left shoulder. There was a thick dark line across his throat, just under his chin, and beneath it was the pool of blood that had spawned the rivulet running into the drain. His left leg was bent unnaturally, and there was a strange bulge high on his thigh, almost at the hip. Nora's eyes recorded all of this in a split-second stare, and then she said, "*No, Jerry*," and started toward him.

"Don't." Frank had her arm again, his grip rougher than before.

"*Look at him! He's—*"

"Dead. He's dead. Don't go over there, don't touch him. We need to leave now."

She started to fight him, twist her arm loose, but then her eyes focused on the bulge on Jerry's leg again and for the first time she understood what it was. The bone. That was the bone pushing at the skin, trying to escape. They'd broken his leg. That understanding brought the nausea on in a wave, and she started to sink to her knees. Frank caught her and kept her upright, moved her back toward the door. Her jaw went slack, and for an instant she was sure she'd be ill, but then he had her outside and into the fresh air.

"Oh, no, Jerry." She was on her knees on the pavement now, aware of a sudden heat in her face and neck. "No, Jerry, what did they do, what happened to him, what did they do to him?"

She tried to get to her feet, and Frank put his hand on her shoulder and shoved her gently back.

"Stay down. I'm calling the police."

She put her hands flat on the gravel and squeezed them into fists, wanting to hold something, watching idly as one short fingernail split against the stone.

"Did you see his leg?" she said. Frank was talking in a low voice into his phone. She repeated the question, and still he talked only into the phone. Her hands were trembling now on the gravel. She asked the question a third time as he put the phone back into his pocket and knelt beside her, wrapped his arm around her back.

"Did you see his leg?"

"Yes." His voice was soft.

"They hurt him," she said.

"I know."

"They did that to his leg."

"I know."

From the time he'd called Nora and left the first message the night before, Frank had tried diligently to convince himself that most of this was undue worry. That his impression of the men who'd come to her body shop was inflated by the adrenaline of the moment, that bad memories of a man he barely knew had driven him to exaggeration and paranoia. All of that ended when he stepped into the body shop with Nora behind him and saw Jerry Dolson tied to the car, his blood drying on the floor. There'd been no exaggeration, no paranoia. He knew these men now, not by name, maybe, but he knew them. Waiting for the police with his arm around Nora's back as she wept, Frank felt a pang of desire to see his father in a form he'd been sure he would never wish to recall—with gun in hand.

These men were good, but his father had been better. Faster of body and faster of mind, a deadlier shot, superior in every quality of combat. The image of his father as the violent but righteous crusader, an idea that Frank had come to love as a child and loathe as an adult, returned to him in a desperate ache. *Come back,* he thought as he felt Nora's jerking sobs under his hand. *Come back and make this right. Settle this in the only way that it can be settled properly—in blood. You could do that. I cannot.*

His world disappeared into a cacophony of sirens then, three police cars arriving in succession, men emerging with weapons drawn as if there were anything they could do.

Eighteen

They separated Frank from Nora almost immediately, and for the next six hours he didn't see her again. None of the cops bothered to search him for a weapon at first, but he was conscious of the gun in his shoulder holster, and eventually told the officer who seemed to be in charge of the scene that he was carrying. The guy didn't handle it well, took the gun and then searched Frank with rough hands, as if he might have voluntarily given up the pistol only to attack them with a knife a few minutes later.

At first it was nothing but local cops, small-town guys who all seemed to achieve a certain level of shock with the realization that someone had been tortured and murdered at noon on a Saturday in the middle of town. They ran through the basic motions, asked Frank the basic questions, but nobody seemed focused, a high level of confusion permeating the group.

He was left alone in an interrogation room at the little Tomahawk police station for more than an hour. People came and went outside, talking in soft voices, and he caught snippets of their words, muttered curses and musings, references to Mowery. Tomahawk's police department had just hit the big time, and Frank probably understood this better than they did.

When the door finally opened again, the cop who entered wasn't one he'd seen before. Even before the guy settled into a chair across the table and introduced himself, Frank knew he was an outsider. He was about fifty, with a receding hairline and weathered skin, bony shoulders poking at his shirt. When he looked at Frank, one eye drifted just a touch, seemed to gaze off to the left and up.

"Mr. Temple, my name is Ron Atkins. Feel free to call me Ron. How are you doing?"

"Fine," Frank said. "Who are you with?"

Atkins raised an eyebrow. "You imply I'm from a different agency than the one that brought you here."

"I do."

"What makes you think that, might I ask?"

"You don't look excited."

Atkins considered Frank for a long moment after that, then gave him a few slow nods. "Interesting observation, Mr. Temple. No, I am not excited. There's nothing exciting about what we're dealing with here."

"Rest of the cops seem to think so."

"Agreed. That'll pass with time."

"So who are you with?"

The repeated question seemed to irritate Atkins, causing a quick, hard flicker of his eyes before he answered.

"I'm with the FBI, Mr. Temple."

"Milwaukee?"

Atkins's eyebrow went up again. "No, Wausau. We maintain a small field office there."

Frank nodded. If Atkins had come in from Milwaukee already, that would have told him something, suggested that the cops here were already getting a sense of things, maybe knew something about who these guys really were. Nobody from the FBI responded to a murder otherwise. But if he'd just made the hour-long drive from Wausau, maybe it wasn't quite as strange. There weren't a lot of homicides up here, certainly not of this nature, and Frank guessed the FBI office in Wausau wasn't swamped. Probably welcomed the chance to step in, give this one a look.

"Not a real good start to your weekend, is what I'm hearing," Atkins said. "First you had this trouble yesterday in which, according to what I've been told, you performed quite admirably. Then, not twenty-four hours later, you found a murder victim in the same building."

Atkins cocked his head at Frank. "No way to start a vacation, right?"

"Nope."

"So you are here on vacation?"

"Yes."

"That's what brings most people here. Most people, though, they don't have a string of bad luck like you're experiencing."

"I wouldn't think so." Even this early in the conversation, Frank had reached two conclusions about Atkins: First, he was smart, and deserving of respect. Second, Frank didn't like him.

"You rent a cabin up here, is that it?"

"Own one."

"Really? Very nice. Out there on the Willow Flowage, is it?"

"Yes."

"How'd you come into possession of the cabin, might I ask?"

Here was the reason Frank didn't like him, drifting out in these casual questions. The man had come here to ask about Frank's father. Either he knew the name, or somebody had done the homework.

"It was in the family," Frank said. "But I don't see what relevance that has to the poor bastard we found with his leg broken and his throat cut, Mr. Atkins. Ron."

"I understand that. I'm going to ask you for a little patience. See, I may find relevance in places you don't."

"Tell you what," Frank said, "let's go ahead and talk about my dad."

Atkins pursed his lips into a little smile but looked at the tabletop instead of Frank. "Your father. Yes, I've heard about him."

"A lot of people have. And, hate to tell you this, but he's been dead for seven years. Tough to blame him for this one."

"I've heard a few terms used concerning your father—"

"I've used a few of them myself."

"I believe it. But I'm talking about his, uh, entrepreneur-ship, you see. Because the man didn't just kill people. He made money doing it, for a while. One of those terms that people use is 'hit man.'"

"I've heard it."

"Right. So—and I understand how frustrating this has to be for you, trust me—when a cop ends up beaten half to death outside of a body shop on a Friday and another man ends up killed in the same body shop on a Saturday, and the key witness to both events is, well, the son of a hit man . . ."

"This is what brings the FBI up from Wausau," Frank said.

Atkins nodded with a theatrical sense of apology. "Like I said, Mr. Temple, I understand this may not be fair to you, but sometimes we have to endure a little extra suffering along the line just because of our families. That happens to everybody, in one way or another."

I could tell you some of the ways, Frank thought. *Could tell you what it's like to be seventeen years old and fooling around with your girlfriend, biggest concern in the world just trying to get her shirt off, when your father comes home and walks into your bedroom. And for a minute, Mr. Atkins, you're still worried about the girl and about his reaction and this all seems like a major crisis. Seems like that until he says,* Son, we're going to need to be alone right now, *and something in his eyes tells you that the pending conversation has nothing to do with anything as innocent as you and the girl.*

"So I understand, is what I'm trying to say," Atkins said. "But I've still got to ask the questions."

"Yeah," Frank said. "I kind of figured you would."

"Right off the bat, I'm curious about this: I was told you were wearing a gun when the police got down to the body shop. A gun, I might add, with your father's initials stamped into the stock. FT II would be him, right? You're FT III?"

Frank nodded.

"You always carry the gun?"

"No."

"Okay. Then you come up here on vacation, a fishing trip, and you think, yeah, this seems like the time and place to pack a pistol?"

Frank looked at Atkins for a long time before he said, "It had started to seem like a dangerous town."

Atkins nodded. "Almost from the moment you arrived."

Nineteen

This couldn't be her life. The longer Nora thought about it, the less sense it made. Hit men, tracking devices, murder? No, they didn't fit. None of those things belonged.

Yet there they were, the reality hammered home by the parade of police interviewers. *Can you describe* . . . they'd say, time and time again. Of course she could describe it. Jerry had been murdered. Try seeing that and forgetting it. She'd be able to describe that scene for a long time, far longer than any of the things she *wanted* to remember. The way his head had hung at that unnatural angle, the way the bone had bulged from his thigh . . . this couldn't be her life.

She'd gone through a few rounds of interviews and one short talk with some sort of grief counselor who'd left a card and told her something about the pain of those left behind lingering longer than the pain of those who suffered. What that meant, Nora had no clue. The idea seemed to be that Nora would suffer more than Jerry, but the grief counselor hadn't seen Jerry's leg.

The only thing that stood out in all the talking was the lead cop's disclosure that no tracking device had been found in the locker. He wanted to know if it could have been left somewhere else, and she gave them permission—as if they needed it at this point—to search the whole shop, but she knew it was gone. That's what they'd come for, and now it was gone. The only physical link she'd had to them was missing.

The last visitor was a man in an ill-fitting brown suit who showed his badge almost immediately, the only person who'd done so all day. FBI, it said. That surprised and comforted her. About time somebody like this was involved.

The reassurance his presence provided didn't last long. After some of the same preliminary questions, his focus shifted to Frank Temple and stayed there. How long had she known Mr. Temple? Just a day, huh? Was she aware of his father's story? Oh, Mr. Temple had already offered that. Interesting. What else had he said?

That's how it went for more than an hour. One thing was settled—she didn't need to do that Internet research to verify Frank's story. Mr. Atkins of the FBI did a fine job of that.

"You seem to be suspicious of Frank," she said. "Is that my imagination?"

"Suspicious?" Atkins leaned away from the table and hooked one ankle over his knee. "That's getting ahead of the game, Ms. Stafford. I'm just gathering information."

His words reeked of insincerity, though, and she felt instantly sorry for Frank. This was the price he paid for the family he'd been born into. When she walked through the streets of Tomahawk, people stopped her and told her stories about how wonderful her father was, asked after his condition; strangers gave her hugs on a regular basis simply because of her father's history in the town. Frank's experience was quite different.

"I understand you need to gather information," she said, "but Frank was nothing but a help. I've already told you what he did yesterday."

"Yes, I know. But when you consider his background, Ms. Stafford, you can surely understand any heightened curiosity we might have."

Heightened curiosity? Now, there was a good FBI phrase. A minute ago he'd denied being suspicious of Frank, but now he admitted to *heightened curiosity.* Huge difference, clearly.

"Whatever his father did when Frank was essentially a child really seems insignificant to this situation," she said.

"Perhaps."

"You disagree?"

"Let me ask you this—has Mr. Temple told you anything of what he's been doing for the past seven years?"

"I just met him yesterday. Obviously I don't know his life story."

"That's a no, then?"

"He told me he's been a student."

"He's been enrolled in school for a grand total of six semesters in seven years. Those six semesters were scattered among five different schools, in five different states. He has lived in at least ten different states for short times. His highest level of employment is as a bartender, his longest stint at that five months, yet he's paid his rent, bills, and tuition in full and on time."

"Wonderful. So your point is that he's a model citizen?"

Atkins gave her a long, unpleasant stare. Things were becoming contentious, and she knew part of her defensiveness was a product of guilt. She'd basically berated Frank as they'd driven back to town, dismissing his concerns and suspecting him of lies. Then there was Jerry, a terrible but undeniable support for Frank's story. His concern had clearly been genuine and well founded.

"My point," Atkins said, "is that there are many unknowns about Frank Temple the Third. He leads a nomadic lifestyle, maintains few connections to his past, and somehow generates a steady cash flow. It is a pattern, Ms. Stafford, not unlike many of the men in his father's profession."

She pulled her head back and stared at him. "You're kidding, right?"

"I'm making observations, not accusations."

"Well, I made an observation myself today, and that's that Frank doesn't like to talk about his father and is very ashamed of what the man did."

"Shame is one reason to avoid talking about his father. There are other possibilities."

"You're suggesting he followed in his footsteps? Frank was *seventeen* when his father died. I've never heard of a seventeen-year-old assassin."

Atkins just looked at her, studying her face, silent.

"Why aren't you asking about Vaughn?" she said.

"This is the man who drove the Lexus?"

"Yes. He's the one who caused all of this. He's the one who brought these murderers into my shop."

"You were with Mr. Temple and Vaughn at the same time," Atkins said, switching tracks. "Although he called himself Dave O'Connor at the time, right?"

"What do you know about him? Who is he?"

Atkins ignored her. "Did you sense any familiarity between the two men?"

"Frank and Vaughn?" She shook her head. "Absolutely not. I mean, they'd just gotten in an accident. So they had about twenty minutes of familiarity before I met them. That was as much as I sensed, too."

"You let the Lexus driver leave without seeing a driver's license or insurance information?"

"He gave me cash. I've explained that to everyone already. It was a mistake, but I can't fix it now. I can't fix any of this now."

"And you have no idea where he went?"

She should answer that question, tell him about the island cabin and the car in the woods. That was the right thing to do, certainly, but she was remembering Frank's reluctance to bring the police into this, the idea he had that it might make her even more of a threat to these men who had such evil ways of dealing with threats. The less involvement the better, right? Knowing nothing was better than knowing something. If you knew something, you were a loose end. Isn't that what Frank had called her? A loose end. Just like Jerry. She wanted to be clueless again. Wanted to be a bystander. She *was* a bystander, damn it—and wouldn't it be safer, ultimately, to stick to that role? She thought of that and of Jerry's blood running into the floor drain, and she shook her head.

"When he took my car he said he was going to Rhine-lander."

She waited for him outside the police station as evening descended, the sky tinged with wispy purple clouds that stood stark against a backdrop of pinks and oranges. Down the street, loud music blared from speakers near the river, some sort of evening event commencing.

Jerry was dead. He'd been a cantankerous, combative employee from day one, but he'd also been the only person she was close to in the entire town. Time with Jerry made up about ninety percent of her human interaction since she'd arrived in Tomahawk, and understanding that he was gone filled her with the chill of loss. With Jerry went the shop. She couldn't run it alone. Running it with just the two of them had seemed impossible at first, but they'd made it work. The reason for that, she knew, was Jerry's willingness to stick around. He might not have liked working for her, but he'd done it, and without him the shop that her grandfather had opened sixty-eight years earlier would have already been out of business.

She was feeling the threatening rise of more tears when the door opened and Frank Temple stepped out of the station and came down the steps to join her. He held his jacket in his fist, and she saw for the first time that he was wearing a gun in a holster on the side of his chest.

"Where'd you get that?"

He didn't look at her. "Had it on when we left the cabin. Cops seemed to want to keep it, but I made a compelling case against that by pointing out that nobody was killed with a gun today."

There was a bristle to him she'd not seen before, a darkness in his voice. Atkins, probably. If he'd asked *her* so many questions about Frank's past and his family, it could only have been worse for Frank.

The door to the police station opened again, and two cops in uniform stepped out and stared at them.

"Is your car still around?" Frank asked.

"At the shop. They were going to give me a ride, but I wanted to wait for you."

"Let's walk down there, then."

They started down the sidewalk, falling in step together quickly and silently.

"The FBI was here," she said.

"Uh-huh."

"I was surprised . . . I mean, I'm glad that the police are getting help, but I was surprised by that."

He was looking at his feet and still holding the jacket in his hand, that gun open and obvious now, as if it were some sort of statement. "The question is whether I'm the only reason they're involved."

She wasn't sure how to respond to that.

"Because if I am," he said, "then it's somewhat discouraging. I understand it, sure, but having the FBI investigate me is not going to help with this mess."

"He seemed pretty interested in you."

"Yeah, he did. As much as that pisses me off, it's no shock. I just wonder if I'm the heart and soul of their interest, or if I'm part of a package." He turned to face her. "Did Atkins say a word to you about Vaughn?"

She thought about it, then shook her head. "Not until I brought him up. When I asked about him, Atkins just wanted to know whether you seemed familiar with Vaughn. Up until that point the only thing he'd wanted to talk about was . . ."

"Me," Frank said.

She nodded.

"Okay," he said. "That's basically the same response I got, like Atkins was completely uninterested in Vaughn. Since he should be *very* interested in him, I'm going to guess that my wonderful, well-known name is not the only draw that attracted our VIP from Wausau. They've got something on Vaughn already. That Lexus rang some bells somewhere, down in Florida maybe, or on the FBI computers. They got excited about him, and then my name was an extra wild card in the deck. They don't know what to make of it yet."

"And they don't know where he is."

The look he gave her then was both knowing and in-trigued. "You didn't mention Ezra's find?"

"No. Did you?"

He shook his head. "Figured it was your play, and if you told them, they'd be back around with more questions. When that didn't happen, I assumed you'd decided not to say anything."

"I don't know why I didn't," she said. "I just . . . there was a lot going through my mind."

"You didn't say anything because you saw what hap-pened this afternoon."

Blunt, but true. There had been a lot going through her mind, yes, but it was the memory of that blood dripping into the floor drain that made the decision for her.

"You remember what I said about loose ends?" he asked.

She nodded. "I was thinking about that the whole time. That, and everything you said about the guy who owns the cabin, Devin, and how everyone around him is so . . ."

"Deadly."

"I guess that's the word."

"It's the only word that counts right now. Whoever fol-lowed Vaughn up here made a clear statement today, and we've got to listen to it."

"Doesn't that mean I *should* have told the FBI about the car?"

"You were the one who chose not to," he said. "I didn't instruct you on that. So what's your reasoning? Why didn't you tell them?"

She stopped walking, and he went a couple of paces ahead before turning back to her.

"I didn't tell them," she said, "because I'm scared."

"You should be."

"And there was a moment in our conversation this morn-ing when you seemed to suggest that it would better to distance myself from the whole thing."

"I did think that, but as of right now, you have no dis-tance. I don't think there's much chance of getting any back, either."

"So what do we do?"

"I'm not sure yet. Here's what I can tell you—the police in this town, with or without Mr. Atkins of the Wausau office of the FBI, aren't ready to deal with these guys. So I don't think you made a poor decision. I don't think that at all."

"So what do we do?" she repeated.

He looked at her, then down, his eyes seeming to settle on the butt of his gun.

"There are only two things I'm certain of right now. First one is that we should talk to Ezra."

"We should talk to a *fishing guide*?"

"He's a bit more than that, Nora."

"Okay. And the other thing you're certain of?"

He started to walk again, the gun bouncing a little with each step.

"That if you go home tonight, you probably die."

Twenty

Grady hadn't dated much since Adrian left. The occasional setup, or maybe somebody he'd meet at a party and see once or twice again, but nothing serious. He had a date for Saturday night, though, a woman who worked computers at one of the major Chicago banks and had been assigned to help Grady review hundreds of transactions. He was with a team that was trying to trace terrorism dollars now, the new concern, and Helen was the liaison the bank had offered up to the Bureau. They'd spent the better part of two weeks together, going over numbers that led nowhere, and Grady had enjoyed her very much. Good-looking, personable, and able to laugh at herself, which was certainly not a trait Adrian had possessed. He wouldn't have asked her out; there was a professionalism issue as excuse, but the reality was that he'd never been good at that, getting around to the actual question. Two days after he'd broken off from the project, though, she called him at work and asked if he wanted to go to dinner. It was the first time a woman had ever done that with Grady.

He was in a good mood as Saturday afternoon wore down, went for a long run along the lake and then spent an extra ten minutes stretching, felt the week's tension leave his muscles and fade into the air. When he got back to the apartment he showered and—this was embarrassing—tried on three different shirt-and-pants combinations, feeling like a high school kid. He'd just decided on a black button-down with a dark green pair of gabardines, was still threading the belt around his waist, when the phone rang. Not the home number, but his cell, which meant it wasn't a call that he could ignore. He fastened the belt and answered the phone.

"Agent Morgan?"

"Speaking."

"Ron Atkins calling from Wausau."

Wausau? Grady knew there was a field office up there, but what in the hell could Wausau have cooking on a Saturday evening that required his attention?

"What can I do for you?" Grady said, standing before the full-length mirror and taking inventory, trying to ignore the gray hair.

"I'm sorry to bother you on a Saturday night like this, but I've been doing a little research, and it looks like you're the foremost expert we've got on Frank Temple."

Grady watched his face change in the mirror, saw it drape with concern and alarm.

"Which one?" he said. *Please say the dead one, Atkins. Tell me it's old, tell me it's something very old.*

"The son," Atkins said. "Frank the Third."

Grady turned away from the mirror and walked out to the living room, the sick taste of defeat rising in his mouth. Wausau. Shit, he should have remembered. That town was maybe fifty miles from the cabin, that infamous family cabin Frank had spoken of with such warmth, the one he wasn't sure he could ever return to, the one his father had purchased with Matteson and the other soldier, Ballard.

"What's happening?" Grady said.

"I'm still trying to figure that out. Right now here's what I know: The Temple kid blew into town yesterday, with a couple of real bad boys from Miami on his heels, and we've already got one body in the morgue and a cop recovering in the hospital."

Real bad boys from Miami on his heels. The words spun through Grady's brain like whirring blades, and he sank down onto the couch knowing that the kid had done it. He'd gone down to Miami to settle up, he'd put three bullets into Devin Matteson's body, and Grady had sent him there.

"I've been told," Atkins said, "that you spent some time with the kid."

"Yes."

"And you brought his father down."

"He brought himself down."

"What? Oh, sure. Sure. The thing is, you know, it seems the apple didn't fall far from the tree, right? Like father like son and all that? You pick whatever cliché you want, because they all apply here."

"I wouldn't rush to that judgment."

"What rush? He's been adrift for damn near a decade now, floating all over the country without a job but with a seemingly inexhaustible supply of cash."

The supply was exhaustible—probably getting close to exhausted by now, actually—and Grady was well aware of its source. Frank's father had been clever with his banking, setting up some hidden trusts and offshore accounts that his son could use. Frank, though, actually told Grady about their existence. Explained his father's final conversation with him, which included information on the money. By the time the kid disclosed this, Grady was beginning to feel overwhelmed by his guilt, and the sort of trust Frank was showing made it worse. So instead of shutting the money down, as he should have, Grady merely warned Frank that he ought to separate himself from a bloody slush fund like that.

"I spent some time with him," Grady said into the phone, "and he seemed to have his head on right."

"Did you not hear me say I've got one dead up here already?"

"I heard that, and I understand what you're looking at. But let's not start painting Frank as the same as his father right away, all right? Not right away."

The disbelief, tinged with disgust, was clear in Atkins's voice as he said, "Yeah, when a contract killer's son floats into town, wearing a gun and leaving bodies in his wake, I suppose he really could just be on a fishing trip."

"He was wearing a gun?"

"Uh-huh. Smith & Wesson with his father's initials engraved on the stock."

Grady pressed his eyes shut. That was the suicide gun. "Tell me what you know, Atkins."

"These guys from Miami, they showed up yesterday and attacked a woman who owns a body shop here. The same body shop where Temple's car ended up after an accident a few miles north of town. Temple interceded—and I'll admit that the woman hasn't claimed any sense of familiarity between Temple and the pricks who went after her. But by the end of the day the cops somehow lost both of these guys, which takes some doing."

"Why attack the body shop owner?"

"I'm getting to that. They went after her yesterday, then killed one of her employees today. Hung him off the front end of a car and cut his throat. Nasty scene. The way it looks is that they've lost track of Temple and figured the people at the body shop were the last who'd seen him, you know, the best chance of finding out where he went. There's a guy named Vaughn Duncan involved, too, and supposedly these guys are interested in his car."

"Who is Duncan?"

"A prison guard from Florida, part of this whole shit storm that's come up north."

"Frank's not from Florida."

"Maybe not, but his old man certainly had some ties down there. Duncan's car was the one that had the tracking device. Allegedly."

"And he's a prison guard in Florida."

"Was. Evidently he called in and quit a few days ago, no warning, no two-weeks notice, hasn't even filled out the paperwork or met any of the usual requirements. The people down there are less than happy with Mr. Duncan. Seems he came into some serious cash about a year ago, too, source unknown. Guy's working as a prison guard and driving a Lexus, you know something's wrong."

"What prison?"

"Coleman."

"Which part of Coleman? It's a big complex."

There was a rustle of papers and then Atkins said, "Phase One. That mean something to you?"

Yes, it certainly did. Manuel DeCaster was locked up in Coleman Phase One. He was the big boss, the ruthless bastard who'd employed Frank's father, probably still employed Devin Matteson. This was not good news.

"Well," Atkins said. "You got any ideas? Anything I should be checking out?"

As an FBI agent, as a law enforcement officer, Grady had to tell him. Had to drop that Matteson name and news of the recent shooting, fill Atkins in on the back story. He needed to draw connections for Atkins, get the investigation rolling in the direction it clearly needed to go in. But he couldn't do it. Not yet. Not without talking to Frank. So for the second time in his Bureau career—and the second time involving Frank Temple III—Grady ignored those professional obligations, ignored his oath. In the end, he settled for a cop-out. Not a bold-faced lie, but a delay.

"I'm not sure," he told Atkins, "but I know some people I can ask. Let me call around a bit and get back to you."

Atkins seemed satisfied with that. Probably more so than he would have been if he'd known the first person Grady was going to call was Frank himself.

He still had the number, but when he called, all he got was an error message saying it had been disconnected. One perk of working for the FBI, though—if the kid had a number, Grady could find it.

He called Helen next, canceled the date with what he hoped she knew was a sincere apology, and then headed for the office. Another perk of working for the FBI—when you told a woman a work emergency had come up, she tended to believe you.

He thought about Devin Matteson as he drove, about that blood debt he'd chosen not to mention to Atkins. Grady could remember a day, maybe two months after the suicide, when young Frank told him quite emphatically that his father had never killed a good man. *The victims were all evil,* he'd said, *and I know you can say he was no better, but the question is, was he any worse?*

Grady had argued with him that day, told Frank that no one was entitled to make a character judgment that ended another man's life—but what had he told himself, not long after that conversation, to justify the misconception he was allowing to flourish?

Devin Matteson was a bad man. That's what he told himself. Devin Matteson was an evil bastard of the first order, a killer and drug runner and thief, as corrupt as they got. So who cared if the kid thought Devin was the one who'd given up his father? Who cared if he thought Devin was the one who had, essentially, put the gun barrel into his father's mouth?

Nobody cared. Allowing him to think those things couldn't do any harm, really, so long as Frank knew better than to take action, seek retribution.

For a long time, Grady had been sure he knew better.

It was a good thing, Ezra Ballard decided as he looked at the clock for the fifth time in ten minutes, that he'd never had children. He wouldn't have done well with the constant worry.

He'd left the note on Frank's door at two that afternoon, stopping by the cabin to find that Frank was missing, which wasn't a surprise until Ezra noticed the boat was on the beach. If he wasn't fishing and he had no car, where'd he gone? A walk, maybe. That was the only answer. Ezra scrawled a note and used a fishhook to fasten it to the door, then left expecting to hear from his friend's son within a few hours.

It was dark now, had been for thirty minutes at least, and the phone hadn't rung. Ezra actually lifted it from its handset a few times, just to check the dial tone. He wished the kid would call. There was something riding the air today that Ezra didn't like, something that had taken his mind for most of the day, left him distracted, answering questions only after they'd been repeated. The woman had been in the water again this morning, that beautiful woman swimming alone in the cold lake. No sign of the gray-haired companion, no movement from the car hidden in the trees. Maybe that was good. Maybe they were nobodies, nothing to worry about.

He couldn't believe that anymore, though. Not after hearing Frank's story about the attack on Nora Stafford, two men with guns arriving in pursuit of a car whose driver had now joined that woman.

Whoever this gray-haired son of a bitch on the island was, he couldn't be anyone Ezra wanted around. Now Temple's boy was at risk, and that sweetheart of a girl who'd taken over Bud Stafford's shop, and none of that was good.

So what to do about it? Maybe nothing. Maybe it would be best to just wait it out, take his fishing parties after walleye and muskie and come home and smoke a pipe and read a book, and eventually the man and the woman would go away and things would be back to normal.

That was one option. An option he favored until the headlights of a truck washed over his driveway and Frank Temple III arrived, not alone, but with young Nora from the body shop, and right then, even before they got out of the truck, Ezra understood that this thing was not going to be one he could wait out.

They came onto the porch and sat with him and told him what had happened. He listened without speaking, as was his way. People commented on this often, as if it were strange behavior. Ezra didn't understand any other way to listen. When somebody was telling you something, particularly something important, you shut up and listened and thought about what they were saying. If you were always opening your own mouth, or thinking about what you were going to say, how much did you really hear? Ezra heard it all. Heard it, and considered it.

What he heard now, this description of a man with bound hands and a cut throat, took him back to a place he'd left long ago. Not Vietnam, either, no place so far away. Detroit was across a lake, not an ocean, but to Ezra it was home to more bad memories than Vietnam. He'd seen men die in both places, but the deaths in Detroit were a different sort of killing. In thirty years in Tomahawk, he hadn't encountered anything like them again. A throat laid open in pursuit of a dollar gained, a bullet through the eye to avenge a dollar lost, those things did not happen here. *Hadn't* happened here, at least.

But now they'd come to him, Temple's son and the girl had, and they were right to do so. He could see the doubt in Nora's eyes, could see her taking in him and his cabin and wondering what Frank was thinking, why they were on this porch instead of in a police station somewhere. Frank understood, though. He'd learned some things from his father, some things he wished not to know. In this circumstance, at least, they would help him. Ezra hoped the kid appreciated that.

"I didn't think she should go home," Frank concluded. "Am I wrong? Are these guys already out of town, trying to disappear?"

"No," Ezra said. "You weren't wrong, and they aren't gone yet."

He was sure of that, though he hadn't seen the men personally, knew nothing of them. What he did know, just from Frank's story, was that these two were professionals who'd come all the way up here to do a job. The job didn't involve beating up Mowery or killing Jerry Dolson, and because these things were happening it was clear that the job was not done. Also clear, then, was the notion that they would not leave until it was.

The girl was tougher than he might have guessed. He could tell that in the way she stood and listened. Frightened, sure, but not panicked. Not frozen. There was a quality of disbelief to her at times, as if she hadn't reconciled with everything that had happened yet, but that was reasonable. Expected.

"So what's your advice?" Frank said. "Should we go back to the cops?"

"I don't think we'll be able to decide that until we find out exactly who the visitors are, and what they're running from."

"How do we do that?"

"Well," Ezra said, "I'd imagine asking them directly would be a good start."

Frank and Nora stood there and stared at him, no sound but the buzzing insects filling the air for a while.

"We're going there?" Frank said. "To the island?"

"I think we should."

"Without the police."

"Son, you were the one telling *me* the risks with the police."

"I know, but . . . you're saying we go out there now?"

Ezra shook his head. "It were up to me, I'd wait till daylight. You go out there in the middle of the night, you're gonna provoke a different sort of reaction."

Frank didn't respond, and Nora Stafford looked unsettled. Ezra spread his hands and leaned forward, the chair creaking beneath him.

"Listen—you two are worried. Scared. That makes sense. And you're trying to decide what to do that will leave you the safest. Also makes sense. But you can't do that until you understand the situation. That gray-haired guy and that woman, they aren't the same cut as these men that rolled into town on their heels, but they've got some answers. Some things we need to hear."

Frank nodded slowly. "All right. So you and I go out there in the morning and try to get them to talk."

"It's my recommendation, yes."

"No," Nora said, and Ezra thought she was objecting to the whole idea until she said, "You're not going to leave me sitting in some cabin while you go out there to talk to them. I won't do it."

Nobody answered her at first. Ezra wasn't thrilled with the idea; Nora's involvement had already gone too far, in his opinion.

"They came into my shop and they killed my employee, my friend, a man who'd worked for my family for years," she said. "If anyone here deserves some answers, it's not you guys. It's me."

Tough to argue with that. Ezra just said, "That's what you want to do? Talk to them in person?"

"From what I've heard, it seems to be what you think is best. But if anyone goes out there, they'll be taking me with them."

"Fine," Ezra said. "We'll all go, then. First thing in the morning."

"What if they leave?" Nora asked.

"Be tough to leave that island," Ezra said, "without a boat."

Frank's eyebrows rose. "You're going to steal it?"

"Not steal it. Might disrupt it a touch, is all."

"What if they see you?" Nora said. "Won't that cause problems?"

Ezra smiled at her, and Frank answered for him.

"They won't see him, Nora."

Her head was swiveling between them, her lips slightly parted, eyes intense, not saying a word. Frank looked to her.

"You're in more jeopardy here than anybody. What do you think?"

"I think," she said after a long pause, "that we should know what it's all about. If they can tell us that, then I like Ezra's idea."

It was quiet for a few minutes, and then Ezra said, "You feel safe at your cabin?"

"I do," Frank said.

Ezra nodded. "You'll be safe there tonight." Ezra had a boat and a rifle with a night scope. Yes, they'd be safe tonight.

"All right," he said. "I think I ought to go address that boat on the island. You all go on back home. Rest. It's done for the day, all right? I believe that. Any trouble does come up, I'll be around, and I see you got your dad's gun in case you need it."

Frank looked down at the gun, then back at Ezra. "How the hell can you tell it's his gun when it's holstered and I'm standing in the dark?"

Ezra walked to his truck.

Twenty-one

Grady found an active cell number easily enough, but he couldn't get through to Frank. He called five times over two hours, got nothing but an immediate voice mail, indicating the phone was turned off. He left two messages. No details, just his numbers and an urgent request to call.

What to do now? He owed Atkins information. Every hour that ticked by made him feel guiltier about that, more aware of the ramifications. If Frank was really responsible for shooting Devin Matteson, then what in the hell was Grady thinking, trying to protect him?

It would help if he would answer the damn phone. One conversation, no matter how brief, would give Grady some guidance. Some sense of how to proceed. Finally, frustrated, he picked up the phone again and called Saul down in Miami. Maybe Jimmy would have insight by now, some new development.

Saul answered on the first ring, his voice tinged with irritation. "Shit, Grady, I was gonna call you tomorrow. Should have known you couldn't wait on it till morning like a normal person."

"Wait on what, Jimmy?"

"The hell do you think? Matteson."

"You've heard about what's going on up there?"

"Up there? What . . . look, Grady, why are you calling?"

Grady stood up, the office not feeling so warm anymore, and said, "Did Matteson die in the hospital?"

If he had, then it became murder. Not just attempted, but the real deal.

"Die? Uh, no, Grady. The boy is loose."

"What?"

"Matteson bailed out of the hospital under his own power sometime this afternoon. Hasn't been heard from since."

"I thought he was in critical condition."

"He had been initially. Like I told you yesterday, he was recovering unusually well, but not well enough to be out of the hospital. Doctors seem to think he just signed his own death sentence, and nobody down here has a clue what motivated him to go. He wasn't facing charges for anything, so it doesn't really make sense."

He's coming for Frank, Grady thought. *Oh, shit, he is coming to Wisconsin and he is going to kill Frank.*

Then Saul said, "Best bet is he's looking for the wife," and everything changed.

"The wife?" Grady said, the word leaving his mouth as if he'd never said it before, didn't understand the meaning.

"Yeah, of course. Oh, wait, I hadn't heard about her the last time we talked, had I? That news came in a little later. Remember when I said there weren't any suspects?"

"Yes."

"Well, that's been blown out of the water. Nobody can find Matteson's wife. Originally the cops thought it was no big deal, she was just MIA, but now their idea is that she took off. Ran. Which makes her—"

"The suspect," Grady finished. Did this clear Frank? It had to, right?

"You got it," Saul said. "Problem with that is there were no signs of a rift with Matteson, no indications of an affair. But, still, until she turns up, that's what'll occupy the focus. Could be she's dead, too. Could be—"

"Devin left the hospital today," Grady said, no longer interested in hearing the theories, suddenly sure he knew more than anyone in Miami did.

"That's right. Nobody knows where he's headed, either."

"I do," Grady said.

"What are you talking about?"

"I think I know where he's headed. I could be wrong, but I doubt it."

The irritation left Saul's voice. "What's going on up there, Grady?"

"I don't know yet, but here's my advice: If you want to find Matteson, you check on the ways out of Miami to Wisconsin. Check every flight that left there yesterday with any destination in Wisconsin. Could be he's driving, but I doubt it. I think he'll be in a hurry."

"How do you know this?"

"I'll fill you in soon. First I've got a question: Does the name Vaughn Duncan mean anything to you?"

"Nope."

"Check him out," Grady said. "He's a prison guard from Coleman, and he's up in Wisconsin, tangling with Frank Temple and a couple others. Check him out and get back to me."

He hung up on Saul's demands for more information.

The cabin was dark when they entered, and the memory of Jerry's body sickened Nora as she followed Frank through the door. She'd felt so in control as they'd walked into the shop that afternoon. In charge, ready to take on the world. These guys had shown up and caused trouble, but now she was going to set them straight. It would be that simple. Then she'd gone through the door and seen the body and the blood, and everything she believed changed.

There was no blood here, nothing out of place in the cabin, no traces of unwanted visitors. Even so, she was nervous until he got all the lights on and showed her around the place. He was still wearing the gun, and she was troubled to realize that it comforted her. She'd never cared for guns before.

"I thought about taking you back to your house so you could get some things together," he said, walking back into the living room, "but it wasn't worth the risk. If they're watching anyplace, it would probably be your house."

"Right."

"Ezra keeps the place stocked even though nobody's here," he said. "There's an extra toothbrush in the bathroom, soap and shampoo, should be everything you need. Well, I don't know what you—"

"Don't worry; I won't require any feminine products."

She'd been trying to make fun of him, get a laugh and reduce that tension he'd acquired. It didn't work. He just nodded, still looking ill at ease.

"I was joking," she said.

"Yeah. Look, you can take whatever bedroom you want."

"What's wrong?"

He frowned. "Nothing. Just telling you to make yourself at home."

"You seem anything but comfortable with me right now. Maybe I should go to a hotel. Maybe that would be best."

It was quiet for a moment, and then he said, "I'm not like them. I need you to understand that. I'm not anything like them."

She stared at him. "The guys who killed Jerry? Are you kidding me? Of course you're not anything like them."

He leaned against the wall, looked down to the gun, back up at her.

"I'm not like him, either."

"Your father."

He nodded.

"I don't think otherwise."

His eyes were so damn sad when he said, "You would have liked him."

She had no idea how to answer that.

"Everybody did," he said. "You would have, too."

"Is that what scares you the most?"

"What?"

"That you loved him. That you thought he was good."

He looked at her for a while without speaking, and then he walked to the door and went outside.

* * *

She found an open case of beer in the refrigerator, took two bottles, and went after him. He was sitting on the log wall that held the soil back from the beach. He didn't look away from the water until she handed him the beer.

"Thanks." He took the bottle and pointed at the lake with it. "I can see why Ezra never left."

"It's a gorgeous place." The air was warm again tonight, but the sky was overcast, only a handful of stars showing. The wind that had blown so hard in the morning was almost gone now, nothing left but a few gentle puffs trying to catch up. It had been one of those weird warm weeks, each day feeling more like summer than spring, then settling down overnight until you woke to a cold sunrise.

"You don't need to worry," she said, "about anything I heard today. Nothing the cops told me was different from what you'd told me this morning. I'm not scared of you. I don't think you're dangerous."

"Then the old man failed. He spent a lot of time trying to make me dangerous. It would break his heart to hear you say that."

She thought of the way he'd come across the body shop, unarmed, the day before. How long had it taken him to knock that guy out with the wrench? Two seconds, tops. So was he dangerous? Maybe he could be, but she wasn't scared of him. It wasn't that sort of quality.

"I'm sorry," he said. "I'm not going to make you sit here and be my therapist. It's just that a day like today puts him in my mind more than normal. Just being up here, seeing this place and seeing Ezra . . . it works on me."

"I believe that."

He drank more of the beer, leaned back from the wall, and braced the heels of his hands on the grass. She could feel a prickle in the middle of her back, touched off by sitting out here in the open, surrounded by darkness. Wasn't he afraid? Didn't seem to be. Either he thought they were completely safe here, or he thought he'd sense any trouble before it came.

"Where's your mother?" She surprised herself by asking

the question; one second it had been in her head and the next she'd spoken it, without ever planning to. There was just something about him right now that made her curious, some rootless quality, as if he'd always been alone, drifting along in the company of bad memories.

"Baltimore."

"That's where you grew up?"

"No. That's where she is now."

"Were they divorced?"

"Not officially. They were together until I was fifteen. She picked up on some changes that I missed, I guess, or maybe he had more trouble facing her than me. Anyhow, things got bad, he moved out, got an apartment. They were still married, and he was always saying they'd get back together."

"Are you close to her?"

The personal questions that had bothered him so visibly the previous night now seemed almost welcome, taken in stride.

"Not by happy-family standards, I guess, but in a different way. A deeper way, maybe. We're all we have, you know? To go through something like we did . . . that's a different sort of bond than what I'd like to have, but it's there. We talk on the phone, I see her every now and again, holidays, that sort of thing."

He drummed his fingers on the beer bottle. "She moved back to Baltimore, where my aunt lived. Got remarried a few years ago. And that's great for her, don't get me wrong, but the first time I saw the guy . . ."

"What?" Nora prompted when he left the sentence unfinished.

He shook his head. "It's not an impressive thing to admit, a little too much testosterone in it, but when I met him I was just so disgusted. And angry. Because he's this little guy with a paunch and a soft chin, a pharmaceutical sales rep who wanted to take me *golfing,* and I took one look at him and thought, *You've got to be kidding me.* Because he was so, so far away from what my father had been."

He lifted the beer, took a drink. "Later that night, though? I thought about that, and realized that of course he would *have* to be. For her. He would have to be so far from what my father had been."

She was sitting with her knees pulled up to her chest, arms around them, facing the water. The way he was leaning back put him behind her, so she couldn't see his face, just hear his voice. He seemed more comfortable that way.

"He killed people, and he took money for it, and that seems so *obviously* evil to most people . . . but I wish they'd met him," he said. "Not that they would change their minds, or should. But now he's a monster, you know? And there is no more one-dimensional character than a monster. If Dad was anything, it was multidimensional. He wasn't all darkness. Sometimes I wish that he had been."

"I'm sorry," she said. What a horribly hollow phrase.

The silence was interrupted by the soft sound of a motor somewhere out on the lake. It was too quiet to be a big engine; maybe one of those trolling motors, instead. She couldn't see any lights. Only when she sat up straighter to stare out at the water did Frank speak.

"It's Ezra."

"That's him in his boat?"

"Yes."

"How do you know? There are no lights. What if it's—"

"It's not them. Whoever's in that boat took it out around the sandbar, and you don't do that by dumb luck."

It was clear he'd been aware of the boat for some time.

"You're sure it's him," she said.

"Yeah. I knew he'd spend the night out there."

"How did you know?"

"Because he takes his responsibilities seriously," Frank said. "And tonight, we're on that list."

"Is Ezra from the South?"

"No."

"He talks like it. Has that drawl, the twang."

"Uh-huh."

"Where's he from?"

"Detroit."

"Detroit?" She raised her eyebrows. "Wow. I wouldn't have guessed that. He talks like he's from someplace far away from there."

"Yes," Frank said. "He does."

The motor had disappeared now; she could hear only the gentle thumping of water on the beach and the occasional creaking of a tree in the woods behind them. How was Ezra intending to watch over them from the water, in the dark? Must have some of those night-vision goggles. Or perhaps he could see in the dark. She could imagine Frank informing her of that detail in his detached, matter-of-fact voice: *Ezra can sense heat from a thousand yards away. He'll know if anyone else shows up.*

She was smiling at that, her own private joke, when Frank said, "So what's your story?"

"What do you mean?" She turned back to him.

"You're from Minneapolis. Your dad lived up here, ran that body shop, and then he had a stroke."

"Yes."

"So what else is keeping you here?"

"That's not enough?"

He leaned forward, so that she could see his face again, and lifted the beer to his lips. "Could be. I'm asking you if that's all there is."

All the months she'd been up here now, and nobody else had asked. Everyone just assumed it was all about her father, trusted her good intentions. Now Frank picked them apart as if the ulterior motive couldn't be more obvious.

"I came for Dad," she said carefully. "He needs someone here, and I don't want that shop to close."

He didn't answer.

"But there might have been some things going on in my life that made staying here seem more appealing."

"Okay."

There was a long pause, an obvious cue for him to inquire further, but he didn't.

"I was engaged," she said.

"Yeah?"

She nodded. "Had been for three years."

"Long time to wait."

"That's what he said."

Frank's laugh, low and genuine, caught her by surprise and relaxed her. She leaned back and twisted a little, facing him directly.

"The wedding date was set for a month ago, in fact. Came and went and here I remain. I had his full support when I came out here, after Dad's stroke. Longer I stayed, though, the pushier he became about me coming back to Minneapolis. And I realized a couple of things. One was that I didn't want my father to be alone in a nursing home, nobody coming to see him, his shop going out of business, all the rest of that. It seemed so wrong."

"And the other?" Frank said.

"The other was that I didn't want to get married. I'd been dating him for five years, living with him for two, and yet I kept coming up with delays."

"Just reluctant, then? No specific reason, no epiphany?"

She started to nod, then stopped, wondering if agreement would be a lie. There had been an epiphany of sorts. A party not long after their engagement, when Seth had turned to a group of people to introduce Nora and said, *This is my fiancée.* She'd waited for the *Nora* to follow, but it never came. A simple thing, maybe, a minuscule issue of semantics, but in that moment it hadn't felt simple or minuscule. It felt chilling. Because she knew that he hadn't misspoken, knew that her identity, at least in his mind, had already been completed. The name was irrelevant; she was his fiancée. His possession. Standing there in an uncomfortable dress making phony smiles at people she'd never truly trust, she flashed forward twenty years and saw herself introduced as *This is my wife,* again no name behind it, then saw herself kissing his neck and running her hands along his back so he'd write a check for her daughter's trip to Europe, saw herself doing that and not even recognizing it for what it was.

A powerful moment, one that had stayed with her as few

others had and one that she'd never discussed with anyone, and would not discuss now, with Frank. It was a bit too much, a bit too personal.

"When I had to come up here, it was the first time I'd been on my own in a long while," she said instead. "It felt good. The other thing, and this was a good deal more personal, was that he made too much money. Not millions or anything, but enough that he wanted me to forget about a day job and concentrate on my art."

"Generally considered a positive thing."

"That's what I thought. First I had my mother and my stepfather taking care of me, spoiled little shit that I was, and then the future husband promising to do the same thing. Wonderful, right? But when I came up here and started going through my dad's things, really looking at his life, at how hard he and my grandfather had worked to make a living off that crappy little shop . . ."

"Made you feel soft?"

"Made me realize I *am* soft. My dad got up at three in the morning when it snowed, ran the plow till eight, then came back and opened his shop up and worked all day. Would run the plow again in the evening, if he had to. Did that all winter, for thirty years. When I went back through their books, I saw that there was *never* a time when that shop did more than struggle to keep bills paid, but they kept them paid. For sixty-eight years, they kept them paid."

The wind blew hair into her face and she pushed it back.

"I've never worked for anything. Not that counted. I worked for good grades, worked on my art, but that's not the same. I've never *had* to work hard, never had my back to the wall in any way in my entire life. I suppose it's awfully childish of me to say that like it's a bad thing. I suppose I should just be grateful."

"Is that what the fiancé told you?"

"Among other things."

"So you called it off?"

"He gave me an ultimatum."

"Poor bastard. Hate to bluff on a play like that."

"I guess."

"A name," Frank said. "I require a name."

"Seth."

"Horrible."

"Someone named Frank is criticizing another guy's name?"

"Frank was half of the first names of the Hardy Boys. It doesn't get any more solid than that."

She was laughing again, and he seemed to have drawn closer without ever moving, and there was a sudden intimacy to the evening that absolutely did not belong. Even while understanding that it didn't belong, she didn't want it to go away, either. There was a pause that went on a few beats too long, his face close to hers.

"This is where you tell me what a shitty kisser Seth was," Frank said. "To inspire me."

"Inspire you to what?"

He didn't respond.

"Can't do it," she said. "He was actually a very good kisser."

"She sets the bar high," Frank said, and then his hand was sliding across the back of her neck and pulling her forward and his lips were on hers and, what do you know, he *was* better than Seth.

Twenty-two

It was the first time he'd watched anyone kiss through a rifle scope. When Ezra realized what they were doing, he dropped the gun and looked skyward, despondent. Just what this mess needed. What the hell was the kid thinking?

He lifted the gun again, watched them for a few seconds, Nora Stafford beautiful even bathed in the wavering green light of the scope. Okay, *that* was what the kid was thinking. On second look, even through the scope, it made a hell of a lot of sense. Well, good for Frank.

Very good, really. Ezra hadn't liked the boy's look this evening. Reminded him too much of other men he'd known, in other places. It wasn't the way he wanted to see the young Temple go. The girl could be good for him. Once they got this shit cleared up, got those sons of bitches from Florida or wherever they were from sent on their way, the girl could be a wonderful thing for Frank. Ezra hadn't seen her many times, but enough to know that she was a different cut than others her age. As was Frank. Certainly, as was Frank.

Ezra went into the water two hundred feet from the island, swam naked through the cold lake, spent all of thirty seconds on the motor, and then swam off into the darkness again, leaving the outboard disabled. Whole thing had taken maybe five minutes, but they were minutes that took him back to those other places, those other times. Damn, but the three of them had been close once. You got a different sort of close in combat. He'd read a couple of textbooks on the brotherhood of battle once, written by psychologists sitting in university offices in towns that held peace rallies even when the country wasn't at war. Read just enough to know that the authors didn't understand their subject, and then gave up and moved on to other books.

The lake had healed Ezra. That was something none of the psychologists would understand, but it was as true as anything he'd ever known. This place had *healed* him. He liked to believe the violence had drained away slowly, that the lake and forests had soaked it up, taken it from him. What he feared, time to time, was that it hadn't drained away at all. That it was just a little better hidden.

He was esteemed throughout the area as a hunter, but what he never told anyone was that he'd let the real trophies pass by. He'd looked at some amazing bucks in the scope, and once at a bear that went a good eighty pounds beyond any he'd ever seen in these woods, and he'd turned away from them. Let them go in peace. Just to prove he didn't even have to hunt, didn't have to kill, didn't have to squeeze the trigger ever again if he didn't want to.

The lake had done that for him.

He was glad when Frank and Nora stood up and went into the cabin, left him to watch nothing but the building and the woods through his scope. He didn't want to watch people through the scope anymore.

They'd been kissing for a while when Nora put her palm on his chest and pushed him back.

"What?" he said, breaking away. "I shouldn't have done that?"

"No, it's just"—she was smiling at him—"not really the night for it, you know?"

He was looking at her hard, trying to read her, but she'd turned back to the lake.

"Is he still out there?" she asked.

"Ezra? Yes."

"I wonder if he was watching that little display."

"Probably."

"He must think I'm a slut."

"I doubt it. But if you want to try to convince him . . ."

She laughed at that and got to her feet, dusted off her pants. He stood up, too, stretched, and tried not to stare at the lake, searching for the boat the way she had.

"Look," he said, "I'm sorry. If I did anything—"

"It's fine." She held her hands up, palms out. "Relax, okay. You didn't do anything wrong, I just don't want to let that moment turn into something it shouldn't."

"You can trust me," he said and immediately regretted it. He was coming on too strong, overreacting to her withdrawal. She was right—this wasn't the night for it. Not at all. But his first thought when she'd pushed him back was that she was scared of him. It had been in his mind earlier, when he brought her to the cabin, and hadn't left yet. He was not like the rest of these people who had invaded her life, and he *had* to have her understand that. He was not dangerous.

"I do trust you," she said, but now the awkwardness between them was evident. "Don't worry about it. It's cold, though. So maybe we can go inside?"

She rubbed her upper arms in a false gesture, and he just nodded and walked to the door and held it for her, thinking that there was a reason he was so concerned about whether she was afraid of him, and it came from a place of guilt. Even while he implored her to trust him, while he said he would protect her, he was also asking her to believe in a complete fraud—the idea that his connection to all of this was circumstantial, an extraordinary coincidence. It had been easier to ask her to believe that than to tell her that he'd come here to kill someone. What would she do if he told her that? What sort of response would that little disclosure provoke?

They drank another beer but kept their distance. She sat on the couch, and he took the chair beside it. They spoke in soft voices for about an hour, and the conversation slowed and vanished, and after a while he realized she was asleep. He repositioned her on the couch, got a pillow under her head and a blanket over her body, then sat beside her and willed sleep to stay at bay. Wasn't fair to make Ezra do all the watching.

He thought about his cell phone at some point as he sat there in the dark, got quietly to his feet, and went to find it. He'd turned it off after going into the police station, and now he turned it back on, heard a chime indicating a message was waiting. The sound seemed loud in the quiet house, and he looked over at Nora. She didn't move, and her breathing stayed slow and deep. He played the message.

Grady Morgan. The sound of Grady's voice hit him as hard as Ezra's had a few days earlier, maybe even harder. Frank scarcely took in the content of the message at first, just that voice. There was a tension to it, maybe even some anger.

Grady had heard about the day's events, of course. Frank should have expected that. As soon as Atkins showed up, he should have expected that Grady would get a call. If he'd been thinking, he would have preempted Atkins, explained things and given Grady some warning. Now Grady had heard only Atkins's side of things, and he was worried.

Frank looked at the clock, saw it was nearly one. Late for a call, but Grady's tone had some urgency. He probably wouldn't mind.

After one more check to ensure that Nora was sleeping soundly, Frank slipped out the door and into the night to make the call.

Grady had been asleep for about an hour when the phone rang. He turned onto his elbow, reached out and grabbed the receiver, mumbled a hello that was thick with sleep.

"It's Frank."

Grady said, "What the hell kind of trouble did you get into?"

"Atkins didn't tell you?"

"I've heard what he said. Now I'm asking *you*."

"Can't tell you anything different except that these guys are involved with Devin. That much seems clear."

"Frank . . ." He wanted to ask the question, *had* to ask it, but it didn't leave his lips.

"What?"

"Here's how I'm going to phrase it. And, damn it, you tell me the truth. Were you down in Miami when it got started?"

Say no, say no, say no. Don't make this my fault, Frank, don't tell me that a man is dead and you're going to prison because of the lies I told so many years ago . . .

"Grady, I haven't been to Miami since my dad took me down eight years ago. I don't intend to head that way, either."

Grady moved the phone away from his mouth so Frank couldn't hear that exhalation of pure relief. It didn't sound like Frank was lying. He'd been nowhere near Miami, had not put those bullets into Devin Matteson.

Grady said, "So you're telling me that—"

"What happened in Miami? You seem to know a lot more than I do."

"Devin Matteson was shot."

Silence filled the line. Grady's eyes were adjusting to the dark, turning shadows into furniture around the room. He sat and waited.

"Just shot," Frank said at last, "or killed?"

"Shot. Three times in the back. But he didn't die."

"Of course not," Frank said. "Wouldn't be that easy."

"Listen . . . are you telling me the truth? You really have nothing to do with Matteson?"

"I do not."

"Then why are you up there?"

"You still want the truth? Because I heard he was headed this way."

"Who told you that?"

"Ezra Ballard."

"Well, I wish you hadn't gone up there," Grady said. "You should have called me. Now look at what it's turning into. Stay away from Ballard, and stay away from whatever ideas he's got."

"Who said he's got any? But I don't want to argue with

you. Tell me what you know about Devin. Who took him out?"

Grady sighed and rubbed his eyes. "Nobody knows. But his wife went MIA the same night he got popped, so that's taking the focus."

"You mean she might have done it?"

"That, or she bolted with whoever did."

"His wife disappeared." Frank's voice seemed to have tightened.

"Yes."

"You got a description of her? Know anything about her?"

Grady paused. "Why are you asking?"

"You surprised to hear I'm interested in whoever shot Devin?"

Grady didn't like that answer. He'd spent enough time talking to Frank to recognize when he was being evasive.

"Agent Atkins was telling me about the guy you got tangled up with," he said. "Vaughn."

"Is that his name?" Frank said, but it sounded false.

"Yeah, it's his name."

"Told us his name was Dave. That's about all I can offer. That, and he's a nervous little prick. Jumpy. Doesn't fit the mold for the rest of them. What do you know about him?"

"Nothing, yet. But people in Miami are looking into him."

"That's where he's from?"

"Originally. He works at Coleman, though. As a guard."

"Coleman," Frank echoed, and Grady knew he remembered, knew he was thinking about Manuel DeCaster, drawing all the same connections Grady had.

"Atkins seems to think the guy is still in your area, though," he said. "Thinks that's what today's killing was about."

"Yeah, that's the simple math."

"Do you know where he is?"

Silence.

"Frank, if you know, tell me."

"I hadn't seen the guy before yesterday, and I haven't seen him since."

Again the evasiveness. Grady said, "Frank, listen to me—I want you to leave. Get in your car first thing in the morning, and get out of there. Will you do that?"

"Atkins might not like it."

"I'll deal with Atkins. You need to get out of there."

"Devin's going to make it? Three bullets weren't enough?"

"He was recovering."

"Was?"

Grady hesitated. "Yeah."

"So what changed?"

"He's gone, Frank. He left the hospital against doctor's orders, and he's gone. Now, I don't know what the hell is going on up there, but I think he wants a part of it. And you need to be gone when he gets there. All right? You need to be *gone*."

Frank didn't say anything, but his breathing had changed, slowed.

"Are you listening, Frank? Get out of there, first thing in the morning."

"I don't have a car," Frank said, and there was something in his tone that made Grady get out of bed and onto his feet.

"Look, I'll drive up there myself. I'll drive up and talk to this Atkins guy and then you can ride back down with me. Leave them to figure it out. That's what you've got to do, Frank."

"No, Grady. You stay down there. Okay? You stay down there."

"Frank—"

"Thanks for the insight, though. This is important to know."

"If you know where Vaughn is, you've got to tell—"

"I'll talk to you soon, Grady. Thanks again."

He hung up, and Grady swore loudly into the dead phone.

The conversation had ended too fast. Grady should have told him. It was time now. He had to tell him. He turned the light on, and blinked against the harsh brightness until he could see the numbers clear enough to call back.

Frank had turned the phone off again.

Twenty-three

The flashlight blinked three times, then stopped. Ezra waited for the pause, then hit the lights on his boat, just tapped them on and right back off, enough to show Frank that he understood the signal.

It was almost two in the morning, and Frank wanted Ezra to come in? This couldn't be good. Ezra ignored the outboard—too noisy—and turned the trolling motor on, brought the boat in to the beach with no sound but that soft electric whir. Frank met him in the shallows, waded out, and took the bow line and threaded it through the U-bolt Ezra and Frank's father had bored into the log wall long ago.

"You all right?" Ezra stepped off the boat and onto firm ground.

"We're fine."

"Then what's the problem?"

There were no lights on the boat or outside the cabin, and Frank's face was only a few shades lighter than the shadows that surrounded it.

"Devin's on his way."

The wind was blowing warm and steady out of the southwest, and Ezra turned his face into it, breathed it in.

"How do you know?"

"Just talked to Grady Morgan. You remember him?"

"FBI."

"That's right."

"Didn't seem to be my biggest fan."

"Didn't know you."

"Sure," Ezra said. "Well, what did Mr. Morgan have to say?"

What Frank told him then made some sense. Made a lot of sense, actually, because the one thing Ezra had never been able to get his head around was why Devin would possibly have called him and told him to open the cabin up. The only reason he could have understood was if it had been a taunt, Devin deciding he'd screw with an old man's head, make it damn clear that Ezra no longer intimidated him or never had. Problem with that was the tone of the call. The message had been simple, businesslike, as if he'd never had a problem with Ezra. The answer, Ezra understood now, was that it hadn't been Devin who made the call. The other guy, Vaughn, had apparently understood Ezra's role as caretaker, but it didn't seem he knew the back story.

"He's out of the hospital," Ezra said when Frank was done, "with three bullets in him?"

"That's what I've been told." Frank was wearing jeans and a T-shirt, and Ezra could see the muscles of his chest and shoulders under the shirt, taut and hard in the easy, natural way they could be only when you were young. Ezra could remember when he had looked like that. Could remember when Frank's father had looked like that. The boy's features didn't resemble his father, he'd taken after his mother in that way, but the way he stood now, the energy in his words, the eagerness for battle . . . those traits ran warm through his blood.

"Sounds like Devin's hurt bad, then," Ezra said. "Hell, he might not make it up here, son."

"But you know he's coming," Frank said. "You know he is. That's his wife out there on that island, and either she shot him or Vaughn did. They betrayed him, tried to kill him. You think he could be headed anywhere else?"

Ezra didn't answer, and after a few beats of silence Frank said, "He gave my father up. Brought him into it, and then turned right around and gave him up to save his own ass."

"I know the story, son."

Frank extended his arm, pointed out across the dark water. "He's coming for them, Ezra. The people out there on that island. Why? Because they tried to take him down, and that's something I sure as hell respect. They did our work for us."

"Unsuccessfully."

"Fine. Unsuccessfully. But I'm not going to let that son of a bitch come out here, to the place my father and his father and you and me all shared, and kill those two, Ezra. I'm not."

"At least one of those two is headed for jail, Frank. You don't want to interfere with that."

"You want to see them go? You want to see them go to jail for shooting *Devin*? Don't you remember—"

"I remember it all," Ezra said, and there was a depth of anger he hadn't heard to his own voice in a long time. "Don't stand there and ask me if I remember. It goes back a hell of a lot farther than you, back to places you'll never see and can't imagine. Understand *that,* son?"

There was fury in his words, and he was leaning into Frank, his face close, but the boy didn't back away. Just stood there and held Ezra's eyes for a long time.

"Yeah," Frank said at last. "I understand that. Now you listen to yourself, hear what you just said, and explain to me how in the *hell* you're going let Devin go out to that island."

"Didn't say I would. I'm telling you there's another option here."

"The police? Shit, Ezra. You want somebody to go to jail for trying to kill *Devin*?"

Ezra looked away, out into the lake, and said, "What do you want to do, then?"

"To get them out of here," Frank said. "Is that so much to ask? We get them out of here. If he catches them somewhere else, fine, but he's not going to settle up here. Not on this lake."

"Get them out of here," Ezra echoed. "That's your goal?"

"It's what I said."

"And when you get in the middle of it? What then? Devin comes at you, or comes at the girl inside your cabin, the same way his boys already have?"

"If that happens," Frank said, "we deal with it."

Ezra gave a low, ugly laugh. "That's what you're hoping for. You want to hang that son of a bitch from one of these pines, but you also want it to be justified."

"It's already justified."

"Bullshit, son. Not in a way you can accept it's not, and you know that."

Frank didn't answer. The wind picked up and the water splashed into the logs below them and something rustled through the woods a few yards away.

"It's going into action tomorrow," Frank said eventually. "Whether it's cops or Devin or those two assholes he sent up here, somebody is going out to that island. Are we going to let them do it? Are we going to step aside and wait for that, pretend we don't know anything?"

Ezra took a few steps away, knelt and dipped his hand into the lake, cupped his palm and held the water. It was cool against his skin, cool enough that the hairs on his arm rose in a ripple. He kept his fingers tight, held the water until it slipped through the fractional gaps and fell back into the lake, and then he turned to his old comrade's son.

"No," he said. "No, we're not going to step aside and wait for that."

Twenty-four

Grady woke sometime before dawn with the knowledge that he had to play it straight with Atkins.

There was no way around it. Not at this point. He kept hearing Frank's insistence that Grady stay in Chicago, hearing the way he'd said, *I don't have a car,* when Grady urged him to leave. The kid was waiting for Devin, no doubt about it, and the smart money said he was going to get him, too.

Someone needed to intercede, and Atkins would be more than happy to do so. If Grady's suspicion turned out to be accurate, and Frank did know where Vaughn Duncan was holed up, it was going to turn into an ugly day. But that was the sort of ugly day that paled in comparison to the one they'd see if Frank met Devin Matteson up in those woods.

It wasn't yet six, too early to call Atkins, and Grady lay awake in the bed for almost an hour, watching sunlight fill the empty room and wondering how much of this was his fault.

It had been an anonymous tip, damn it. That's what he told people from the beginning, what he'd assured them, and there were only a few people within the Bureau who knew the truth. On one level, he'd almost been showing *kindness* to Frank by telling him the tip had come from Matteson. It had seemed, back then, a lesser punishment to the boy, who was already reeling. Matteson was a worthless piece of shit, so what did Grady care if he'd added another layer of tarnish to the man's name? Even in the worst-case scenario, one in which the kid plotted some act of vengeance, all that stood to be lost was Matteson, right? And that would be a damn favor to the community.

Except Matteson wasn't all that stood to be lost. Grady had forgotten about the avenger. He could be lost, too.

At ten to seven he called Atkins and got no answer, left a message. At seven twenty, pacing the apartment with a cup of coffee going cold in his hand, he called again and left another message. Five minutes later Atkins finally called back.

"Didn't hear the phone," he said. "I was in the shower, sorry. What do you have for me?"

Grady lifted the cup, took a swallow of room-temperature coffee, and said, "I think Frank Temple knows where all the excitement is headed."

"Pardon?"

"He didn't kill anyone," Grady said, "and I'm almost certain he's more a bystander than anything else, but I think he might know where Vaughn Duncan is."

"Why do you think this?"

"I spoke with him last night, and when I asked where Duncan was, he was very guarded. Evasive. That's not Frank's style. He doesn't like to lie, and I think he was trying to avoid that last night by refusing to answer the question. If he didn't know, or didn't have some idea, at least, he would have told me that."

A long pause.

"You there?" Grady said.

"I'm here." The other agent's voice was drawn tight with anger. "I'm just wondering who I'll have to call in Chicago to make a formal complaint."

"Because I talked to Frank? Listen, Atkins, you don't—"

"No, I'm not going to listen. What you just did is such a flagrant breach of conduct . . . what the hell were you thinking? I tell you this kid is a *suspect*, I ask you for input, not to get on the damn phone and—"

"I knew I could get you some answers."

"Bullshit. And even if you did think that, you don't make a call like that without informing me first."

"Atkins, you're missing the point."

"This is one of the most egregious—"

"Vaughn Duncan may be up there with another man's wife," Grady said. "You want to know who the man is, or not?"

Silence.

"A guy named Devin Matteson was shot in Florida a few days ago. Matteson is a key player for Manuel DeCaster. That name mean anything to you?"

"No."

"Well, it does down in Florida. He's one of the worst they've got, and one of the most powerful. He's in prison now, in Coleman, and about seven years ago Frank Temple's father was making hits for him."

Atkins didn't make a sound, but Grady could almost *hear* the battle going on within him, curiosity fighting anger.

"Matteson won't tell the police who shot him. But his wife is missing. So it's not much of a puzzle, is it? And now this guard from Coleman, Vaughn Duncan, he's up at that lake, and there's a woman with him," Grady said. "You want to take odds on who the woman is, I've got a retirement account I'll put on Matteson's wife."

Atkins started to speak, but Grady rushed ahead. "And Matteson's missing, he's out of the hospital, he's gone. You understand what that means? He's coming north, Atkins. I would bet every dime I have that he is coming up to that lake."

"And I'm still supposed to believe the coincidence," Atkins said. His voice was clipped, tight.

"What coincidence? That Frank's up there?"

"That's the one. Bystander? *Bystander?* You out of your mind, Morgan? You really believe, and expect me to believe, that this kid just *happened* to smack his Jeep into his own father's filthy history? That's an *accident*?"

No. It wasn't an accident. Couldn't be. Grady wanted to believe that it was, but he knew better. Frank's presence on that lake wasn't a fluke. That was why it was so important for Atkins to intercede now.

"Look," Grady said, "I'm not going to waste my time or yours discussing what I think about that kid. I'm telling you that—"

"I cannot believe you called him. You son of a bitch, you called a *suspect* and warned him—"

"He knows where Vaughn is and he knows Devin is coming for him!" Grady shouted. "Would you shut up long enough to understand that, Atkins? You want to bitch and moan about me, do it Monday. Shit, call Quantico, call Washington, call anybody you want. Right now that doesn't mean a damn thing. What matters is that you've got a dangerous son of a bitch headed your way to settle up with his wife and this other guy, and Frank Temple knows that."

"How does he know that?"

"Because I told him. And I'd tell him again today, and if you want to get me fired over that, knock yourself out. But you've got something up there waiting to *explode*, and you need to deal with it."

"Temple is at his cabin?" Atkins said, his voice still angry, but lower.

"Yeah. It's out on some lake—"

"I know where it is."

"Okay." Grady hesitated, then said, "If he's not there, he might be with a man named Ezra Ballard. You need to get him away from Ballard."

"Who is he?"

"He was in special forces with Frank's father. They were tight."

"Special forces with Frank's father," Atkins echoed. "You're kidding me, right? Morgan, this is unbelievable. I needed to know all of this yesterday!"

"You know it now," Grady said.

"I will tell you this, Morgan: If you call that kid again today I'll see that charges are brought, do you understand?"

"I won't call him, if you get your ass moving and get out

there. And I'm headed that way, Atkins. I'll leave now, but I don't know how long the drive is."

"Keep your car in the garage, asshole. I don't want you within a hundred miles of this."

"I'm coming up."

"Yeah? Well, if I see you, I'm putting you in handcuffs."

Atkins hung up. Grady stood with the phone in his hand for a minute, then set it on the counter, poured his coffee into the sink, and picked up his car keys.

Frank had coffee going by the time Nora woke up. Her hair was fuzzed out an extra six inches from static, and when she looked at him it was with one open eye, the other squinted almost shut.

"What time is it?"

"Ten past seven."

"Have you heard from Ezra?"

"I expect he's on his way." Ezra's boat had been missing when the sun rose. Frank had even used binoculars to search for it, but found no trace.

"Then we'll go to the island," she said.

"Yes." Frank took the coffeepot and poured a cup, then brought it to Nora. Seeing her this way, bleary-eyed and sleepy, made him want to lean down and kiss her forehead, but he didn't. He wasn't sure how she'd react to him this morning, with the alcohol and that brief moment of romance in a tense, fear-filled night now pushed aside by sleep and daylight.

He returned to the kitchen and poured his own coffee, waited for her to express a new concern, wonder aloud whether they should call the cops. She didn't say anything, though. Just drank the coffee and smoothed her hair with her palm, then rose and went into the bathroom, reemerging five minutes later looking more awake, fresher.

"Did you sleep?" she said.

"No."

"Aren't you tired?"

"No," he said, and this was the truth. Anticipation of Devin's arrival provided more fuel than sleep would have. He was ready for him, but Nora was a problem. He and Ezra had discussed that before Ezra slipped back into his boat and out into the lake.

Frank would not deceive her. Couldn't do that. But he knew, and had tried to explain to Ezra, that she was not going to be kept off that island. He remembered the steel in her voice when she'd said, *If anyone here deserves answers, it's not you guys. It's me.* She was right. He wished she weren't a part of it, but she was, and he needed to decide what to tell her, how to explain what he was going to do. That would have to come after they heard what the pair on the island had to say.

He left in her in the cabin and walked out into the day, found the air to be uncommonly still, the gray water like dirty glass. He stood with his coffee in hand and turned in a full circle, took in the lake and the trees and the sky.

Which direction would Devin come from? Would he drive right up to the dam, launch a boat and head out to the island, or would there be more to it than that? He knew they were on the island. Surely his advance team of gunslingers had reported that back to Miami, and while Tomahawk might have been a mysterious destination for them, it would not be to Devin. By now the island was anything but a hiding spot to the two who waited on it. Frank saw the game plan clearer this morning, understood that Jerry Dolson's murder had been merely routine maintenance, the removal of one of those loose ends he'd been worried about from the start. Either by then or soon after, the pursuit had effectively ended. The men from Miami knew about the island, had to know by now, and yet they had not moved on it. That meant one thing: They were waiting on Devin.

"He'll be here today," Frank said. He'd spoken in a soft voice, but it still rang out loud. There was no trace of wind to whip the words away.

Ezra arrived by boat, and when he saw that Nora still intended to go to the island with them, he didn't object. She watched his eyes go back and forth between Frank and her and wondered what he was thinking. Had he seen them outside the night before, as Frank predicted? Probably. There was something about Ezra that gave you the feeling he'd been watching you for a long time.

"All right," he said as she and Frank walked down to the boat. "We're going out there to hear the story. Their side of it, at least. That's all we're doing right now. Whatever happens next will depend on what we hear."

He was staring at Frank while he said it, but Frank wasn't paying attention. He was looking up in the direction of the road; his gaze seemed unfocused.

"Okay," Nora told Ezra, because it seemed as if he deserved some sort of response, and then he offered a hand and guided her as she stepped onto the boat. There was a mammoth outboard on the back, a motor of disproportionate size to the actual craft, and Ezra positioned her on the rear seat with her back to it. Frank took the seat in front of her, and Ezra settled in without a word and turned the key and the larger motor came to life with the throaty, muscular sound that reminded Nora of the better cars they'd had in the shop, those with expensive, fine-turned engines.

"Okay," Ezra said, spinning the wheel and pointing them out into the lake. "Let's go see what the hell we're looking at."

He shoved the throttle forward and the motor behind her roared with delight and then the front end of the boat rose several feet out of the water and if Ezra said anything else Nora could not hear it.

Frank sat staring straight ahead, his clothes rippling as they tore across the lake. Behind the wheel, Ezra was impassive, his face shaded by a baseball cap with a Ranger Boats logo and his eyes hidden by Oakley sunglasses. They both wore light jackets that Nora knew concealed guns. As she sat there clutching the boat seat under her butt and squinting against the force of the wind, she felt a surge of doubt. They were essentially strangers, Frank and Ezra, and she'd put an awful lot of trust in them with this trip to the island. No one, *no one* had any idea where she was.

The sun was creeping out, sparkling off the water, and though her hair was streaming out behind her like a flag in gale-force winds, the trees on shore were still, untouched by any breeze. It was too calm, and that probably meant rain by the afternoon. The humidity felt wrong for so early in the day.

They went past one enormous rock that jutted angrily out of the water, then through a cluster of islands, and came out in a large bay that seemed even more desolate, only two other boats in sight. Ezra slowed and worked his way around what appeared to be a sandbar, then brought the motor back to a roar and the front of the boat lifted again and they were off, tearing past a bay filled with stumps and half-trees that seemed like menacing guards to the empty shoreline.

Nora shifted on her seat and thought about reaching out and tapping Ezra's shoulder, asking him to stop and turn around. *Take me back,* she could say. *I've been thinking about it, and this is wrong. We shouldn't come out alone. We should leave that to the FBI and the police. They'll know how to protect me; it's what they do.*

Ezra actually turned and looked at her then, and for a split second she wondered if she'd voiced her thoughts aloud, but then he faced the water again and she'd let the moment pass without saying a word.

A few minutes later he did slow the boat, and the motor quieted and Nora's hair fell back around her shoulders. Out here there was nothing to look at but trees and water, no sign of another boat. Then she saw an island ahead, over Frank's shoulder, partially blocked by his body.

"Shit." This came from Frank. "There's somebody down there, Ezra. Somebody on shore."

Ezra leaned to the side for a clearer look. "Sure is. And it looks like the fella's having a bit of trouble with his boat motor. Might be we should stop by and offer a bit of assistance."

"He'll recognize Nora and me."

"Bound to happen sooner or later." Ezra brought the boat's speed down even more, eased in closer to the shore, and Nora looked over Frank's shoulder and saw the man and the boat for the first time. It was the gray-haired Lexus driver, Vaughn, and he was looking up from the motor, his attention focused on the approaching craft. Nora slid down into the seat and tilted her head a bit, trying to put herself back behind Frank, out of Vaughn's sight.

"Little trouble?" Ezra said, shouting over the sound of the motor.

Vaughn waved them away. "Nothing I can't handle."

"Sure about that? Doesn't look like it's going well."

"It's not a problem."

"Tell ya what," Ezra yelled. "How about I come in and give it a look, and then you and me and your girlfriend have a chat? I'm the caretaker of this cabin. Feeling a bit guilty about the way I been neglecting you all."

Though Ezra's voice had been friendly, it produced a new rigidity to Vaughn's body. He took a step back and let his hands fall away from the motor, studying them carefully now.

"The caretaker?" he asked. He was speaking to Ezra, but his eyes seemed to be on Frank.

"Uh-huh. That place has been my responsibility for a damn long time."

"We're doing fine," Vaughn said, and the boat had drifted so Nora could no longer see him. She sat up straighter to compensate, and when she did Vaughn's eyes locked on her face and she felt the recognition across the water a split second before he reached behind his back.

"Don't." It was a single word, spoken and not shouted, but somehow Ezra's voice still seemed to boom out across the water and shake the trees. Nora saw that his arm was extended, his gun pointing at Vaughn. How in the world had he gotten that out so fast?

Vaughn stood with his arm behind his back and didn't say a word. Ezra kept his gun pointed while he adjusted the wheel with his left hand, bringing the boat in close to shore, the water now shallow enough that Nora could see the bottom. Frank had been keeping his back to Vaughn, but when he heard Ezra's one-word command he finally turned, and Vaughn's eyes flicked to him.

"How you doing?" Frank said. "You owe the lady here a car, and owe both of us some answers."

"Don't hurt her," Vaughn said. His voice was high and it cracked on the last word. Nora felt a moment's confusion—*don't hurt me?*—before she realized that he was talking about the woman on the island.

"Nobody here has done any hurting, or intends to," Ezra said. "But your buddies have. And we need to talk about that. Now put that gun of yours on the bottom of your boat, and then catch the bow line when Frank tosses it to you."

Vaughn dropped the gun. It took him four tries to catch the bow line and pull them to the beach.

Twenty-five

Vaughn was back to that damn chattering even before they were all ashore, the same routine he'd gone through while waiting with Frank for the tow truck two days earlier.

". . . and I don't know what you've been told or what you think, but I was going to come back on Monday and give you the money I owed you, which, you know, there's no reason to be pulling guns on me, your car is fine, I promise it's fine, and I didn't know any—"

"Stop," Ezra said.

Vaughn stopped. His face reminded Frank of a dog his mother had when he was a kid, a beagle that would always sit with its tongue hanging out. Frank's father would say, *Put your tongue back*, and the dog would snap his jaws shut, hiding the tongue, and look at Frank's dad with a perplexed expression. Vaughn looked about as sure of himself as the dog used to.

"Gonna be plenty of time for you to talk," Ezra said, "but I figure we should all be present and accounted for. You could work on slowing down a touch, too, give us a chance to hear what the hell it is you're saying."

Vaughn nodded, and Ezra gestured up at the cabin.

"She in there?"

Another nod.

"Then let's go up and have us a seat and bit of conversation."

They walked across the beach to a trail that led up the bluff. Vaughn went first, slipping a few times, his footwork awkward and clumsy. Frank was last, following Nora, who walked easily. He didn't know what she was thinking. Probably hadn't been real encouraged by the way Vaughn had reached for that gun.

The cabin was in remarkable shape for a building that had sat empty for so long, but Frank didn't marvel over it. He expected no less from Ezra, who would take care of an empty cabin that didn't belong to him better than most men would ever care for their own homes. Vaughn took the steps up to the porch with a quickened stride and was talking before he reached the door.

"Renee? We got some company. Man here says he's the caretaker—" Vaughn twisted the doorknob and pushed the door open and stepped into the house just as the blond woman stepped out. Frank saw the gun in her hand, then saw it in Ezra's eye socket. She just stepped onto the porch and stuck the gun in his eye, no hesitation.

"You reach under your jacket any farther," the woman said, speaking to Frank without taking her eyes off Ezra, "and I'll kill him."

"Shit, Renee, what are you doing?" Vaughn was standing in the doorway, jaw slack.

Renee Matteson. That would be the full name. She was something to watch. Even in this moment, when the only ready-to-shoot gun was the one in her hand, Frank was taken with her. So poised, so strong. He let his hand fall away from his jacket and took one step backward.

She'd stuck the gun into Ezra's eye with enough force to open up the skin and start a small trickle of blood. Now Ezra cleared his throat and said, "This isn't a real good way to get things started."

"He's the caretaker—" Vaughn began, but she cut him off.

"Caretaker my ass. I saw his gun, Vaughn."

"We're not the ones you should be scared of," Frank said. "Though you should know that they are not far away."

"He makes a good point," Ezra said, the blood flowing down his cheek. "Perhaps it would be best to save the gun-play for those gents of whom he speaks."

The blond woman, Renee, was staring Ezra in the eye, their faces separated only by the length of her arm and the gun.

"What I'm saying is, the way things are developing, y'all are going to need your bullets," Ezra said. "Hate to see you waste one on me."

"Maybe if I took out my gun and set it down," Frank said, his voice loud, and he made the slightest motion with his arm. It was enough, as he'd hoped it would be. She looked at him instead of squeezing the trigger as she'd promised, and when she did Ezra snapped his head sideways and his arm moved with the speed of a whip, laced up and then down and then Renee's hand was in his own and her gun was pointed at the ground. Frank had the Smith & Wesson out by the time that was done.

"Damn, son," Ezra said. "You think you'd have gotten that out fast enough if she *didn't* look your way?"

"Felt pretty sure she would."

"Me, too, but I was a little less excited about testing the theory. Always the man with the gun in his eye who's the bigger fan of patience, though."

He said all this with the casual delivery of a man in a barber's chair, working the gun out of Renee's fingers as he talked.

"Now, we got lots of guns around, everybody noticed that? Way too many guns. I'm thinking it'd be nice to put 'em all away, every one, and then just do some talking. Hell, this porch is nice enough. Let's have us a seat out here, enjoy the day."

He stepped back when he had possession of her gun, put it into his waistband, and motioned at the porch. She hadn't moved throughout all of this, seemingly hadn't *blinked*, just stood there and held his eyes with a stare so cold it seemed like it could pass through Ezra and carry out to the lake, put a skim of ice on the water.

"I could have killed you, and I didn't," she said. "Now let's see if that was a mistake."

She turned from him, walked to an old wooden bench beside the door, and sat down. Vaughn sat beside her and reached for her arm, but she shrugged away from his touch and slid to the other end of the bench.

"All right," she said. "Talk."

"I think that's *your* job," Nora said. The sound of her voice surprised Frank; hell, it seemed to surprise everyone. She'd been so still and quiet it was as if they'd forgotten her presence. When they all turned to look at her, she met the stares with a shrug.

"What? We didn't come out here to tell them who *we* are. We're not the ones responsible for getting good, innocent people killed. I want to hear *their* story, not mine." She jabbed a finger at Renee and Vaughn.

Renee looked at Nora for a long time, as if she were intrigued. Frank tried to guess her age, and couldn't. She had the body of a young woman, but her face carried some lines and her eyes were those of someone older. Or were they just tired?

"Where are the police?" she said. "You found us, so why not tell them to come out here and ask the questions?"

"It wasn't my idea," Nora answered, "but I listened to it."

Renee nodded as if that made sense, then turned to Ezra. "You're really the caretaker? You're how these two found us?"

"Yes."

"Then your name is Ezra."

"Uh-huh."

She nodded. "I've heard about you."

"From Devin," Ezra said, and Frank felt an unpleasant tingle at the sound of the name. "Where is he?"

"Dead," she answered.

Frank and Ezra had agreed the previous night that they wouldn't share any information at first, just hear the story as these two were prepared to tell it. Now, after hearing Renee proclaim her husband dead, Ezra merely nodded in Frank's direction.

"You don't know young Frank, I take it?"

Renee turned her cool gaze to Frank and searched his face. He was standing about five feet from her. She shook her head.

"I'm sorry, I don't know who he is." Talking as if she and Ezra were the only people on the porch.

"Last name of Temple," Frank said. "That help you any?"

Vaughn looked from one to the other with confusion on his face, but Renee got it.

"Your father," she said. "Devin and your father—"

"Killed people together."

"The way I heard it, that wasn't a joint project."

"Then you heard it wrong," he said. "And allow me to be the first to congratulate you on Devin's demise. You're better off with him gone. Everybody is."

She came up off the bench in a smooth, fast motion and slapped him in the face. The sound of the blow made Vaughn step toward them, hands out, but he didn't touch anyone. Nora made a soft sound of surprise, and Ezra just stood there and watched. Frank took the slap and looked down at Renee with his cheek stinging, didn't say a word.

"Now that we got the greetings out of the way," Ezra said, "maybe we ought to talk about the people who are still alive, sort out things with the dead at another time. Seems that you two have led a pair of unfriendly types into the area. Some innocent people suffered as a result. I think it's time to hear what it's all about."

The woman stood where she was for a long time, staring at Frank, challenging him to say another harsh word about her husband. He had none. His mind was too occupied by what that slap meant, by the way she'd risen so fast to defend Devin. It was not the action of a woman who'd wanted him dead. The idea he'd had, then, that they would come out to this island and meet with the two people who'd put bullets into Devin's back, no longer seemed to be the case.

The reality had just spun away from the expectation, driven by the palm of her hand against his face. He looked at her and felt the tingle on his cheek, the heat of the blow fading into cold needles, and with it the truth he'd wanted.

"I'll tell you what it's all about," Vaughn said as Renee finally turned and stalked back toward the bench, "it's about *these* two innocent people"—he waved his hand between Renee and himself—"suffering for Devin's mistakes."

"Explain," Ezra said.

"You know about Devin, you know what he does."

"Right," Ezra said, "but what do *you* do?"

Vaughn leaned forward on the bench, ducked his head so his eyes were hidden.

"I work—*worked*—at a prison in Florida. I'd been at it for about twelve years when I met Devin. Or when he approached me, would be a better way of saying it. I'd done the job right until then, too. I had."

"Because nobody had ever offered him any money before then," Renee said, and the scorn in her voice seemed to drop Vaughn's head even lower.

"What did he pay you for?" Ezra said. "Smuggling to people on the inside?"

"Right idea," Vaughn said, "wrong direction."

"You were taking something *out* of the prison?"

"Instructions," Frank said. This made sense already, had since Grady's call the night before. "He was a postman, Ezra. A messenger. For Manuel DeCaster."

An image of a newspaper photograph was trapped in Frank's mind, a picture of DeCaster as he was led out of the courthouse on the eve of a guilty verdict. The man's sallow, jailhouse skin was contorted into a sneer of contempt. He looked nothing like a man whose world had crumbled, and more like an emperor amused by the weak efforts of peasants hoping to overthrow him. And why not? With men like Devin Matteson to handle business on the outside and men like Vaughn to carry the messages, maybe his rule hadn't been all that interrupted by steel bars and block walls and barbed wire.

"Yes," Vaughn said. "Manuel DeCaster."

"The big boss," Ezra said, his voice dropping into an even slower drawl. "So Devin recruited you to work as the messenger, keep DeCaster in touch with the outside world in ways that monitored phone calls and visits could not."

"That was the idea," Vaughn said.

"I understand how that could have brought some trouble down around you," Ezra said, "but these boys that followed you into Tomahawk, they aren't the police sort of trouble."

"No."

"So who are they?"

"They work for DeCaster. I don't know how they found us."

"You left them an easy trail," Frank said. "There was a tracking device in your car. That's how they got here, and I'm wondering when they had a chance to put it on your vehicle."

Vaughn stared at Frank in confusion, mouth half open, but Renee Matteson lifted her hands to her temples, eyes going wide and then squeezing shut.

"What?" Frank said.

"I should have remembered," she said. "Damn it, I should have remembered."

"You knew about the device?" Ezra said.

She shook her head. "No. Well, not specifically, but I knew they'd been following him. A long time ago, Devin was following him."

"Devin was *following* me?"

"At first," she said, nodding, "he wanted to be sure he could trust you. Wanted to know what you were doing, where you were going. I didn't think about there being a device on the car, and that was so long ago . . . that was a year ago . . . and it was *Devin,* not the bastards who shot him."

"But they would have known about it," Frank said. It made sense. Devin and the rest of DeCaster's team would have wanted to follow Vaughn at first, make sure there were no covert meetings with cops, no betrayals.

"How many of them are there?" Renee asked.

"Two that we know of," Frank said, thinking that this changed everything, made Devin's role less important, the whole thing less personal. If these two were hiding from DeCaster's crew, then it was no mystery why Devin had fled from the hospital. His survival odds were better on the run than inside, waiting for someone to come by and finish the job. This was bad, very bad. Stepping into the middle of a personal vendetta between Devin and these two was one thing. Stepping into the middle of a power struggle that ran back to Manuel DeCaster was a damn death sentence.

"Two that you know of? Well, there will be more than that if they call for help," Vaughn said.

"All right," Ezra said. "So we got some bad boys and big troubles. Everybody pretty well understood that. You're dancing, though. I asked what it was you did to attract this. Haven't heard that one answered."

"I didn't do shit. Devin, he got his eyes on the throne. The longer Manuel sat in a cell, the cockier Devin got. He started talking about what he could do on his own, talking about eliminating people closest to Manuel, starting with his cousins, who were key to the whole operation, guys who are so damn mean that when you look at them—"

"Slow down," Ezra said, "and just tell us what happened. It ain't that hard."

Vaughn took a deep breath and ran a hand through his hair, completely avoiding Renee's hard gaze.

"I'm *trying* to tell you what happened. You want it in two sentences or something? Fine, here you go: Devin was going to kill DeCaster's cousins and two other guys, Cubans who were involved with him. He wanted a housecleaning."

"And this had what to do with you?"

"He needed someone to lie to DeCaster. You know, tell him that one thing was happening while something else really was, and work it the other way, too, get the information he needed."

"You agreed."

"It was a lot of dollars."

"Someone smelled it out?" Frank said. "Killed Devin before he made his play?"

"Yes. Then they came for me, and Renee. Still *are* coming for us, I guess."

Ezra was looking hard at Frank, a question in his eyes, and Frank met the gaze and shook his head ever so slightly. Ezra frowned but broke the stare. Frank knew what he was wondering—whether they should tell these people that Devin was alive—and he wasn't ready to do that. Not yet. There were too many questions here, too many possibilities and problems and angles, a dizzying new scenario appearing. And a disappointing one. Frank felt that in the pit of his stomach, a hard ache of disappointment. He'd come out here hoping to align himself with these two and against Devin, see it boil down to the type of finale he'd wanted for so long. That wasn't going to happen, though. There was still a chance that Devin was headed this way, but he wouldn't be arriving with vengeance on his mind. Rather, he'd be on the run. Same as these two.

"Why Renee?" Nora said, breaking the silence that had gathered. "If Devin's dead, what's the point of killing his wife?"

"Renee was around a lot," Vaughn said. "She knows things that could hurt them, hurt DeCaster. So do I. Now that they know Devin violated their trust, they'll try to clean up the mess that surrounded him. Besides, they killed her husband. If anyone in the world is motivated to try to hurt these guys by going to the police, it's Renee."

Nora turned to Renee. "Then why *don't* you go to the police? This guy and your husband are the ones that did something wrong."

Renee smiled at her, and there was genuine warmth in it, something that Frank hadn't been able to imagine on her face until then.

"I lived with Devin for nine years. You have any idea the things I know that the police would *love* to hear?"

The explanation didn't seem to satisfy Nora, but Frank understood what she did not: Renee's world was one in which cops were the enemy. Her husband's death—the death she believed in, at least—wouldn't change that outlook. Cops were to be feared and never trusted. It didn't make sense until you'd spent a decade or so living with that worldview.

"We'd been here just one day," Vaughn said, "when I left to get some food, supplies. I was coming back from that when Frank here hit my car."

Frank didn't want to hear him return to that, didn't want anyone dwelling on the incredible coincidence of Frank hitting this guy's car, a guy who just happened to be with Devin's wife. The longer people thought about a coincidence like that, the more unreasonable it seemed, and he wasn't quite ready to explain to Renee that he'd really come up here intending to kill her husband.

"Why did you come here?" Ezra said, and for a moment Frank thought the question was directed at him, that Ezra had somehow stepped inside his thoughts. Then he realized he was asking Renee.

"It's what Devin told Vaughn to do," Renee said.

Vaughn nodded. "Right before he got killed, he was getting worried about things, told me that if anything happened I needed to get Renee out fast. He told me to bring her here, because nobody else knew it existed. Nobody down there, at least."

"Well," Ezra said, "that was a hell of plan. But there's a problem, buddy. They sure as shit know about it now."

Twenty-six

Traffic in Chicago was always a bitch, but Grady was helped by it being a Sunday morning, and made his way out of the city and into Wisconsin by eight, doing eighty-five up I-90. If anyone stopped him, he'd flash the badge and go on his way. He had a map on the seat beside him, and the Willow Flowage was way up there, just south of Michigan's Upper Peninsula. Looked like a five-hour drive at best, and that was counting on forgiving traffic and no delays.

He should have left last night. As soon as Frank had hung up the phone, Grady should have been in the car. Hopefully it wouldn't matter. Hopefully Atkins was already out there. He'd be giving Frank hell, of course, but that didn't matter so long as he was getting Frank off the lake and out of Devin Matteson's path. With any luck they'd have Matteson's wife and her boyfriend, the prison guard, in custody by noon, and by the time Matteson *did* arrive it would be over, nothing left but the shouting.

His phone rang just before nine, and he answered expecting Atkins and hoping for good news.

It was someone from the Bureau, but not Atkins.

"Good news," Jim Saul said, "you won't have to worry about picking up any speeding tickets in Miami. Police down here love you dearly. Hell, get drunk and drive naked down the strip. They won't care. Of course, that wouldn't be far out of the ordinary for this town, either."

"Why do they love me?"

"Vaughn Duncan."

"You turn something up?"

"Turned a murder warrant up. The Miami police guys had one complete fingerprint and one partial on a casing they found in the parking lot where Matteson was shot. Shooter got two of the casings but left one behind, lost it in the gravel. Either he panicked and didn't want to take the time to find it, or it was too dark and he couldn't. Anyhow, Miami PD ran the print through IAFIS and didn't get a match. Surprising, right, because they were betting whoever took Matteson out had a record."

"Right."

"Well, no match on IAFIS, which means no record, at least not one of substance. And the cops down here were confused, because the print on the shell indicates whoever popped Matteson wasn't a pro, and that seems wrong. Then you throw this guy Duncan at me, and I call around and find out he decided to quit his job up at Coleman without giving any notice, and I think, hmm, the good folks at Coleman probably have his prints on file."

"They matched?"

"Bet your ass they did. Nothing on IAFIS because he didn't have a record, but once we got the prints from Coleman and compared them, they matched up. I had some unhappy people down here, bitching about turning this around on a weekend, but I assured them I had a first-rate tip."

"Duncan shot Matteson, then left with the wife?"

"That's the flavor of the month, yes. The print is enough for the warrant. Now, you care to tell me where you're getting this information?"

"Wisconsin," Grady said, "and now I've got to make a call up there. I'll talk to you soon, Jimmy—"

"Hang on, hang on. I also had the flights checked. Miami to Wisconsin. Guy matching Devin's description got a private charter to some place called Rhinelander, flew out late yesterday, real late."

"Rhinelander." Grady felt numb, even though this was

what he'd been expecting. The map beside him showed Rhinelander clear enough. It was about thirty miles from the Willow Flowage.

"Yeah. Like I said, private charter, and it landed in Rhinelander just after midnight—"

"I gotta go, Jimmy."

Grady hung up and found Atkins's number, dialed it as a car behind him blew the horn, Grady letting his own car drift into the next lane. He veered back to the right and slowed, held the phone to his ear. It was answered immediately.

"He's not here, Morgan. He's not at his cabin, and I'm getting pretty damn pissed off because I think when he talked to you he heard something that made him bolt."

"No," Grady said. "He's not gone. Trust me."

"Trust you. Sure."

"Listen, Atkins, I'm on my way north—"

"I told you to stay the hell away from here."

"I know that, but I thought maybe you'd want some help serving the murder warrant."

"Warrant?"

"That's right. You got a pen handy, Atkins? I think you're going to want to write some of this down."

The conversation might have gone on all morning and into the afternoon if nothing had interrupted them. Ezra and Frank were prying for more information, sorting through the mess of memories Vaughn and Renee offered, when Nora's cell phone began to ring. She'd slipped it into her pocket before leaving Frank's cabin, and the first two times it rang she simply put her hand inside her pocket and silenced the phone. On the third call, though, she took it out and checked the display and saw the call was from the receptionist desk at her father's nursing home.

"Give me a minute," she said and started to walk off the porch. Renee's eyes went wary, though, and Nora realized she was probably afraid that the call was from the police. Might as well stay on the porch, then. Relax the woman.

She answered and said hello and Barbara, a receptionist whom Nora had seen several times a week at the nursing home since arriving in Tomahawk, burst into a tirade of worry and concern.

"I don't know how he got the newspaper or who brought it to him, Nora, I really don't, but your father saw this article and he is *beside himself* because he doesn't understand it but he knows it's bad. He's so worried, and we are, too. We were worried even before, but now that he's seen it, I really think you need to come down and show him you're okay. They've got a photograph of all the police cars outside your shop, and he keeps looking at that, and he won't let us take it away."

Nora squeezed her eyes shut. Wonderful. Of course he would have seen or heard about it by now, and of course he'd be panicked. How could she have forgotten that, or ignored it till now?

"Barb, can you put him on the phone? Let me say a few things to him, and then I'll come in and visit. Please?"

"Nora, I don't think you understand—he's not able to talk on the phone right now. He was extremely agitated. We had to give him some tranquilizers to get him calmed down. If there's any way at all you can get in here to see him, that's what I'd suggest. He's not going to be calm until he sees you."

What could she do? She hesitated, felt annoyance and disbelief in Barb's silence at the other end of the line, then promised to be in as soon as possible. When she hung up, everyone on the porch was staring at her.

"It's my father," she said. "He's in a nursing home, and somehow he got his hands on a newspaper. He doesn't understand what happened, but he's worried about me." She looked at Frank. "I need to go see him."

He looked irritated, but said, "All right. We'll take you. Ezra?"

Ezra worked his tongue around his mouth, looking at the lake. "There are two boats. Why don't you take her back in mine, and I'll stay here."

"Don't trust us enough to leave?" Renee said.

"You want to be left alone if your buddies show up?"

"No," she said.

"I was thinking an extra body wouldn't hurt anything," Ezra agreed, "and we still got some talking to do. So, Frank, you take Nora in and get her to her father. You stay with her, okay, and keep your eyes sharp. You know why."

"Yeah, I do."

Ezra nodded, looked at Nora. "That work? Time you get this settled with your dad, maybe we'll have a better idea of what the hell needs to happen out here. Y'all can come back out, and we'll see what we've got."

"All right."

"You got a phone?" Frank said to Ezra. "A way we can get you if we need to?"

"Most times it doesn't work on the water, but I'll give you the number. It'll ring, if nothing else."

He ran Ezra's boat hard all the way back across the lake, a stupid thing to do considering his lack of recent knowledge of the sandbars and stumps, but one that had an advantage. When the motor was roaring and the boat was sluicing through the wind and water, conversation was impossible, and right now Frank didn't want to talk. His mind was at turns back on that island, and the house of his boyhood, and in a Florida prison he'd never seen.

Everything he'd hoped for last night when he'd stood on the dark beach with Ezra was gone, obliterated. The situation wasn't what he'd desired, and it appeared a good deal worse. It was also, he knew, his fault. That any of them were involved in this now was his fault. He'd come up here after Devin, come up with blood in his eyes, eager for a confrontation, and because of that he'd caused the accident with Vaughn and set all of this in motion. You couldn't run from this, the legacy of bullets and bodies. Seven years he'd dodged it, bouncing around the country and avoiding anything to do with his father. Then one phone call from Ezra had pulled him north, and the result was this: They were right in the crosshairs of a bloody feud that should never have involved any of them. Particularly Nora.

It was time to get out. Time to hand the whole mess over to the people who should have had it from the beginning, to let Atkins and the FBI take it and hope he and Nora and Ezra could get the hell away from here before the fallout.

The good thing about running Ezra's boat almost wide open was that it gave him a moment of peace; the bad thing was that he made the trip in too short a time. They were back at the cabin with the motor cut and the boat's hull nestling into the shallows before he'd worked anything out. Not that extra time would have helped, though. He already knew what he had to do, which was get out of here, and stay gone.

He wanted to drive, but it was Nora's truck and she had the keys. She got in the driver's seat, and he opened the passenger door and sat down. The motor was started but she hadn't put the truck in gear before she spoke.

"Do you think we can help them?"

This was the reason he'd run the boat at full throttle, the exact question he'd wanted to drown under the whine of the wind. He'd hoped Nora would not want to help them. Trying to help Vaughn and Renee would be nothing but an exercise in futility. Either DeCaster would get them or the police would. The fact that Devin was alive and missing was only an added problem, one that would make pursuit of Renee all the more imperative. If they had Renee, they could force Devin back to the surface. Maybe. Knowing what Frank knew about Devin, it seemed just as likely he'd leave his own wife to pay the price for his greed.

"Well?" Nora said when he didn't answer. Her face was beautiful in the half-light of the shade in which she'd parked, those earnest eyes speckled by shifting shadows.

"Her husband isn't dead," Frank said.

"What?"

"He's alive. Somebody shot him, that was true, but he didn't die. He was in the hospital until yesterday, and then he took off."

She turned and stared out of the windshield, then back at him. "What are you talking about? How do you know this?"

He inhaled, looked away. "I talked to a guy last night."

"Last night?"

"Around two in the morning. You were asleep. He's with the FBI, was part of the group that investigated my dad. He told me that Devin had been shot, told me that he'd left the hospital and no one knew where he was."

Her face was incredulous at first, uncomprehending, and then the anger began to show as she reviewed the timeline.

"You knew this last night, and didn't tell me?"

"I wanted to see what the situation was first. The way it was told to me, Renee and Vaughn were responsible for shooting Devin. Tried to kill him and run off together, or something."

She frowned. "How do you know that's not true?"

"The way she slapped me. That was sincere. She wouldn't have had that sort of reaction if she wanted her husband dead."

Nora started to nod, then stopped. "Wait a second. You knew that her husband is still alive, and you didn't tell *her*? She thinks he's dead! Why didn't you tell her?"

"Let the FBI tell her," he said. Then, after a pause, "You know, it was a damn nice opportunity. I got to keep him from existing for a little while. Next best thing to actually killing him."

"*What?*"

"I told you what happened to my father," he said. "Devin's the piece of shit who turned him in to the police. Devin, the same guy who recruited him and then made sure he stayed on board, he turned him in."

When she didn't respond, he plunged forward. "Listen, don't think for a moment I'm defending what my dad did. I'm not. He earned his fate, Nora, and I understand that better than anyone. But Devin? Devin earned his, too, and he walked away from it. Still is, somehow. Three bullets in the back and he's still walking away."

She was shaking her head now, not wanting to hear any more.

"What are you really doing here?" she said. "Why did you come here? It's not an accident. None of this could *possibly* be an accident."

His fingers had curled into his palms, and now he flattened them on the seat, breathed, looked at her.

"I came here to kill Devin."

"Devin? He's not even here."

"I thought he would be. Ezra thought he would be. Ezra called, told me Devin was coming back . . ."

"And you came to kill him," she finished.

"I'd like to pretend that's not the truth," he said. "I'd like to think, to hope, that if it had happened as I'd expected and he'd been out on that island, I would have been able to stop myself. To walk right to the brink and then turn around and leave. But I doubt I could have."

It was quiet. The windows in the truck were up and the air-conditioning was off, making the inside of the cab muggy. Sweat was starting to run down his spine. He was having trouble looking at her now.

"Think what you want of me," he said, "but I've told you the truth. And I'm sorry you're involved. You have no idea how sorry I am about that."

The silence went on for a while, but then something changed in the engine noise, an increase in pitch as it acclimated to the long idle without ever being put into gear, and the sound seemed to jar something loose in Nora.

"What do we do?" she said, voice soft.

"I think you ought to call your FBI guy, Atkins. Tell him where they can be found. It won't cause Ezra any trouble. It's got nothing to do with him."

He felt guilty about that, leaving Ezra on the island with no warning that they were turning the whole mess over to the police, but ultimately it was the thing to do.

Nora's eyes narrowed, lines showing on her forehead. "What? Now you *do* want me to talk to the police?"

"I think you should."

"You want to go to the police?" She repeated it again, as if it were incomprehensible.

"No, I want *you* to. I'd actually love it if you could drop me off someplace where I could rent a car. That would be a big favor."

"What are you talking about?"

"I need a car, Nora. I've got nothing to drive."

"Where are you going?"

"I'll work that out. If the cops, or anybody else, want to find me, they can track me down. I've committed no crimes, and there's no reason I have to stay here."

"You're leaving? You're *leaving*?" She leaned toward him, spat the repeated the question in his face, eyes aflame.

"I'm not going to die for Devin's wife, Nora. I'm not going to kill for her, either. I stay and try to help, it's going down one way or the other. Grady, the FBI agent I talked to, this was his advice, to just get in a car and get the hell away from here and keep on going. He was right, too. I just should have listened to it earlier."

"You're going to leave the rest of us behind?" She looked at Frank as if she'd lost all hope of communicating and shook her head. "And I'm supposed to go the police alone?"

Before he could respond she lifted her hand. "You know what, I can't think about this right now. Before I deal with any of this, I've got to go see my dad, show him that I'm not *dead*, and then I can take you to get a rental car so you can run away, and then I will decide what in the world I tell the police."

She put the truck into gear, backed up, and started down the gravel drive.

Twenty-seven

It was as if the lake were angry with him. As if it knew what Ezra was doing out here, had listened to his conversation with Frank the night before and heard him relent, heard him plan for violence. The day that had dawned so beautifully was turning ugly, dark clouds massing in the west, the surface choppy beneath a temperamental wind, waves slapping at the beach.

A storm on the way, for sure, and though it had been a few days building—you didn't enjoy weather this warm and this humid in the spring without paying a price for it eventually—Ezra still had the sense that it was his fault somehow, that he'd triggered the unpleasant change.

The situation was not what they'd expected, and it looked more dangerous. Handling Devin was one thing. Handling Devin and a few of his friends, even, was one thing. This, though—this could turn into a team effort, maybe already had. Who knew how many men the two from Miami had called in now. And here was Ezra, sitting on this island that he'd once loved so dearly, waiting for it to come his way.

He'd made a mistake. No, a series of them. First in calling Frank Temple's son to begin with, then in agreeing to the boy's proposal last night, and now in letting Frank and the girl go off alone. They shouldn't have separated like that.

Throughout the morning's conversation, Ezra had wondered whether Frank would break the news that Devin was alive. Once, he'd looked hard at him, trying to convey the question, and had gotten a brief shake of the head. Apparently that had settled it, at least in Frank's mind. But did he not intend to tell her at some point? Surely he did. Ezra guessed that Frank probably wanted to call his FBI friend, Morgan, again. Maybe bleed him for more information, maybe provide him with some. Until then, until Frank returned or offered some word, Ezra had nothing to do but wait.

He stood on the porch with his gun in his hand and watched the weather turn, listened to the soft voices from inside. Every now and then they rose a bit, usually Renee's first and then Vaughn's. Some sort of a dispute. He'd started out inside the cabin with them but didn't like it, all those walls closing him in and blocking him from the world outside.

He didn't trust either of them. Particularly Vaughn. Oh, the story they'd told had made sense enough, but something still felt off. When you got right down to it, what felt off started with the fact that they were together at all. It was an odd pairing. And while Ezra now understood Vaughn's involvement, how he'd been nothing more than a courier for Devin and DeCaster, there was still something in him that didn't fit.

The wind died off abruptly, just faded as if it had been sucked beneath the lake, the surface going glassy, and in the short lull before it began to blow again, Ezra figured out what it was about Vaughn that felt so wrong.

He wasn't dangerous. That was the problem. Wasn't . . . competent. Had still been pulling the outboard cord on his boat long after he should have noticed the tiny feed tube from the gas line had been removed, had drawn his gun clumsily, had talked too much and seen too little. No, he wasn't competent in the way that Devin would be, or in the way that you'd expect from Devin's hired guns.

Of course, Vaughn wasn't a hired gun—that had already been established—but here he was with Renee Matteson, supposedly charged with her protection. That didn't make much sense. Because if you really feared for your wife, if you were really laying emergency plans, wouldn't you want her with another type of bodyguard? Someone less like Vaughn and more like . . . Ezra?

Vaughn must have earned the trust—but so far, Ezra couldn't see how.

Nora was startled when the nursing home sign appeared; the entire ride had been made in an almost dreamlike state. The last two days had felt that way to her, though, a constant sense of the surreal, of disconnect from the life she knew. That was what happened when violence stepped inside your world. Renee Matteson must know the feeling well.

Neither of them had spoken during the drive, and Frank didn't say anything when she pulled into the nursing home parking lot. There were visitors' spaces right by the front doors, but she avoided them today, drove all the way to the employee lot in the back of the building. If anyone was watching for her, they wouldn't expect her to park there, or to walk in through the employee entrance. She couldn't help feeling proud of her awareness, the ability to think of something like that on the fly.

When she turned off the engine and started to get out of the truck, Frank reached for his own door handle.

"No," she said. "I'll go in alone. You can wait here."

"It would be safer—"

"*No*. I don't want to frighten my dad, or get the nurses talking, or anything else. Nobody's going to jump out of a closet and snatch me away. It'll be fifteen minutes. You can wait."

He sat there looking at her, then swung his door shut, relenting. For an instant she felt bad about her tone. Those damn sad eyes of his, working on her once again. Always confident, always strong, but always sad. She'd never seen anything else quite like them.

Then she remembered why he'd come here—to kill—and most of the guilt evaporated.

"I'll make it quick," she said, "and then we'll get you a car and you can take off."

"Take your time with your father," Frank answered. "He loves you, and he's worried."

He didn't look at her when he said it. She hesitated only a moment, then slammed the door and walked away from the truck.

The employee entrance was at the back of the building, a single door with a keycard lock that was never used, or at least not during the workday. Nora had seen plenty of people come and go without pausing to use a card. The door was open today, and she stepped through and found herself in a hallway that led around to the front desk. Barb gave Nora a startled look when she emerged from the back but didn't question it.

"Hello. He's doing a lot better since we gave him the sedatives, but I know he wants to see you. Go on down."

"Thank you."

"I hope everything's all right? It's such a horrible thing . . ." Barb let the sentence dangle, peering over her bifocals at Nora, obviously hoping to hear some details of the most exciting news Tomahawk had heard in years.

"Horrible," Nora echoed, nodding, and then she turned and walked away, chased by a sigh of disappointment from Barb, who'd probably been waiting all day for some insider information. Nora should have sent her out into the parking lot to talk with Frank. *His dad was a real-life hit man, Barb. Might sign an autograph if you ask nicely.*

The door to her dad's room was closed, and it creaked when she pushed it open. He was sitting up in bed and turned to face her when he heard the sound. His face split into that smile, and she felt her own do the same.

"Hi, Dad."

"You were *worried*," he said, meaning he was worried about her.

"I know. I'm sorry." She crossed the room and leaned down to him, kissed his cheek and gave him a hug. He smelled like aftershave. It was one of the things he insisted on; every morning he needed a dab of Old Spice. Something about that smell and thirty years of wearing it had stuck in his brain after the stroke.

She saw the newspaper on his bed, the word *murder* in a huge bold font across the top. What an awful thing for him to see, to struggle to understand. Who in the world had let him get a copy of the damn thing, anyhow? Didn't people around here have more sense than that?

She folded the paper without reading the story or looking at the photographs and tucked it into the wastebasket. Her father watched her.

"It sounds like a problem," he said, speaking carefully. "You have a real problem."

That one almost put her on her knees, driven either by laughter or tears. *Yes, Dad, it's a problem. You have no idea just how much of a problem I'm looking at right now.*

"It's going to be fine," she said. "Everything's all right. We had a bad day. It's done, though."

She sat on the bed, and he turned in his chair so he could keep his hand on her leg, some of the confusion and fear draining from his face. She was here now, he could reach out and touch her, and even if he didn't understand the rest of it, that was enough.

Had Nora been in a less hostile mood, Frank would have inquired as to why she parked in the back corner of the lot. It wasn't the ideal position as far as he was concerned; any watchers would probably be in front of the building or on the main road, and back here Frank couldn't see shit, had no hope of knowing what was going on. Also, the front of the building had wide banks of windows looking out on the parking lot, which meant that any attempt on their truck would be visible to those inside. Not so from their current position.

She wasn't in a mind-set that welcomed debate, though, so he'd decided to just let her go inside and talk to her father, hope for the best. He hadn't seen the Charger when they pulled in. The part of his brain that was most connected to his father's ghost whispered that of course he wouldn't see the Charger, there was no way these guys would still be using it, but he tried to shut that voice out. It was a matter of minutes now. That was what he was down to in Tomahawk. Minutes. Wait for Nora to finish here, then go rent a car, and be two or three hundred miles away by the time the sun went down.

Two or three hundred miles *west*. That's what he decided as he sat in the passenger seat and waited for her to return. Most of his wanderings had been devoted to the East Coast or the Midwest. Why not give the Rockies a shot? Some state like Montana or Wyoming might feel more like home to him than any place had in a long time. It was a wild region, populated with private people. A damn fine mix, as far as he was concerned.

You've got acres of trees on the north side of the building, offering protection for a watcher as well as a clear view of the entrance to the nursing home.

The ghost was back, offering reminders Frank didn't want to hear. There was no need to worry about this place, act like some commando preparing for a raid. It was a nursing home, and chances were the pair from Miami didn't even know Nora's father was a resident.

Now that you're in the back corner of the lot, you can't see a damn thing, but if someone's in those trees, they saw you come in, and they're making plans for action. You can't make a counterattack plan, because you have no idea what the hell's going on, and won't until it's too late.

It was like a chorus that caught in your brain and refused to be cast aside. He could almost see his father leaning against the side of the truck, gesturing around the parking lot with one of the cigarettes he was always promising to stop smoking. Frank tried to will the memory away, keep thinking of the Rockies, of places he'd never been and where he had no history, wide-open places with wide-open possibilities.

You're already beaten, son. You let yourself get separated from the only person you had to take care of, the only body

*that needed guarding. How the hell are you supposed to help
her from the parking lot if something goes down inside?*

Frank drummed his fingers on the armrest, tried to think
of a song to hum. Ten minutes had passed now. How long
would she take? Probably not much longer. She wanted to
get rid of him. Was disgusted by his, what, cowardice? Was
that what she thought? Hell with her if she did. She was
nothing but a stranger anyhow. Different place, different
circumstances, he'd have been attracted to her, sure. Would
still be tasting her lips from the previous night, remembering the way her hair had felt against his neck. This wasn't
the place, though, and these weren't the circumstances.

*You can't see her. Don't even know what room she's in,
don't know a damn thing about the layout of that place,
haven't bothered to get out of the truck and into a protected
position in case there's trouble, or even clear your gun—
my gun—from the holster.*

He kept drumming his fingers awkwardly, the sound uneven, no rhythm at all. Why couldn't he think of any songs?

Nora spent twenty minutes with her father before she stood.
It hadn't been enough time for either of them, but she had
Frank waiting in the truck and Renee, Vaughn, and Ezra wait-
ing on the island.

"I'll come back tomorrow, Dad. First thing in the morning. Okay?"

His face dropped as if an invisible hand had slid over it
and tugged the eyes down, the mouth into a frown. She knelt
beside his chair, squeezed his hand.

"Everything's okay, Dad. I promise. And I will see *you*,"
she kissed his cheek again, "in the morning."

She released his hand—it was always hard to leave, but
this was an entirely new feeling—and walked to the door
without looking back. If she looked into his face again, saw
the disappointment and worry and confusion, always the confusion, she knew she'd fall apart, end up in tears on the floor.
Better to leave with her head high and her stride purposeful,

have him thinking everything was okay and she was in control.

As soon as she stepped into the hallway, she closed the door behind her, hearing a soft click as it latched. The hallway was empty, and she turned to the left and started back toward the entrance, made it about three steps before the door to a vacant room across from her father's swung open and a hand encircled her mouth and pulled her into the room. She saw a gun in her face, and even though she couldn't see the man who held it yet, she knew it was the one whose hand had left bruises on her arm two days earlier.

"Three things," he said, his lips close to her ear. "First, there's a nurse in the room next to your dad's. Second, anybody screams or causes a problem, I'm going to begin shooting. Third"—he paused as someone laughed in a room a few doors down—"I'm the only person in this building with a gun. So if the shooting starts, a lot of people are going to get hurt. Including the old man you just left in that room."

Frank had wanted to come in with her. Frank and his *gun* had wanted to come in. She'd left him in the parking lot instead. But how could she have known . . . *the newspaper.* She'd seen the warning and ignored it, wondered who would possibly have given that paper to her father. The answer: someone who wanted to make sure Nora came by to see him. She could hear Barb's voice on the voice again: *We're not sure how he got it.* This guy had been waiting here for a while. Probably all morning. They were smart, too. When she didn't turn up at her house last night, they'd had to go in search of a way to find her. It wouldn't have taken much research to learn that the only personal connection Nora had to Tomahawk was in this nursing home.

The hand on her mouth released slowly, air filling her lungs again.

"Good girl," he said. "It would have been very bad if you'd screamed. Very bad."

He was talking in a strong whisper, and he reached out and twisted the lock, trapping them inside.

"We're going to be leaving through that window," he

said, gesturing at the large open window with the screen already removed. "Thanks for parking where you did. Makes this a lot easier."

She swallowed, thinking of how clever she'd felt, parking in the rear of the lot to hide the truck. It was hidden, all right. Hidden from anyone who might come to her aid.

"First thing you need to do is make a phone call to your friend in the truck," he said. "You tell him that a very good shot is watching him through a scope right now. You tell him to take that gun out from under his jacket, hold it in the air for a second, and then put it in the glove compartment."

She didn't respond. He smiled at her. His face and clothes were as she'd remembered, but the ornate belt buckle was gone. Maybe he thought it stood out too much. Maybe he'd gotten Jerry's blood on it.

"If you don't have Frank's cell phone number," he said, "I can provide it. Yes, honey, we're all caught up on the research. Now, do you want to call or should I?"

She called.

Twenty-eight

His fingers froze on the armrest when the cell phone rang. Jumpy. He took the phone out, saw it was Nora's number. She was probably calling to order him out of the truck, not wanting to see him when she came outside.

"There's a problem," she said when he answered. Tension in her voice, but not the angry sort.

"What?"

"One of them is inside with me, and the other is watching you through a gun scope." Speaking softly but clearly. "I've been asked to tell you to take your gun out, hold it in the air for a second, and then put it inside the glove compartment. If you don't listen, they will shoot you."

Told you, told you, told you! the ghost screamed at him. *It's over now, son, over because you got lazy and dumb and told yourself that wouldn't matter. It* always *matters.*

"You're with your father?" Frank said. "This guy was waiting in your father's room?"

"No, I—" There was a rustle, a whisper, and then her voice returned. "Frank, put the gun in the glove compartment, and do it fast."

Shit. He hadn't seen anyone watching, had no proof that this thing about the guy with the scope wasn't a bluff, but he had to listen. He already knew there could be someone in those woods north of the building. Had been trying to ignore the notion for the last ten minutes. Moving slowly, he reached inside his jacket with his free hand and withdrew the Smith & Wesson, held it in the air, then squeezed the phone between his ear and shoulder while he opened the glove compartment and put the weapon inside.

"I put the gun away."

More whispering, then, "We're coming outside. He wants you to get behind the wheel and keep your hands above the dash. If you see anyone else, look normal."

The call was disconnected, but he kept the phone at his ear as he slid across the seat, banging his knees on the gearshift. Without looking at the display, he punched the CALL button with his thumb. That would bring up a list of previously called numbers, and Ezra's number, entered just before leaving the island, would be at the top of the list. *Most times it doesn't work on the water, but I'll give you the number. It'll ring, if nothing else.*

Frank hit the CALL button again, keeping the phone up and hoping the watcher wasn't going to be aware of exactly when the call from inside the nursing home had ended. Still, he wouldn't have much time, because as soon as Nora and the guy with her left the building, it would be obvious that Frank should no longer have the phone to his ear.

One ring, then two, no answer, and right then he saw them—Nora and the man he'd knocked out in the body shop, rounding the corner of the building. Either there was another door, or they'd gone through a window. Odds were good nobody in the building had seen them leave. He closed the phone without getting an answer, dropped it into his lap, and thought, *Figure it out, Ezra, figure it out. There's trouble on the way.*

Nora walked to the truck quickly but without obvious fear, eyes up, stride steady. That was a good word for her, steady. She'd hung together through all of this, with the one exception coming when they'd found Jerry's body. Brave girl. She didn't deserve this.

Frank noticed the door was locked when they were about ten feet from the truck and leaned over to unlock it. When he moved, the gun in the tall guy's hand showed for the first time, rising fast. Frank unlocked the door and leaned back, held his hands up again, indicating it hadn't been an aggressive move, no suicidal idiot sitting in this truck, no, sir. The gun dropped, and then the door was open and Nora was inside the truck and sitting beside him, the tall guy piling in behind her.

"Keys," the guy said, and Nora fished her keys out and passed them to Frank.

"Start it up and drive out of here. Take a right out of the parking lot, and go straight until I say something else. Keep both hands on the wheel, keep the speed down, and keep your mouth shut."

Simple enough. Frank did as he was told, made a right turn away from the nursing home without anyone stopping them or even seeing them. They'd gone about a half mile before he noticed that Nora's leg was trembling against his.

Ezra rotated the cell phone in his palm and stared out across the water. The wind was coming at the island in uneven gusts, pushing tendrils of gray clouds ahead of it. Just one boat had passed in all the time he'd been out here, and he'd recognized it as Dwight Simonton's pontoon. Unthreatening. A peaceful afternoon, a lonely lake.

But there was the phone in his hand, small and still and silent since those two rings, just two, that had come in from Frank Temple's son. Ezra didn't like the two rings. Liked it even less that there had been no second attempt.

He'd thought about calling Frank himself. Would take maybe ten seconds of conversation to clarify the situation.

He didn't call, though. Because if it hadn't been a mistake, if Frank had intended to hang up that quickly, without getting a chance to talk to Ezra or leave a message, then the afternoon was about to get interesting. Either Frank had been interrupted in his attempt to call—an option that prickled at the back of Ezra's neck—or he'd made the call as a warning. One or the other. Or a mistake.

Ezra felt Frank would understand the effect of an aborted call like that, would anticipate the worry on Ezra's end. That belief tilted the scales, ever so slightly, in the direction of trouble. No matter how gentle a shift that was, it was something he had to listen to. If you ignored it, the first chance you'd have to regret it wouldn't come until too late.

He was alone on the porch. Vaughn and Renee were still inside, though he hadn't heard much conversation from them. Vaughn had looked shifty, even angry, the last time Ezra was inside, but the woman seemed to have taken a measure of comfort now that some time had passed. She would listen to Ezra willingly, and Vaughn, if it came down to it, would listen to Ezra because he would be given no other choice. Ezra went to the door.

"You two got any rain gear?"

They were sitting together in the living room, Vaughn speaking to Renee in a harsh whisper, and when Ezra entered and spoke they both looked at him as if they didn't understand the language.

"What?" Renee said.

"Rain gear? If not, don't worry about it. I got a few of those emergency ponchos in the boat, if we need 'em. Chances are, we're going to need 'em, too. Those clouds don't look like kidders to me."

Vaughn stood up. "What are you talking about? If it rains, we've got a roof over our heads."

"Not anymore." Ezra was turning down the blinds now, the sunlight disappearing from the room in strips. "We're going on a boat ride, kids. And we're going on it in a hurry."

Now Renee was on her feet, too. "What's wrong?"

"Nothing's wrong," Vaughn said. "This guy's crazy. What the hell are you talking about, boat rides?"

"Shut up," Ezra said, and the argument died on Vaughn's lips. There was still anger in his eyes, his forehead lined with dislike, but he quit talking. He was scared of Ezra, and that would make things easier.

"They're coming, aren't they," Renee said, and there was neither question nor alarm in her voice. Just a calm, if disappointed, understanding.

"They could be," Ezra said. "And I'll tell you this—an

island is a damn tricky place to sneak away from. So best to get off it early."

"Where are we going?"

"Not quite sure about that one yet, but we'll need a boat, and we'll need to move fast."

"I want my gun back," Vaughn said. "If they're coming for us, I want my damn gun."

Ezra gave him a cool, even gaze until Vaughn looked away.

"When it comes time for shooting," he said, "I'll see that you got something to do it with."

Three times the man with the gun instructed a turn. Those were the only three times the silence was broken. They'd gone maybe five miles, were well out of town and into the woods, before he told Frank to stop. They were at a ramshackle bar with CLOSED and FOR SALE signs in the windows, an ancient gas pump out front. Frank drove behind the building, following instructions, then parked and cut the motor. Nothing around them but the deserted building and the trees, with buzzing insects and wind-tossed cattails indicating a marsh about a hundred feet behind the bar. Frank turned away from it. It would take a long time before a body dumped in that marsh was found.

"Now we sit here and we wait and nobody says a word," the guy with the gun said. His weapon was a Beretta, resting against his knee and angled toward Frank.

They sat for five minutes, maybe ten, and then gravel crunched under tires as someone left the paved road and drove into the parking lot. A few seconds later the new arrival appeared around the building. A van, light blue with darkly tinted windows, suburban-looking, about as anonymous as a vehicle could get. It pulled in beside the truck, and the driver climbed out. Shorter than the guy inside the truck, but quicker, more graceful in his movements. Strong, too. Frank remembered that from the way the guy had whipped his gun into Mowery's face beside the police car.

"Out," the guy beside Nora said, and Frank opened the

door and stepped out onto the dusty parking circle, a warm gust of wind flapping his shirt against his body. It was his first opportunity to see the second man face-to-face, and he didn't like the way the guy stared at him as if they'd already met, a sense of the familiar in his gaze. The guy held that look for a long moment, then turned away from Frank and slid the van's side door open, and Frank found himself staring at Devin Matteson.

The last time Frank had seen him—the only time—it had been eight years earlier, in Miami. He hadn't been around him long, maybe an hour, just enough for the dislike to put down roots, but what he remembered from that meeting was two qualities: arrogance and strength. The strength was no longer present.

Devin was leaning sideways against the seat so that he could face out, a gun resting in his lap, but it looked like just keeping his head up was taking a real effort. His usual deep tan and strong jawline had turned into a junkie's face, fish-belly complexion with hazy, red-rimmed eyes and muscle lines that seemed given to tremors. Bulges showed under his shirt, and Frank realized after a second look that they weren't bulges from a holster but from bandages.

Vaughn was lying. Had to be, because this no longer made any sense: The two men who'd arrived pursuing Vaughn and Renee were indeed here, but Devin was with them. Vaughn's story had just come unhinged, but right now, staring his old nemesis in the face, Frank had no concept of the truth, just understanding of the lie.

"This is a crazy damn world, you know?" Devin said, and his voice came from some tight, trapped place in his chest. "I mean, I send two guys up here to do a job, and who do they tell me got in the way but Frank Temple Junior."

"The Third," Frank said.

"Huh?"

"Frank Temple the Third. No junior here."

Devin looked at Frank for a long moment, and then gave a low laugh as his eyes went to his shorter partner.

"You believe that? It's his son, no question. *No junior here.*"

He laughed again, and the other guy gave an awkward smile, as if he didn't know what was so amusing but felt obligated to share in the fun. Devin's laughter swept through Frank as pure white rage. He willed himself still, willed himself silent. Let the prick laugh. Let him enjoy this. Let him think that Frank didn't know what had happened those many years earlier, and then, when the time was right, let him pay.

Devin stopped laughing, but it wasn't clear if it was because the humor had passed or because he'd run out of breath. He waited for a moment, jaw clenching, eyes watering, and when he looked up and spoke again his voice had less energy and a darker tone.

"You want to tell me, Temple *the Third,* what the hell you're doing here?"

Frank said, "I came to send you home."

"What?"

"Ezra Ballard told me that you were coming back. We didn't think that should happen."

Devin gave him a look caught between anger and wonder. "Ballard's a crazy old bastard. I don't know what he told you, kid, but it was all bullshit. Me giving your old man up? That's a lie."

This time Frank didn't think he'd be able to will the anger down, thought it was going to tug his foundation loose and sweep him away with it, send him rushing into that van, the other two and their guns be damned. But he fought it down again, didn't say a word.

"Whatever," Devin said. "I don't give a shit what you two think. I'll tell you what I told Ballard—whoever tipped the FBI, it wasn't me. Supposed to be somebody close to your dad, though. Hell, could have been you."

Frank was halfway to the van when the tall man stepped in and swung his gun sideways, going for his throat. Frank blocked it, got his hand up and met the guy's forearm with his own, was still moving forward, still heading for Devin, when the second man placed the barrel of a gun against Frank's cheek.

He stopped then, had to, and the tall guy turned his gun over and pressed it into Frank's ribs, two guns against him now, two fingers on the trigger. Devin hadn't moved, just sat there and watched with his own gun still on his lap.

"Your old man never shut up about you," he said. "All this bullshit, telling everybody how fast you were, how good with a pistol. On and on. And you know what I finally figured out? He had to keep talking about it, because he knew you were a pussy. He knew that, and it shamed him."

He got out of the van slowly, almost went down once, but when the tall man moved to help him he put up his hand and shook his head. He steadied himself, took a couple of steps toward Frank, until they were face-to-face. The tall man had moved back toward Nora, but the other one kept his gun on Frank's cheek.

"How did you hook up with Vaughn Duncan?" Devin said. "Did he find you, or did you find him?"

This provided an answer to a question Frank hadn't even really had time to consider yet: If Devin was already here, why hadn't he just gone out to the island? Frank was the reason. Frank was the wild card, the development Devin hadn't been able to understand. Frank and Nora—loose ends.

"I drove him off the road," Frank said, each word coming slow, the pressure of the gun working against his jaw muscles, "because I thought he was you, and I was going to kill him. Like I said, it's why I came up here."

Devin Matteson stared at him for a long time. "You're serious," he said. "You're *serious*."

It wasn't a question. Devin looked away, at each of his partners and then at Nora, and shook his head, limped a few steps back, so he could lean on the van.

"Well, hell, kid," he said. "Sorry to disappoint. It wasn't me, was it? But you and him, you guys got something to share. You wanted to kill me, he tried."

It took a second for Frank to process that. Then the truth that had felt so close when Renee slapped him—the reality of her loyalty to Devin imprinted on his cheek, stinging his flesh—finally arrived, came screeching up in a cloud of smoke, engine revving. Vaughn was after Renee. You didn't have a chance to take a woman like Renee away from a man like Devin. Not when he was alive.

"Vaughn shot you," Frank said.

"Three times," Devin said.

"That's not what your wife thinks," Nora said, and everyone but Frank turned to look at her.

"My wife," Devin said, offering the phrase guardedly, as if he were afraid of its power. "You've seen her."

Nora nodded.

"She's here. With Vaughn."

"Yes. But she thinks you're dead."

Devin said, "AJ," and waved his hand at the man who held the gun to Frank's face. The gun dropped away and the man stepped back, cleared some space so Devin could see Nora clearly.

"Tell me," Devin said, "what they told you."

Nora told him. Frank heard her words but wasn't focused on them, was instead staring at Devin and trying to smell out the lie. He *had* to be lying, didn't he? Vaughn had shot him? But Frank could see that now, could see it in the way Vaughn and Renee had interacted, his obvious adoration for her. And Vaughn had told the story, provided all the details, details that were clearly lies. Everything Renee knew about the reasons they'd fled came from Vaughn. None of it had come from Devin, at least not the way she'd told it to them that morning.

"I cannot believe he had the balls," Devin said when Nora was done, his voice barely audible. "That cocksucker . . . he planned it for a while. Spent some real time on it. Had a story ready for her. And I'm laying in the hospital and he's up here with my *wife*."

He banged the butt of his gun against the van, then again, and again, until the effort took his strength and he had to wait a minute to get it back, hanging against the door.

"You thought she left you for him?" Frank said, and Devin's eyes slid unpleasantly back to him. "That's why you didn't name the shooter for the police? You thought she was involved?"

Devin waited for a moment, then said, "I wanted to conduct my own investigation. That's all."

"Then how did these two"—Frank nodded at the other men—"get here before you?"

"I sent them. When they told me he'd come here, I left so I could see it to the end in person."

"If this is the truth," Nora said, and her voice was wavering, "then why did you bastards have to kill Jerry? Why did you have to do that? You knew Vaughn was going to that island!"

"Unfortunately," Devin said, nothing showing in his bleary eyes, "I was out of communication with these two for a while. So they had to keep following the trail."

That justified it to him. It was enough. Frank looked at Nora, saw the shock and horror in her face, and wondered if she understood what else this meant. She was playing Jerry's role now: a liability.

"They're on that island?" Devin said, ignoring her question, stepping away from the van again, closer to Frank. "They're on *my* island? Vaughn and my wife?"

Frank nodded.

"Who's with them?"

He didn't say anything. Neither did Nora. But Devin stared into Frank's eyes and said, "Ballard. He's out there with them, isn't he?"

Frank still didn't respond, but Devin was nodding his head, already convinced.

"Okay," he said. "AJ, King, get them in the van. We're close, boys. We're close."

Twenty-nine

Past Madison and gaining on Stevens Point, maybe two hours away if he could keep this speed up. Grady was driving hard and staring at the clock, willing it to tick a little slower.

He wanted to call Frank, see if the kid had his phone on today, if he'd answer. There was news to share, damn it. Atkins hadn't been kidding when he said he'd press charges over another phone call, though, and Grady had the sense that Frank was done talking to him anyhow. He had a plan of some sort, was putting something in motion.

If Duncan was good for the murder, as the fingerprint suggested, then this thing was shaping up exactly as Grady had feared: Devin Matteson was headed out to that lake to settle the score, and Frank Temple had placed himself in the way.

By the time he passed the first exit for Stevens Point he couldn't wait for news anymore, grabbed the phone and called Atkins again.

"He's still gone," Atkins said, without bothering to exchange a greeting. "I've also tried to find the guy you mentioned, Ballard, but he's MIA as well. Thing is, there's a boat down here now."

"Where?"

"At Temple's cabin. There was a small boat the first time I came out, little aluminum thing, but now there's a fancy bass boat on the beach. I called in to check the numbers, and it comes back to Ballard."

"But they're not inside."

"No, they're not inside," Atkins snapped, his tone icy. "There was a truck here this morning, too, registered to that girl at the body shop, and now that's gone and this damn boat is here and none of them are where I can find them. This is fantastic, Morgan. I've got a murder warrant ready to go, and these assholes know where the guy is, and now I can't find them."

"You got anybody else involved?"

"Couple of the locals are running around, trying to turn the girl up. Said she was just in at some nursing home visiting her father, so I guess she's all right. But I'm the only one out here at the lake."

"You probably ought to have some help."

"I'll get help when I find out where the son of a bitch *is,* Morgan. And I can't do that until your buddy shows his face again."

"Wait there," Grady said. "If Ballard's boat is there, they'll probably be coming back to it."

"I'm going to wait for maybe twenty minutes, and then I'm going back to check Ballard's house. But I'll give it another twenty."

Devin Matteson made them all ride in the van, first instructing Nora to write a note that said, *Out of gas, back soon, please don't tow,* for display in the windshield of her truck. She hadn't thought much of it then, but after she was in the van and they were in motion, the note began to disturb her. It would keep anyone who found the truck from immediate concern and imply that Nora had been under her own power when she left the vehicle behind. Those were only temporary effects, of course, but the fact that Devin had considered them made something bitter bloom in her stomach. He was good at these things, kidnapping and murder, so good that the little moves like that note came to him effortlessly, it seemed. Came the way things did after a lot of practice.

AJ was driving and sat alone in the front, Nora in the middle row beside Devin Matteson, Frank all the way in back with the man called King. Devin and King and AJ were all wearing guns. AJ had two, actually; he'd paused long enough to take Frank's gun out of the truck before they left. It lay on the floor in front of the passenger seat now. She could hear it slide around when they took sharp curves.

Devin Matteson's true condition began to show itself during the van ride. He'd looked bad initially, unhealthy, but once they were in the van Nora saw that he'd held it together well for that first encounter. Now he seemed to struggle with every turn and bend, wincing at the motions, patting his chest lightly with his hand. By the time they'd gone five miles his face was bathed in sweat, his breathing audible across the van.

There was nothing between her and the end of this but twenty minutes in the van, another twenty in a boat. The fear should have been intense, cloaking her, forcing her into hysterical sobbing. That seemed right, at least. Instead, she was just sitting here, swaying gently with the van's motion, listening to the rasping breaths of the man with the gun beside her, numb.

They were going to die. While she believed the story Devin had told, at least the portion about Vaughn, she couldn't believe that meant any change in her fate. She'd seen these men face-to-face, watched them commit crimes. After all that, they weren't going to simply head home after finding Vaughn, trusting that she and Frank would pretend none of this had happened.

So we're going to die. She almost nodded as if confirming the silent, internal voice. It was true. If things went according to plan for these men, there would be more killing before the end of the day, and it wasn't going to stop with Vaughn.

All this over a murder, she thought. *No, wait, it wasn't even a murder. He didn't kill Devin, he just tried. And now how many others will die because of that? How many innocent people are going to atone for one man's attempted killing?*

The interior of the van darkened as they drove north, the sun pushed beneath ivory clouds that looked a good deal more ominous to the west. She watched the shadows play across the seats and tried to think of a way to stop this. The moves that came to mind were all in hindsight, though, things she could have done and had chosen not to do. Atkins of the FBI sat somewhere in Tomahawk, awaiting her call. If she'd called him instead of getting in the boat with Frank and Ezra . . .

Ezra. The thought of him was the closest thing to comfort she could come up with. He was capable, always in control, and, if what Frank had said about him was true, the sort of man who could deal with these bastards. The odds weren't with Ezra, though. He was without warning, he was without preparation, he was without the support of favorable numbers. He was also all she had to hold her hope.

The van rumbled over a stretch of rough pavement, and she looked back out the window, saw with surprise that they were already on County Y, minutes from the cabin. It was all going to happen fast now, too fast. She sat up straighter, wanting to turn and look at Frank, but King's hand came down immediately, pressed hard into her shoulder, brought her back into the seat.

The van came to a stop, and she looked up again and saw the lake through the windshield, the water darker and tossed by a gusting wind. For a moment the lake held her attention, but then she heard AJ swear softly, and when she leaned to the left for a clearer view she saw that there was a car parked beside Frank's cabin. A white Buick sedan, nobody sitting inside.

"Whose car?" Devin said, leaning close to her, his face shiny with sweat.

Silence.

"*Whose car?*"

"I don't know," she said. Frank didn't speak. Maybe he knew who it was. Someone he'd arranged to meet at the cabin before all of this had started.

That idea died an immediate death when Atkins, the FBI

agent, walked around the corner of the cabin. He had a sheaf of papers in his hand, and when he saw the van he folded the papers and tucked them into his back pocket, cocking his head and studying the van and AJ behind the wheel.

"Who is that?" AJ said.

Nora didn't answer, just stared at Atkins as if he were the ghost of a loved one, someone you'd known you'd never see again no matter how badly you hoped for it. At that moment, Atkins reached into his suit jacket. AJ tensed, but then Atkins's hand was back out, with a badge in it. Nora's muscles went soft, liquid. What was he doing? Don't pull a badge, pull a *gun*.

"Handle it," Devin said, and then he pressed the gun into Nora's stomach as AJ opened the door.

"Not a sound," Devin said. "King? Don't let either of them make a sound."

AJ stepped out into the wind, said, "Is there a problem, sir?" and then slammed the door.

"No," Nora said softly. She couldn't let this happen. Couldn't let AJ talk his way out of this, send their best chance at rescue off in that Buick, oblivious. King's hand descended onto her shoulder again, tightened into the nerves, held her against the seat.

AJ was walking toward Atkins with a leisurely stride, one hand in his jacket pocket, the other cupped to his ear as if struggling to hear over the sound of the wind. Atkins walked forward to meet him, still holding the badge in the air, waving with his free hand at Frank's cabin.

"Oh, shit," Frank said, and King's hand left her shoulder and went to Frank's throat as AJ closed the gap to a few feet and Nora finally realized what was about to happen, that AJ's goal had never been to fool Atkins with talk. She screamed then, and Atkins jerked, looked toward the van and took a fumbling step backward and AJ's hand came up out of his jacket and into the FBI agent's stomach.

Atkins hunched, as if caught by an unexpected stomach cramp, and then AJ's hand rose higher and Atkins rocked back onto his heels and kept going, landed on his back with the handle of the knife rising out of his sternum as if AJ had planted a flag there. It was the last thing Nora saw before King slammed his rough hand across her mouth and pulled her backward, dragging her head behind the seat, telling her to shut up or she'd die, too.

It was like that, with her back arched and her neck strained to its limits, staring into the backseat upside down, that her eyes finally found Frank's. King's gun was shoved against Frank's head, but Frank seemed unaware of it. He'd turned his eyes away from the scene outside for only a moment, just long enough to meet hers, and what she saw there was nothing like what he had to be seeing in her own face, not fear or sorrow but the dark shadows of rage.

Thirty

"We didn't need this. Damn it, we didn't *need this!*"

Devin was standing above Atkins's body, staring at AJ, his face now stricken by both pain and anger.

"You said handle it, man."

"Handle it, shit, you think that means you *gut* the guy? An *FBI agent*? This is something we needed?"

AJ showed a ghost of a smile, spread his hands. "Dev . . . what can I say? You know, it's done. I'll deal with it."

Frank, watching him, thought, *He did it because he likes it.* That was all. Devin was dangerous, but Devin had a brain. This wild son of a bitch, AJ, he was closer to the edge. Bloodthirsty, driven by it. He'd killed Atkins because it was not only what he knew to do but what he liked to do. Any guilt over his own stupidity, over the additional attention this was going to bring down around them, was buried beneath the pure pleasure he'd taken in the moment.

"I mean, I saw a badge, you know? I saw a badge, Dev, I just reacted." AJ was watching Devin, the knife gone and the gun back in his hand. It was a Glock, and he kept rubbing his thumb over the butt as he looked at Devin. There was a strange symbol tattooed on the back of his hand. A lefty, too. Frank had only known one left-handed shooter, but that guy had been damn accurate.

"You'll deal with it." Devin shook his head, disgusted, and stared at the corpse at their feet for a long time. When he finally looked up, his eyes found Frank, lingered there, and then he nodded.

"All right," he said. "We'll make it work."

He made Frank drag the body down to the boat, a crimson smear marking their path over the grass, the trail of blood leading right to the cabin door. That's what the cops would see, Frank knew, and what the newspaper and TV people would use for drama. When they were all dead and the cops came up here to sort out the mess, all they'd see was that trail of blood leading to the door of a dead murderer, and the Temple name would be infamous again, Frank accepting the baton from his father. He understood that perfectly as he followed Devin's instructions and handled the body, leaving fingerprints all over the corpse of an FBI agent who'd surely voiced his suspicions of Frank to colleagues already.

Devin hadn't wanted this complication, but he knew how to deal with it.

"Take that anchor line," he said, "and loop it around his neck. Make it tight."

Frank was standing in the shallows, knee deep in the lake, the body slumped facedown in the water as he wrapped the line around Atkins's neck. Devin stood above him on dry land, using a tree for support and studying the lake with the gun held down against his leg, checking for other boats. There weren't any, though. The weather was on Devin's side, rain starting to fall now and thunder crackling just a few miles west, a good storm on the way. A Sunday before fishing season, with a storm coming in, guaranteed an empty lake. Empty except for them and those on the island.

Atkins was the first of at least three victims today if things went Devin's way. He was clearly aware of the possibilities left by making Frank handle the body, but he might not appreciate just how well this would work, might not know that Atkins was already investigating Frank, the hit man's son. Some quick, quiet killing at the island and a fast trip out of town were the only things keeping the trio from

Miami from disappearing like phantoms, leaving the police to try making sense of a situation they'd probably never understand.

Grady. Frank thought of him as he secured Atkins in the anchor line. Grady was an element Devin didn't know about, couldn't plan for. Grady had been putting the puzzle together for everyone, and he'd know where to start when Atkins was announced as missing or the body was found. He wouldn't believe it was Frank's doing. Would he?

Shit, what would it matter? If nobody was left but Grady, let them think what they wanted.

Devin was weaker than Frank had thought at first, hardly able to stand. He'd taken a long time just to cross the short stretch of yard to the tree he leaned against now, and his pain was visible even from down here in the water, his face pale and shiny, his mouth always hanging open to help with breathing. The day's killing would be done at his whim but not by his hands. That was fitting.

Frank finished tying Atkins to the line and set the anchor back into the stern, the body now tied in the middle of the line. Then AJ waved at Frank with the gun.

"Get in."

Frank climbed into the boat, and then Nora and King followed suit and AJ turned back to look at his boss. Devin pushed off the tree, took a wavering step toward them, and then leaned backward and clutched for the tree again, used it to regain his balance.

"Dev . . ." AJ started toward him, but Devin was already in motion again, trying to walk toward them. He made it four steps before his legs buckled and he went down. AJ caught him by the shoulders, helped him up.

"You got to get out of here, man," AJ was saying as Devin struggled for his breath. "Got to get to a—"

"Shut up." Devin had his hands on his knees. "You know what I'm here to do."

"I'm telling you, we can do it for you."

"No."

AJ looked back at the boat, then down at Devin. "Dev, you aren't going to make it in that boat. You aren't. And it's starting to rain, man. Gonna turn ugly soon."

Devin didn't respond, just took in fast, panting breaths.

"We'll go get him," AJ said. "We'll get him, and we'll bring him back to you. All right? Him and Renee. We'll bring Renee back, Dev. You got to stay here, though. Out in that boat, man . . ."

Devin rose slowly, stared at the group already waiting in the boat, his eyes lingering on Frank the longest.

"All right," he said. "You go out there and bring them back, and do it *fast,* damn it, do it fast."

"Right." AJ was nodding. "Out and back, man, nothing to it."

"Take them both," Devin said. "This crazy old shit that's out there, he's good."

"He's nothing, Dev, don't worry about—"

"No." Devin shook his head. "He's *good*, okay? That's why you need them. You make sure he knows you've got the girl, too. Make that good and clear."

"We got it, Dev. Now let me get you inside."

AJ left Devin there in the yard and walked back to the boat, extended his hand to Frank, and asked for the key. Frank reached in his pocket and took it out, the key to the last place of clean memories he had with his father, and then he passed it over so Devin Matteson could go inside and wait for somebody else to finish his bloody work.

AJ took the key and went back to Devin, helped him across the yard and into the cabin, Frank watching them go, thinking, *I'll be back for you, you son of a bitch. It won't be these two coming back. It'll be me.*

Ezra was on the island, and whether he'd gotten Frank's aborted phone call or not, they would not be surprising him, not by approaching in a loud boat in the middle of a storm. He'd be waiting, and he'd be ready, and then it would be done. Let Ezra handle these two, and then Frank would come back for Devin.

The door reopened and AJ stepped out, started in their

direction, then pulled up short and returned to the van, opened the driver's door, and leaned inside to grab the extra gun, Frank's father's gun. It was the second time he'd gone back for it—the first, he'd made sure not to leave it in the glove compartment of the truck—and each time Frank had felt relief. He wanted the gun to travel with them, as if it somehow represented protection no matter the hands that held it.

They were close now, the island no more than twenty minutes away. He had no grand plan, no idea how to stop this from happening except to run directly to Ezra and hope for the best.

"Start the motor," AJ said, stepping on board and coming back to sit behind Frank.

The big outboard fired at once, smooth and powerful and as loud as a damn train. Ezra had more horsepower on the back of that boat than was in most cars. Frank put the motor in reverse and kept the throttle low until the prop had pulled them into deeper water, then spun the wheel and slammed the throttle forward.

The rain was driving hard now, blowing into their faces and speckling the surface of the lake. Water ran down Frank's neck and under his shirt, dripped into his eyes. After they were around the sandbar, into the middle of the lake, AJ leaned over the side of the boat and there was a flash of silver from his knife and then the anchor line parted and slipped overboard and Atkins's body drifted away. His white face was turned up as the anchor tugged it slowly beneath the lake, a ghostly sinking shadow. It was probably twenty-five or thirty feet deep out here. He might surface soon, he might not. If the body stayed wrapped in the anchor line and tangled in any of the stumps that lined the bottom, Agent Atkins might be a resident of the Willow Flowage for a long time.

"Go on!" AJ yelled, and Frank increased the speed, hardly aware that he'd slowed to watch the body.

Devin wanted AJ to have hostages, had made that clear before he'd sent them off without him. Hostages gave AJ a bargaining chip for use with Ezra, leverage to force the situation into his favor. One thing was certain, though: AJ had never had a hostage like Frank Temple III.

Frank held tight to that idea as he squinted against the wind and the spray, pushing the boat ahead fast and hard. All those lessons his father had offered, those violent skills that he'd provided and that Frank had spent seven years trying to suppress, they were about to have a purpose. These assholes might have known Frank's father, but they didn't know him well enough. Contract killer or not, Frank Temple II was at heart a teacher—and his son had excelled at the lessons.

There wasn't a real road within two miles of where Ezra sat. A couple of trails led up to the Nekoosa Kennedy Fire Lane, but even if Ezra got them out of the boat and through the woods to the fire lane, what would he have accomplished? They'd still be a long, long walk from safety, with the boat marking their entrance point into the woods. Find the boat, and it wouldn't be hard to understand where they were headed if you had a map. He had a feeling these boys would have a map.

"We're just going to *sit* here?" Vaughn said. "We left the cabin to come up here and sit in a boat? If they don't kill us, the lightning will!"

The lightning was a concern, although Ezra didn't admit it, or even bother to respond to Vaughn at all. The rain was falling now, and the dark thunderheads were on top of them. They needed to get out of the boat and on land for the duration of the storm if nothing else, even though that wasn't what he wanted. Not for the first time since they'd left, he wondered if he'd made a mistake by coming north. Frank could have made that call from Tomahawk, more than thirty minutes away. With time like that, they could have gotten to Ezra's truck.

It was a risk he couldn't have chanced, though. You planned for the worst-case scenario, and the worst-case scenario put these bastards close and coming closer. Circumstance like that, you had to run away from them, not into them. So he'd run, taken the boat into the deepest reaches of Langley Bay, one of the most secluded spots on the lake, with the only approach coming from the water. That meant going *back* required crossing a hell of a lot of water, too. He turned and looked at the motor on the stern. Stupid little outboard, nine-point-nine horse. It would take them five times as long to get across the lake with it as Ezra's boat, with the two-twenty-five knocking away.

"If they're out here to find us, they'll search the whole lake," Renee said. She was sitting in the middle seat of the little aluminum boat, and it rocked as she leaned toward him. She was wearing one of the ponchos Ezra kept in the boat, but there was rain on her neck, sliding slowly down to her collarbone. "They won't get discouraged and give up."

He understood that, didn't need it told to him. Truth was, Ezra had some doubts now, and he wasn't used to doubts. There was a time when something like this, combat prepara-tions and a retreat into the woods, felt as natural to him as a trip to the movies, simple and almost fun. Hell, back then it felt *more* natural than a trip to the movies, but that time was long ago. Today, shaken out of years of a peaceful existence, maybe he'd slipped. Maybe he'd made a mistake. What the hell were they accomplishing, really, sitting out here in a boat with no idea what was happening on land? Even if his worst suspicions were accurate, then the real concerns were Frank and Nora. These two were at least temporarily safe. The others might not be.

"We can't just sit here," Vaughn said again, and his voice made Ezra prickle, filled him with an urge to smack the gray-haired son of a bitch onto the floor of the boat. The hell they couldn't just sit here. Ezra had sat in worse places than this. Spent nine hours—*nine hours*—on his face in a mud hole filled with water that smelled like piss, trying not to breathe while an entire battalion of Vietcong milled around the jungle not thirty yards from him. How well would Vaughn have handled that?

Ezra's stomach was clenched, his mind unsettled in a

way it never had been before in a situation like this. It wasn't fear that had him shaken up; no, it was something even more disturbing than that—uncertainty. It was a good way to get yourself, and others, killed. He needed his old mind back, the old instincts, the old moves. Everything he needed now had that word in front of it: *old*. He'd spent decades trying to become someone different than he was, and now he was afraid that he'd succeeded at the task.

Thirty-one

The island showed itself as a dark silhouette against the gray sky, each tree taking on a gradual shape as they neared from the south. Frank was tempted to keep running, head straight into the shore. That'd change some things up, for sure. All four of them in the water, it'd be a matter of who surfaced fastest and who held on to their guns. Since he didn't have any of the guns, though, probably wasn't the wisest choice.

"This is it?" AJ was leaning down to make his words heard over the wind, his face close to Frank's, the gun within reaching distance. Frank looked at it and wondered if he could get his hands on it, whether he could move fast enough. He thought he probably could, but then there was the one they called King to worry about, and Nora directly behind him, in line to accept any bullet that passed through his body.

"Well?" AJ pressed closer, raised the gun a few inches. "Is it?"

Frank nodded, throttled down, the island maybe fifty yards away now, the cabin visible between the trees.

"All right," AJ said, and his voice was different now, softer and measured. "All right. Bring it in slow, kid. Everybody look happy. We're all friends, remember."

He had the gun pressed into Frank's chest.

Thunder hammered through the sky again, and the darkness was such that the trees across the bay seemed to disappear into a night sky. It couldn't be later than one in the afternoon.

Frank was staring up at the house and the trees closest to it, trying to imagine where Ezra was. He'd be watching them approach, Frank was certain of that. The motor was loud, even over the thunder and wind, and Ezra wouldn't ignore it. So where was he? Frank couldn't see him anywhere in the trees, but they were dark and whipped by the wind, branches tossing. The beach was close now, twenty feet ahead, and Frank had the motor throttled all the way down.

"Take us in," AJ said.

"All the way?"

"Yes."

Frank gave the throttle a quick hit, goosing the motor enough to send them toward shore with a hard push, and then cut the engine, had the blades off by the time the boat scraped into the gravelly bank.

"Get her out," AJ said, speaking to King. "Get out her out fast and keep that gun in her back. Come on!"

King rose awkwardly, a big man with land legs, then pulled Nora up, his gun in her back as instructed. He stepped out and got one foot down in the water, almost fell clearing the other one. Nora was submerged nearly up to her knees.

"Move," AJ said, giving Frank's stomach an encouraging twist with the gun barrel. "Out and into the trees."

Frank went up to the front of the boat, passing AJ to do so, that familiar Smith & Wesson just inches from his hand for a second. He cleared the front of the boat with a jump, got almost out of the water, soaking only his shoes before joining King and Nora on the beach. Then AJ was out, and everyone was looking at him and waiting for instructions except for Frank, who kept his eyes on the trees by the cabin. Ezra was in there somewhere. Had to be. Why not shoot? Surely he saw the guns.

Take them, Ezra, he thought. *Damn it, take them!*

No shots came. No sound at all except for more thunder and the howl of the wind across the lake and AJ ordering everyone up to the house.

Frank was shoved into the lead, and he climbed the trail with a cold fear sliding through his body, squeezing his chest. He'd put everything on Ezra, every chance any of them had left, and now Ezra was nowhere to be found. What if Frank had been wrong? What if Ezra hadn't gotten the phone call or been alarmed by it, hadn't heard the motor, was completely unprepared for any of this? If Ezra wasn't ready, that left nobody but Frank for the job.

They came up over the hill, and the cabin came into view. AJ stepped closer to Frank, wrapped one hand in his shirt to keep them together, used the other to press the gun against Frank's kidneys.

"That door going to be locked?"

"I don't know."

"If it is, you call out for Ballard."

Up the steps of the porch as the rain began to fall faster, pattering through the leaves and beading on the floorboards, then to the door, Frank's hand closing around the knob as AJ released his shirt and reached back for his second gun. Locked.

"Call his name," AJ said, hissing it in Frank's ear, and Frank opened his mouth and a laugh came out instead of a name.

"The boat," he said and laughed again, turning away from the door.

"What?"

"It's gone. *They're* gone."

How in the hell had he missed that? Staring at that island so intently as he'd brought them in, scanning the trees, double-checking every shadow, and he'd forgotten the damn boat. They were gone, all right, gone in the boat and into the storm, and that meant Ezra had understood the warning.

"They took the boat and left," he said. AJ shoved him aside and raised his foot and slammed it into the center of the door, tore the hasp out of the frame and burst into the dark house, calling for King to stay on the porch.

They waited while he searched the place, found it as empty as Frank already knew it would be.

"Where did they go?" AJ returned with a snarl, his hand so tight on his gun that the muscles and veins in his forearm stood out. All of the composure and calm were gone now, nothing but fury left behind.

"They left in the boat," Frank said again.

"I know that!" AJ grabbed Frank's throat and drove him backward, slammed him into the cabin wall and pressed the gun into his mouth, banging the muzzle through his teeth. Nora screamed, and King said something in a harsh whisper. Frank couldn't see either of them, couldn't see anything but AJ's face and the gun. The metal was cold against his tongue.

"You know where they are," AJ said, the words slow and soft. "You *know*, and don't lie again, do *not* lie again. You got one chance, and you tell it right this time. Did they go to the police?"

Frank shook his head ever so slightly, not wanting to tamper with that gun.

"He doesn't know!" Nora shouted from somewhere behind AJ. "They were here when we left!"

"Shut up." AJ's eyes never left Frank's. "He knows, and he's got one chance to tell me."

The voice was back then, Frank's father's voice, whispering again.

Trust Ezra. You already did once, and that was a bigger risk than this, because you weren't sure he'd gotten the warning. Now you know he did. He's ready for them, son.

"He doesn't know," Nora said again, her voice tight with tears.

But you do know. Have a general idea, at least, because you know what I would have done. You learned from me. Don't want to remember it now, but you learned from me, listened to all the old stories and remember every damn one and who did I learn from? Ezra.

AJ pulled the gun back slowly, the spit-covered barrel sliding out of Frank's mouth.

"Where are they?" he said.

"On the lake."

AJ's head canted to the right, into a shadow. "Where on the lake?"

Frank swallowed, worked his tongue around his mouth, still tasting the metal of the gun. The last taste his father had ever had in this life.

"The north end. That's as much as I can tell you. They were here when we left. They're gone now, and they didn't tell me where they were going. He knew you were coming, somehow."

AJ's anger seemed barely tempered by a need to believe Frank.

"Then why would they still be on the lake?"

Frank looked past AJ's shoulder, saw Nora watching him.

"He wasn't sure how much time he had before you got here. Couldn't even know for sure that Nora and I had ever gotten away from my cabin. And since he wasn't sure, he couldn't risk going south to get back to the boat ramp or to the cabin. Too much of a chance he'd run straight into you. So he'd go north."

"What's north?"

"Nothing," Frank said. "Nothing but water and woods."

Nine times Grady had called; nine times Atkins had failed to answer. What in the hell was going on?

He'd driven past Wausau and into a rainstorm, cruise control set at ninety now and still nobody stopping him. All he could hope for at this point, as Tomahawk neared and his wipers slapped back and forth at the highest speed setting, was that Atkins couldn't take his calls because he was too busy with Frank. Interviewing him in some safe room in a building far away from Vaughn Duncan and Devin Matteson, maybe. Or maybe it was already done; maybe Matteson and Duncan were both in handcuffs, and Atkins was preparing for the mountain of paperwork that lay ahead.

Maybe a lot of things. As many optimistic options as Grady could produce, he couldn't believe any of them. Not today. Because it was a karmic world, Grady believed that in his heart, and he'd spent too many days and too many years telling himself that he could always make up for his lie, that there would always be time, somewhere down the road, to sit down with Frank Temple and set him straight, give him the truth and apologize and explain why he'd done it, explain that they'd wanted so badly to take Devin down that a little misdirection had seemed so, so insignificant.

The gambit hadn't paid off, though, and so Grady kept that damn watch on Frank Temple out of a little fondness and a lot of guilt and reminded himself often of a personal pact that one day, if it ever seemed necessary, he would tell the kid that it hadn't been Devin who gave up his father.

Grady had let seven years roll by, twenty-five hundred days, and had never said a word. Because it hadn't mattered, not anymore—Frank had swallowed the lie, but it hadn't hurt him, and now, after all this time, there was no way that it could.

Wrong. It was going to hurt him now. Frank and who knew how many others. And all Grady could do was streak up the interstate through the rain, destined to be too late.

As they had so many times in the past, Ezra's ears warned of disaster before his eyes. For a moment he questioned it over the noise of the storm, but then the wind abated for just a moment, as if the lake were going to give him *one* break today, and that was enough to confirm his suspicions: There was a boat on the water.

He could hear the engine faintly, this one riding a lower and stronger pitch than the little outboard under his hand would create. It was a familiar sound, the growl of a Merc two-twenty-five pounding hard, the rhythm of his daily life in the summers.

"What?" Renee said, seeing his face.

"There's a boat coming."

"Could be anybody," Vaughn said. "Let's go, man. Faster we get back to the car, faster we're out of here."

The fear was returning to his voice now, that jerky panic that he'd talked with earlier in the day.

"No." Ezra shook his head. It could be Frank, alone, but something told him it wasn't, told him that the game was in play now.

"You don't even know it's them. I can't see any boat—"

"It's them," Ezra said. "I know the sound of my own boat."

He looked down at the throttle under his hand, knowing that it would dictate what happened next as much as anything would. His boat ate up the water faster than anything else on this lake. Trying to outrun them with the little nine-point-nine would be like a car chase between a Lamborghini and a dump truck.

"It could be that kid and the girl," Vaughn said. "Just them."

"Could be," Ezra said, even though he knew it wasn't. "If it is, we'll know soon. Right now, we got to get ready."

The best scenario would be to ditch the boat and take to the trees and get ready to do some shooting. If he were in his own boat, this bullshit would be over before it got started. He still had his rifle in the boat, with a night scope that would work just fine in this weather. Take that and head into the trees and then he could make damn sure these boys would have a rude welcome. Should never have left it in the boat. Damn. It was the little things that killed you, the missed details and slips of timing, and Ezra felt those stacking up on him now, things that he wouldn't have missed in another time and another place. He was out of practice, had been *happy* to be out of practice, but now it was proving to be a dangerous thing.

When they got to the island and saw it was empty, the boat missing, they'd begin calculating the situation just as he was, and whoever came out ahead in this fight would be the one who thought it through the best, saw the moves before anybody made them. Combat was a thinking man's game, always had been.

So think, then. Think hard and well and think *fast* damn it.

He looked back at Renee and Vaughn, saw them waiting on him with anxious faces, and nodded to himself. Step one, separate these two. It seemed like a bad idea at first blush, but that was almost a good thing, because it meant the boys in Ezra's boat wouldn't expect it. Generally you'd want to keep everyone together, protect one another, seek safety in numbers. The second layer of this move, and the one that probably meant the most, was that the men from Florida wanted Renee and Vaughn together, not separate. So if things played out poorly, if these men caught them, better to make it happen one at a time. That would slow things down, and when you slowed things down you had more time to come up with a countermeasure.

"Is there any way we can get help?" Renee said.

Ezra took his cell phone out to humor her. Nobody could get here fast enough, and anybody who might wasn't going to be the sort of cop who could help with these guys. It'd be a Fish and Wildlife officer or a sheriff's deputy or some other poor bastard who'd do nothing but add to the death toll.

"No signal," Ezra said, the whitest of lies, because the phone showed just one tiny bar, the barest hint of a connection. "We got to get moving again. First thing we're going to do is split up."

Renee was silent. Vaughn said, his voice wary, "Split up *how*?"

"You and me are going to be on the shore," Ezra said, gesturing north of where they sat, "and she's going to stay on this island. Temporarily."

"No way." Vaughn shook his head. "No chance I'm leaving her alone. You're a damn coward."

"We're splitting up to protect her," he said, speaking to Vaughn and pointing at Renee. "She stays here while we go across to the main shore, and we'll make sure they *know* that we're going there. We'll beach the boat in the open, make it obvious."

"No," Vaughn said, but Ezra ignored him and spoke to Renee.

"You're a swimmer, right?"

"Yes."

"How good?"

"Very."

He pointed west across the water as lightning lit up the bay. "Can you make that shore?"

It was a hell of a swim, but she nodded.

"All right. Anything happens and you're on your own, that's the one to shoot for. Walk far enough, you'll hit a fire lane."

"I'm *not* leaving her!" Vaughn spun toward Ezra, leaning close. "You want to go on and lead them into the woods, do it, man. Go ahead. But I came here to take care of her, and I am going to do it."

"No," Ezra said. "You're not."

Vaughn stared at Ezra with a strange flicker in his eyes. It surprised Ezra, almost made him want to lean back, a crazy quality in the look.

"You want to take care of her," Ezra said, "then you'll help me occupy these boys."

"I'm not—"

"Please, Vaughn," Renee said, and her voice was gentler than Ezra had heard before. "Please."

That stopped him, and he looked away from Ezra and stared at Renee. "I can take care of you," he said. "We don't need to listen to him, Renee. We don't need him."

"Yes, we do," she said, tone stronger now.

Ezra couldn't hear his boat's engine anymore. That meant they were stopped, which probably meant they were at the island, checking the empty cabin.

"We got to go," Ezra said, "and you're coming with me."

Vaughn sat in a furious silence while Renee climbed off the boat and into the puddles and mud onshore.

Ezra reached under his seat and found the gun he'd taken from her on the porch, the one she'd stuck in his eye. "Here."

She took the gun, and Ezra gave her a good-luck nod and then pushed the boat offshore, sent them back into the water as she walked toward the trees. Before he fired up the motor, he reached behind his back and withdrew the gun he'd taken from Vaughn on the beach earlier that day, held it out.

"You ever actually used this?" he said.

Vaughn's eyes were dark and small, his face wet with rain.

"Yes," he said. "I've used it. Probably in ways you wouldn't guess."

"Fantastic," Ezra said. "Maybe you'll get to tell me the story sometime. Right now, it's time to move."

He pressed the gun into Vaughn's palm.

Thirty-two

They were back in the boat as the rain billowed down at them like laundry tossing on the line, flapping in gentle gusts, but each gust was a solid wall of water. Nora's hair clung to her neck in tangles, water running into her mouth and eyes, the whole world gone wet, lake and sky blending into a liquid universe. She sat in the back with King's hand locked into her arm, his gun close, as Frank started the engine and took them back out into the lake.

AJ's mood was different than it had been before the island, wilder, his self-control held together by a few overstretched threads. She wasn't sure if it was the realization of what he'd done back at the cabin catching up with him or more a sense of anticipation—it was now clear that Ezra knew they were coming.

But did he? Was he really somewhere north of here, taking refuge in the storm with Renee and Vaughn? Or had Frank been lying, saying whatever it took to get that gun out of his mouth?

The engine roared louder behind her and the boat lifted again, shoving her backward, tightening King's grip on her arm. She'd have another set of bruises from him now, more blue streaks from his big ugly hands.

They hammered across the lake, the bow banging against windblown waves, and for some reason her thoughts turned to her mother, always wanting Nora married off and tucked away from the world, and Nora suddenly wondering if this was why. The world could send its evil blowing into your life disguised as something as innocent as a car with a smashed front end, and you'd never see it coming.

But she should have seen it coming. Had known even as she pocketed the two thousand dollars that her father wouldn't have done it, that he'd have demanded ID and some more information, or maybe refused the car altogether.

Her focus should probably have been on the hand that was digging into her arm and the guns around her, but she couldn't take her mind off the earnest, pleading look on the face of the man she'd believed to be Dave O'Connor as he'd put the cash into her palm and assured her he could be trusted. She closed her eyes, reopened them, tried to see the lake instead of the mistake that had taken her here.

This far north, there was nothing to see except wilderness. The trees lined the shore in unbroken formation, like soldiers from some ancient battle massed and ready for action. Here and there stumps and weathered trees jutted out of the water, and the sky was empty of the osprey and eagles and gulls that normally filled it, empty of everything but roiling clouds and sheets of rain. AJ was speaking into Frank's ear and pointing, sending Frank along first one shore and then the other, cutting back and forth across the lake, searching for Ezra and the others. It was a random, worthless method, even Nora knew that. Someone like Ezra would be able to hide the boat so well that they'd never find it, not if they spent the whole weekend out here. He probably had it onshore by now, dragged into the woods and covered with branches and underbrush, utterly invisible.

So what then? What would AJ and his near-the-breaking-point temper do when he realized they'd never find the boat?

She hadn't formulated an answer to that question yet when Frank abruptly dropped the throttle and the boat sloshed to a stop, rocking on its own wake. Nora stared over his shoulder and felt her stomach dip with horror and astonishment—the boat was dead ahead. Not hidden at all, completely unconcealed, in fact, just sitting there on the flooded main shore, tied among the trees, dead center in the bay, visible from a hundred yards out even in the storm.

What was Ezra thinking? Had he lost his mind?

Ezra sat in the wet leaves for a long time with Vaughn at his side, thinking about the line he'd uttered as Ezra passed him the pistol and asked if he knew how to use it. *I've used it. Probably in ways you wouldn't guess.*

He thought about that and about the way Vaughn had re-acted to being separated from Renee, the sort of desperate need he'd shown for her, took those two moments and put them together with the worry he'd had before, the notion that Vaughn was not the sort of man Devin seemed likely to turn to in a time of crisis. He considered all of those things for a while as they sat in the rain and waited for their pursu-ers, and after a long time he turned to Vaughn and said, "Devin's alive."

Vaughn had been staring out at the lake, and now he con-tinued to do that, but everything in him seemed to shut down, not a breath coming, not a blink.

"He is alive," Ezra repeated. "Left the hospital yesterday. Hasn't been seen since. The way Frank heard it from the FBI, they think Devin might have been headed this way."

This time, Vaughn got himself together enough to muster an attempt. He cocked his head, turned away from the water to face Ezra, and said, "I don't know if I believe you, but if you're serious, then that's good news."

Ezra said, "No. It is not good news for you."

"I don't understand," Vaughn said.

"I think I do," Ezra said. "I think I understand."

Vaughn's tongue slipped out of his mouth and ran across his lips, as if they needed moisture even with the rain beat-ing off his face.

"Now," Ezra said, "it being just the two of us out here in the rain, and Devin's wife far from hearing range, I'd like to ask you a question and receive an honest answer. Did you shoot him?"

"What? Man, we sat on that porch and I *told you*—"

"I know what you told me," Ezra said, "and this time I'm asking for the truth."

A gust of wind blew hard for a few seconds, bending the treetops and showering Ezra and Vaughn with water, and then it faded and the rain slowed and the woods grew quiet around them.

"I'm the only chance you've got today," Ezra said. "You better *know* that, friend. I'm it. And I need the truth."

There was a long pause, and then Vaughn said, "She's scared of him. That's all it was. She doesn't love him. How could you, guy like that? But how do you leave him, too? I'd be scared, if I was her."

"You think she's in love with you?" Ezra said. "Because I didn't see that."

Vaughn tensed, a quick flash of anger. "She could be. She might be. Man, you haven't seen us, you don't know what you're talking about. I spent times with her, so many times, when she was telling me how much she liked all the ways I was different from him, how a guy . . ."

His voice trailed off, but Ezra understood what Vaughn never would, that Renee had been part of the game, packaged with the cash to keep this guy happy and playing for Devin's team. Someone in law enforcement, buying him off might not be enough protection. Devin would have wanted to bring Vaughn in close, lure him as near as possible so he could be watched. You looked for something that kept a guy like Vaughn on the hook. Renee, it seemed, had played that role awfully well.

"Were you having an affair with her?" Ezra asked. "Sleeping together?"

Vaughn shook his head. "No. It wasn't there yet. But she was scared of him, and I know she wanted to leave him, I *know that for a fact*."

He hissed the last line at Ezra, spit showing on his lips.

"All right," Ezra said slowly. Then, "Why'd you run *here*? Of all the places you could have gone, you came here?"

Vaughn didn't offer an answer, but after a moment Ezra gave himself one. "You needed someplace that would seem like Devin's idea. To convince her."

That got a nod. "He'd talked about it once. Right at the beginning. Offered me the place if I wanted to stay there, you know, a vacation or whatever. Wrote your name down"— he nodded at Ezra—"and said I should just call you and say when I was coming. He acted like it was funny, though. Seemed real entertained by it."

"He would have been," Ezra said. "I promised him if he ever came back here, I'd kill him. He probably thought it would be real damn funny if you called me and said he'd sent you. If you thought you'd killed the guy, though, why did you need to run at all?"

"To be with her," Vaughn said, his voice barely audible. "To be with her, away from the rest of it. To show her what I could be. That I could take care of her. That I could be like him, only . . . better. If she knew that he'd trusted me, if she knew . . ."

He looked up at Ezra, hope filling his eyes. "You won't tell her. Will you? You hate him, too. You understand."

"I am a damn fool," Ezra said. "An old fool."

"What?"

Ezra stared down at him, felt contempt for Vaughn and loathing for himself rising warm out of his belly.

"People are dead, and more are going to die," he said. "For you. And I'm out here protecting you."

"You think I wanted that? Think I wanted any of you people anywhere *near* us?"

Ezra didn't answer.

"You won't tell her," Vaughn repeated. "Right? You said you'd promised to kill Devin. You just told me that. So you understand."

So he understood. This sniveling, murdering little shit was looking Ezra in the eyes and seeing a kindred spirit.

"I will tell her that her husband is alive," Ezra said.

"What?"

"He is alive," Ezra said, "and she deserves to know that. You didn't kill him, and now whatever you were hoping to pull off with her, it's over."

"It's not over," Vaughn said, speaking carefully, "if Devin is dead."

It was quiet for a minute, his suggestion hanging in the air.

"No," Ezra said. "No, we're not killing anybody so you can get his wife. I'm not being a part of that."

"You said you *wanted* to kill him." Vaughn was pushing off the ground, his body rising with his voice. "You just *told* me that the reason he didn't come back up here anymore was because you said you'd kill him. So what do you care, man? It's nothing to you."

Nothing to him. Vaughn was right about that. Yet here Ezra sat with him in the wet woods with a gun in his hand and a bloody mess headed his way. He started to speak but stopped when he heard a motor.

They were here. He leaned out of the trees and looked across the water, Vaughn joining him, and saw his boat out in the lake, coming to a stop about a hundred yards from shore. Ezra could see four figures in the boat, recognize Nora but none of the others. It could be Frank behind the wheel. Yes, that was probably Frank. They'd make him run the boat.

"Is Devin out there?" Vaughn said. "If he's out there, man, kill him and let's be done with it. Just let us go. Let me take Renee and go."

"*Shut up.*" Ezra wanted to lift his gun and bring it down in the middle of Vaughn's face, hit him again and again until his lips were smashed into his teeth and he couldn't say another word.

The motor came back to life, and the boat was headed their way, coming into shore. Ezra watched them come, saw that it was indeed Frank behind the motor, and wished again for his rifle. It would be over now, if he had his rifle. Instead, they had to wait and let the battle come to them. It wasn't what he wanted.

They landed the boat, and Ezra rolled back against the base of the tree, looked at Vaughn, and said, "They're coming onshore, and we'll let them come, okay? These guns, they don't have the range we need. So we've got to sit here and wait, wait *quietly*."

Vaughn didn't answer or even nod, just looked at Ezra with blank eyes. A hell of a combat partner he was going to be. It was up to Ezra, nobody backing him up out here, no Frank Temple or Dan Matteson like in the old days.

"When they come on shore," Ezra began, but he was interrupted from further instructions by the sound of another motor. What the hell? From where he stood, he could only see his boat, and the big Merc was shut down. He shifted a few steps to the side, knelt again, found the little aluminum boat. Yes, there was someone on board, starting the engine. Frank was on the beach, pushing the aluminum boat back into the water. Ezra had wedged it well into the sand.

Frank got the boat free, climbed in with the tall man who was at the motor, and then both boats pulled away, out into open water. Kept going until they were a good two hundred yards offshore, and then the anchor went out from the little boat, which was pitching hard in the wind.

"Shit," Ezra said, watching them. This was a good move. A damn good move. They didn't want to have to follow Ezra into the woods and leave both boats on shore. If they made a mistake and let Ezra double back and return to the boats, that would be end of it. With just two guys, they also couldn't afford to leave one guarding the boats. The solution, one Ezra would have considered if he were in their shoes and felt good about how much time he had, was to remove one of the boats. With this storm keeping the lake desolate, they had the time.

"What are they doing?" Vaughn said, whispering even though there was no chance of being heard down on the beach.

"They're moving one of the boats offshore. Far enough away that we can't get to it. Then they'll come back."

They would come back in his boat, which was bigger and

faster and also possessed the most important quality for this situation: It required a key to start. Take the key with you and the boat was dead in the water, unlike the little boat with the outboard and its pull cord. Ezra had no second key hidden away on the boat, but he could probably hotwire the thing if he had enough time. Finding that sort of time, though, was difficult when people were shooting at you.

Far out on the water, an exchange was taking place on the two boats, men stepping off one and into the other. They'd anchored almost directly across from the island where Ezra had left Renee, no more than fifty yards from its shore, and he hoped she was well hidden.

The exchange was completed, and it looked like Ezra had been right and they were taking the little boat on their return trip. The showdown was coming, and Vaughn didn't matter anymore, could be dealt with later, after this last bit had played out.

If the first goal was to separate Nora from AJ and King, then Frank supposed he should count this as progress. It was hard to believe that, though, as he watched King bind Nora's hands behind her back with duct tape, then wrap her ankles together. She'd given up on fighting him by then, but when he advanced on her with the piece for her mouth, she spoke.

"No. Please don't cover my mouth."

He snapped the tape over her face, wrapped it around her jaw until it tangled in her hair, and then added another, shorter strip. The fear grew in her eyes when her mouth was covered, and Frank wondered if she was claustrophobic. They had her stretched out in the small boat they'd taken. AJ kept his gun on Frank while King handled the tape work, and Frank had put up a little bit of an argument, just enough to let them think he opposed this. In reality, it was for the best. He felt bad for Nora, couldn't meet her eyes because the panic that showed there was tough to take, but he knew it would be easier if he was alone with these two. Nora was a liability, an extra concern anytime he decided to take action. With that eliminated, he was a little freer. Now the only person who would die immediately if he screwed up was himself.

"You're staying with her," AJ told King, and that quickly all of Frank's hope for this situation began to disappear. "Wait till we're on the shore. The minute we hit that, you start watching the clock, all right?"

No, Frank thought. *No clocks, no countdowns, please don't say that.*

"Ten minutes go by, you put a bullet in her head. No hesitation."

"Won't be a problem," King said, and he leaned down close to Nora's horrified face, stroked her cheek with the back of his hand. "Won't be a problem at all, will it, hon?"

The lake and the land surrounding it seemed to tilt and spin around Frank, that time limit—*ten minutes, ten minutes, ten minutes*—scorching through his brain, every possible scenario filtering through, none of them any good. It was too little time.

"You can't—" Frank wasn't even sure what words would have followed, because they never got the chance to develop. AJ hit him backhanded with the gun, caught him flush in the face and knocked him back into the boat, almost over the side and into the water. Blood left his nose, ran down his chin, and onto his shirt.

"Get up," AJ said.

Frank stayed down, looking at his own blood.

"Get up!" AJ screamed it this time, then almost lost his balance in a wild kick aimed at Frank's chest that instead hit the seat above him. The boat was rolling in the windblown chop. Frank got to his feet, fat red drops of blood speckling his jeans.

"Start the engine," AJ said, shoving him into the seat behind the wheel. "And take us back. We're almost done."

Frank turned the key over and the motor growled and then they were in motion, pulling away from the aluminum boat where Nora—*ten minutes, ten minutes, ten minutes*—waited bound and gagged and alone with King.

A sharp ache cut into Frank's ribs as AJ leaned forward,

pressing the gun against him, and shouted, *"Faster!"* into his ear. Nothing to do from this position that wouldn't generate a bullet in the lungs, and the only power Frank controlled— the boat—was useless now, too. If he rolled it or wrecked it and somehow pulled off the miracle of escaping unharmed, King would still be back on the boat with Nora, watching and ready to produce the planned result without the ten-minute wait. Whatever happened would have to happen in the woods, and it would have to happen fast. Frank leaned over the wheel, holding his shirt to his bloody nose, and slammed the boat through the lashing water. As the blood began to clot and the wind tore at his eyes, he tried to coax some insight or reassurance or reminder of old lessons from that voice in his head one more time. None came. The old man had said his piece.

"Slow down and land it," AJ shouted. There was no real beach on this part of the shore, just trees giving way to rocks. The water was high this early in the year, and some of the smaller trees near the shore were almost submerged, only the tops showing. Frank brought the boat in among them, felt the stern shudder as the prop chewed through some branches. The rain was driving into the trees, swept by that strong western wind. It was going to be a wet, slippery climb to the top of the slope.

"Tie it up," AJ shouted, pointing at the half-submerged tree just off the bow. "Cut the motor and tie it up!"

Frank got the stern line tied to one of the protruding limbs, but the wind had pushed the boat backward so quickly that the bow was now facing away from the island, toward the thin shape that was the boat with Nora and King.

"All right," AJ said, tearing the key out of the ignition and sliding it into his pocket. "You lead the way, and stay close."

Stay close so Ezra would have trouble getting a clean shot. Frank stepped out of the boat and sank up to his waist, would have sunk deeper if his feet hadn't found a stump. AJ splashed over the side behind him, and then they were both stumbling through the water, pushing branches aside. The water was cold, crawled up through Frank's legs and into his chest even though he was already drenched from the rain. He slogged through the small trees and stumps, slipping and splashing until he was out of the water except for his feet, facing a muddy slope lined with small saplings that seemed to grow horizontally. Then one more step and his foot touched the gravel bank and he felt like it was coming down on a land mine, that clock—*ten minutes, ten minutes, ten minutes*—starting to tick back on the boat.

"Start climbing," AJ said, his breath warm on Frank's neck. He was staying right at Frank's back, determined not to give Ezra a shot.

He fought his way up the slope, using the saplings for handholds, his feet sinking into the muck, his brain counting seconds and subtracting them from ten minutes. They got to the top of the hill and stood gasping for breath and staring into dark trees that were shaking with wind and rain. No one in sight.

"Ballard!" AJ shoved Frank forward again, toward the trees, and bellowed the name. "Ezra Ballard, if you hear this, you listen sharp. Out on the boat is the girl from the body shop. Nora, I believe is the name. You know Nora, don't you?"

They were into the woods now, and AJ paused when a prolonged ripple of thunder threatened to drown out his words. The thunder passed, and after one flash of lightning, he began to shout again.

"The minute we landed, you started to run out of time. That girl's got ten minutes of life left. Those ten run out, and she takes a bullet right in her beautiful face."

They were fifty yards into the woods now, walking without purpose, and Frank realized AJ was banking completely on the assumption that Ezra was close enough to hear him. What if he wasn't, though? They were just going to walk around out here, shouting into the wind, until ten minutes were gone and Nora was dead?

"You can stop that," AJ yelled. "What I want is Vaughn and Renee! You send them out and this is done. Renee, babe, you hear me? Devin is alive. Devin is alive!"

Eight minutes. That's what Frank expected they had left. Maybe seven? The climb up the slope might have taken longer than he thought. Either way, it was time to act. He'd been waiting on Ezra, praying for Ezra, but the woods around them were silent except for the rain and the echoes of AJ's shouts.

"Come on! Let me know you hear me!" AJ screamed it, his voice fading on the last word, and then went quiet and they both listened. There was no sound.

Thirty-three

What Ezra thought, kneeling in the wet earth beside a fallen pine, was of another word with *old* tacked on the front of it, the sort that had been tormenting him. *Old game.* Unlike those phrases that had run through his mind earlier, this one wasn't a negative, had no doubts chasing it. Instead, it was an *old* of familiarity, as in *old friend.*

Old game meant Ezra knew the game. Had played it well. Few were better at it, in fact, and this son of a bitch shouting into the trees wasn't going to be one of them. There were no doubts now, because there were no decisions to make. Only one outcome would work.

"Seven minutes!" Another shout. "That's how long you've got to cooperate!"

To cooperate? No, friend, you do not understand. The seven minutes may be accurate, and important, but the cooperation? Not a part of the game that I play. Those minutes mean something altogether different to me.

How long I have to kill your friend on the boat.

The shouting man and Frank were already twenty yards behind Ezra and Vaughn and pushing farther away, walking in a straight line and making so much noise that there was no way they could hear anyone around them. Ezra might have taken a shot if he'd had to, but the one thing this guy did that was smart was stay pressed against Frank, preventing a clean line of fire. That was all right, though. If the time limit was honest, then the guy who mattered most wasn't in the woods anyhow. He was back in the boat with Nora, well out of handgun range.

A damn good thing, then, that this idiot had just ferried Ezra's rifle back across the lake and left it behind in the boat.

He let them push on, still shouting, for another fifteen steps, and then turned back to Vaughn, who was stretched out on his face in the wet leaves and dirt. Ezra nudged him with the toe of his boot, and Vaughn lifted a mud-streaked face.

"I'm going to the boat. You're staying here."

Vaughn had a wild, unfocused look, the one he'd been wearing ever since Ezra had told him that he would not kill Devin, that he would not preserve these lies for Renee.

"Stay here," Ezra repeated. "If he comes back, shoot him."

"No, don't—" But Ezra was already moving, taking advantage of another roll of thunder that offered some additional sound cover. He moved on his belly, using his knees and forearms, a quiet and fast crawl that had saved his life more than once. Saved his old life, saved old Ezra.

They walked deep into the woods with AJ shouting out a constant stream of threats and explanations, intimidation and coercion. None of it got a response. The rain was falling harder than ever, slapping through the trees beneath steady rolls of thunder. When the lake was out of sight, AJ grabbed a fistful of Frank's shirt and shoved, pointing him so they were now walking north, parallel to the shore.

"You start talking now," AJ said. "Make that old bastard hear you. Only a couple minutes left."

AJ was right; there couldn't be much time left at all— three minutes, maybe—and still Frank hadn't made a move, just walked along and waited as if some great opportunity were going to present itself. That wasn't going to happen.

"I said talk," AJ hissed.

"Ezra!" Frank called, and his voice sounded wooden and too soft. He shouted louder. "Ezra, if you can hear us, answer, or people are going to die. Nora's back there on that boat. Answer us!"

The answer Frank wanted Ezra to provide was a bullet right between AJ's eyes, but neither it nor a verbal response was offered.

"Old man is going to let her die," AJ said. "You believe that shit?"

Frank started to yell again, then stopped, his eyes going toward a spot fifty feet ahead. The ground seemed to give way there, dipped down a short, steep hill and then rose again on the other side, a sort of sinkhole. It was the best spot he'd have, and he shifted slightly to the left, walking toward it, AJ so distracted by searching the trees that he didn't notice or, if he did, didn't react. The hole would give Frank a chance. Make a move on AJ right now and his first instinct would be to fire. With the gun pressed against his spine, that wasn't an instinct Frank wanted to encourage. Make a move that started a fall, though, and do it fast enough, and the shooting response might not be AJ's first instinct. Catching himself, stopping the fall, would come first. Right?

Better be right. If it wasn't, then Frank was dead.

"Keep talking," AJ said. His voice was tense and he jerked his head around constantly, peering into every shadow, shaking rain out of his eyes, his confidence slipping. These dark woods were not home to him. His sort of killing was done in different places, under streetlights and in alleys and at construction sites. He didn't like it out here, didn't trust himself the same way in this environment. Good.

"Ezra, damn it, *answer us*!" Frank shouted, completely unaware of the words leaving his mouth, focused instead on a quick mental rehearsal, choreographing the move he was going to need to make.

AJ was behind him, holding the gun against Frank's back. That was okay, though. He'd done it this way before, down in that basement in Chicago, his father coaching him through the steps. This was the normal position, the way you held a gun on somebody when you were sure he couldn't take it away from you. Stand behind him and jam the gun into his back and you had the illusion of total power and control. No way the guy in front could move fast enough to take the gun from you, right? No way.

It could be done, though, had been done before.

Take the gun away from me, Frank. Come on, kid, too slow. You don't have a chance. You know how many times you'd have died already, trying this? So slow, so slow. Come on, try again. Oh, shit, almost had it that time.

They'd practiced it over and over until Frank could pull it off every time, one of his father's favorite routines because it showcased Frank's speed, and Frank Temple II had *loved* his son's speed. Today the circumstances were right, too. AJ was standing against Frank's back, thinking that this was the proper approach because he was using Frank for protection, for a shield. It was also keeping him close, though, and close was where Frank needed him to be.

They were closing in on that dip in the earth, a simple, unimpressive slope that held Nora's best chance at life. The drop-off was in full view now, and Frank saw it was maybe ten feet from top to bottom. It would be a simple step sideways and a sweep of his right arm and leg, have to do it *damn* fast, but if he pulled it off he could send AJ down the slope.

Your gun is on his back. Tucked in his belt on his back, and if you make a perfect grab, you might get it. Don't even worry about the gun in his hand. Just get him in front of you and headed down the hill and then go for the gun in his belt.

The drop-off was just in front of them, almost there, but AJ was pulling him away from it now. Shit, he couldn't let that happen, needed the hill. Frank stopped, bringing AJ up with him, and pointed into the trees.

"What?" AJ said.

"Somebody moving, I think. I don't know . . ." Frank started walking again, toward the imaginary source of noise, and AJ followed. They were walking alongside the drop-off, and Frank's pulse was drilling away but his breathing seemed frozen. Four more steps, now two, now one . . .

In the end, he didn't go with the move he'd rehearsed in his mind, that sidestep and sweep. It had sounded good, sounded like the only thing to try, but in the second that he moved, instinct took over and some subconscious part of his brain told him it wasn't going to work. Instead of sidestepping he simply spun, a full, fast pivot that took his back away from the gun as he lifted his left arm and held it out straight and kept on turning, caught AJ across the shoulder and drove him forward.

It turned out he'd been wrong; AJ's first instinct still was to fire. The gun went off a half second after Frank had spun away from it, tore through the air inches from his flesh. Then his arm hit and knocked AJ toward the drop-off. They were a step too far away, and AJ might have been able to recover if Frank hadn't gotten a foot against the back of his knee as well, ruining any chance of balance he'd had left. AJ stumbled and fell and there was the gun in his belt, right there, all Frank had to do was reach out and . . .

He got it. His fingers closed on the stock and then AJ was gone and tumbling through the wet leaves and broken branches to the bottom and the Smith & Wesson was out of Frank's left hand and into his right and lifted and aimed.

For one fleeting second, he waited. Just long enough for AJ to land at the bottom of the drop-off and turn back to Frank and start to lift his own weapon. Frank let all of that happen, let him get that close, and then he squeezed the trigger once and killed him with a single round below his right eye socket.

Thirty-four

They'd been alone on the boat for maybe five minutes before King began to talk to Nora.

"Uh-oh," he said, turning back to her with a slight smile. He'd been standing, or trying to stand, in the pitching boat and watching AJ and Frank head off.

"Know where they are now, baby? On the shore. And you know what that means." He tilted his wrist, looked at it, and then frowned. "Damn. Look who forgot his watch. That's no good. How am I going to know when ten minutes go by?"

He leaned close to her, and she tried to slide away but found it impossible with both hands and feet bound. His face, long and angular and covered with rough stubble, was against hers, his breath on her cheek.

"I'll have to guess," he said. "You know, estimate? I was always bad at that, though. Thought five minutes felt like ten."

The wind rose again in a hard gust, and the boat rolled. He put out his hand to catch himself, falling almost on top of her, his legs heavy against hers. Somewhere in her stomach liquid churned, threatening to rise. No, no, no, she couldn't be sick, not with that tape over her mouth. Get sick and she'd choke on it, die, make this even easier on him.

"Look at that," King said, pushing her sideways, running his fingertips along her forearm, over the bruises he'd left two days earlier. "Little love marks. They from me? I bet they are."

She was stretched out on the seat, and he was on his knees now in the bottom of the boat, not even looking at the island, just staring into her face as the wind pulled his shirt tight across his chest and the rain dripped down his face and onto hers. He reached out and took her hair in his hand, squeezed hard enough to make her eyes sting.

"It was dumb-shit luck that kid showed up when he did. Too bad, because we were going to have some fun, you and I. Might still have some." He rocked his hand left to right, jerking her head sideways. "I take that tape off your mouth, we could have some *serious* fun. But you might be a biter. Yeah, I could see that. You're the type, aren't you? Angry little bitch. So maybe that tape stays."

He lifted her by her hair, and she would have screamed if the tape didn't prevent it. Her eyes were streaming now, nose following suit, the pain demanding a physical response. He pushed her back against the side of the boat and leaned against her, pressing his body down on hers. The sudden change was almost too much for the boat; they rocked hard to one side, and he pulled back at the last possible second, the boat rolling with him. What if he hadn't recovered? What if they'd just kept going over, ended up in the water, with tape over her mouth and her hands and feet bound? She'd die then, too. That or wait the ten minutes.

"That tape stays," he said, flicking his index finger off her mouth, smashing her lip back against her teeth. "Keep you from biting. Tape on the hands can stay, too. You won't need those."

He moved suddenly, slammed her head back against the boat hard enough to make her vision blur, and then he got to his feet and moved back to the bow, leaned against it, and stared into the woods. She tilted her head, tried to see what he was looking at. The angle wasn't right, though, and she couldn't turn any farther without rolling her whole body over. Didn't want to do that, and draw his attention back, so instead she kept craning her neck in that awkward position and tried to see where the boat had gone.

She couldn't see the boat, could hardly see the main shore.

There was another island that she could see, but that wasn't where AJ had taken Frank. She let her eyes pass over that shore and then started to look away, wanting to ease that awful pressure on her neck, when she saw motion.

There was someone on the island. No, couldn't be. She was seeing things, some weird reflection, the sun playing tricks even behind the dark clouds. Where had it gone? Wait, there it was again. Yes, someone was moving through the trees on the island just beside them.

Nora kept herself in that awkward position, the pain momentarily irrelevant, and stared. Now the motion was gone, but she was positive she'd seen someone, and not where the boat had been beached. So had the boat been a trick, a ruse?

King turned back from the bow then, and Nora moved her head, but it was a second too slow. He'd seen her staring out across the water, seen the intense look in her eyes, and he followed it.

"Son of a bitch," he said, lifting the gun, and Nora knew she'd just ruined someone's chance to escape.

Ezra crawled to the top of the rise and paused, looking out across the angry gray lake. There was the boat, a few hundred yards out, small but visible. Wait till he had it in the scope. Wouldn't be small then, no, sir. Be nice and clear, a perfect picture of some poor bastard waiting to die.

He couldn't hear the shouting anymore, which could be good or bad. Maybe the idiot was out of shouting range now, and maybe he was quietly working his way back to the boat. Ezra didn't know, and he wasn't going to waste time worrying about it. Time was slipping away, and he needed to get out to his boat. They'd tied it up right in the middle of the stumps and partially submerged trees that surrounded this part of the shore. He could hear a rapping sound as the hull banged against a stump, and it made him like these bastards even a little less. Ezra took damn good care of that boat.

Maybe twenty feet of fairly open ground to cover before he reached the lake and had to plunge into that mess of branches and water, fight his way out to the boat. It would take about thirty seconds to get on board, but he'd be in the open the whole time, and if whoever was out there with Nora had a rifle, Ezra might die before he ever got to take a shot. Nothing to do about that, though. Times came when you had to gamble, that was all. Ezra had gambled before, and still had the dice in his hand.

He got his breathing steadied and thought about doing a countdown, ten seconds and then move, but decided the hell with it. A countdown didn't make it any easier, and he didn't have seconds to waste. He pushed off the ground with his hands and went upright for the first time since he'd left Vaughn, got his feet moving and ran down the hill.

It was a slippery, dangerous mess in the rain, and twice he almost went down on his face, righted himself somehow and kept moving, hit the water knee deep and sloshed through it as quietly as he could, hunching now, trying to stay below the boat. The whole procedure seemed loud as hell to him, but out there on the lake with the wind whipping across the bay he doubted they'd hear. If they were watching close enough they would have seen him by now, which meant he needed to get the gun out fast.

No shots came; no motor roared to life. He waded out to the stern, the water up almost to his armpits, and then braced his hands on the side of the boat and heaved. Damn, it was hard work. He was weighted down with water and wet clothes, and his upper body wasn't what it used to be. He got over, though, flopped across the side and slid down to the floor, lay there breathing hard for a few seconds and waiting for a shot that didn't come.

Still silent. He pushed himself into a sitting position and cast one glance at the console, saw the empty ignition. They'd taken the key, as he'd feared. That could be dealt with later, though. Right now, he needed the rifle.

He'd left it in the storage compartment under the floor, a space designed for fishing rods. He flipped the latch and lifted the cover and peered inside, felt a moment's horror when he saw nothing but rods. But there it was, tucked all the way against the side, a gun that had never seemed as beautiful as it did now.

It was a custom-built bolt-action rifle that Ezra had paid an absurd amount for six years earlier, and it was also the best long-range gun he'd ever held, one that would make the Browning A-Bolt and the Remington 700 look like pawn-shop pickups. A high-velocity cartridge rested inside, wait-ing to head out of that perfect bore at twenty-eight hundred feet per second. Each round that left this gun was a gorgeous product of engineering.

He pulled the rifle free and closed the storage compart-ment, then slipped the cover off the scope. It was a Yukon night-vision scope, a piece of equipment that cost more than Ezra had paid for some cars but that had seemed only an ap-propriate pairing for the rifle. He'd often chastised himself for both purchases, which felt like obscene wastes of money when he was in a rational mood. Today, it all felt incredibly cheap. He couldn't believe they'd ferried it right across the lake to him so unwittingly. His own enemy had delivered him his sword. Mercy be on their souls now.

Crawling back toward the outboard, he pressed himself in against the bench seat and lifted the gun barrel, rested it on the stern. Then he lowered his cheek to his shoulder, closed one eye, put the other to the scope.

A night-vision scope, even a good one like this, didn't demand total or near-total darkness for use. It had an infra-red illuminator that could be engaged for such conditions, but today the standard image tube was all Ezra would need. It gathered the natural light and enhanced it, and in this storm that would work fine. He slid the rifle left a few inches to bring the boat into view, tweaked the scope to clarify the scene.

The shouting man had not lied. There were two people in the boat, Nora Stafford and a big son of a bitch with a gun in his right hand. Nora had tape over her mouth, and the guy with the gun was—hold on a second, he had just lifted the gun.

The shot rang out loud and clear even in the wind and

rain, and for a second Ezra was absolutely baffled, because the guy was turned away from Ezra and firing across the lake. *What the hell?* Ezra thought, and then he got it: *Renee.* The tall man had spotted Renee and opened fire without bothering to see who the hell he was shooting at.

"Shit," he whispered and brought the crosshairs down quick, sighted along the big man's chest, his finger tight on the trigger. It was a hell of a long shot, even with the scope, at least a hundred and sixty yards. Tougher still because the guy was standing sideways from Ezra's position, offering only his profile. All these details ran through Ezra's mind fast and then were pushed aside because the son of a bitch had fired again and Ezra couldn't let him continue. He clenched his teeth together, steadied his breathing, and pulled the trigger.

It was maybe the best shot he'd ever made. Certainly the best he'd made so quickly. The bullet hit the guy in the neck, blew a cloud of blood into the air, and then he was falling forward, collapsing against the side of the boat. Shit, he'd fallen right on Nora. As Ezra watched through the scope, the boat tipped dangerously to the left. For a moment he thought the body would slide into the water and the boat would right itself, but somehow the guy hung up on the side. The boat rocked back to the right, but then Nora struggled beneath the body and her motion made it roll to the left again. There was a half-second pause where equilibrium was still possible, but she kept thrashing and the little boat overbalanced and tipped, spilling them both into the water.

"Damn!" Ezra lowered the gun and peered out, as if that would somehow help him see, then lifted it again and looked back through the scope. He hadn't meant to send them both into the water like that, but it wasn't the worst thing that could have happened. He'd seen the bullet's impact, knew that it had missed Nora, hitting at least three feet above her. She could swim, surely, or at least hang on to the upside-down boat until Ezra could get out there.

He kept the scope to his eye and watched the water and saw nothing. Nobody moving, nobody splashing. What the hell was she doing? Surely she hadn't been knocked out in the fall.

Then he remembered the tape.

Thirty-five

Nora didn't know *what* had happened. One second King was standing above her and firing at the figure on the island, and the next drops of blood showered across the boat and he collapsed on top of her. Her first thought was that lightning had hit him; her second was that the person on the island had returned fire. Then she felt the boat begin to tip, and the source of King's demise was no longer a concern.

They rolled backward until her hair was almost in the water, and she thrashed against him, trying to push forward, send them the other way. He was too heavy, though, and the tape kept her from using her arms or legs to push him off. She rocked back and threw herself forward again, a desperate heave, and still he was on top of her, his blood dripping through her hair and down her cheek. The wind gusted again, shook the boat just enough to worsen the lopsided weight, and they slid back toward the water. She had a fraction of a second to suck air in through her nose and brace for the cold, and then they were over the side and she was sinking.

She fell fast and soundlessly, dropped through the frigid water with a sense of terror and helplessness she'd never felt and couldn't have imagined before, strong and healthy and uninjured and dying all the same.

Bunched up the way she was, unable to kick with her feet or pull with her arms, she sank quickly, dropped all the way to the bottom. Her eyes were open, and she could see the shimmer of light that was the surface, knew that she would die staring up at it.

Then she bounced. She'd landed on her ass, but a final violent twist got her feet under her, and she realized that the tape had taken every important motion away from her except one: She could bend her knees.

She pressed her feet into the lake bottom and bent at the knees and pushed off as hard as she could, shot upward again. The lake wasn't deep here, maybe ten feet, and that one massive push was enough get her to the surface. Enough for one gasping inhalation through her nose. Then she sank again.

This time she was equally sure she'd die on the bottom. The little bit of air she'd gotten didn't feel like nearly enough, but she also didn't need to wait for the bounce this time, knew what she had to do, and so she landed with her feet out, almost upright. One more bend and push, one more rise, but she knew it was futile even as she headed toward the surface. She wasn't getting enough air with these brief appearances above the water, and the adrenaline-fueled strength was fading fast. She could manage another rise or two, maybe, but eventually she wouldn't come up fast enough and she'd frantically try for a breath and take in water instead, drown, and sink back to the bottom, this time for good.

She hit the surface, got a little more air this time, then sank again without ever seeing anything but angry dark clouds. Her feet hit the bottom and she went through that hopeless routine one more time, probably the last repetition she could manage, bend and push. This time she came up under the boat.

Her first reaction to breaking the surface beneath the upside-down boat was panic, but it saved her life. Instead of simply sinking again, she instinctively jerked her head backward, as if to clear herself out from under the boat. She didn't clear it, of course, but instead drilled the back of her skull against the aluminum frame, wedged between one of the seat brackets and the side of the boat.

She stuck. Only temporarily, for a few seconds, but it was enough to hold her head out of the water so she could get a breath and realize what had happened. Then she felt herself sliding away from the bracket, ready to sink again, and responded by arching her back. The motion forced her head back against the bracket and lifted her legs, and her body slid into an awkward floating position, as close to a survival float as you could possibly achieve with no arms to balance you. It wouldn't have been possible without the bracket there under her head, but it worked now.

Breathe. That was all she had to do, all she needed to worry about for this moment, just sucking air in through her nose, trying to get as much oxygen into her lungs as possible before she slipped out of this position and sank again. She hauled the air in, her chest rising and falling, got in at least five breaths before she began to slide away from the bracket again.

She tried to repeat the motion that had worked before, arching her back and lifting her legs, but this time she couldn't find the bracket, and her head kept sliding away.

No, no, no. Come back, I can stay alive here, I can stay alive . . .

The water was over her face and she was sinking again when she realized that it hadn't been her head sliding away from the bracket, but the other way around. The boat was moving, pushed aside. She watched it move as she dropped, was three feet deep and still going when legs bumped against her back and then an arm encircled her, wrapped around her neck and hooked under her chin and lifted.

A second later she broke the surface, blinked water out of her eyes, and stared at Renee, unable to utter a single word of thanks because of that damn tape.

Ezra dropped the rifle and got to his feet, hardly conscious of the assailant who still lingered in the woods behind him, and looked around his boat for some way to help.

The key was gone, and he didn't have time to hotwire the ignition. That left no power source but the electric trolling motor, and though it would surely be too slow it was the only chance he had. Ezra couldn't make a swim like that, not anymore.

A swim. The thought triggered a memory of Renee and the initial source of the shooting. She was so much closer to the overturned boat, and she could swim. Had she seen what happened? Did she know Nora was in the water?

He turned back to search the lake for her, but then something moved onshore behind him, and he whirled back to face it, reaching for the rifle.

"Shit," he said and picked up the rifle but left it pointed down. The movement on shore was from Vaughn, who had just stepped out of the trees, holding his gun ahead of him with a wavering grip.

"Come on!" Ezra yelled, turning to the trolling motor, a hopeless effort but the best he could now make for Nora. "Get out here."

Get Vaughn and go after Nora. That's what Ezra was thinking as he stepped up into the bow, the gun held loosely at his side, his eyes scanning the woods to see if anyone else was approaching. No, just Vaughn, and why wouldn't he hurry, and lower that damn gun before somebody got—

Vaughn fired from the shoreline, and for a second Ezra was so stunned he didn't react, but then he realized it hadn't been an accident and he got both hands around the rifle and lifted it as Vaughn took a second shot, missing again, and a third.

The third round caught Ezra in his right side, blew through his ribs and out of his back and splattered blood and flesh off the windshield that guarded the steering console. He tried to keep lifting the rifle, to get it aimed at Vaughn, but the bullet had spun him and now he was stumbling. His knees banged off the side of the boat and he couldn't right himself, flipped over the side and fell into the tangled branches of a partially submerged tree. The branches snapped under him, and he dropped into the water as Vaughn fired again, missing again. Ezra tried to lift the rifle, but it was too heavy now. Or was it even in his hand?

Another branch snapped, and he dropped again, and then the gray sky was fading into an odd red mist and Ezra couldn't focus anymore, couldn't see to fire even if he'd had the gun ready to shoot. The red mist spun into black and then shattered into jagged points of light, and Ezra Ballard closed his eyes and welcomed the water.

Renee got the tape off Nora's hands first, which allowed her to hang on to the boat while Renee freed her feet. The feeling of power, of *life*, that came back to Nora as she moved her legs and arms was intense. She could support herself again, move again, was no longer helpless. She tore the tape off her mouth, smacked her lips together and sucked in a grateful breath of air and rain, tasted the fresh water on her stale tongue.

"Thank you," she said. "Thank you."

The rain was hammering the overturned boat, a sound like a drum corps, but even so they both stopped talking and listened as another sound, a series of cracks, echoed over the water.

"Guns," Renee said. "Somebody's shooting."

Nora didn't say anything. The strength was already fading from her newly freed legs, and even the gentle kick needed to stay upright seemed difficult.

"Can we roll it over?" she said.

"The boat?" Renee shifted in the water, looked at the capsized boat as if surprised that Nora would want to be inside it. She was treading water easily, her breathing steady. Beneath the surface, her arms and feet moved in ghostly circles, her hair fanning out around her shoulders.

"Let's roll it," Nora said and leaned back and tried to push the craft up, succeeded only in driving herself deeper in the water.

"All right. We can try." Renee swam closer, dipped under the boat, and braced her hands on the edge, as Nora had. "On three."

It took them two tries, but they flipped it. The motor was the key; once that weight had shifted enough, it overbalanced the boat and did the rest of the work for them. By the time the boat was finally floating upright, though, they didn't have the strength left to climb into it. They waited for a few seconds, hanging off the side, and then tried again. This time Nora made it easily, then turned back and got her hand around Renee's forearm and helped her into the boat.

They sat there on the bottom of the boat, getting their breath back and staring at one another. The water had been freezing, but now Nora felt even colder as the wind fanned over them.

"Where are the others?" Renee reached up and gathered a handful of her hair, ran her hand down it in a fist, squeezing the water out. Her eyes were on the lake, away from Nora.

"On the island. Well, one of them is dead. The guy they left on the boat with me is dead. I think someone shot him. That's why we tipped over." Nora took a deep breath, wiped water from her eyes, and said, "And Devin is waiting at Frank's cabin."

Renee sat with her hand still wrapped in her wet hair and stared at Nora with a look that made Nora's neck prickle.

"What did you say?"

"Your husband is waiting at Frank's cabin."

Renee said, "You're confused," but Nora was already shaking her head.

"He's alive, and he's there," she said. "He's not in good shape, but he's alive. Vaughn shot him."

Renee let go of her hair. Her mouth was parted slightly, her eyes distant. "Vaughn shot him?"

"That's what Devin said." Nora watched the other woman's face, then added, "That's what Devin said while he put me and Frank into a van at gunpoint and came out here and had an FBI agent murdered at the cabin. The one named AJ killed him with a knife."

The words slid by Renee without any apparent effect. She said, "Vaughn shot Devin. I've been up here with him, and he's the one who shot Devin. He tried to kill Devin."

"Yes," Nora said.

Renee was looking at the lake without seeming to see anything. She said it again. "Vaughn shot him."

Nora was shivering violently now, the wind and her drenched clothing combining to drop her body temperature.

"Can we start the motor?" Renee said.

Nora turned and looked at it. The thing had been upside down for a while, but it still looked in place, everything as it should be.

"Probably."

"Try to start it, please."

"Where are we going?" Nora asked as she moved for the stern.

"To my husband. But first we're going to stop at that island. I left a gun there."

When he heard the first shot, Frank was down in the hole with AJ, relieving the body of its gun and the boat key. The sound almost dropped him to his knees, overwhelming him with a sense of defeat. He was too late. Ten minutes had gone by and Nora Stafford was dead. He'd let her die.

Then there was another shot, and a third, and it was this last one that got him moving again, because it hadn't come from a handgun. He recognized it as a rifle shot, and King didn't have a rifle.

He was running toward the shots but angled too far to the left and ran into a tangle of undergrowth that he and AJ had not encountered on their walk into the woods. At first he tried to push through it, but that was a bad idea, and he fought his way back out of it and ran parallel to the lake, looking for a gap in the brush that would let him get back down to the shore and to the boat.

He heard voices—it sounded like Ezra—and then there was another volley of shots, three in succession. Who was shooting? He slapped branches aside and cleared the trees, found himself at the top of a muddy bluff, Ezra's boat screened from sight. Out on the water, the smaller boat, where Nora and King should be waiting, seemed to have overturned and was now floating upside down in the lake. He could see people in the water.

The bluff was steep and slick with wet mud, but he fought his way down it, turning his feet sideways to limit his momentum, his shoes plowing furrows in the soggy earth, and then he was in the water up to his knees, splashing down the shore toward the collection of stumps and trees where he'd left Ezra's boat.

As he stumbled through the water, something began to happen with the boat out in the lake. It rose in the air once, then twice, and finally it flipped back over, resting upright again. Two people climbed onto it, and even from out here Frank could see that neither one was tall enough to be King. What the hell had happened? Was Ezra out there with Nora somehow? Or Renee?

When he came around the bluff, Ezra's boat appeared, and he saw Vaughn on board, standing in the stern, using the trolling motor to pull away from the island.

"Hey!" Frank shouted. *"Hey!"*

Vaughn turned at the sound, lifted a gun, and fired two wild shots that hit in the water some twenty feet to Frank's right.

"Stop shooting, you idiot! It's me! It's Frank!"

Vaughn was still holding the gun, but he stopped firing, hesitating, and Frank yelled, "Bring it over here! I've got the key!"

Vaughn looked down at the big, silent engine on the stern and then lowered his gun. He was struggling with the trolling motor, didn't seem to understand how to use it, and Frank, trying to go out to meet the boat, was now in water up to his chest, holding the gun high to keep it from going under.

Vaughn finally got the boat pointed in the right direction, and when it reached him Frank caught the side, took one deep breath, and heaved up, got his knee on the side, and used that leverage to force his way onto the boat.

He was collapsed on the starboard seat, fighting for breath, when Vaughn let go of the trolling motor and turned to him with the gun held out in a shaking hand.

"Give me the key."

Frank stared at him. "What? Get that gun out of my face, asshole."

"Give me the key!"

Out on the lake a motor coughed several times and then caught, and both Frank and Vaughn looked toward the sound and saw that the aluminum boat was in motion again, headed toward another island, away from them. Vaughn kept staring after it, and Frank planted his feet on the floor, then rose and swept Vaughn's gun down and away, hit him once in the chest with a closed fist. It knocked Vaughn back against the steering console, and Frank locked his left hand around Vaughn's wrist and twisted until the fingers opened up and the gun fell to the bottom of the boat.

"What the hell's the matter with you?" he said, his face close to Vaughn's, whose entire body seemed to be shaking. "You could have killed me, you stupid bastard."

Frank knelt and picked up the gun, wedged it beneath the seat, out of the way, and then put the key in the ignition and twisted. As the motor came to life, Vaughn moved away, and Frank straightened and stared out at the departing aluminum boat. It looked like Nora was at the motor. There was no way she'd hear him, so he lifted his arm and waved it in a slow arc. Finally she saw him and lifted her own hand, but kept taking the boat away, toward the other island.

"What's she doing?" Frank said, dropping to the seat and moving his hand to the throttle.

"Renee was on that island," Vaughn said.

"I think she's on the boat now. What happened to the one who was with Nora on the boat, though?"

Vaughn didn't answer.

"What about Ezra?" Frank twisted the wheel and turned the boat to go in pursuit of Nora and Renee.

"They shot him," Vaughn said.

Frank spun to face him. "What?"

Vaughn nodded, his jaw trembling. "Somebody shot him. He's dead."

"*Who* shot him?"

"I don't know."

"Well, where is he?"

Vaughn lifted an unsteady hand and pointed at the water.

Thirty-six

The sickness that had come and gone during those first few shots returned to Frank as he drove Ezra's boat away from the island where his father's old friend had been killed, was somewhere in the water now, joining Atkins, their blood spilling into the lake.

He imagined the bodies down there among the weeds and the stumps, fish swimming past, crimson clouds rising from the wounds and dissipating into the gray water, water that slapped gently against the log wall back at the cabin where Devin Matteson waited. It was on Devin, all that blood in the water, two more lives taken, adding to that total that included everyone Frank's father had killed, included Frank's father, who'd fired a bullet into his own mouth with the very gun Frank now held in his hand. *All* of this was on Devin, Atkins and Ezra and even the two thugs Devin had brought with him, the body count rising at his whim while he sat removed from it all, untouched.

That would end today. Frank was going back to that cabin and he was going to kill him. That would be the last of it. He'd kill Devin, and the others could call the police, and then let it end however it would end. He couldn't think about that, didn't care about it, nothing mattering anymore but getting back across this damn lake to put a bullet into Devin Matteson's heart.

"I'm sorry, Ezra." He whispered it, and if Vaughn heard

he did not react. There was some shared responsibility here, and all of his hatred for Devin didn't blind him to that. Ezra was dead, and Frank had a role in that. He'd come here for blood, and now he'd seen plenty of it, hadn't he? None from the correct source, though. That was the last thing he could make right, the only thing.

Nora had taken the other boat into the beach of the island, and as they approached Frank could see that she was still in the stern while Renee was onshore.

"What are you going to do?" Vaughn said. He was in the seat beside Frank, hands trembling on his thighs.

"We're going to get them and get out of here," Frank said. He'd brought Ezra's boat in alongside the other, was staring across at Nora, who looked back at him without saying a word. There were red streaks across her face from the tape that had covered her mouth.

"You okay?" he said, dropping the motor to idle, speaking as his boat thumped against hers.

"I'm here," she said.

"Ezra's dead."

She stared at him.

"Vaughn says they shot him. He's dead."

Nora didn't answer. What did he expect her to say, anyhow? He said, "Get in this boat, and we'll leave that one behind."

She nodded and got to her feet, and he reached out a hand to help her step over. As he did it, he turned to Renee, who was walking down from the island. She was moving at a fast, confident pace, stepped right into the lake without breaking stride, moving toward his boat, a gun in her hand.

"Hey," he said. "Get in. We're leaving."

She kept walking, the water up to her knees now. She hadn't even glanced at Frank; her eyes were locked on Vaughn.

"Put that gun down," Frank said.

She didn't say a word. Just walked along the boat toward Vaughn. Frank's own weapon was on the seat, and he turned and reached for it, thinking Vaughn might do the same, but instead Vaughn rose, climbing over the side of the boat and splashing into waist-deep water, moving toward Renee.

"Renee," he said. He had his hands outstretched, reaching for her. "Forgive me. It was for you. I love you so much, and you could never understand that, you couldn't see it, baby forgive me I did it because I love you so—"

He was a few feet away, still moving through the water toward her, still reaching for her, when she lifted the gun and fired. The bullet hit him in the temple and knocked him backward, snapped his head back and turned his eyes to the sky before he dropped into the water and then beneath it.

Frank had just gotten his hand on his own gun, and Nora was still standing in the rear of her boat, waiting to step across. She said something, some whispered gasp or oath or prayer, and Frank stood where he was, in a frozen reach for his gun, as Vaughn's body sank.

"Let go of that."

Renee's voice finally tugged Frank's eyes away from the spot where Vaughn had collapsed into the water, and he saw she was pointing the gun at him now.

"Let go of it and step back," Renee said. "We're leaving now. Just like you said."

Frank opened his fingers and dropped the gun back onto the seat and stepped away.

"Turn off that engine, and go over there and help her in," Renee said. "I'm not going to hurt either of you. Okay? But you're taking me back to my husband now."

Frank cut the engine and walked to the side of the boat and extended his hand for Nora's. She just stared at him, and Renee said, "Girl, get in the damn boat," and Nora took Frank's hand and stepped out of one boat and into the next.

"Okay," Renee said. "Now help me in. And, please, don't try to take this gun. We don't need that. I don't want to hurt anyone."

Frank didn't move, didn't speak. Renee stood there in the water holding the gun and staring at him with challenging eyes.

"He shot my husband," she said. "Shot him, and then brought me up here. I don't give a damn if you think I was wrong."

"He deserved it," Frank said. "Absolutely had earned it."

She looked at him strangely, and finally nodded. "Yes."

Her body looked incredibly small under those saturated clothes, her hair plastered against her face and neck, but her eyes were hard and her jaw was set. The gun looked comfortable in her hands, as if she'd held a few before.

"Help me into the boat," she said. "Now."

He walked into the bow, and she slogged through the water to get closer. He reached for her and she extended her free hand, grasped his, her palm smooth and slippery with lake water. When he had a firm hold he leaned back and pulled against her weight, not hard, just what was needed to give her an awkward lift and prove she'd need to use the other hand to help. She hesitated, looking once into his eyes as if searching for a sign of treachery, and then she put the gun down on the bow, still in her hand but temporarily useless as she tried to push off and get over the side.

Frank slid his foot over and placed it on her wrist, the fine bones trapped under his heel.

"Don't," she said, looking back at him. This time her face changed as she saw what was in his eyes now, what she'd missed in her first study.

"Let go," he said.

"Stop. I told you I wasn't going to hurt—"

He shifted his weight, pressed down on her wrist, and her words cut off in a gasp and then her fingers loosened and she released the gun and slid back off the bow. Frank leaned down and took the gun, worked it into his hand before lifting his foot and freeing her.

"Fine," she said. "You want the damn gun, keep it. I just want to get back to my husband. Let's get the hell out of here."

She stretched her hands up to him again, like a child wanting to be held. He stood where he was and looked down into her face.

"You killed Vaughn in cold blood."

"He deserved it. You said so yourself."

"Yes, I did. And you believe that what you did was right."

"Absolutely." She'd dropped her hands again, was watching him with wary expression.

He nodded. "Good. You and I, we think alike."

"Okay," she said. "So let's go."

He turned from her and faced Nora, who was standing in the back of the boat watching this all unfold with a horrified expression. There were splatters of blood on her arm. Vaughn's blood, probably.

"Nora," Frank said, "I'm going to have to ask you to get back in the other boat."

"What?"

"Please," he said, voice gentle. "If you'd get back into the other boat, I'd like you to take Renee and go to the dam. You know how to get there? Good. There's a bait shop right there, just down the road. Go there, and call the police."

"Frank . . ."

"Take the other boat and go get help," he repeated. "Please."

"Where are *you* going?"

He didn't answer.

"No," she said, shaking her head. "Frank, let's all go get help together. Don't go back for him. Let the police—"

"*Nora.*" He spoke with a stronger voice, and the emphasis made him move his gun hand, almost involuntarily. He hadn't meant it as a threatening gesture, but her eyes went to the gun and fear rode through them, and when she looked at him again he felt sickened.

"It's safer for you this way," he said, but she was already moving, had stepped over the side and back into the smaller boat, moving out of fear. Fear of him, of the gun in his hand and what he might do with it.

"Where's he going?" Renee said, her voice sharp with alarm. "What's he talking about? *Where are you going?*"

He didn't answer, just walked to the steering console and brought the motor to life and pulled away from them, trying not to see Nora, trying not to remember the way she'd looked when he'd moved the gun. He'd turn his mind elsewhere, to the things that needed remembering, things like Ezra's body under the water and Devin waiting at the cabin.

Thirty-seven

Ezra liked the trees. Loved the trees. They belonged on land, high above the water, but instead they were in it, supporting him, holding him to the surface. The trees didn't want to let him sink.

He imagined the bottom was way down there, forty or fifty feet at least. Maybe more. The trees that held him were massive. Oaks probably, or maybe birch? They were big boys, that was for sure. He hadn't realized how high the lake had risen this spring. All the years he'd been out here, the water had never covered fifty-foot trees. Lucky thing for Ezra this was the year. It must have been a hell of a flood. Strange he couldn't remember it.

Consciousness was difficult to hold, and the sky swam above him, but the trees kept his head out of the water and kept him breathing. There were moments when he'd start to slip, and the water would lap at his chin, but then—and this was the *damnedest* thing—the trees would grow. *Grow.* Right then in the moment he needed them most, they'd strain skyward and lift him an inch or two, whatever he needed. They were amazing trees.

He'd tried to use the branches to pull himself farther away, toward the shore, but pulling set off wild bells of pain, so he stopped that and just hung on, floating and waiting. No sense in going anywhere. The trees would grow when he needed them.

Vaughn was gone. Ezra had seen him take the boat, had managed to focus on that and actually lift his head a bit. Then the boat had moved away from him, down the shore and into deeper water, and there had been more gunfire, and though Ezra had no idea where it was coming from or who was causing it, he knew it was bad.

For a while he was waiting to die and not afraid of it at all, patient as could be. This was where he wanted to end. He wanted to bleed his life out into this lake, this beautiful lake that had given that very life to him. It was fine to end out here. It was right. He'd broken the vow he'd made so many years ago when he'd first come to this place, had taken a man's life once more, and the lake would not allow that. Had not allowed that, had sent Vaughn to punish him. All those years in the jungle with men who excelled at combat, and more years back in Detroit with some of the meanest sons of bitches ever walked the earth, and Ezra had gotten shot by someone like *Vaughn*? It was tough to get your head around a thing like that.

So he'd killed again and the lake had punished him, but then it had sent the trees to hold him up, and that was confusing, because he'd been ready to die and the trees would not let him. He didn't understand that. Perhaps the trees were a gesture of forgiveness. The lake had healed him once, and maybe it would heal him again.

A low grinding sound filled his brain, and for a while he was sure it was a motor, but then it went away, fading until it sounded like a drill bit chewing through wood. Maybe there was no sound, and that was just the pain fooling with his head. A bullet could do things like that to you.

A sprinkling rain started again, much lighter now, and it felt good on Ezra's face, helped to push the fog back. He thought he'd been floating above the surface, but now, after a hard blink to focus, he realized that the water only rose up to his shoulders. The water really wasn't that deep down here. Maybe if he reached with his foot . . .

Son of a bitch, he could touch the bottom. Now how was

that possible? The bottom should be way down there, at the base of the tree trunks, fifty feet away.

He tilted his head to the left, studied the tree that held him. The branches weren't so thick. In fact, they were little more than twigs. He wasn't in a tree at all. It was a bush, really, one of the wild tangles that grew along the shore. He was very close to shore, had his feet on the ground.

Ezra was not going to die out here. Not today.

Grady had stayed on 51 too long, had missed a turn that he should have taken, though he wasn't sure what it would have been. His state map was useless up here, he hadn't seen a single sign for the Willow Flowage, and Atkins wouldn't answer his phone.

He finally gave up as a gas station came into view, the highway a two-lane now, and pulled off and into the parking lot, got out of his car and ran inside and shoved past an overweight woman who gasped in indignation.

"Hey." The shaggy-haired kid behind the counter was looking down at the register, and when Grady stepped up he just lifted a finger, asking for a minute.

"*Hey!*" Grady said and slapped the countertop. When the kid looked up at him, a haughty expression on his face, Grady showed him the badge. "I need you to tell me how to get to Willow Flowage."

"Shit, man, FBI? For real?"

"Just tell me how to get there."

The kid frowned, offended, and pointed out the window. "Straight across the highway, man. Swamp Lake Road. Take that all the way in to County Y, then take that to Willow Dam."

"Swamp Lake to County Y to Willow Dam?"

"Yeah. What's going on?"

"Nothing. Look, I need to get to a cabin out there. I have no idea where it is. Could be anywhere on the lake."

The kid shook his head, and now the fat woman was standing close, listening with undisguised interest and clutching an armful of soda bottles to her large breasts.

"Not many cabins *on* the lake out there. Not many at all. You sure it's on the lake?"

"Yes," Grady said. "A guy named Frank Temple owns it."

That widened the kid's eyes. "No shit? I heard all about him."

"Fantastic. You know where—"

"Yeah, yeah, I can get you there."

"How long of a drive?"

"Maybe twenty."

Twenty minutes. Okay, that wasn't bad. Grady still had a chance. He would not be too late. He would *not* be too late.

A gentle rain faded to nothing as Frank crossed the lake, the clouds still heavy and dark but quiet now, the wind settling, the surface of the lake smoothing again.

Frank ran the boat at full throttle, knowing that the big engine would give him just enough time. He'd make it to the cabin maybe ten, fifteen minutes before Nora and Renee got to the dam, and that would be more than sufficient. It wasn't going to take long at all, maybe thirty seconds, walk through the door, put the gun in Devin's face, squeeze the trigger.

Simple.

And a long time coming.

And *right*.

Yes, damn it, it was the right thing to do. Ezra was dead, and so was Atkins, and Nora could easily have joined them. Forget Frank's father, forget the betrayal, forget the past entirely—Devin had earned it *today*. Earned more than handcuffs and a cell. It was time to bring him to an end.

The gun in Frank's hand was the Ruger he'd taken from Renee, and he discarded it as he crossed the lake, took the Smith & Wesson back, loving the feel of it, that FT II engraved on the stock. *Here's a bullet from the old man, Devin. Enjoy it. I know he will. Wherever he is, heaven or hell or somewhere in between, I know he will.*

He was utterly alone on the lake, even when he came through the Forks and out into the southern portion where the most boat traffic could usually be found. Nobody was going to venture out after a storm like that, with more rain threatening.

He dropped the speed as he neared the cabin, came in close to the shore and with the engine as quiet as possible until he saw the cabin. The van waited alone beside it. Nobody had noticed Atkins's absence yet, or if they had, they didn't know where to start looking for him. The cabin had one main window that looked out on the water, so Devin could be watching the lake right now, waiting for a boat to come in, sizing up the situation. If he saw it was Frank alone, he'd be ready.

Frank cut the engine and let the boat drift into the weeds. He was several hundred yards from the cabin and doubted Devin had seen or heard him. Possibly he'd heard the engine, but he couldn't see this portion of the shore without coming outside, and the yard was empty except for that van.

He got out of the boat in the shallows, wrapped the bow line around a downed tree, and then climbed up the bank and into the woods and headed toward the cabin. He walked quietly but quickly, with his head up and the gun held down against his leg, finger hooked in the trigger guard.

Through the trees and into the yard without a shot fired or even a sound. Across the yard and to the door, still nothing. Hand on the knob, still nothing. He paused for one deep breath, slipped his finger completely around the trigger and tensed it, then twisted the knob and threw the door open and stepped into the cabin in a shooter's stance, gun raised, ready to kill.

Devin was on the floor. Stretched out on his side, one cheek on the linoleum, his body slightly curled, as if he'd been going for the fetal position but couldn't make it. His gun lay on a table beside the couch, out of reach, and Frank could see that he'd fallen from the couch onto the floor. There was a small puddle on the floor near his mouth, bile maybe mixed with traces of blood. For a second, Frank thought he was dead. Then he lifted his head.

He twisted to see the door, his hazy eyes taking Frank in before flicking to the gun on the table, several feet away, no chance of reaching it. When he moved, it was away from the table, rolling into a sitting position with his back against the wall.

"Where's my wife?"

Frank stepped farther into the cabin, then reached back and swung the door shut behind him, never taking his eyes off Devin.

"She's fine," he said, "but you're never going to see her again."

"No?" Devin brought his head off the wall, and for a moment the light in his eyes seemed to fade, as if that small motion had still been too much.

"No." Frank came closer. "The rest of them are dead. Your boy, AJ? I took his gun and I shot him with it. One round right through the eye. I watched him die, and then I came back. For you."

Devin didn't speak. He had his lips parted, was sucking air in through his mouth in slow, audible breaths.

"He had a chance," Frank said. "Hell, he had better than that. He was holding both of the guns. Wasn't enough. But I'll give you the same chance."

"Yeah?"

"Go for the gun," Frank said, nodding at the table. "I'll let you get your hand on it. I'm going to give you that much."

Devin just stared at him. Frank's hand, so damn steady when he'd fired that bullet into AJ's face, was beginning to tremble. He ran his thumb up and down the stock, took another step into the room.

Just shoot him. Quit the bullshit, quit talking, and just *shoot* him.

"Going to kill me?" Devin said.

"Yes. Unless you get that gun first. I told you, better move for it."

"You have to wait until I've got the gun, is that it?"

"I'm giving you a chance."

"Your dad," Devin said, "wouldn't have needed to wait."

"I'm not my dad," Frank said.

Devin smiled. It was a dying man's smile, a look not of

hopelessness but of disinterest, and Frank hated him for it. Hated him for being in this condition, so weak. He wanted him at full strength, wanted the best the prick had to offer, and then Frank would still be better than him. He'd be better, and he'd kill him, and it would be done, *finally,* it would be done.

"Get up!" Frank screamed. "Get up and go for the gun, you piece of shit!"

Again the smile, and Devin just shook his head. "Can't reach it."

Frank ran to the table and kicked its legs, upending it and spilling Devin's gun to the floor. It hit a few feet away from him, slid to a stop almost within reach.

"Pick it up!"

Devin shook his head again, and this time Frank went for him. He hit him backhanded with the Smith & Wesson, caught the side of his skull, knocked him away from the wall and back to the floor. He let out a soft moan of pain but didn't move, didn't reach for the gun. Frank reached down with his free hand and caught Devin's neck, dragged him upright, and then slammed his head into the wall, still screaming at him to pick up the gun. He banged his head off the wall again, and then a third time, and then he dropped to one knee and jammed the barrel of his father's gun into Devin's mouth.

It was then, down on his knee with his finger on the trigger, that he saw Devin was unconscious.

He let go of Devin's neck and pulled the gun out of his mouth and Devin's head fell onto his right shoulder and the torso went with it. He landed with his body bent awkwardly, one lip peeled back by the floor, a trace of blood showing in his mouth now.

Frank laid his fingers against Devin's neck, felt the pulse there. He was not dead.

He got to his feet and stared down as Devin's eyes fluttered but stayed closed. He took the gun and laid it against the back of Devin's skull, held it there for a few seconds, feeling the trigger under his finger.

I'd find him and I'd kill him.

Damn right you would. Damn right. You're a good boy. Check that—a good man.

It's justified, Frank had told Ezra. It is already justified. And Ezra's response? *Bullshit, son. Not in a way you can accept it's not, and you know that.*

Devin made some sound, a muffled grunt, and stirred but did not wake. Frank moved the gun across the back of his head, traced a circle in Devin's hair with the muzzle. He thought again of Nora, of the fear in her eyes as she'd looked at him, and then he pulled the gun back and walked away. He picked up the table and set it back where it belonged, beneath his grandfather's posthumous Silver Star. He looked at the medal for a moment, and then he dropped his eyes to the gun in his hand, and he ejected the clip into his palm. He took Devin's gun from the floor and emptied that clip as well, and then he walked into the kitchen and set both guns on the counter, put the clips into his pocket, and ran cold water onto a towel.

When he turned off the water he could hear a boat motor, and he stood at the sink with his head cocked and listened. Something small, and headed this way. He went to the window, looked out at the lake, and saw the aluminum boat approaching, Nora up front and Renee at the tiller. Not surprising that Renee had refused to go to the dam.

He slapped at Devin's neck with the wet towel, then held it over his face and squeezed a trickle of cold water onto his forehead and cheeks. The eyes opened, swam, then focused on Frank.

"Get up," Frank said. "Your wife's coming."

When they arrived, Devin was sitting up against the wall, Frank standing in the kitchen with his back against the counter, near the guns. Renee came through the door first, saw Frank and said, "If you—" but then her eyes found Devin and she stopped talking and turned from Frank and ran to her husband.

"Baby," he said, and he reached for her with one arm as she fell to her knees in front of him, almost in the exact position Frank had taken when he put his father's suicide gun in Devin's mouth.

Nora stepped inside, stood in the doorway staring at Renee on the floor with Devin before she looked at Frank. Her eyes searched his, then flicked to the guns on the counter.

"They're empty," he said, and he pushed off the counter and walked into the living room. Renee turned at the sound of his approach, a protective motion, covering Devin with her body.

"Get him up," Frank said, "and get out of here."

"All right."

"The keys to the van are inside it, I think. You've got to get him out there, though. I'm not helping. If I touch him again, I'm going to kill him."

She just nodded.

Frank turned and walked outside, leaving the empty guns on the counter. Nora followed him, and a few minutes later Renee appeared, with Devin on his feet but leaning heavily against her. Frank and Nora stood together beside the cabin and watched as she got the van door open and got him inside.

"You're letting them go," Nora said.

He shook his head. "They aren't going far. He's got to get to a hospital. Anybody can see that."

She didn't answer. Renee slammed the van door shut and walked toward the driver's door. She paused for a moment in front of the van and looked back at them.

"Thank you," she said. "And I'm sorry. I'm so sorry."

There was a beat of silence, and then Frank said, "You know what he does. You know what he is. So how the hell do you love him so clean?"

"Hon," she said, "whoever said anything about it being clean?"

Frank looked away from her, out at the lake. He didn't turn when the doors opened, didn't turn when the engine started, didn't turn when they drove up the gravel drive.

When the sound of the van had faded and they were alone, Nora said, "Is there a phone inside?"

"No."

"Mine's ruined. The water."

"Yeah. Mine, too."

"Where can we go to call the police?"

He waved toward the drive, and then they turned and started up it together, not speaking, stepping over puddles and through the mud. They were halfway to the main road when they heard the hum of an engine and the crunch of tires and Nora said, "Are they coming back?"

They weren't coming back. It was a car, not a van, and when it slid to a stop and the door opened and Grady Morgan stood up and stared at them, all Frank could say was "You're too late, Grady. Too late."

Grady looked over his shoulder and then back at Frank. "Who was that? Who was in that van?"

"Devin Matteson and his wife," Frank said.

"I can't let them drive away from here."

"Sure you can," Frank said. "You never saw them. Didn't know who it was. Didn't ask me about it just now."

Grady looked at Frank for a long time and said, "I've lied about him before. I guess I can do it again. Now what the hell happened out here?"

Thirty-eight

Six hours later, Frank and Nora long departed in police custody, Ezra Ballard evacuated to some hospital, first by boat and then by helicopter, Grady stood alone at the shore and stared out into the dark lake where several bodies waited to be found.

Atkins was dead. Another agent, one who'd been trying to do the job right, was dead, and Grady would see that blood on his hands for the rest of his days, understood that it was the end of his career long before anyone back in Chicago would.

Too late. That was the first thing Frank Temple's son had said to him. Grady had been too late.

Frank had no idea, either. He had no idea.

Seven years of watching that kid, keeping tabs on him, and it had never been about protecting Frank from anything. It had always been about protecting Grady, about covering his own ass. He'd never had the courage to approach the kid and tell him the truth and apologize, and now they were bringing body after body out of this damn lake, one of them a dead agent, a colleague.

Too late. Yes, Frank, I was too late.

Grady Morgan and the Seven-Year Lie. He could have gotten the nerve just a year ago, six years too late and still it would have been in time for this. If he'd tracked Frank down then and told him the truth, how much blood would have been spilled? Not as much, that was for sure. There would have been some, Devin Matteson's gunmen would have seen to that, but not as many people would have died, certainly not Atkins. If Frank had known Devin wasn't responsible for his father's demise, he never would have headed north, never would have seen Vaughn Duncan or had anything to do with it. Those two from Miami would have made their way north quietly, killed Duncan and taken Renee home to see her husband.

It was a sick world, Grady thought, when you could stand on the shore of a beautiful lake like this and long for one murder. One murder that would have saved the others. Everybody with their damn score to settle, and Frank in the midst of it with one that didn't need settling.

He was done with the Bureau. Wouldn't have to be—all of this was indirect involvement, he was close to retirement, and the Bureau loved to handle such things quietly and in-house—but he knew he'd resign now. Should have seven years ago, but it wasn't too late to do it now, and he felt he owed Atkins that much. Atkins wouldn't have wanted a guy like Grady left in his Bureau.

The truth would start with Frank, though. The hell with the people in Chicago who would hear it next; Frank was the one that mattered.

He didn't see him again until the next morning, and while there were still cops moving around the lake—and still divers looking for Atkins—they were alone in the cabin, sitting with their backs to the window that looked out on the lake and its grisly activity.

Ezra Ballard was alive and recovering from a single gunshot that had blown through his ribs and wreaked some internal havoc but left him to see another day, and that's what Frank wanted to talk about at first.

"He'll make it," Frank said after he finished filling Grady in on all the medical details Grady had already heard.

"Yes."

"One of the few, though. One of the few, and you don't

need to tell me how much of that is my responsibility, Grady. I understand it."

"That's not the way anyone else is telling it," Grady said. "You see the papers? You're on the front page."

"So was my dad."

"They're saying different things about you, though."

Frank didn't respond to that.

"You let Devin go," Grady said. "Had him and let him go, there at the end. I saw the reports."

A nod.

"It was the right thing to do," Grady said, and his voice was so rigid, grandfatherly, none of the relief coming through in it. And it *was* relief, because a day earlier when the kid stood in this room with a gun in his hand he had somehow done the right thing, despite all the energy Grady had invested into priming him for the wrong thing.

"Anybody heard about him?" Frank said. "Has he turned up somewhere?"

Grady shook his head.

"I was sure that he would," Frank said. "Sure of it. He'll need a hospital. I'd be surprised if he didn't, at least. Nobody's blaming me for letting him walk, though. Wasn't my job, they keep saying."

"It was the right thing to do," Grady said again. "And I need to explain that to you."

"I get it, Grady."

"No, Frank. No, you do not."

Frank tilted his head and squinted against the sunlight, and Grady finally opened his mouth and let the truth out.

"I was seventeen years old," Frank said when he was done. It was the first thing he'd said in a long time, Grady doing all the talking, speaking too fast, trying to rush out as much as he could before Frank went nuts, blew up.

He never blew up. Just sat there and listened and didn't show a thing, and it took Grady back to those first few conversations in the house in Kenilworth and made his cowardice and corruption play through his eyes again, everything here so damn similar except that this time Frank was an adult and Grady was telling the truth.

"I know," Grady said. "Frank, I know. You were a child, and one who'd suffered a loss, and we—"

"Turned me into a gun."

"What?"

"That's what you said he wanted to do. My father. That he'd raised me to kill. And while you were saying that about him, you were loading me up and pointing me at Devin."

"We didn't want *you* to go after him. We thought that you might know something, and we needed to push the right buttons to see if . . ." Grady stopped talking and shook his head. "Shit, you've got me defending it now. I'm not going to. It's like I said, Frank, I'm telling the truth now, and it had to start with you."

Frank stood up and walked to the window, looked out at the lake. There was a flat-bottomed boat within sight, divers adjusting their masks before going back in, still searching for Atkins.

"You are a bastard," Frank said, but it was without any venom at all, or even energy.

"I'm going to resign."

"I don't care about that. Why would I care if you kept your damn job?"

Grady didn't say anything.

"I'd just turned eighteen," Frank said, "when I called Ezra Ballard and begged him to go to Miami with me to kill Devin. Begged him. He said he wouldn't, so I said I'd go alone, and he made a compromise with me. Said as long as Devin stayed down there, the hell with him, let him rot. But we'd never let him come back here. Never."

Grady was sitting on the couch with his elbows on his knees, staring up at Frank, who hadn't turned from the window, didn't even seem to care that Grady was still in the room.

"Kudos," Frank said, "on a job well done, Grady. You set out to convince me that Devin deserved retribution, get me fired up about it, *consumed* by it, right? Well, you got the job done. Yes, sir, you got it done."

"I want you to know," Grady began, but Frank continued talking as if he hadn't heard him.

"I was *relieved* when Ezra told me the prick was coming back. Well, not at first. At first I had some sense. But then this fat bastard professor asked me if I'd write a memoir, and it was like fate, right, confirmation that there would be no getting away from this legacy, ever. Then I was relieved, Grady. I was absolutely relieved. Because I could finally welcome it."

He stopped looking at the search boat then, turned to face Grady. "Devin was important to me. He gave me somebody to hate, somebody to blame, who wasn't my father. I'm not saying he was enough for me to give the old man a pass, but he was enough to distract me. To redirect some things."

"I understand that."

"I came up here to kill the guy for no reason, is what you tell me now. But he's still a piece of a shit. You know that. They're looking for one of his bodies out there right now. So maybe I should have gone ahead and done it."

Grady shook his head. "No."

"It would have made sense to me then," Frank said, "because I had my reasons. Now I don't. But other people have still got theirs, right? So maybe I should have done it for their reasons. Why are they any less valid than mine?"

Grady was quiet. Frank said, "How many sorts of crimes has Devin been involved with, you think?"

"Plenty."

"No, give me a number."

"I don't know, Frank. What, dozens?"

"Dozens," Frank said, nodding. "And deaths? How many deaths?"

"The same. There's a reason we wanted him so bad, Frank."

"Yeah. That's my point. There were plenty of reasons." He looked around the cabin. "I had him here yesterday with a gun in his mouth and my finger on the trigger. And if the son of a bitch hadn't been so sick, if he hadn't looked like he was dying, I probably would have pulled it."

"It's good that you didn't."

"Is it?" Frank said. "I don't know about that, Grady. I don't know. But I don't want to be the one who has to decide. I do not want to play that role."

They stayed in the living room for a long time without speaking, and eventually Grady stood and said he was leaving.

"Devin didn't give my father up," Frank said. He wasn't looking at Grady.

"No."

"Somebody did."

Grady was silent.

"It was an anonymous tip, says the legend. From someone close to him."

Grady had given his word never to reveal that source. There were divers out in that lake who were proof that Grady's word wasn't worth a damn, though, and maybe Frank was entitled to it by now. Surely he was entitled to it by now.

"I'll tell you," he said, "and this time it'll be the truth."

Frank was shaking his head. "No," he said, and Grady would always remember the awkward way he finished it—"I would like not to know."

Grady nodded, and he left, and he did not tell him. Would never tell him, or anyone, about that day when an attractive woman whose dark hair and skin were contrasted by striking blue eyes came into his office and said, *I would like to talk with you about my husband.*

When they'd finished that day, he'd praised her bravery, lauded her for doing the right thing. She'd looked at him as if he were insane. *Brave?* she said. *Doing the right thing? It's got nothing to do with that. I'd never have told you anything. I love him. But he's going to ruin my son, Mr. Morgan. And I cannot let that happen.*

Thirty-nine

They let Ezra out of the hospital seven days after he went in, and Frank picked him up in his own truck, drove south from Minocqua with the windows down and fresh air blowing in, the highway filled with cars towing boats, the first weekend of fishing season under way.

"How've the dogs been?" Ezra asked.

"Disgruntled."

"Good. Nice to see some concern on the home front."

"The doctors say when you'll be able to get back out on the boat, back to work?"

"They might have, but I don't recall listening to it. I think it'll be soon."

Frank had already tried offering apologies to Ezra, tried to explain how he'd have handled things differently if he'd understood the situation, how he should never have believed Vaughn. Ezra had cut him off every time, not interested in hearing it, not needing to hear.

"What about Devin?" Ezra said. "Any word?"

Frank just shook his head. During the first few days he'd been sure news about Devin was on its way. The memory of his face there at the end left Frank convinced he'd turn up in a hospital somewhere—or dead. That was the preferred option, that he would turn up dead and Frank would able to shake his head and think about just how little would have been accomplished if he'd pulled the trigger, realize that he'd have removed nothing more than a few days of pain from Devin's existence. Yes, that was what should happen.

It hadn't happened, though. The days ticked by and no word came, Devin and Renee still gone.

"He's got the right sort of friends for this," Ezra said. "People who can help him disappear."

"He does," Frank agreed, and he could feel his finger on the trigger again, see that circle he'd traced in Devin's hair with the gun barrel.

"You talked to Nora?" Ezra said.

"Called a few times. Haven't heard back from her."

"She still in town, though? Or has she gone home, after all this?"

"I'm not sure."

"How about you? Headed home soon?"

"Headed where?" Frank answered, and Ezra nodded, and they drove on in silence.

Nora didn't get back to the shop for five days. The cops had taken Vaughn's Lexus, and now she had no cars left but the Mazda that Jerry had refused to repaint. Nobody to fix any cars that came in, either. She tried to finish the Mazda herself, spent three days on the paint job, creating runs and streaks and then sanding them back down and starting over and making it worse. By the third day the car was an absolute disaster, and she finally called another shop across town and towed it over to them. The owner, a man who'd known her father well, painted it in one day and then had it towed back to her shop, with her check for the work sitting on the driver's seat.

She called the car's owner to tell him it was ready, and he came over immediately, more anxious for conversation than for the car. He'd read about her in the papers, he said. Hell of a story.

He left with the car, and then it was just her and an empty shop. No business, no employees. More bills on the way.

Frank Temple had called a few times, left messages. Why did he want to see her so bad before he took off again? Did he think there was some sort of closure for this, some nice, neat wrap-up to such awful events? She didn't call back. It was surprising that he was even still in town.

Her mother called daily, first to politely urge her to return home, then to demand it. Nora said she was considering her options, and then she called the local newspaper and put out an ad for a new body man and painter.

The ad ran for a week, and she interviewed two guys. Told them she'd be in touch, but the truth was they couldn't handle the job, and she couldn't pay them even if they could. That Friday, she answered her father's constant question honestly for the first time, told him, no, we don't have any cars. Then his face fell, and she responded with a lie, promised some were on the way in, that things would be *too* busy by the first of the week.

The shop was lost, and she supposed she should have felt relief at that. It ended the uncertainty, at least. She could go home now. So why did she feel so damn sad? Her father was part of it, of course—the idea of leaving him in this town without any family still haunted her—but today she was more aware than ever of what had always helped her linger: She didn't know what came next. It was that simple, that sad. While her peers were caught up with their families or careers, she still waited for the road sign that told her which way to turn. Tomahawk, and Stafford's Collision and Custom, had provided a welcome delay. Now the delay was past and the uncertainty remained and, worst of all, she'd failed at the one goal she'd set. The family shop was closing, and not on Stafford terms.

The next Monday found her alone in the empty shop. The phone rang several times, but it was always a long distance number. Reporters, not customers. It was nearly noon and she was getting ready to leave for lunch when Frank Temple came through the door.

"Hey," he said, letting it close softly behind him. He looked good, all the bruises and nicks gone. The black-and-blue streaks on her arms were gone, too, but she continued to wear long sleeves every day.

"Hi," she said. "I know, I owe you a call. It's been hectic, though. I figured you might have left town already."

"No." He looked around, taking in the quiet place, her sitting alone in the little office. She felt pathetic, didn't want him to see it.

"How are things?" he said, and she meant to tell him they were fine, she really did, but somehow the truth came out instead. She wasn't weepy about it, wasn't sentimental, just told it like it was. She was going to have to close the shop, and that was that. Head back to Madison, or maybe, much as she hated to think of it, to her stepfather's house in Minneapolis.

"I saw your ad," he said. "If you hired somebody new, couldn't you get it going again?"

"The truth is, I couldn't afford to pay anyone until we'd made some money, and that takes time. Most body men don't want to work on spec. And really, I need two people, because most aren't going to be able to do what Jerry did."

He nodded. "How much would you need to make it till then?"

What was this about? She didn't like the question.

"I don't know," she said, "but it's going to be more than a bank will want to loan a company that's already overextended and has no employees and no customers."

He nodded again, just taking all of this in as if it were minor stuff.

"I was thinking I'd like to invest in something," he said. "I've got some money left, and rather than burn through it and then go looking for income, I thought it would be a good idea to put it into something promising. An up-and-coming business, something like that. Or maybe one with some history. Some tradition. You know, a proven entity."

She was shaking her head before he was done.

"I don't take handouts. It's generous, a very sweet offer, but no."

"I don't give handouts," he said. "Maybe you missed the investment part of what I said? I'm thinking of something different entirely. More like being a partner."

She kept right on shaking her head.

"I don't want a partner. If I can't do it alone, then I'll just get out."

"You know," Frank said, "being strong doesn't necessarily mean being alone."

She looked at him for a long time, then pulled her chair closer to the desk.

"Dad told me the only partner worth having was one who'd get his hands dirty, share the job side by side."

"Then I'll share the job."

"You don't know anything about fixing cars."

"No," he said, "but we can find some people who do. And I'm pretty sure I could drive a plow in the winter."

"In the winter." She said it carefully, a verification.

"Made more sense to me that way," Frank said. "But if you want me to drive the damn plow in the summer, Nora, I'll do it."

He stopped talking and looked her in the eye, and she saw something surprising there, a deep and powerful quality of need.

"You could think about it," he said. "You could do that much, couldn't you? I don't want to go. I'd like to stay here. It's the best chance I've got."

They sealed the deal on a handshake. It was a start.

Here's an excerpt from *The Silent Hour*— the next thriller by Michael Koryta, available soon in hardcover from Minotaur Books:

He'd sharpened his knife just an hour before the killing. The police, prosecutor, and media would all later make great use of this fact. Pre-meditation, they said. Proof of intent, they said. Cold-blooded murder, they said.

All Parker Harrison had to say was that he often sharpened his knife in the evening.

It wasn't much of a defense.

Harrison, an unemployed groundskeeper at the time of his arrest for murder, took a guilty plea that gave him a term of life in prison but allowed the possibility of parole, the sort of sentence that seems absurd to normal people but apparently makes sense to lawyers.

The guilty plea prevented a trial, and that meant Harrison's tenure as the media's villain of the moment was short-lived. Some editors and TV anchors around the state no doubt grumbled when they saw he was going to disappear quietly behind bars, taking a good bloody story with him. On the day of his arrest, he'd offered something special. Something none of them had seen before.

The victim was a man named John Maxwell, who was the new boyfriend of Harrison's former lover, Molly Nelson. The killing occurred in Nelson's rental house in the hills south of Xenia, Ohio, a town made infamous for a devastating tornado that occurred the same year Harrison was born, destroying homes, schools and churches while killing thirty-four people and leaving nearly ten thousand—including the infant Harrison and his family—homeless. It wasn't the first storm of breathtaking malevolence to pass through the little town: the Shawnee had named the area "place of the devil winds" more than a century earlier. The winds certainly touched Harrison's life, and a few decades later the locals would claim the devil clearly had, too. A Xenia native who was half-Shawnee, Harrison had been separated from Nelson for more than a year before he returned to town and reunited for one night together. It was passionate and borderline violent, beginning in a shouting match and culminating in intercourse on the floor. Evidence technicians later agreed that the abrasions found on Harrison's knees were rug-burns from that night, and had no relevance to the killing that took place two days later.

After the night of sex and shouting, Nelson told Harrison she was done with him, that it was time to move on. Time to move *away*. Get out of town, she said, find something else to occupy your attention.

Apparently she didn't convince him. Harrison returned to her house two nights later, hoping, he would say, for more conversation. The police would insist he returned with murder on his mind and a recently sharpened knife in his truck. Harrison's story, of an argument that the new boyfriend turned into a physical contest, was never proved or disproved because there was no trial. What went undisputed was the result of the night: Harrison punched Nelson once in the jaw as she went for the phone, interrupting her as she hit the last of those three digits needed to summon help, and then turned on Maxwell and killed him with the knife. Harrison disconnected the phone, but a police car had already been dispatched, and a single sheriff's deputy entered the house through an open side door to find Nelson unconscious and Harrison sitting on the kitchen floor beside Maxwell's body, his cupped hands cradling a pool of blood. He was attempting, he later explained, to put the blood back into the corpse. To return it to Maxwell, to restore him to life. He was, he later explained, probably in shock.

That detail, of the attempt to return the blood, added a new twist on a classic small-town horror story, and the crime received significant media coverage. Front-page articles in the papers, precious minutes on the TV news. The murder was well documented, but I don't remember it. I was an infant when Harrison was arrested, and his name meant nothing to me until almost three decades later, when the letters started. . . .